The Olympus Device:
Book One

By

Joe Nobody

Copyright © 2013-2014
Kemah Bay Marketing, LLC
All rights reserved.
Edited by:
E. T. Ivester
Contributors:
D. Allen
www.holdingyourground.com

Other Books by Joe Nobody:

A few disclosures...

The physics behind the rail gun are being explored by the United States Navy as of this writing.

Technically, the weapon described in this tome is a coil gun. For readability's sake, I used with the more commonly used description of "rail gun" in depicting technology that moves a projectile via magnetic fields. Both categories of devices do exist.

It should also be noted that I took fictional liberties with the known laws of physics, or perhaps I should state the "unknown laws of physics." No one really yet understands what would happen if the situations described in this book did occur. Perhaps the story is closer to reality than a work of pure fiction.

While super-hero devices, like Iron Man's suit or Batman's cave of wonders are great entertainment, the real story is how a man copes with such power. How would you react if you held the Olympus Device?

Joe Nobody

Day 1

The green LED glowed brightly for a moment, then faded back to powerless oblivion. Dusty raised his hand to give the uncooperative connection a good thump, but reconsidered at the last moment. *It must be the weld*, he thought. *There's nothing else it could be.*

Lowering the welding mask over his face, he peered through the narrow rectangle of dark green glass, making minute adjustments to the mixture of gases fueling his torch. Content with the size, color, and shape of the flame, he shifted his weight, positioning just perfectly for the delicate operation.

"I thought I'd find you out here," sounded a greeting. "Have you finished the choke on my shot...? What the hell is that, Dusty?"

Sighing, Dusty closed the valve, extinguishing the flame. Lifting the welder's shield, he turned to face the visitor. "Hey, Hank. How's it going?"

"I'm doing well, thanks for asking," replied the always cheery man. "Dusty, what is that... that thing?"

"It's a little experiment I've been working on for about a year. It's called a rail gun. I read about the US Navy experimenting with larger ones in *Popular Science* a while back, and I thought I'd try to build a miniature. So far, I've failed miserably."

Hank couldn't seem to pull his eyes away from the contraption, stepping around Dusty while staring like a boy in a bicycle store. "What's it supposed to do?"

"It fires a projectile just like a regular gun, but it uses magnetic fields to propel the bullet rather than gunpowder."

Finally pulling his gaze away, Hank shrugged his shoulders and replied, "So? What good would that do?"

"In theory, you can propel an object much faster with magnets than you can with a chemical reaction, like burning smokeless powder. So far, that theory isn't working out so well."

Turning his attention back to the device secured in the workbench vise, Hank pointed and said, "How's it work?"

"The barrel is actually formed by rare earth magnets from China. I shaped them like doughnuts. The projectile is pushed and pulled down the tube - kind of like a shish kabob through doughnut holes. Magnets become stronger if you surge electrical current through them, so if you time the jolt of power just right, each ring pulls the steel bullet through the barrel while the previous one pushes... hopefully faster and faster as the projectile moves from one magnet's influence to the next."

Hank scratched his head, obviously in deep study of the rifle-like invention. "What's this right here?"

"That's a cordless drill battery I had laying around - the drill broke last year."

"You expect to shoot a bullet using a drill battery?"

Dusty grinned at his friend's skepticism. "Yes, but not how you would think. I ordered a Taser off the web, and I'm using some of the electronics from it. They use an ultracapacitor to store up a lot of juice, so I used that to power the magnets, just like the Taser generates all its power from a small battery."

Hank knew his neighbor would eventually grow frustrated with his questions, but couldn't keep his curiosity in check. "So what do you think is wrong with it?"

"I've got a bad weld on one of the coils... at least that's what I think it is."

"Well, what are you waiting on? Let's fix it, and let's see if it works."

Shaking his head at the innocent contradiction, Dusty handed his guest a spare mask from the bench. After making sure Hank's eyes were protected, he set about re-welding the problematic connection. After a few touches with the super-hot flame, the procedure was completed.

Without lifting the shield, Dusty moved to the computer keyboard and pushed a key with his gloved finger. The display on the laptop flashed once and then refreshed. The green LED on the weapon's stock glowed brightly – and remained illuminated.

Lifting his mask, Dusty turned and smiled at his friend. "I think that was it. The computer says all systems are go."

"Let's shoot the damn thing, Dusty. I've gotta see this."

The gunsmith scratched his chin, eventually shrugging his shoulders and declaring, "Why not?"

Motioning for Hank to follow, Dusty moved to the back wall of his workshop where the two men began stacking hay. "I normally test a good deer rifle with bales stacked two deep. Today, just to be safe, let's stack three."

"Three! Now, Dusty... you don't think that contraption of yours is really more powerful than a good ole' 30-06, do ya?"

"Better safe than sorry."

Nodding his agreement, Hank pitched in and helped finish constructing the organic bullet stop. Dusty then pulled a tri-pod from a corner and set about mounting a small movie camera on top of the stand. Noticing his friend's inquisitive expression, he said, "If it works, I want to send a video to my brother."

"Sounds like a little sibling rivalry still lurks. How's the professor doing by the way?"

"He seems happy enough at A&M. I don't know how he stands living in the big city like that, but he claims to be enjoying his research."

Hank grunted, "College Station is hardly the big city, Dusty. You need to get out more."

Ignoring the jab, Dusty pulled another piece of equipment from a nearby shelf. "I want to set up the chronograph so we can get a velocity measurement. The software I'm burning into a chip is the key to the whole system, and knowing how fast the projectile is moving will help me with fine tuning."

The gunsmith reached into a glass jar next to his invention and pulled out a single, shiny, steel ball bearing. Holding up the marble-sized metal, he declared, "Our missile."

Dusty flicked a switch on the gun's stock, and the magnets started spinning. He dropped the projectile into the breach of the weapon.

Always the perfectionist, he examined the unit closely, taking a small penlight from his shirt pocket and shining the beam on the ball bearing. Motioning Hank to come take a closer look, he pointed and said, "See how it floats in the chamber? It should stay levitated the entire trip down the barrel... never touching anything. That way there's no resistance – no friction."

"That looks like a magician's trick. How did you get it to float in mid-air like that?"

"The magnetic poles are pushing equally on all sides of the ball bearing. It took me three weeks of machining to mill them down to just the right shape. After that, I had to order bearings from eight different companies before I found a supplier who manufactured product to extreme tolerances. These are from Russia."

"What are the bearings normally used for?"

"Jet engines... military jet engines."

Hank grunted, "Don't you just love the internet?"

Moving back to the rail gun, Dusty adjusted the power setting, the red LED numbers showing *02*. "I'm going to give it two percent for the first shot. I just want to see if the ball bearing will move at all. We'll turn up the power if this works."

After one last check to make sure everything was in order, Dusty motioned for Hank to lower his mask for eye protection – just in case. Once he was sure his visitor was protected, he hovered a finger over the keyboard, inhaled, and pressed down.

It was difficult for Dusty to tell exactly what happened, the welding mask restricting both his view and hearing. His first thought was that the weapon had exploded. He pivoted, finding Hank lying on the ground, slowly raising himself to an elbow and surrounded by what looked like smoke.

Rushing to his friend's side, Dusty bent and shouted, "Hank! Are you okay?"

Hank seemed not to hear the question or was unable to respond. Dusty started visually inspecting the man's torso, looking for any sort of wound. He couldn't see any bleeding or physical damage.

Slowly, the prone man raised a shaky hand and lifted his protective mask. Staring with a look of terror in his eyes, Hank's mouth started moving, but no words came out. He pointed a trembling finger.

Dusty turned his head, his gaze naturally following his friend's gesture.

Dusty inhaled sharply and dropped his mask on the floor. Both men remained silent for several moments, staring at what had been the back wall of the workshop just a few seconds before.

The three-thick bales had been completely cut in half. Behind them, a hole almost four feet in diameter had been punched through the cinderblock, the back wall of Dusty's shop now equipped with a new opening into his backyard. It wasn't smoke he'd seen a moment before. It was dust – a small cloud of pulverized cinder block now settling around the shop.

It was what they saw through the new hole that was truly shocking. Fifty yards behind the building, a truck-sized boulder had been split through the middle, each half lying on the ground like a ripe melon split with a cleaver.

Hank finally managed to speak. "Look at what you did to Pilgrim Rock."

Dusty couldn't believe his eyes. He and his brother had played on that rock since they were old enough to toddle. It had been their fort, castle, and outpost during countless afternoons of childhood adventure. Now it sat in two pieces, wisps of vapor rising into the air.

After helping his friend to his feet, Dusty walked to the blackened ends of hay, carefully touching the tips as if expecting them to be hot. Glancing back at Hank, he announced, "They're ice cold." He then moved to scoop up a handful of the crumbled cinder block. "This feels like it has been in a freezer."

Going back to the only eyewitness, Dusty grabbed the shocked man by the shoulders. "Hank – what happened? What did you see?"

"I... I don't know. It was like a streak of black lightening or something."

Remembering the video camera, the gunsmith removed the small device from the stand and hit the rewind button. Focusing on the small, fold-out screen, he watched, frustrated as one frame showed the pre-shot room intact, the next displaying the destroyed bales.

His next stop was the chronograph. With his mouth dropped open, Dusty stared blankly at the screen. He finally managed to stutter, "That's impossible," as he looked at a message on the device's readout – a display that indicated an error. Turning back to Hank, he declared, "That device is rated to measure speeds up to 9,999 feet per second. There's no way. That's impossible."

Both men stood staring at the rail gun for several moments, trying to reconcile what had just happened.

"What are you going to do?" Hank finally managed.

Dusty's voice was low and calm. "I'm going to take your advice, my old friend. I'm going to get out more... I'm going to visit Mitch."

Hank shook his head, "I think I'm going to visit a bottle – I need a drink."

Day 2

The day wasn't old enough to be hot. Driving with the windows down provided more than enough comfort despite the slow speed required to navigate the narrow lane. The driveway wasn't really anything more than a gap in the fence with a mailbox, the grass thinned from the passing of the occasional tire. More from habit than need, Dusty pulled the pickup under the drooping branches of an ancient cypress, the wisps of foliage brushing harmlessly over the windshield as he rolled under the umbrella of shade.

After exiting the truck, he parted the low hanging growth and approached a broad, shady porch. A slightly arthritic, red tick hound dog guarded the area, barely raising its head to acknowledge the newcomer.

"Hello, Roscoe," Dusty greeted. The only response was a single thump of the animal's tail on the wooden floor. Taking a knee and scratching behind one of hound's droopy ears, Dusty softly instructed, "Now, Roscoe, don't get all excited."

The sarcasm was clearly lost on Roscoe, who managed two half-hearted wags of his tail in response. Switching ears, Dusty took a moment to scan the homestead.

The old Barlow place was just over 200 acres, and in Dusty's opinion, some of the best land in the Fort Davis area. A modest, single-story home dominated the grassy floor of a valley, the flatland bordered on three sides by steep, black faced walls of volcanic rock. A large barn and smaller outbuilding stood toward the back of the cut, their rough, aged gray façades evidence that the property was once a working ranch.

Blooming beds of seasonal fauna now surrounded the home, a sure sign of a woman's touch. Hanging baskets, dripping with ivy, framed the porch, a small fountain of tumbling water adding to the relaxed atmosphere of the retreat. Dusty smiled, approving of both the color and the obvious pride of ownership indicative of the landscaping. This land hadn't always benefited from such considerations.

Old man Barlow wouldn't have bothered with such trivial pursuits. He had earned a reputation as a man more concerned with counting his money than wasteful investments in frivolous gardening or home décor. He'd passed away some five years ago, wealthy and alone. Dusty would have never used the word "happy" in describing the old gruff, terms like sourpuss or codger more in tune with the value of his life.

The sound of the nearby screen door interrupted his sequence of memories, as well as the manipulation of Roscoe's ear.

"I thought I heard someone out here. What brings you over this way, Mr. Durham Weathers?"

Dusty removed his hat and shyly looked down. "I'm sorry to drop by unannounced, Miss Grace, but I'm going to be taking a trip tomorrow and wanted to check on my Last Will and Testament."

Grace's tone became gentler. "Durham, you know you're always welcome here, announced or not. Come on in."

The lady of the house held the door open for Dusty to pass, the narrow entrance bringing their bodies physically close. She smelled of vanilla and softness, the shine of her blond hair drawing his eye. If she noticed he hesitated too long in the doorway, she didn't let it show.

Dusty entered the living room and paused. He began to justify his visit. "I'm taking the plane to College

Station early tomorrow. I've not seen Mitch or his family in quite a while. That's a long flight for me, and, well, I reasoned it best to have my affairs in order before I left. Otherwise, I wouldn't be bothering you."

Grace, placing her hand on hip, threw Dusty a look of "Stop being silly," but didn't say anything. "Can I offer you a glass of iced tea or coffee? I just made a fresh pot."

"A cup of java sounds great, if it wouldn't be a…," Dusty started, but Grace waved him off and turned toward the kitchen before he could finish.

He didn't feel like sitting, instead deciding to mentally dissect the montage of pictures hanging on a nearby wall. The first frame held a college degree from the University of Texas School of Law, the ornate document proclaiming one Grace Amber Kennedy as having been awarded a Juris Doctorate. The next cluster of images held countless awards and honors issued by the State of Texas and numerous legal associations. Finally, his gaze settled on a small group of personal photographs.

Dusty struggled with the words to describe Grace Kennedy. *Beautiful* seemed like an understatement - *attractive* sounded almost insulting. Any woman equipped with such a disarming smile, petite frame, and healthy skin was desirable, and surely Miss Grace was all of that. Adding proven intelligence and an extensive track record of professional success to the mix elevated her well beyond mere physical descriptions. Silly words like *stunning* and *gorgeous* began entering the male mind. He dismissed the labels as shallow, overused, and cliché.

There was another aspect to the woman – a depth that was difficult to identify. *The answer is in these pictures*, he concluded. *I know it is. I've looked at these old photos a dozen times, and I still can't put my finger on it.*

There was a young, smiling Grace with her parents, a cap and gown identifying the event, then another image of a slightly older girl, a wedding photo taken with a handsome, clean-cut young man. The marriage was soon followed with several pictures of a newborn baby, smiling underneath a billowing, pink hair bow, despite the baldhead. *Amber was her name*, he remembered. The big Texan sighed and shook his head at the tragedy that had befallen what seemed like a storybook existence. Grace's husband and child had died in an automobile accident nine years ago.

On and on, the wall memories continued. An older Grace, sophisticated in her formal gown, posing with a clearly prestigious award. Another clipping from *The Dallas Tribune*, proclaiming a milestone in her legal career.

"Durham Weathers," interrupted her voice behind him. "Haven't you studied those old pictures a million times already?"

Smiling, Dusty turned to see her carrying a lime-green serving tray, complete with two mugs, a matching pot, and small containers of milk and sugar. Grace was the only person who refused to call him by anything other than his formal name, claiming she liked the handle better than Dusty.

She motioned him to the couch while she set the tray on the table and began filling the cups.

With coffee in hand, she chose the loveseat, studying her guest with an intense gaze over the rim of her mug.

"You're not being honest with me," she finally proclaimed. "Something else is troubling you besides the flying. What's going on, Durham?"

As was common with many of their conversations, things weren't exactly following Dusty's pre-rehearsed plan.

"It's no big deal," he lied. "Like I said, I've not seen Mitch in a while, and it's a long trip. Besides, I've had you working on those documents for what – almost a year? It's high time I got off my lazy duff and finished things up."

The look on the lawyer's face clearly indicated she didn't buy it, but she decided not to press. *It would be rude to question him*, she reasoned. *Our relationship doesn't work that way.* Setting down her cup, she rose and announced, "I'll go back to the office and find the file. You should review the contents to make sure they still represent your wishes."

Relieved at being off the hook, Dusty watched as she sauntered to the back of the house where he knew a spare bedroom had been converted into her workspace. "That was close," he whispered.

Of all the mornings for that man to show up, thought Grace. *He had to pick the day I was planning on working in the garden.*

Standing in front of the mirror, she determined there wasn't anything she could do about the old jeans and plaid work shirt – he'd notice a wardrobe change in a heartbeat. Hastily pulling a brush through her tresses, she decided that was about the best she could do without being obvious. Mildly frustrated, she strolled to the office, trying to remember where she'd left his file.

The man was a puzzle, and Grace Kennedy wasn't a fan of unsolved mysteries. He had been the first to befriend her when she moved to Fort Davis. They had quickly developed a causal friendship, his warm smile and western, gentlemanly demeanor welcomed by a lady who had just struck out on a new adventure in life.

While his friendship was unquestionably genuine, above all he treated her with respect. Unlike the parade of men that came calling back in Dallas, Durham Weathers was interested neither in her money, nor in a quick trip to bed. It was the perfect prescription, exactly what the relocated newcomer had needed – at the time.

After the accident, she'd mourned for months, isolating herself in an empty home, wandering aimlessly, staring out the windows at nothing. Because there *was* nothing. Time eventually healed the pain, but didn't fill the void she felt inside.

The realization dawned that she had to do something, *anything* to fill the deep, dark hole that had been drilled into her soul by a cruel world. It came gradually, beginning as a soft glow of light, enough energy to clean out his closet. The success of that effort fueled more ambition. Amber's room was next – a gut wrenching exercise of filling boxes and converting the nursery into a spare bedroom that would probably never see a guest.

After recovering from that exhaustive effort, she resolved to fill her life with a professional challenge big enough to overshadow the gaping chasm in her heart. Her unused degree was the key – unlocking a doorway that she burst through, channeling all of her energies with a determination to dominate.

Dallas was a diverse, target rich environment for an attorney. After emerging onto the legal landscape, it quickly became obvious that corporate law was where the money lay, intellectual property the best game in town. And she played that game hard.

Within two years, her shingle was known by the key players at the Fortune 100 corporations. Another year, and she was turning clients away. Ruthless, tough, strikingly beautiful, and seemingly made of ice, Ms. Kennedy quickly became known as the most eligible bachelorette in town. Some of the power-players viewed her potential conquest as a trophy, others as a method to climb the ladder of success. All of them were out of their league.

As time passed, and the accolades multiplied, Grace became bored and frustrated. Her immersion into law had become stale, her personal life entwined by reputation and polluted by a mundane cast of male characters who all seemed so shallow... unfulfilling.

She'd fallen into a trap. Mired in layers of personal and professional reputation, it had all become a game with rules that were dynamic and not always obvious. She began to feel herself changing to meet the expectations of others. Men who failed to woo her advanced reports of a cold woman, so she allowed the ice queen to emerge in all her scorn and glory. Business associates advertised an unrelenting, uncompromising assailant, so the queen bitch joined her arsenal of personality traits. It was all so dishonest – as false as the façade of a Hollywood movie set.

Without fanfare or ceremony, she made the decision to leave it all behind. The complexity wasn't fun anymore – she needed something simpler, cleaner – more wholesome. As was typical of her analytical mind, Grace plied into research. After a few weeks, she settled on the western end of the Lone Star State. Her visit to the Barlow property sealed the deal.

She soon discovered that the perceived need for the slower pace associated with a small town wasn't going to be a panacea of wellness. Fortunately, she met Durham early on, and he helped smooth the transition. They had become fast friends, always flirting with a deeper relationship, but that never happened. Some unknown factor seemed to prevent a more meaningful connection.

Finding the file, she straightened herself and then made for the living room.

"Durham, I finally found it. Take a moment and read through everything just to make sure. If it's correct, I'll run to the courthouse in a few days and register the document with the county clerk."

Dusty accepted the thin manila folder and began his review. His last wishes hadn't changed, with half of his worldly assets going to his son, the other to his brother. "It looks good," he announced. "I was planning on leaving before first light in the morning. Is there any chance you'll be heading into town this afternoon?"

"If that's what my client wants, then that's what I'll do," she replied with a nod. "More importantly though, I'll do it for my friend."

She wanted to say more, but the words didn't come. He paused at the door, seeming to hesitate, acting as if he too had something on his mind.

Just like that, he was gone. She watched his truck pull out of the driveway and then walked over to Roscoe. Gently rubbing the animal's head, she contemplated, "Why is it I can't find my tongue when he's here? Why do the words come after he's left? I feel like a schoolgirl - a silly, shy thing who's scared of her own feelings."

Day 3 - Morning

Grace accelerated the Jeep beyond her comfort level, taking her eye from the road just long enough to glance at the dashboard clock. "I can't believe the alarm clock picked this morning to misbehave," she grumbled.

Her stress level was already high – the result of driving on a strange road, darkness still prevailing an hour before sunrise. Her discomfort was elevated further due to the fact that she wasn't sure exactly what time Durham would be taking off. The fresh thermos of coffee beside her was an offering – a small comfort that she hoped would send a message to him, a message that she cared.

Something about his demeanor yesterday kept troubling her - his stoic expression, the urgency to finish the Will, his resolve to have it filed with the county immediately. The look in his eyes had haunted her since he'd left. It was if he were saying goodbye.

Maybe she was overreacting, perhaps misreading his mood. There was no way to be sure. Still, the entire episode had motivated her to rise early and brew the fresh roast. Her inner voice said it was worth venturing out in the dark and driving around the countryside at the strange hour. She wanted to see him again, to make sure he realized that he was important to her.

After he'd left, it occurred to her that Durham was like a soldier preparing to ship out for war - too polite and honorable to expose his own fears, too conscious of her feelings to express any internal doubt. He seemed burdened with the uncertainty of the future. Grace didn't know what battles he anticipated, but he evidently expected some sort of fight. He obviously wasn't confident in the outcome.

Why is it so important that he knows I care? She asked herself, the same question popping into her mind a dozen times since getting out of bed at a gawd-awful hour.

She'd never forget the kind, gentle guidance he'd offered when she first arrived in Fort Davis. *Maybe she simply wanted to return the favor to a troubled friend.* No, it was more than that.

Her mind drifted back as the Jeep negotiated the rural lanes. The Barlow ranch had been unoccupied for over two years when she'd found it online. The heirs were trying to fatten the windfall of their inheritance by overcharging for the property. Compared to the corporate players back in Dallas, manipulating two spoiled brats into a fair settlement for the homestead had been child's play. Acquiring the estate had been easy compared to the daunting task of making it livable.

In the big city, she'd simply hire the work out. Plumbing, electrical, structure, roofing – whatever maintenance needed to be done, Grace sought and contracted professionals. Not so in Fort Davis. The few independents available locally had full schedules, sometimes months in advance. She later found that most locals did their own work, leaving the artisans for the really difficult jobs. Unfortunately, Grace didn't have a clue how to do much more around a house than change a light bulb.

The other unanticipated issue was the town itself. A new, single woman moving to the small berg was one thing – a lady lawyer quite another. Durham had once commented, "You're too smart, too successful, too beautiful, and too much woman for the good folk of Fort Davis to swallow without choking. Let them accept you one bite at a time, little by little. They're good people –

they'll come around." And they had - with Durham's guidance.

Eventually, the hard glances she received from the townsfolk faded into neutral expressions, a short time later, honest smiles. The town's women finally judged their men safe from Grace's seduction - early rumors of her nymphomania, lack of morals, and trollop-like behavior proving unfounded.

In the big city, you lose individuality, she reasoned. *No one knows you or what you're about. In a small town, everyone knows you and what you're about.* It was a tradeoff, one she struggled with at first, but gladly accepted as time wore on.

Convincing the town's gossip hounds that she wasn't an invading courtesan from the east had taken a deft, knowledgeable touch. Her respect for Durham Weathers had grown.

Making the final turn, the headlights pointed at a small gravel lane. She knew it would lead to a barn where Durham kept his plane. She was relieved to see the craft still on the ground – she'd made it in time.

As she approached, the words she wanted him to hear began to form. *I want to tell him that I'm not going to hurt him like Maria did. I want him to know that my feelings are stronger than I've let on.*

She parked the Jeep beside the barn, picking up the thermos while practicing her speech.

He'd seen the headlights coming across the pasture. Curious who would be out this time of the morning, he greeted her at the corner.

"Well, my, my, counselor – what brings you out this way at such an early hour?"

Smiling shyly, she offered the jug of coffee. "I wanted to bring this out so you'd stay awake while flying.

I can't have anything happening to my best paying client."

His laugh was warm, his skin warmer as it brushed her hand accepting the thermos. "Really, Grace... I don't know what to say. This was very kind of you."

"I've not felt right since you left yesterday. Don't get me wrong, I'm not trying to nose into your business, but I can tell you're worried about something. I didn't want you to leave without my saying a few things."

Motioning for her to follow, he led them into the barn and gestured for her to sit on a bale of hay. "I can't offer the same accommodations as those you extended yesterday, but they're comfortable enough if you excuse the odor of the straw."

Grace sat and patted the bale beside her. Once Durham was seated, she looked him directly in the eyes. "That's just the point I came out here to make. I don't mind the smell — I like it. I'm happy here, Durham. This life isn't just enough for me... it's what I want. The only thing that would make it better is if I had someone like you to share it with."

His eyes didn't panic — such a reaction her worst fear. Instead, they remained gentle, a slight smile showing at the corners of his mouth. "I know I'm not the most approachable fella around. Shoot, I might even be a little standoffish. But you've got to understand — I was deeply hurt when Maria left. The fact that she wasn't leaving *me* so much as leaving *Fort Davis* made it worse. Then you come rolling in from the big city... a successful, sophisticated gal by any measure... it's just confusing. My wife left me because she was bored, unchallenged, and longing for a faster pace in life. She wanted everything you had. Then you come into the picture, just the opposite, claiming you crave a slower rhythm — a more relaxed environment. I hope you can see how a man might not put it all together… how I might hesitate at opening up my insides again… exposing myself to the real possibility of hurt."

He paused, looking down at his boots as if trying to gather his thoughts. "I'm glad you said those words, Grace. They make me feel warm inside. I've been worried you were going to change your mind and decide this life wasn't for you. If you're here to stay, I'd like nothing more than to see if we're a match."

"That's all I'm proposing, Mr. Weathers," she replied with a smile.

"When I get back, I want you to come over first thing. I'll fire up the grill and marinade some steaks. You can bring over some of that fancy wine, and we will sit and talk like a man and a woman, not a lawyer and a client or two friends."

"That sounds absolutely wonderful. You've got a date."

~  ~

The concrete landing strips of Easterwood Regional Airport appeared out the starboard window, right where the GPS said they would be. Dusty adjusted the trim and radioed the ground controller for permission to land. The response was immediate, directing him to runway 04/22.

Touching down on the wide, smooth pavement was a pleasure compared to his rough, dirt strip at home. The old crop duster seemed to appreciate the luxury as well, achieving wheels down without incident or complaint. A few minutes later, he rolled the Rockwell Thrush Commander to a numbered spot on the visitor's tarmac, shut down the engine, and reflected on what had been a beautiful day of flying.

Climbing down from the small cockpit, Dusty stretched gingerly, lifting his arms and twisting at the hips. The first priority after securing the plane would be a visit to the men's room – a necessity after four straight hours in a vibrating cockpit and accented by a now empty thermos of coffee. His mind drifted back to Grace and her visit that morning, an omen of good luck and something to look forward to when he got back.

Stiffly walking around the small craft, he couldn't help but feel a sense of pride. The Thrush had been a part of his life for almost 20 years – as much a member of the family as any nonliving object could be. At one point, when it looked like he and Mitch were going to lose the ranch, the plane had provided financial salvation.

Years later, when times were better, Dusty could have afforded practically any private plane on the market, but wouldn't hear of it. Instead, he'd set about restoring and updating the old crop sprayer – making her better than new. Now she was a classic, sporting a bright, canary yellow paint job accented with coal-black lettering.

He decided to leave all of his belongings in the cramped storage area behind the pilot's seat, except one. Pulling a small, portfolio-sized, aluminum case from the back, Dusty made for the main building. He didn't feel comfortable leaving the rail gun behind.

After visiting the facilities, he filed the necessary paperwork, ordered gasoline, and called his brother to report his safe arrival. "Glad you're safe, brother. I'll be there in ten minutes," responded an upbeat Mitch.

Dusty had two other bags stuffed inside the enclosed space of the Thrush. One was a pull-along containing his personal clothing and toiletries, the other a shopping bag filled with gifts for his sister-in-law, niece and nephew. Retrieving his Resistol hat, he felt ready to face the day.

A voice sounded across the tarmac, Mitch rounding the corner with a smile on his face. "I sure am glad to see the old Commander made it down safely," he teased. "Oh, and you too, brother."

The two siblings embraced and then sized each other up. "What's it been, Mitch? Almost two years?"

"Noooo," replied the younger Weathers. "It was Christmas of ..." his voice trailing off as he consulted his mental calendar. "Oh my gawd, Dusty. It *has* been two years."

Patting his brother on the shoulder, Dusty stated, "You don't look like you've aged a day, young man. It must be Mrs. Weathers' good cooking. How are the kids?"

"Oh, they're fine... looking forward to seeing Uncle Dusty. Come on," Mitch waved, "let's get going. You'll see everybody tonight. We've got work to do."

Mitch bent to help Dusty with his baggage, pausing as his brother reached first for the metal case. Looking up, he asked, "Is that the device?"

"Yes. I built it with a folding stock, so everything fits in this small case. I figured you wouldn't want me walking around the campus of A&M carrying a full sized rifle bag."

The two men strolled across the lot in silence, Mitch leading them to a Honda Sedan parked nearby. Dusty's bags went into the trunk, the weapon riding on his lap.

Entering the campus, Mitch nodded at the case in his brother's hands. "I scrutinized the video you emailed me over a dozen times. I'm really puzzled by the effect – a real mystery. Don't worry though; we've got some of the world's most sophisticated measuring equipment here. We'll figure it out if anyone can."

A short time later, they pulled into a reserved parking spot, the sign indicating the space was assigned to "Department Head – Thermal Dynamics – Dr. Mitchell Weathers."

Dusty glanced at his brother and let out a low wolf whistle. "I always said you were the smart one of the bunch, *Doctor* Weathers. I wish dad could be here to see that."

"That's just not true. You've always been every bit as bright as I am, just not as focused. You were playing football and courting every girl in the county. I couldn't get a date and sucked at sports, so there wasn't much left for me to do except study."

With a sincere voice, Dusty responded. "Mitch – all teasing aside – I'm super proud of what you've accomplished."

Waving off the compliment, it was Mitch's turn to become serious. "I owe it all to you. When dad died, you were the one who worked three jobs and did without. It was you who drove that old, beat-up truck so we could save money for school. If anybody needs to have his back patted, it's you."

The praise embarrassed Dusty. As usual, he handled the compliment by changing the subject. Tapping the case on his lap, he said, "Well, now I need your help. I've sewn together a "Frankin'gun" – a monster created in the depths of my secret laboratory. Problem is, I can't tell you how or why it functions."

Switching off the Honda, Mitch snorted at the analogy. "Does it only fire on a full moon?

Mitch's comment sparked an ongoing contest as they walked through the campus, each trying to one-up the other with old movie analogies. Growing up in the remote mountains, a single channel out of Midland Station reached their second-hand television via the foil-covered rabbit ears. Every Saturday night, that channel broadcasted a classic monster or horror movie – an event rarely missed by the young Weathers boys.

Using Mitch's magnetic key card, they eventually entered a building labeled "Anderson Hall," and proceeded through a maze of seemingly endless corridors. Dusty felt as though he had been swallowed by some huge beast. After descending two flights of stairs, they came to a large metallic door that looked more like the entrance to a bank vault than a college lab.

The super-thick steel portal required not only Mitch's entry pass, but his thumbprint as well. Noticing his brother's curiosity, he commented, "We've got some top secret stuff stored down here. We run all kinds of experiments for the military and other government agencies."

The locks hummed, and then a heavy thump sounded from the doorframe. Mitch reached for the handle and swung the enormous door open with surprisingly little effort. "Balance," he responded to his brother's inquisitive expression.

They entered a cavernous space that, to Dusty's eyes, looked more like a movie set from the latest Hollywood science fiction blockbuster than any classroom he'd ever seen. Stainless steel devices lined one wall, multi-colored wires and copper sleeves protruding here and there. Bright yellow stickers warned of high voltage, while other labels declared "Danger – Radiation."

An island of computer monitors and blinking lights dominated the center of the space. A half dozen office chairs scattered about. "That looks like mission control at NASA," Dusty commented, "At least what it looked like on TV."

Laughing, Mitch boasted, "We're a few years ahead of NASA technology here. Those guys down at Johnson would give their left arm for some of this gear."

"That's nice, bro, but let's get our priorities straight here. Do you have a coffeemaker?"

Chuckling, Mitch disappeared behind a wall of equipment and soon returned, rolling out what essentially appeared to be a huge water pipe on wheels. Even to Dusty's uneducated eye, it was clear that the device wasn't used to pump liquid. About 12 feet long with a diameter large enough for a man to crawl through; the tube was ringed with reinforced steel bands, electronic black boxes, and various valves and fittings. It too contained numerous warning labels.

"This is a ballistics tube. The design was actually created in Germany to test naval and tank cannons. You can fire just about anything into this baby's throat, and she'll provide very accurate measurements of energy, velocity… you name it."

"That thing can handle a tank's gun?"

"Sure can," Mitch replied with pride in his voice. "Each of these first sections contains a baffle that holds 5,000 pounds of compressed air. The next four feet is filled with vaporized iodine – about the heaviest gas you can get. The last six feet is filled with plain old H2O. Firing a projectile into this unit is worse than firing a gun under water – about 50 times more resistance."

Dusty was skeptical, but had to trust the expert. "Can it make espresso?"

Ignoring the remark, Mitch again vanished, returning with a heavy, steel table lined with robotic arms, each appendage equipped with fierce-looking metal claws. "Can you set your gun in here?"

"Now hold on a minute, Mitch. I built this thing using bailing wire and paperclips. That thing looks... ummmm... nasty."

Smirking, the professor pointed at the table top and said, "This is probably the world's most sophisticated vise. Those grasps measure rigidity, tensile strength, and molecular density over 1,000 times per second. You could sit a sleeping newborn on that table, and that machine could change the diaper without the baby waking up."

"Can it make blonde roast?"

"No! We'll get coffee later."

Shrugging his shoulders, Dusty began uncasing the rail gun. Mitch couldn't help his curiosity, almost getting in the way, trying to watch his brother assemble the device. "Do you need any special tools?"

"Naw," replied the gunsmith. Snapping the stock around and inserting the drill battery, Dusty handed the professor the weapon. "Here ya go – all done."

Reaching as if he were being offered a poisonous snake, Mitch accepted the weapon and then hefted its weight. Turning to the robo-vise, he sat the gun on the table, and then moved to one of the computer consoles.

A few keystrokes later, the stainless steel arms snapped alive, spinning quickly to lift the rail gun from the surface. Satisfied with the subject's position, the professor initiated another computer command causing the lights to dim.

Dusty watched, fascinated as green and red laser beams shot out of the ceiling, their granular twinkling of light dancing back and forth, up and down his invention. A few moments later the procedure was complete, the lights brightening to their previous level.

"I just did a complete 3D blueprint of the gun," Mitch announced. "I think we're almost ready for a test shot."

The doctor proceeded to position several large lenses around the gun and its automated cradle. "These are high speed cameras and radar imaging systems. I'm setting up a Doppler device as well, although I'm not sure we'll need it."

Eventually the rail gun was surrounded by an impressive assortment of equipment, antennas and lenses, some of which looked, to Dusty, like the distorted faces of giant bugs.

"Ready," announced the professor.

Reaching into the case for the tube of ball bearings, Dusty took one last look around and hesitated. "Mitch, I'm not so sure this is a good idea. You saw the video – this thing punched right through three bales of hay, a cinderblock wall, and split Pilgrim rock right in half."

Smiling, Mitch spun his chair around and teased, "I was going to speak to you about that later. That rock held some of my fondest childhood memories. We must have played around, over, and on that hunk of stone a million times. I'm kind of pissed that you broke it, brother."

Not to be outdone, Dusty countered. "My most vivid memory of that eyesore was you tumbling off and breaking your arm. Dad went to his grave thinking I pushed you off. I was stuck doing your chores for eight weeks until your arm healed."

Both men broke out laughing, the incident causing them to recall days long past. "He never did believe you, did he? I think Pilgrim Rock was a pirate ship that day."

Dusty became serious again. "Yes, I think it was. I also remember telling you not to go so far out on the ledge, and you ignored Blackbeard's orders." Dusty walked to his brother's side, putting his hand on the younger man's shoulder. "Just like then, I'm warning you now. Don't underestimate this thing, Mitch. The last thing in the world I want to do is harm some of this fancy equipment down here and get you in trouble."

Mitch considered his brother's words and nodded. "You said in your email that you could adjust the power. What setting did you use on that first test shot?"

"Two."

"Two out of…?"

"One hundred."

"Shit."

Looking back and forth between the gun and the ballistic tube, Mitch made his decision. "Let's try five."

"Okay, little brother. But I want it on the record – I'm not doing your chores this time. Can one of these doo-dads you've got in here record that agreement?"

Laughing, Mitch asked, "How do you load this thing?"

Dusty moved to the table, pausing a moment as if the robot arms were going to attack him. He hit the power button on the weapon's stock and watched as the magnets started rotating. The professor put his hand on Dusty's arm – a signal to stop.

"Why do you rotate the magnets?"

"It came to me after a year of machining and ruining over a dozen of the expensive things. I could never get the magnetic fields to evenly balance. If I spin them, I get the benefit of centrifugal force. Watch."

Dusty opened the breech and placed the ball bearing inside, smiling at the look on his brother's face when the small steel ball floated perfectly in the air.

Under his breath, Mitch mumbled. "You've achieved spiral levitation using the cog of a household drill. Amazing."

On a roll, the inventor continued his tour. "See how I machined that shape into the magnets? I was turning an old Winchester on the lathe and put some of the shavings into a plastic bag. I spent hours and hours moving different shapes over those flakes of iron to see how the magnetic field made them react. I settled on this configuration after a lot of trial and error – it seemed the most efficient."

Impressed, Mitch asked, "Is it ready?"

"Yup. Let me adjust the power."

While Dusty turned the LED to read "05," Mitch opened a nearby desk drawer and retrieved two pairs of safety glasses and headphones. Handing one set to his brother, he returned to the computer console and said, "Let her rip."

Dusty moved to the rail gun, verified the LED glowed green and pulled the trigger.

Unlike before, the shot was clearly noticeable. A sharp clap, like a mini-thunderbolt, reverberated through the lab. Before the echo had faded, alarm klaxons and strobe lights ignited throughout the space.

Mitch jumped up from his chair and rushed to a white cabinet mounted on the wall. Pulling open the door, he retrieved two masks, complete with clear tubing and a canister at the end. Throwing one to Dusty, he yelled, "Put this on!"

The gunsmith from Fort Davis didn't have to be told twice, quickly following his brother's instructions.

Mitch returned to his computer, his fingers flying over the keyboard. Dusty felt his ears pop, a sensation similar to a quick altitude change in his plane. "I'm flushing the air with overpressure," mumbled Mitch through his mask. "Those alarms indicate some sort of gas was released into the lab."

Another minute passed, and then the alarms ceased. Removing his mask, Mitch gingerly sampled the air and then nodded at his brother. "It's safe," he promised.

"What the hell was that all about, Mitch?"

"I'm not sure," the professor paused, his eyes locking on the ballistics tube.

Dusty followed his gaze to the tube and inhaled sharply. The once smooth, heavy steel surface was crinkled – the skin looking like a child's pruned feet after staying in the tub for too long. "Holy shit," was all he could think to say.

Mitch approached the massive machine, his pace measured by both caution and amazement. Touching the surface of the tube, he quickly withdrew, shaking the limb as if in pain. "It's freezing cold," he turned and informed Dusty.

Mitch orbited the destroyed equipment twice, his brother behind him, tracing the professor's footsteps. The end cap of the tube had completely vanished, water and all. Several hairline fractures appeared on the surface, their presence explaining the alarms. "Minute particles of the iodine must have escaped and set off the sensors. It couldn't have been much though – we would've gotten very sick."

Finally satisfied with the visual inspection, Mitch turned back to the computers and waved his brother to join him. Still too hyper to sit, Dusty stood and watched over the professor's shoulder as the first monitor displayed a pre-shot image of the rail gun.

"Watch," Mitch said, tapping the screen.

The image slowly advanced, Dusty's finger entering the frame in slow motion, moving to pull the trigger. Mitch adjusted the movie's speed with the mouse, eventually freezing the display when a small cloud appeared around the barrel of the rail gun.

The image looked like a cigar smoker had blown a perfect smoke ring around the magnets. The next frame was even more puzzling.

A pencil-thick, black line appeared, almost as if the rail gun had emitted a dark laser beam instead of a projectile. The dark line ran perfectly straight until disappearing into the mouth of the ballistics tube.

Mitch rubbed his chin, mumbling, "What the hell," as his hands moved to the keyboard. He inhaled sharply when the monitor changed its image.

The area surrounding the black line morphed into a blurred swirl of reds and yellows. Features of the gun, table, and ballistics tube were still discernible, but appeared as some sort of psychedelic, acid rock music video. Everything was colored oddly, except the black line. "That's impossible," muttered Mitch.

"What?"

Tapping the screen with his finger, Mitch said, "This image is showing the infrared spectrum, or the heat every object is emitting. That black line is actually absorbing light, and that's impossible."

Again the doctor manipulated the computer, this time the same picture coloring with hues of pinks and blues – except the still-black line. "No," Mitch said, "That can't be."

Dusty didn't bother this time, his brother clearly troubled by what his instruments were telling him.

"I wonder what the speed is," Mitch blurted out while pivoting the chair to a different screen. Again, the two men watched the same video recording, this time with large green numbers at the bottom of the display. Before Dusty realized what was going on, Mitch exhaled and sat back in his chair. "I've always wondered about that."

"What?" Dusty asked shyly, not sure he wanted to know.

"I've always wondered if Mother Nature… the universe… if it would protect itself. I think your rail gun just proved that it will."

"What are you talking about, Mitch?"

Pointing to the green numbers on the monitor, Mitch explained, "This is a speed reading detected by the instruments. It indicates 235,700 kilometers per second. The speed of light is only 298,000."

Dusty shook his head, not sure he was understanding what his brother was saying. "I thought nothing could move faster than the speed of light. Didn't they teach us in high school that anything moving that fast would achieve infinite mass - would weigh as much as the entire universe?"

Smiling, Mitch nodded. "You actually learned something in Mrs. Higgins' physics class!"

"I remember almost failing because I was sitting next to Elizabeth Jordan, and her cheerleader outfit was very short. I kept trying to convince her that Newton was wrong – two objects could occupy the same space at the same time, or at least get damn close."

Mitch was too excited to tease his sibling over past sins. "That was Pauli, not Newton… but anyway, you remember correctly about the infinite mass. If your ball bearing reached the speed of light, it would, in theory, weigh as much as all known matter. It would have so much gravity that the earth would be crushed and compressed, the entire planet ending up a little speck on its surface – so to speak. The entire solar system would soon be sucked into its field… the sun, light, other planets… everything."

"Okay, I think I follow, but what does this have to do with Mother Nature defending herself?"

"The universe is constantly experiencing massive, unimaginable events. Supernova, colliding black holes, quantum strings - the list goes on and on. Huge spikes of energy are created, collisions of matter on a galactic scale – probably a lot of things occurring that we don't even understand. And yet in all the billions and billions of years, no event has resulted in one tiny sub-particle reaching infinite mass. Not by accident or design, it's never happened. My friends over in the quantum physics department would argue that something eventually will reach that speed, but so far there is zero evidence of it ever occurring."

"So? Pardon my ignorance, brother, but if the speed of light is the ultimate universal speed limit, why is that such a puzzle?"

Mitch opened his mouth, an explanation of equations and theory ready to roll off his lips, but then he stopped. "I believe it does happen, and perhaps more often that we might imagine. I think Mother Nature defends herself by opening a door to another dimension and escorts anything approaching that speed limit through the portal."

Turning to point back at the monitor, the professor continued. "This image shows that black line absorbing light. Nothing we know of can absorb all light – except a black hole. Some of my colleagues theorize that a black hole is a gap between dimensions. I think your rail gun, somehow, opened a door to another continuum and escorted the ball bearing, or what was left of it, through – probably to a dimension where the speed of light is faster, and thus, your projectile wouldn't result in infinite mass."

"My drill battery is generating a black hole? Is that what you're saying?"

"No. Your little power cell is ringing the doorbell. Mother Nature, with her infinite potential for energy is opening the door."

"Oh."

Mitch's gaze moved to the rail gun, his expression clearly indicating his mind was off somewhere, trying to piece together what they had just experienced. Shaking his head, he said, "I need a cup of coffee."

"Now you're talking."

Day 3 - Afternoon

High above North America, silhouetted by the deep background of space, the satellite LOEWS-7 fired a microburst of radio waves toward the surface, its beam directed at the antenna farm residing outside Colorado Springs, Colorado.

The signal was transferred by fiber optic cable into the bowels of Cheyenne Mountain, where it was received, decrypted, and processed by computers belonging to the North American Aerospace Defense Command. The end result of the process was a blinking blue light on the monitor of a United States Air Force lieutenant.

Clicking on the computer icon, he watched intently as the display changed to a series of graphs and lines, complete with a message that scrolled across the bottom of the screen, "Warning - Potential EMP event."

Turning to locate his commanding officer, the LT didn't have to look far as the strobe mounted on top of his console had already drawn the senior officer's attention.

"Sir, we've got another one of those odd magnetic events in Texas – this one similar to the occurrence two days ago," he informed the colonel. "Whatever is causing the reading produced a slightly stronger signal just a few minutes ago."

The older man clasped his hands behind his back, a grimace on his face. "Our diagnostics found all of our equipment was functioning properly. What the hell is going on?"

"This event was slightly east of the previous one, sir."

"Overlay a map of North America, Lieutenant."

The computer monitor changed to show a map of Texas, complete with the denotation of major cities and interstate highways. The colonel sighed. "Looks like those damn Aggies are running some sort of experiment at College Station and forgot to notify Homeland Security."

Everyone under the officer's command knew he was a graduate of University of Texas, the archrival of A&M - a fact that was made obvious to anyone with ears during college football season.

"Bring up the magnetic spectrum analysis, son. I'm curious what those dunderheads are doing."

After punching a few keys, the display changed again. The officer studied the data, one hand moving forward to rub his chin. "Okay, so it wasn't a nuclear event, and it doesn't match any known particle acceleration profile. Must be something new."

"The computers flagged it as being similar to an EMP event, sir," the young officer ventured. "Yet the level of electron agitation doesn't match the model."

After a moment of consideration, the officer waved his hand. "It's not our problem, lieutenant. Notify Washington of the situation — we'll let the FBI go chew on some Aggie-ass. Maybe that will teach those prima donnas to follow the rules for a change."

The lieutenant couldn't be positive, but he thought he heard the commander mumble, "Hook'em Horns," as he walked away.

Tom Shultz was about to leave the Bryant, Texas field office of the Federal Bureau of Investigation when his cell phone jingled. Looking at the caller ID displayed on the small screen, he snorted and then tapped the answer button. "Agent Shultz."

"Tommy, this is Fred Monroe down in Houston, how goes it up there in Aggie land?"

Frowning at the informal use of his given name, he barely contained the smart-ass response forming in his throat. The man on the other end of the call was the special agent in charge of the entire Houston office. He answered safely, "Everything's fine, sir. What can I do for you today?"

"I've just gotten off the phone with Washington, Tom. They've got their panties in a wad over some electromagnetic event that just took place up at A&M. The Air Force boys at NORAD are all in a tither because their satellites are squawking - as if they have anything else to do. Anyway, I need you to head over there and kick some ass. Someone at the university is evidently running some sort of experiment and didn't fill out the necessary paperwork to keep Homeland Security in the loop. You know how they are about that shit."

"Yes, sir. I understand. Can you provide me with any additional information?"

"I'll email you the file, Tommy. I appreciate your getting right on this."

Appreciate my ass, thought Shultz, *you big shots down in Houston always think we're just sitting on our hands up here with nothing to do.*

"Yes, sir. I'll head over that way as soon as I receive the information."

Ten seconds after the call disconnected, Shultz's email dinged with a new message. He opened, read, and printed the five pages sent from Houston, then headed for his car.

Mitch and Dusty locked the lab behind them, the professor teasing his brother over his insistence of taking the rail gun along in its hard-sided case.

After working their way through and finally exiting the huge facility, Dusty felt a sense of relief breathing the outside air. The walk to a local coffee shop relaxed the duo even further.

Dusty, in his authentic cowboy garb, stuck out like a sore thumb in the Java Barn. Despite the establishment's name including reference to a rural structure, the atmosphere and décor inside was decidedly bohemian, the clientele several decades behind him in age. The effect, if any, was lost on the two brothers as they gathered their steaming cups and found a quiet corner. Both men had more pressing issues occupying their minds.

"You know what you're carrying around in that case is easily the most significant discovery in the history of mankind, don't you?"

Frowning, Dusty said, "A weapon? I don't know that I buy in to that. How can anything so destructive be considered so important? I should probably go lay it down in the parking lot and start running over it with your car... or a bulldozer."

Mitch grinned at his brother's linear thinking. "In a way, your rail gun is similar to the splitting of the atom. Yes, it can be a horrible weapon, but that discovery also brought about advances in medicine, power generation, and a host of other fields. The developments enabled by nuclear technology pale in comparison to what you've found."

"How so?"

"You've unlocked what most likely is an absolutely clean, renewable power source. Don't you see, brother? With what you've discovered, we can turn the desert green! We can end hunger, probably most disease. There would be no need for poverty. Unlimited... free... clean energy can solve so many of the world's problems. No more wars over oil or riches – every society self-sufficient and focusing their skills on bettering people's lives. You may have just discovered faster than light travel which means we can colonize other worlds. Besides keeping every physicist on the planet busy for the next 20 years, you've no doubt opened the door to countless discoveries that could benefit mankind."

Dusty took a sip of his coffee, pausing a moment to savor the excellent brew. Mitch knew his sibling well, remaining quiet while the older Weathers worked through it all.

"You know what I see?" Dusty began. "I see something that is way, way too powerful for our kind. I don't have much faith in our elected officials or the military. There has been too much abuse, scandal, and outright corruption in the last 20 years for me to have any less jaded opinion. For sure, I don't trust a corporation any further than I can throw it. And that's just talking about the United States. When I think of foreign governments, it goes downhill from there."

"I can't argue with any of that, Dusty. I like math, science, and the elements God created. I don't understand politics or politicians. Still, we can't just throw this opportunity away. There has to be a way to realize, manage, and safeguard the potential of your discovery."

"Now you're talking like a scientist, Mitch. I'm sorry, but I can't think that way. My view is that when people find out about what this baby can do, whole bunches of man's darkest attributes are going to come crawling out of the woodwork. Power is so corruptive, and if what you're telling me is accurate, I'm holding the ultimate corruption right here in this little case. I think we should destroy it."

The concept of destroying such potential, of going backwards, troubled Mitch. If science had always reacted that way, the species would never advance. "There has to be a way, brother. You and I... right now... we're still in shock. Let's take our time and think about this. It's much, much too big a deal to go running off half-cocked and do something stupid."

~  ~

Chief Cassidy looked up from his paperwork to find Agent Shultz standing in his doorway. "Well, well, look what the cat dragged in. If it isn't my favorite federal officer – come all the way down here to the trenches to rub elbows with us common folk."

The FBI agent stepped inside the threshold, smiling at his old friend's greeting. After a quick handshake, the head of the A&M University Police Department continued, "Seriously, Tom, what brings you over our way?"

Producing the report from Houston, Tom verbalized a quick synopsis. "The anti-terror boys are all running around like Chicken Little. There's been an experiment, test, or something on campus, and it registered on a military satellite. Before sending in an armored division to make sure you still control College Station, they asked their A-team, me, to come check it out."

Laughing, Cassidy scanned the paper. Finding the longitude and latitude provided by the Air Force, he turned to a large wall map of the campus. After checking and rechecking the rarely used coordinate system, the chief poked his finger on the map. "I should have known.

That is the physics building, and they've got some pretty serious equipment over there."

"We need to check it out. Houston wants me to scare the crap out of whoever failed to notify our government of their activities. Feathers have been ruffled."

"No problem," replied the local cop. "I play golf with the guy who runs the entire show over there. He's a good egg. A little absent-minded sometimes, can't putt worth a shit, but a good guy nonetheless."

Before long, the two law enforcement officers were motoring toward the main administration building. Shultz was thankful the chief knew exactly where to go, and before long, they were standing outside an office that belonged to one, "Dr. Herman Floss, Dean, College of Science."

A polite receptionist showed the two men into Dr. Floss's inner-sanctum where they were greeted by a tall, thin man in his early 60s. After brief introductions and handshakes were exchanged, Cassidy got right down to business.

"Dean Floss, the United States Air Force has detected an electromagnetic event here on campus. Agent Shultz was directed by Homeland Security to check into the matter and make sure that all national security procedures are being followed."

Shultz added, "In addition, we want to ensure whoever violated current regulations is disciplined by the university and fully understands this is their one and only warning."

The FBI agent's statement caused the stoic dean to frown, but he didn't comment. Reaching for the paper being offered by Captain Cassidy, he mumbled, "Let me see who's working in the lab over there."

The two lawmen watched as Floss turned to his computer and pulled up a complex-looking calendar. The doctor's head swiveled back and forth between the FBI's report and the computer screen. Finally, he spun around to face his visitors. "Gentlemen, there are no experiments scheduled during this time frame at any of our labs. As a matter of fact, the location you've specified, Anderson Hall, doesn't have any activity scheduled all week."

The report caused Shultz's eyes to widen, the unexpected news increasing his pulse. "Can we go investigate that facility, Doctor?"

"Why, yes. Yes, of course we can."

As the three men crossed the campus, Dr. Floss explained. "Professor Weathers is in charge of all of the labs in Anderson Hall. I've asked my assistant to call his office and request he meet us there. I tried his cell, but there is no response. That's not unusual – the shielding around the labs often interferes with the signal."

But when the trio arrived, there was no Professor Weathers. The dean stopped a passing faculty member and asked, "Have you seen Dr. Weathers today?"

"Yes, I saw him this morning. He was walking around with a stranger – a rather rough looking fellow, big guy in a cowboy hat and carrying a metal case of some sort."

After answering a dozen questions of when, where, who, how and why, the now-nervous academic was allowed to continue on his way. Floss, Cassidy, and Shultz entered the building.

"Doctor, are there any high security labs in this building?"

"Yes," answered the dean, "We have three level 4 labs and a single level 5."

"Let's start there," Cassidy suggested, "This place is too huge to search without calling in every officer I have on duty today."

"There's an easier way than that. Just have someone find out where Dr. Weather's key card has been used," Floss replied.

Embarrassed over not thinking of the solution himself, Captain Cassidy pulled his cell phone and five minutes later had the trail of breadcrumbs left by Mitch Weather's key card. Showing Floss the list displaying on his smart phone, he asked, "Any of these the critical labs?"

"Yes, he was in the particle measurement lab when your event occurred. That actually makes sense."

Walking with purpose now, the two law enforcement officers followed Floss to the bank-vault entrance. The dean used his card and thumb to open the huge door, and they entered the lab.

Floss was drawn to the computer monitors while Cassidy and Shultz gawked in awe at the array of technology contained inside. It was Shultz who noticed the crumpled ballistics tube. "Has this piece of equipment always been damaged, Doctor?"

Floss spun around from the computer displays and moved to study Shultz's discovery. The dean's mouth was open as he circled the tube, finally urging the words from his lips, "That's impossible. It would take a nuclear detonation to do this level of damage. What the hell was Mitch doing in here?"

The word "nuclear" focused Shultz's attention even more, the agent starting to wonder if Houston was sending him on a worthless mission after all.

Floss returned to the computers, hunting and pecking on the keyboard. He finally located what he was looking for and turned, saying, "Gentlemen, I've found a video recording of the event."

The two officers moved quickly to stand behind the dean, watching with a rapt gaze as the computer monitor played the video of the rail gun's discharge.

When the dean found the velocity measurements generated by the device, he seemed to lose control of his faculties. Interspersed with a seemingly endless babble of technical terms, the man kept repeating, "That can't be," and "that's impossible."

Frustrated by the long-winded stream of astonished technical jargon, Shultz interrupted. "Professor," he stated in a firm voice, "in your opinion, is the device that was tested in this lab dangerous?"

The dean turned and stared at the two lawmen, his face ashen and voice trembling. "If the satellite hadn't recorded the pulse, I'd say this was a fake – a joke to be played on the internet. Mitch Weathers isn't some prankster - I fear this is real."

"But is it a threat, sir?"

Shaking his head at the officer's apparent naivety, the dean grunted his response. "Would technology so powerful it could collapse the core of a star be dangerous, Agent Shultz?"

"I need to call Houston," whispered a stunned Shultz after the comment.

"I think we need to call Washington," added Cassidy.

"I think we need to call God," mumbled Floss.

Dusty and Mitch exited the Java Barn carrying fresh cups of joe. Not wanting to go back just yet, the two men agreed on a route that would take them through a small park, adding a few blocks to their stroll.

The shade of a nearby bench drew them in, the grassy area calm and inviting. Since the demonstration of the rail gun, their conversation never drifted far off that topic, neither man able to move the other from his core position. Mitch wanted to find a way, any potential, to harness the good from the discovery. Dusty was set on destroying his invention.

Mitch became passionate. "In six months, I can design a generator that will provide 100% clean, 100% renewable energy from your device, all for free. Just think Dusty; this discovery can eradicate electric bills for both individuals and corporations. In two years, we can eliminate every fossil fuel-powered electrical plant in the United States. In ten, we can tear down the dams and decommission the nuclear power reactors. In 20 years, the internal combustion engine will be obsolete. The cost of goods and services will plummet; economic growth will explode. Every nation will be able to feed its people and raise its standard of living. We could build ships that could travel to Mars in days rather than years."

Dusty nodded, seeming to accept his brother's premise. After taking another sip of his coffee, the older Weathers stood and scanned the horizon. "You know, brother, you're right. I shouldn't destroy this thing; I should utilize it for the good of all."

Sweeping his hand across the campus, the gunsmith continued in a low, serious voice. "Now that begs the question. What *is* good for all? And I've decided on the answer. I, Durham Anthony Weathers, am good for all."

The professor's expression made it clear that he was puzzled by his sibling's behavior, but before he could ask, Dusty continued his speech.

"So here's the deal. Since I'm good for all people – since I know best how things should proceed, I'm taking over. I'm going to fly my little plane to Washington and demand to be made emperor. Oh, they'll turn me down at first. I'll have to knock down the Washington Monument, maybe the Smithsonian and definitely the Supreme Court building... and let's not forget the Capital building – but that's okay, we won't need the House or Senate after I'm running the whole show."

Mitch grinned at first, thinking his brother was making some sort of joke, but as Dusty continued, the smile disappeared.

"Now they still may resist, but that's okay. I'll just fly offshore a few miles and fire a shot into the Atlantic at full power. I'm sure the tsunami won't wipe out too much of the east coast – no more than a few million people will die."

The professor shook his head, "Don't fire the gun at full power, Dusty. I'm not quite sure you would survive the aftermath. On a larger scale, that weapon could split the earth's crust... a more powerful model might be able to split the planet in half."

"What about shooting up in the air?" The question meant to be funny.

Mitch sighed, then looked down at the ground. "Again, on a larger scale, hitting the moon might knock it out of orbit, or maybe just cause it to explode. It's not beyond the realm of possibility that a bigger version, if my thinking is correct, would simply cause the sun to collapse on itself and then go nova. The inner planets would all be destroyed shortly after."

Dusty bent at the waist and put his face directly in front of Mitch's, forcing the younger man to look him in the eye. "Don't you see what I mean, Mitch? Damn it, man, this thing is too much. Mankind is not mature enough to handle this sort of power. Some damned old fool is going to get his hands on it, and then we'll all be fucked."

Mitch was becoming desperate to defend his position. "Dusty, how about a compromise? Give me six months to present you with a reasonable plan to manage and control the capabilities you've discovered. If I can't set something up that meets your approval by that time, then we'll destroy the weapon together and forget it ever existed."

The older man rubbed his chin, analyzing the proposal. "And how are you going to set something up without telling everyone the rail gun exists?"

"I don't know, I'll think of something, I'm sure. Hey, what's going on over at Anderson Hall?"

Dusty followed his brother's gaze, back toward the building that housed the lab. At least five police cars on the south side, another half dozen on the west dotting the roadside. The two men could hear numerous sirens in the distance.

"Did someone find the damage in the lab?" Dusty asked.

Before Mitch could answer, a student came by, casually peddling a bicycle. Mitch waved at the kid and said, "What's going on over at the physics building?"

"I don't know for sure," reported the young man. "The FBI and police are over there looking for a guy called Professor Weathers. Something about terrorism was the only snippet of information I heard before they started forcing us to evacuate the building."

After Mitch had thanked the student and sent him on his way, he turned and looked at Dusty with troubled eyes. "I'm not sure how, but the FBI is here. This isn't good. If they've been in the lab, they no doubt saw the videos and know what we've been doing."

"So," questioned Dusty, "We've not broken any laws, have we?"

"Let's go back to your point just a bit ago. The gun is too strong for any one person to control. Do you want to hand it over to the local FBI agent? How about the chief of the campus police? Maybe one of the SWAT guys? Think about that for a minute, Dusty."

"I see your point. I'd better skedaddle out of here until you straighten this all out."

"Give me six months. Hide, run, travel – whatever you need to do, but give me six months to work out my end of the bargain."

Dusty nodded and then moved to hug his brother. After the embrace, he turned and began to walk off when Mitch yelled for him to stop. Reaching in his pocket, the professor pulled out a small thumb drive, a data storage unit. "I almost forgot. I put this in my pocket. This is the only copy of the blueprints the computer scan created of the gun. Keep them safe."

Nodding, Dusty then smiled and winked at his brother. "See you in six months, Mitch, hopefully sooner."

Glancing back at Anderson Hall, the professor noted the rapidly increasing number of police cars. He instinctively knew Dusty needed time, so he tossed the nearly full coffee into a nearby receptacle and turned back for the Java Barn.

~  ~

Dusty headed directly away from the main cluster of police cars around the lab building. He had no idea how many law enforcement officers College Station employed, but it sure looked like every single one of them was converging on the lab.

He found himself in a small area of shops and restaurants with more than a few people strolling along the sidewalks. That was good – he could get lost in the crowd and take a bit to think through his escape. He suddenly realized that a tall guy with a cowboy hat and boots didn't exactly fit in with the average person on the street. The police would have his description soon, if not already.

Two blocks ahead, a police cruiser turned the corner and headed directly at him. Quickly glancing left and right, he spotted an open shop. Ducking inside, he found himself in a campus bookstore. He quickly moved to the rear of the sizable facility, pretending to casually browse while glancing over his shoulder to see if the police were coming in behind him. The squad car passed on by.

The assortment of A&M paraphernalia displayed on the shelves was amazing. Glassware, bumper stickers, shirts, pants... you name it. Stopping in front of a rack of sweatshirts, it occurred to him that he needed a disguise, and this seemed the perfect place to acquire one.

A few minutes later, he was standing in the checkout line, a bundle of A&M logoed clothing in his arms. The girl working the register didn't even look up, scanning the items one by one. Never one who believed in credit cards, Dusty rolled off two $100 bills from his sizable wad and then asked the young lady if the store had a restroom. It did, and tucking his bag under his arm, Dusty headed to the men's room.

Despite the washroom being completely empty, he chose the last stall and breathed a sigh of relief as he locked the door behind him. The commode became his workbench as he quickly began digging through his purchases.

Grimacing, he replaced his best hat, a Resistol Horseshoe model purchased in El Paso long ago, with a baseball cap. The extended bill, pulled low, would make it difficult to get a clear view of his mug. Next, he pulled on a hoodie sweatshirt. Oversized sunglasses rounded out his disguise, the outfit covering much of his head and face.

Loading the backpack was next. Taking the rail gun, batteries and ball bearings out of their hard-sided case, he gently transferred the equipment to the pack. The weapon was followed by the two bottles of water, packages of beef jerky and an extra T-shirt for padding.

After making sure he was still alone in the room, Dusty stood on the seat and pushed one of the square ceiling tiles up and out of the way. The dust falling from above made him sneeze. He carefully stuffed the gun's case in the space above. He eyed the Resistol, common sense telling him to get rid of the big hat, but he couldn't part with it. The tile was fitted back to its original position. He then used toilet paper to wipe up the particles of insulation and dirt that had floated down. It wouldn't be good for someone to wonder what was up there as he sat doing his business. He stuffed the cowboy hat into the pack.

Exiting the stall, he paused to look in the mirror. The disguise wouldn't pass extra-close scrutiny, but if he kept his head slightly bowed, it would be difficult to see his face from any angle.

Laughter sounded outside the door, two college age guys then entering the facility, their conversation focused on the co-ed working the cash register. It was the first test of Dusty's getup. The two fellas passed right by him without a second glance, heading directly to the urinals without missing a beat.

Slinging the pack onto his shoulder, just like he'd seen other students haul books, Dusty made for the bookstore's exit. He froze at the door when the shoplifter alarm began buzzing loudly, the alert causing a sense of panic to well up in his throat. He was tempted to run out of the store, sure the incident would bring some sort of security force rushing to the door. On the other hand, sprinting out of the place would draw the attention of any police officer in the area.

Half-turning to look at the clerk, he shrugged his shoulders while digging the receipt out of his pocket. The girl behind the counter waved him over. "I'm sorry," she said. "I must have forgotten to remove one of the sensors. Turn around."

Dusty did as instructed, and felt the girl tugging on his new hoodie. A click and a snap later, she removed a beige colored button with a special tool and held it up for him to see. "You should be okay now," she said.

"Thanks. I'm trying to surprise my daughter."

"Well, you should probably let me cut that tag off the back of your hat then. It kind of looks a little nerdy."

Embarrassed, he pulled the hat off and let the girl snip the tag. A few moments later, he exited the store.

Normally a man who welcomed being outside, the fresh air no longer gave him a sense of comfort. Instead, he felt exposed, almost vulnerable as he meandered down the front steps.

Trying his best to maintain a normal gait and keep his shoulders slightly slumped, Dusty wandered through the streets of the college town. He tried to remain in the retail section, pretending to window shop while trying to think of a way out.

Renting a car was out of the question. By the time he could locate an agency, his driver's license would be posted everywhere. Stealing a vehicle wasn't realistic either – he didn't know how to hotwire a car. The bus station was probably as off-limits as well. That boiled it down to two options; his plane, or walking out. The latter plan would most likely to get him caught, lost, or shot for trespassing.

As he wandered the sidewalks, Dusty tried desperately to get his bearings on the airport. He knew where it was, the general direction, but the route Mitch had driven into the campus was completely exposed and likely to get him apprehended if he attempted to get there on foot. He tried to think about where he could safely acquire a map of the area, but couldn't come up with a workable solution.

Turning a corner, his heart jumped a beat at the sight of two policemen at the far end of the block, his coronary pace increasing again when they began walking his way. He glanced across the street, hoping a quick jaywalk would avoid the lawmen, but saw a similar patrol on the opposite side.

It would have been too obvious to turn around. Feeling like a rat caught in a trap, Dusty pretended to window shop at a men's clothing store, his mind frantically searching for a way out. A car engine sounded behind him in the street, and in the warped image of the window glass, he saw a vehicle with writing on the side and a contour on the top. *A police car!*

The vehicle pulled up to the curb behind him. Sure, it was a squad car, complete with lights on the roof, Dusty's mind told his legs to run, but they were frozen stiff. About the only thing he could manage was a half glance over his shoulder. It was a taxi, delivering a middle-aged woman to the men's store.

A taxi! That was it! Spinning quickly, he was at the back of the cab before the woman could deposit the change in her purse. Bending slightly, Dusty made eye contact with the driver and asked, "Airport?"

Without a word, the cabbie waved him in, and then they were speeding off. Four blocks of freedom and several glances out the back window later, the blood returned to Dusty's cheeks.

~ ~

Mitch was nursing his third cup of coffee, trying to remain calm at the only open table in the Java Barn. He didn't want the brew, but believed he'd look weird just loitering in the shop.

He didn't pay much heed to the two uniformed police officers when they strolled through the front entrance, assuming they were just stopping in for a quick caffeine fix. With a clear vantage of the counter, his breathing stopped as one of the officers held up a sheet of paper to the kid working the register. He knew it was up when the barista nodded, stood on his tiptoes and scanned the tables. He pointed directly at Mitch.

By the time his vision cleared, the professor was looking at two policemen standing in front of his table. "Professor Weathers," one of them was saying. "Could you please step outside for a moment, sir?"

Mitch couldn't remember his legs ever feeling so weak. He somehow managed to stand, and then one foot was moving in front of the other. It felt like liquid was running down the back of his knees. On the way out, the man in front of him lifted a radio from his belt and reported, "This is 117, and we've located Dr. Weathers at the Java Barn."

"Hold him there," responded a metallic sounding voice through the small speaker.

Mitch was thankful to lean against the hood of the police car, the support allowing him to concentrate on his next move. "What's the problem, officer?" he asked the closest cop.

"I'm not sure, Doctor. We had instructions to locate and detain you immediately. My supervisor is on his way. I'm sure he'll explain everything."

Mitch didn't have to wait long. A government-looking sedan pulled up, a man in a fancier uniform and another in jacket and tie exiting the vehicle. The guy with the tie was clearly in charge.

Extending his hand, the tie said, "Dr. Weathers, I'm glad to see you're okay – we were worried about you."

Mitch accepted the handshake, anticipating a crush, but the grip was only firm. "Why would you be concerned about my well-being? And who are you, anyway?"

"My name is Agent Shultz, FBI. The U. S. Air Force detected an electromagnetic event in your lab. When Dean Floss let us in, we found damaged equipment, but no sign of you. Witnesses and surveillance cameras showed you walking through the building with a rather rough looking character, and we thought you might be being forced to act against your will."

Mitch laughed, partly at the description of Dusty, partly because he'd anticipated immediate arrest. "No, I wasn't being forced to do anything. As far as the man who was with me, he was a colleague of sorts."

Shultz started to say something else, but was interrupted by the beating-disturbance of an approaching helicopter. The agent turned to Mr. Fancy Uniform and said, "Well, so much for calm, cool and collected – Houston is in the building."

Mitch watched the copter fly low over the skyline of College Station, the pilot evidently spotting a safe place to land the noisy machine. When normal conversation was again possible, the FBI man asked, "Professor, would you please accompany me? My superior has just arrived from Houston, and I'm sure he'll want to speak with you."

"Do I have a choice?" Mitch asked, a hint of defiance in his voice.

"Sir, I don't see any reason why you would wish to hinder an investigation. Am I missing something?"

The meaning was clear to Mitch – come along nice, or we'll find a reason to bring you along. He was beginning to seriously dislike law enforcement.

Shultz moved to the sedan and opened the back door, another strong hint that he wanted Mitch to come along. The professor complied with the lawmen's request.

A few minutes later, the men were back in the lab underneath Anderson Hall. Mitch's initial reaction to the throng of law enforcement poking and prying in his lab was protective. "What are all these men doing in here, Dean Floss? They should all leave immediately before something is damaged."

Floss ignored the protest, instead pulling Mitch aside. "What the hell happened in here, Mitch?" the dean asked in a low voice.

"I was asked by a colleague to evaluate a new invention, and it damaged the ballistic tube. I was going to fill out my report after I had a cup of coffee."

Before Floss could comment further, Shultz and another man approached. He didn't offer his hand. "Professor Weathers, I need to know where this man is," said the newcomer as he pointed to an enlarged photo of Dusty, obviously taken by one of the campus's numerous security cameras. "We know he was in the lab with you and is carrying some sort of weapon."

"And who might you be, sir?"

"I am Special Agent in Charge Monroe, FBI. I am responsible for the Central-South region."

"Well, Agent Monroe, I don't know where that man is. I parted company with him at the coffee shop some time ago, and I don't believe he was carrying any sort of weapon."

Monroe's face flushed red, and the man actually leaned closer to Mitch. "I don't have time for this professor. We know that a rifle-shaped object was fired into that tube over there, which Dean Floss claims is practically indestructible. Furthermore, I have the United States Aerospace Defense Command barking up my backside over what they perceive as a nuclear, or near-nuclear event. If that's not dangerous, I don't know what is."

Mitch held his ground, "There was no nuclear event, sir. You'll detect no radiation or other evidence of any sort of isotope in this lab."

Monroe held up another photograph, this one showing an image of the rail gun. "Exactly what is this device, Professor?"

"You don't want to know."

For a moment, Monroe didn't think he had heard the response correctly. His confusion didn't last long. "I most certainly *do* want to know, *Professor*... and I want to know *right now*."

"Trust me, Agent Monroe – no, you don't. No laws have been broken here. I had zero pre-knowledge that the test we performed would generate any side effects detectable by Homeland Security. I will fill out the proper paperwork in due course as per the regulations."

Monroe shifted his weight back on his heels, his chin sticking out in defiance. Turning to Shultz, he flatly instructed, "Arrest Dr. Weathers, Tom. Mirandize him."

Both Mitch and Dean Floss's mouths fell open, the brash move completely unexpected. Shultz played better poker than either of the academics, holding his expression neutral. "What's the charge, sir?"

"Conspiracy, conspiracy to commit an act of terrorism, harboring a terrorist. I'm sure more specific charges will be developed by the Department of Justice."

"Terrorist?" Mitch cried out. "Who the hell do you think is a terrorist?"

"The man who built this weapon," replied Monroe while pointing to the picture. He switched back to the image of Dusty, "This man is a threat to the United States of America."

Dusty was relieved to see the airport parking lot wasn't brim-full of police cars. Paying the cabbie, he rushed over, pulling the blocks from underneath the Thrush's wheels in less than a minute.

He hadn't filed a flight plan, nor checked the weather, but he didn't care. The need to get out of College Station was so vital; he felt it worth the risk. To Dusty, distance equaled time to think, and he desperately wanted to figure everything out. Doing so in a jail cell while strangers poured over the rail gun wasn't what he had in mind.

The old crop duster started on the first turn, and it was a fortunate event. Flashing blue lights swerving into the airport's lot drew his eye, the arrival of the authorities eliminating any chance of radioing for permission to take off.

A quick scan right and left revealed no incoming air traffic as Dusty rolled across the tarmac much faster than normal. He had just applied full power when two policemen came rushing out of the main offices, waving their arms for him to stop. The ground controller was so insistent over the radio that Dusty reached down and turned off the squawking device, the distraction of the annoying voice grating on his already frayed nerves.

The small plane achieved wheels up after a short acceleration down the pavement, Dusty looking over his shoulder in time to see one of the police officers talking into a radio.

The soft drink machine spit out the dollar bill for the third time. With a grunt of displeasure, Colonel Chamberlin snatched the bill away and began flattening it over the edge of the misbehaving device.

"How did a man who struggles with technology as much as you do ever become a pilot?" asked the captain, sitting at a nearby table.

Chamberlin ignored the question and re-inserted his money. After a series of humming and grinding noises, the red LED letters registered $1.00. Looking up with a grin as he punched his drink selection, the colonel answered the question. "Hard work and persistence is how I managed these wings, Captain Taylor... hard work and persistence."

Returning to his game of solitaire, the junior officer grunted, but offered no other comment.

Chamberlin moved to the bulletin board hanging next to the fickle drink machine, intently reading a paper thumbtacked to the cork surface. "If we beat the maintenance team Saturday, we've got a shot at the trophy this year," he commented.

"If I don't come out of my hitting slump, we won't be able to beat the local little league team."

Grinning, Chamberlin turned to the younger man and inquired, "How did a guy who struggles to hit a softball ever manage to become a pilot?"

Before the captain could respond, a sergeant burst into the room. "Sir, we have a scramble order, level Red from NORAD. This is a Noble Eagle roll."

Both pilots vacated the break room, moving quickly for their lockers. They were joined almost immediately by a group of airmen who began assisting with the complex task of donning flight suits.

A short time later, the two pilots were riding across the tarmac of Kelly Field outside San Antonio.

The 182nd Fighter Squadron, known as the Lone Star Gunfighters, was technically a training unit. Staffed with experienced combat pilots and equipped with F-16 Fighting Falcon (block-30) aircraft, the outfit occasionally was tasked with performing missions for Homeland Security as part of Operation Noble Eagle.

Since hijacked aircraft had been used to attack the World Trade Centers on September 11, 2001, the US and Canadian Air Forces have been tasked with providing air patrols over major American cities, successfully executing over 400 missions since the terrorist attack.

A "Red" scramble was a pilot's worst nightmare. Noble Eagle missions almost always involved an unknown civilian aircraft, often a commercial jetliner filled with hundreds of passengers. Every pilot dreaded the day when he would be asked to execute "the order," a command to shoot down such a plane full of innocents.

As they approached their aircraft, Chamberlin's mind was heavy with the concern. He'd personally flown several of these missions, praying each time that he wouldn't have to execute the order, but knowing he would if he had to. The logic was simple – killing 200 in the air might save thousands on the ground. The lesser of two evils. But that didn't make the prospect any easier on his blossoming stomach ulcer.

The two Falcons were an ant mound of activity. Live, air-to-air missiles were being loaded under each wing by the ordnance specialist while the crew chiefs and other maintenance personnel checked every detail of the warplanes.

Each of the pilots performed a quick visual inspection of his aircraft's exterior and then climbed aboard. The two jet fighters were rolling across the runway a few minutes later. Colonel Chamberlin, flying lead, began receiving his mission briefing as he neared the end of the runway.

As the controller's voice sounded in his ear, the Falcon's flight computers were receiving streams of data containing potential vectors, codes, and other necessary information regarding the potential target. The two interceptors were immediately cleared for takeoff, their powerful GE F-110 engines roaring to life.

While the F-16 was nearing the end of its service life, it was still a potent multi-role aircraft. Simple, nimble, and capable of hosting a variety of weapons, the Falcon was still a frontline aircraft for several of America's allies. They were more than capable of handling anything that could cross into American airspace.

The intercept orders received by Colonel Chamberlin were a mixed bag. The airmen were hunting a single-passenger private aircraft, and that was both good and bad news. The pilots were relieved that *the order* wouldn't come into play during this mission, at least not involving hundreds of lives. The problem was this tango, or target, would be difficult to find.

Small, low, slow moving airplanes weren't the intended foe for the Falcon's modern avionics. Chamberlin's bird was built to hunt other jet aircraft and engage them at great distances - if at all possible. In case a standoff missile intercept didn't bring down the adversary, he was ready for a supersonic dogfight. None of these tactics would be effective against a small propeller-driven aircraft.

The colonel knew his radar would be practically worthless in acquiring the target. He also understood that the maximum speed of his quarry was less than the Falcon's stall speed, and that could be a serious handicap.

A crop duster, he mused. *Now why are they scrambling warplanes to hunt a crop duster?*

The vector he'd been given pointed east, northeast. The target's last known position had been College Station. A possible scenario popped into the pilot's mind, and it chilled his soul.

Long ago, he'd attended one of the seemingly endless security briefings so common after 9/11. Texas A&M University maintained one of the largest, deadliest collections of biological samples in the world. Ebola, Yellow Fever, several variety of plague, smallpox and other infectious agents were stored in a high-security facility at the university – the same area his target was last seen leaving.

A crop duster would be equipped with sprayers. Biological weapons were often disbursed as a liquid, suitable for spraying. Chamberlin's mind starting running with the possibility. *Did some crazed idiot steal a batch of smallpox and a crop duster? Is he heading for Austin or*

Dallas with spray tanks full of that shit? What about San Antonio, where my wife and children are right now?

Chamberlin was a career military officer, accustomed to executing orders that occasionally seemed unnecessary, misaligned, or just plain illogical. It was how discipline and the chain of command functioned.

This scramble made absolute sense for a change, and he was confident in his ability to carry out the mission.

Settling in at a cruising altitude, the two hunters flew east at 600 knots.

Day 3 – Late Afternoon

It never occurred to Dusty to fly any direction but west. While he knew heading home was out of the question, his knowledge of several local, unofficial landing strips was significant. The Thrush was capable of setting down just about anywhere that wasn't growing trees, and that was a small comfort to the pilot.

Not only was his home airstrip not an option, he was sure his house would be under surveillance by now. Dark images entered his head, visions of strangers prowling around his workshop, violating his home. He shook it off, concentrating on the things he could control.

Miss Grace was the answer. To Dusty, the image of her calm, logical demeanor was like an oasis filled with cool water to a thirsty man crossing the desert. He had to get there. He needed her counsel.

While he wasn't an expert on the law, he felt comfortable contacting her. She, being his legal representative, wouldn't get in trouble by helping him think through this mess. Or at least he hoped so. *Be honest with yourself*, he reasoned. *You desperately want her advice - and to see that smile.*

He was inventorying the potential landing spots within walking distance of the old Barlow place, when two gray streaks shot past the Thrush's canopy. The pass startled Dusty so severely that he physically lurched against his restraints. The turbulent wake kicked up by the passing fast-movers rattled the Thrush's cockpit – the air disturbed to the point that he had to make quick, minor corrections to maintain level flight.

His mind quickly identified the how, what, and why he'd almost suffered a mid-air collision. After settling all that, the fear began to well up. Someone wanted him, someone serious enough about that desire to send up fighter jets. *The rail-gun cat must be out of the bag*, he reasoned.

Glancing left and right, he tried to locate the two warplanes. Despite the sky being perfectly clear with unlimited visibility, he couldn't find them. They, however, had no trouble tracking him.

Again, seemingly out of nowhere, two flashes of gray metal roared past, closer this time. Dusty, half expecting the pass, got a better look at his antagonists and identified the planes as Falcons – armed Falcons.

He watched the impressive planes this time, following their track as they climbed while making a steeply banked turn. Despite the situation, he acknowledged the beauty in their capabilities – a respect for the power they represented.

The Thrush was outgunned and outmaneuvered. Dusty felt like a cyclist competing at the Indianapolis 500 – there wasn't any way he could outrun his pursuers. While he didn't know their exact specifications, it was clear that speed wasn't the answer to his problem.

The fighter pilots had flown about 200 yards on either side of him with that last pass. He figured they would come closer and closer, eventually damaging the Thrush with their wake. He would either be forced down or crash – the outcome basically the same as far as the military was concerned.

Taking his eye off the warplanes for a moment, he scanned for somewhere to land. He didn't have any local knowledge, so the likelihood of spotting an airport was low. In reality, any field would do, but he didn't want to take too many chances. The terrain below was hilly – not something he was accustomed to gauging from the air.

I wonder how long they can stay on station, he pondered. *Could I land and just wait for them to run out of fuel and leave?* The area below him looked pretty rural. The jet pilots would radio his location and law enforcement would be alerted where to find him. *How long would it take for a county deputy to find him? Could he get airborne again and escape after the jets left to refuel?*

Colonel Chamberlin cupped his ear with his gloved hand, more from the shock of the radio transmission he'd just received than any difficulty understanding the words.

Taylor evidently was puzzled by the order as well, the wingman pulling close to the lead Falcon's port wing, his gesture of "What the hell," clearly visible despite the distance separating the two aircraft.

They had just been given permission to shoot down the crop duster – if necessary.

It was unprecedented. It was "the order."

While taking down an aircraft harboring a single person didn't carry near the psychological weight of an airliner with hundreds of souls on board, it still wasn't taken lightly. The plane they were harassing was technically unarmed and assumed to be piloted by a citizen of the United States. Regardless of Chamberlin's previous fantasy of spray tanks full of deadly biological weapons, he realized that had been pure speculation – unfounded in fact, knowledge, or evidence. Now the justification to kill seemed lacking.

A little surprised at his reaction, the colonel decided he would focus on the "if necessary" part of the order. He'd do his best to *make* it unnecessary. He had no desire to be judge and jury, sentencing a man he didn't know anything about to death.

Pushing his transmit button, the lead pilot informed his wingman of their next tactic. "Two – I'm going to airbrake with a vertical and drop in on the tango. Let's see if I can relate a visual message before things get out of hand."

"Roger that, One."

Searching the ground below resulted in Dusty losing visual contact with the two fighters. Trying to divide his activities between flying, locating a suitable makeshift landing strip, and avoiding another surprise when the jets zoomed past was challenging to say the least.

Pinpointing the hunters came up in the rotation, and he craned his neck all around trying to find his pursuers. At the last moment, he looked up and slightly behind his right shoulder. What he saw made him squint his eyes and brace for the impact, positive he was about to have a mid-air collision with one of the fighters.

The belly of the F-16 was coming down almost on top of the Thrush – and descending rapidly. From Dusty's point-of-view, he understood an insect's perspective right before being squashed by the sole of a shoe. The undercarriage of the warplane looked huge as it dropped toward his canopy.

At the last microsecond, the wing of the Falcon tilted slightly, and then the plane leveled itself with the Thrush. Dusty was looking at the military pilot through the cockpit glass, their wingtips less than 10 feet apart.

The jet's driver looked like a giant, menacing insect with his bubble-eye visor, deformed helmet and breathing mask that was shaped like a giant mandible.

The stall speed of the Falcon was significantly higher than the maximum speed of the Thrush - the jet jockey's hair-raising maneuver required so he could hover next to the slower aircraft for a few moments. He used the time well, relaying what he wanted the private pilot to do, and what would happen if the Commander's aviator didn't comply.

Dusty watched as the officer gestured with sharp, intimidating movements. After pointing to the ground with three quick stabs of his finger, the killer-insect then crossed his throat with one finger – the universal sign for death. *Land the damn plane*, Dusty interpreted, *or I'll kill you*.

Just as fast as it had arrived, the F-16 was gone, peeling off with a bright circle of flame spouting from its exhaust.

The threat didn't have the anticipated effect on the gunsmith. Anger over the injustice of the whole ordeal began forming in his chest – words like abusive, authoritative, and draconian filling his mind. As the old crop duster hummed along, Dusty's temper simmered.

An unusual ground feature off the starboard wing distracted him for a moment, a combination of trees, a small hill, and a field reminding him of a spraying challenge he'd faced long ago. As he studied the terrain, an idea occurred to him – a possible plan of escape.

He scanned for the predators, eventually discovering them off to the south, executing a long, slow turn to come up behind him again. He then checked the sun. If he timed it just right, it might work.

When he was directly between the fighters and the late afternoon sun, he gave the old plane full throttle and put her into a dive. Pulling up less than 20 feet off the ground, he hugged the central Texas landscape as if he were spraying a field.

A line of trees appeared through his front glass, the approaching wall of foliage closing with his propeller at 130 mph. It was going to be close.

At the last possible moment, Dusty yanked the nose up, barely clearing the top of the strand. Like a rollercoaster cresting a high hump, he then pushed her back down as soon as he'd cleared the tree line. The Thrush's dive was such an abrupt change in direction that Dusty thought his stomach was going to come out his nose.

Almost instantaneous with the dive, he banked the small plane hard. He watched in horror as his wingtip approached the ground so close that the waist-high grass below parted in the wake of air as he passed.

Standing almost vertical on its side, the Thrust turned hard. Dusty was pressed down and down in his seat, the G-Force compressing his spin. And then he was in.

The trees and hill were like the rim of a giant soup bowl, the open, flat area of the field in the middle. Keeping the plane in a constant turn, Dusty began circling laps around the edge of the bowl – hugging the forest's edge while hopefully hidden from the birds of prey above.

~ ~

Colonel Chamberlin checked his fuel, mentally calculating how much time they had before heading back to the base. Taylor, as usual, was right on his wing.

It was the captain's voice that signaled the first indication that something was amiss. A simple radio chirp of "One, where did he go?"

Without answering, Chamberlin pointed the nose of the fighter slightly downward in order to provide a clear view of the air in front and below. There was no sign of the little crop duster and its stubborn pilot.

Knowing it was impossible for the plane to have simply disappeared, the two jet pilots slowed their speed and began a systematic search for a bright yellow, moving target. In moments, they passed over where the Commander should have been.

"Two, did he land?"

"One, it was awful quick if he did. Maybe you scared him so bad he crashed."

"Two, there would be some smoke – wouldn't there?"

"One, who knows? I don't see him though."

A tinge of panic began to rise in the colonel's mind – visions of Taylor and him being the laughingstock of the Air Force if they couldn't rein in a little prop-job. "Two," the colonel broadcasted, "You split north, I'll take the south. Low and slow, 20-mile sweep."

"Roger, One. Breaking right."

Separating would double the amount of air space they could search and provide different angles of sight.

Three minutes later, they met up again, no need to transmit their failure. Chamberlin was becoming angry, partly out of embarrassment. Most of his ire, however, was directed at the pilot who was eluding them.

"Two, maybe he did a 180 on us and headed back east. Let's backtrack 30 miles and then sweep forward."

"Roger, One – on your lead."

For 10 minutes, the sophisticated, all-powerful cats searched for the defenseless mouse. The effort produced nothing but a growing frustration and dwindling fuel. Chamberlin's voice developed an edge. "Two, I read 18 minutes to bingo fuel."

"One, concur - 18 is about it."

The lead pilot's thoughts changed to how in the hell he was going to explain losing the target - his mind trying to reconcile what they had done wrong, if anything. When that didn't pan out, he began mentally creating excuses while contemplating the imaginative spin that would be necessary in his report. Taylor might come through this unscathed, but his career was over.

His wingman saved the day. "One, got him," sounded the excited voice. "Bearing 040, angels 20 or less. He's flying laps down in that woods. I would've never seen him, but the sun flashed off his glass."

Even with Taylor's direction, the lead pilot couldn't find Dusty. Not wanting to take the chance of another Houdini-like escape, Chamberlin transmitted, "Two – you've got the lead, my angle is bad."

Dusty was flying to save his life – the most difficult piloting he'd ever attempted. The soup bowl he was hiding in didn't have enough diameter to ever straighten the Thrush's course. Pulling a constant, highly banked turn required all of his attention and skills – one minor distraction would result in his smashing head-on into a thick canopy of trees at 115 mph.

In addition to the difficult flying, it hadn't occurred to him that there was no way to know how long he'd have to stay in the pattern. He couldn't afford to scan the surrounding sky, yet the concept of looping the racetrack for even a single minute after the jets had given up and left, didn't sit well. Every moment he circled was dangerous flying.

In the end, his predicament didn't matter; the gray streak of the two warplanes flashing in front of him at treetop level signaled his scheme had failed. In a way, Dusty was relieved.

Timing it just right, he straightened out the Thrush and rose from his hide. He was exhausted, scared, and tired of the whole encounter. The first priority was to find a place to land the damned plane and wait for the authorities.

A few minutes later, Dusty spied a farm lane that wasn't lined with utility poles – about as good a spot as he could hope for in the rural countryside. He adjusted his course and prepared to set the Thrush down. It soon became clear that he'd noticed the spot too late – the approach was just bad. Keeping low, he decided to circle around rather than make a mistake that would end his life.

~  ~

"One, he's trying to hide again," announced Captain Taylor, completely misunderstanding Dusty's maneuver.

"I see it. I'm sending this guy a message. I'm going to make sure he knows I don't like his little games. Switching to cannon."

Chamberlin's broadcast seemed to take his wingman by surprise, "One... sir?"

Grunting, the flight leader said, "Two, just a warning shot. I want to see that plane on the ground before we head back to Kelly."

The M61A1 Vulcan mini-gun installed in each fighter's nose had been designed to crack the hulls of Soviet era battle tanks. Capable of firing 100 rounds per second, the weapon was so powerful its recoil could actually slow the Falcon's air speed.

When Chamberlin activated the cannon, the display projected onto his canopy changed to bright green crosshairs surrounded by various sighting data. He aligned his aircraft to fire in front of the target, adjusting for the speed and angle of both planes. He squeezed the trigger.

Sounding more like a buzz saw than a gun, a virtual rope of 20mm lead shells exited the 6-barrel mini-gun.

Dusty had it all lined up with good altitude and speed. He was barely 10 feet off the ground when the earth exploded less than 100 yards in front of his plane. Geysers of soil, rock, and vegetation erupted into the air, quickly followed by the flash of the warplanes as they passed overhead.

Somehow, he managed to get the Thrush on the ground, pings and thumps of the debris striking the front of the plane as he passed through the grey cloud of residue raised by the attack.

After he was sure the landing was successful, Dusty started screaming at the circling aircraft, "Why are you shooting at me? I landed, damn it!" It didn't matter that they couldn't hear him; the small relief seemed worth the effort.

Shutting down the engine and still angry, Dusty pulled back the canopy and climbed out onto the wing. He reached back, pulling the A&M backpack from behind the seat.

Deciding to make for a nearby tree line, Dusty started walking across the pasture between his landing spot and the woods. He hadn't traveled more than 30 steps when the two fighters flew over his head so low he physically ducked. His ears rang from the noise generated by their passing engines.

"Good gawd! I set it down, damn it! So what now? Are you going to make me aviator road kill, too?" he screamed.

Something snapped inside the gunsmith from West Texas. Some limit of injustice or fear or outrage was crossed with the low pass of the warplanes. Taking a knee in the open field, Dusty unzipped the backpack and removed the rail gun.

The battery was next, followed by the canister of ball bearings, and then his earplugs. He assembled the gun quickly. Leaving the power at the same 05% setting as had been used in Mitch's lab, Dusty smiled when the LED glowed green.

He'd hunted his share of fowl, the experience initially causing him to lead the circling aircraft by too great a distance. His mind returned to thoughts of Mitch's instruments and the readings showing the gun's projectile moving near the speed of light. He modified his aim, bringing the sites much closer to the nose of the lead fighter.

He pulled the trigger.

The shot's thunder seemed less intense in the open spaces. Dusty thought he saw the mysterious black line, but it was difficult to be sure.

The most powerful explosive devised by man, the splitting of an atom, expands at roughly 9 kilometers per second, creating an atmospheric overpressure traveling at the speed of sound. Despite a diameter of less than an inch, the doorway opened by Dusty's shot expanded at the speed of light, or 41,000 times faster. At that velocity, the blast wave created by the dimensional pipe was devastating. A thin wedge of air, with a density greater than chromium steel, slammed head-on into the F16. Like a giant knife, it sliced through the skin of the aircraft, severing metal, hoses and wiring in its wake.

From Dusty's view on the ground, the lead warplane seemed to wobble in mid-air, almost as if it was suspended on puppet strings.

Chamberlin spied some sort of black streak flash in front of his aircraft, but before the image could register, the entire world of his cockpit went crazy.

Like an anchor had been dropped from the tail of his ship, the plane seemed to hesitate in mid-air, the jolt heaving him forward against his restraints. Then every alarm, light, and indicator on the dash started buzzing and blinking.

The stick went dead. The nose went up, and then down. The plane began spinning like a Frisbee.

The G-Force exerted against the colonel's body was unlike any turn or dive he'd experienced in his 18 plus years of piloting jet aircraft. Quickly exceeding 10 times normal gravity, his head was pinned against the side of the canopy, his helmet weighing the same as 100 pounds, his body tipping the scales at over 2,000.

The force of the spin pulled all of the blood to one side of his torso, and his vision began to tunnel – a sign that his brain wasn't receiving enough oxygen to function.

Adrenaline surged through the pilot's system – his mind screaming that he was about to die. The hormone gave him super-human strength, and he needed it.

The effort to lift his one free arm was off the scale, tendons straining and ligaments being punished. Every muscle in his body protested the abuse, but he kept reaching. Visions of his wife and children filled his mind and made him even more determined to live.

His gloved hand finally closed around the ejection handle, relief surging through his brain. He heaved with the last bit of strength left in his body.

Small, explosive bolts detonated around the canopy. The bubble shaped glass flew away, pulled by the 500 mph slipstream racing past the aircraft.

Rocket motors ignited under the colonel's seat, the effect eliciting even more pain for his already tortured frame. His perch essentially became an aircraft all its own, blasting away from the dying Falcon with spine compressing thrust.

And then everything was quiet.

The red and white stripes of the parachute's fabric were the first thing his re-oxygenated brain registered – the colors beautiful, the air calm, the sensation of floating downward a comfort. It all began coming back to him.

His first priority was the chute, a quick glance assuring him that it had deployed properly. Next was his wingman, but a scan of the sky didn't reveal Taylor's plane. Despite his neck feeling like it was broken, Chamberlin kept pivoting his head in an effort to locate the other aircraft under his command.

On the third pass, he found Taylor – an identical red and white parachute drifting downward about a mile away. *At least he got out*, supposed the flight leader. *I hope his ejection was clean.*

A distant rumble drew his eye to the ground, a ball of black smoke rising into the air. That disturbance was quickly followed by another, almost identical sound. A second column of yellow flame and dark soot rose skyward. The green prairies of central Texas were now scarred with dark smears – the remains of both Falcons scattered across the landscape.

Dusty didn't know how long he'd been standing with his mouth open. Searing pain in his lungs reminded him of the need to breathe. The realization that he'd just shot down two of the world's most advanced fighter jets caused mental paralysis for some unknown period of time. Eventually he shook it off. Like a child who had just broken a neighbor's window with a baseball, his instinct was to run. He desperately wanted to get away from the scene of the crime.

His hands were shaking so badly he couldn't disassemble the rail gun. Instead, he stuffed it into the pack and began trekking back to the Thrush on weak legs, a mixture of guilt and fear filling his chest.

Doing the pre-flight checklist was calming – the structured routine bringing discipline back into his scrambled mind. The crop duster achieved wheels-up four minutes later.

The fact that he'd managed a take off without becoming a third crash site restored some of his confidence. As he gained altitude, the burning debris of his former nemesis came into view, but Dusty couldn't look. He forced his attention on the route ahead and keeping his plane level.

It occurred to him that continuing to head west was folly. The military had stockpiles of aircraft. Visions of angry pilots, scrambling toward rows of waiting war machines filled his mind. He could almost see the need for revenge painted on their stoic faces, almost feel the bloodlust rushing through their veins.

He turned south, choosing that direction for no specific reason.

The desire to flee quickly evaporated, suddenly replaced by the need to hide. "I need to think and gather my wits," he mumbled to no one. "I feel like a big, fat target up here."

A sort of calm came over him, the cold hand of self-preservation finally coming to grips with the panic attempting to take control of his being. For the second time in the last 30 minutes, Dusty began looking for someplace to land his plane.

The landscape below the low flying Thrush was mostly rural, obviously utilized for agriculture. The occasional farmhouse passed by, a campground, a small settlement in the distance.

The sun would be down in a few hours, and Dusty knew finding a suitable spot after dark would be next to impossible.

While he covered the miles, he tried to anticipate what the authorities would do next. Someone would realize the fighters had crashed within minutes, if not seconds. Their last known position was probably already displaying on a computer screen somewhere.

There was also a high probability that some local rancher or passerby was reporting the exact position of the wreckage. The area below was sparsely populated, but not deserted.

He assumed local sheriff's departments would be the first responders – federal officials soon behind. It wouldn't be shocking to learn that additional fighter aircraft had been launched to complete the mission. Perhaps military investigators, medical teams, and pilot recovery units would respond as well.

Regardless of the authorities' reaction, Dusty needed to get out of the air and become invisible, find a spot where he could conceal the Thrush from both ground and airborne searchers. That wasn't an easy ticket to punch.

Thoughts of landing next to a wooded area and covering his plane with limbs and branches were dismissed. He didn't have an axe or saw and most anything he scavenged from the ground would be devoid of foliage. Besides, the effort would take a lot of greenery to cover the plane's bright yellow paint job.

A small, unmanned regional airport *might* be equipped with hangars – covered parking for airplanes. They *might* be unlocked. They *might* not be visited by the local police. His plane *might* not be discovered by another pilot coming or going. Too many, far too many "mights."

Luck was with him as he flew over a small knoll and spotted a large, isolated barn. There had been several such structures beneath his wings, but all had been close by the owners' homes. This particular example sat all alone in the middle of a relatively flat tract of wheat or barley.

Banking to circle the barn, Dusty first checked for nearby structures, but didn't see any other sign of civilization. His next lap was to see if any utility lines or fencing might be in the way. On the third pass, he landed the Thrush and rolled close to the barn.

The old building showed weathered, gray colored, wood plank under a rusted metal roof. It was a two-story affair, a small swing door leading to what was likely a hayloft at one point in time. The main entrance was a doublewide opening, originally built extra wide, so tractors, implements, and other machinery could easily fit inside. From the outside, the growth of weeds around the threshold indicated the barn hadn't been used in some time.

Dusty shut down the Thrush's engine and dismounted, the still-assembled rail gun poking out of the A&M pack slung on his shoulder. He approached cautiously, peeking through the numerous cracks between the rustic planks.

The inside appeared to be absolutely empty, and that was a relief. Dusty had been in his share of old barns, many of which served as storage for junk equipment and unwanted machinery. Whoever owned this property evidently didn't need to store anything inside.

His first attempt at opening the door added to the mounting evidence that the structure was rarely used or visited. The hinges were rusted stiff, protesting with loud screeches as he forced them open. A quick glance confirmed what he'd seen from the outside – a barren, hard-packed, dirt floor was the only thing inside.

He then stepped off the width of the entrance – relieved there would be at least a foot of clearance for each wing. Ten minutes later, the Thrush's propeller was blowing dust and cobwebs all around the interior of its new makeshift hangar.

Dusty stayed in the cockpit until the air settled, making a mental note to measure the opposite door just in case the barn's builders didn't construct it the same size as the one he'd just driven through. He cursed himself for not thinking of that potential problem sooner – a sure sign of his fatigue. Turning the plane around inside would be back breaking work, if it could even be done at all.

After the interior debris had settled, he exited the cockpit and scouted the surrounding countryside again, then pulled the large doors shut. The shelter provided a sense of relief. Not only did it feel good to be hidden from prying eyes, standing on the ground and being surrounded by four walls greatly reduced the number of directions requiring his diligence.

Digging the beef jerky and bottled water from his pack also added to his sense of wellbeing. At least he'd had the forethought to purchase these basics – maybe he wasn't such a bumbling criminal after all.

He began to notice little things, like the sound of birds singing in the distance and the residual smell of hay in the barn. Not only were both a comfort, the experience made him realize that he was recovering quickly from what had been the absolute worst day of his life.

Slowly chewing the jerky and sipping water, Dusty began to ponder his next move. Despite the coziness of his new hideout, it was a short-term solution - an eventual dead end. He'd given his word to Mitch – six months.

Things have changed quite a bit since I made that promise, he reasoned. *The entire US government wasn't after me then. I hadn't shot down any military aircraft when that agreement was made.*

Staring at the rail gun propped nearby, he tried to recall all of the promise within the technology – potential that had caused Mitch to be more optimistic than he could ever remember. Speaking to the gun, he said, "It's all about you, isn't it? You're the cause of all this. Are you worth it? Is your future really that bright?"

The gun didn't answer, but the sound of his own voice helped Dusty achieve a clarity of purpose. He had to save the technology – he had to give Mitch the time he'd promised. But there was something else... some other aspect to his determination. The government's reaction had been completely over-the-top, and that was disturbing.

As he sat nibbling salty meat and sipping tepid water, he tried to reconcile the events of the last few hours. *It all boiled down to a matter of trust,* he determined. He didn't trust his own government – had no faith in his fellow countrymen. *Why was that?* he wondered. What had happened to his once rock-solid, foundational conviction that the United States of America was the greatest country on earth? Why had words like "Land of the Free and Home of the Brave" evaporated into a wisp of adolescent memory?

News coverage came flooding back, troubling headlines of spy agencies monitoring American citizens and prying into private communications. Stories of politically motivated IRS scandals hinted at a punitive federal machine. He recalled worrisome captions that claimed once-trusted agencies, such as the FBI and DEA, circumvented the process of obtaining legal search warrants on a regular basis. He remembered watching footage of overzealous prosecutors twisting facts and spinning circumstantial evidence to achieve convictions. The only word in Dusty's mind that described the leadership of his homeland was "vindictive." *Nothing noble about that*, he supposed.

It wasn't just the feds. Stop and frisk policies were implemented by big city police forces while gun control legislation requiring medical professionals to report "thoughts of violence" were passed at the state level. *Thoughts? Seriously? Now having a bad thought was a crime?* Liberty was eroding, and most of the people seemed not to care. To so many it seemed, liberty was only a statue in New York Harbor.

Dusty's life in West Texas seemed unaffected by it all. Sure, he and Hank would entertain themselves, debating various sides of the issue over coffee at the diner. The two men would play devil's advocate and argue vehemently, each arbitrarily arguing an opposing stance. When their cups were empty, both men would continue with their days, smug in the knowledge that common folk – everyday Americans – were blind to the effect of it all. The citizens of Fort Davis went about their business, buying feed, putting grocery sacks in their SUVs, sending their children off to school and appeared none the worse from the graduated, creeping loss of freedom.

Adding it all up, he came to the conclusion that his lack of trust in the authorities was justified. Launching fighter jets to shoot down a man who was supposed to be innocent until proven guilty was indicative of a larger problem… a problem he couldn't solve. Now he, a freeborn law-abiding American, was in the crosshairs of the unchecked, malicious machine.

Could the rail gun change all that, or would it make things worse? His brother was book smart, but optimistic when it came to the hearts of men, especially powerful men. Still, the only person walking the planet that he trusted 100%, Mitch thought the rail's technology was worth the gamble and sacrifice. His brother's words resonated in Dusty's thoughts. "We can turn the desert green," and "we can end hunger forever, probably eliminate most disease."

Mitch was right, he finally conceded, his mind relinquishing the sweet juice of plotting revenge with great effort. *I will honor our agreement, do my best to follow the plan - for as long as I can.*

That meant hiding. Dusty thought long and hard about where to hide. His natural instinct was somewhere remote… a cave… a deserted island… a mountaintop. While the concept of a desolate existence didn't bother him, the problem of where to find such a place without any time to research or plan was troubling.

It then occurred to him that perhaps isolation wasn't the best option. Wouldn't it be far more difficult to locate a single man among millions of other people? Hide in plain sight? The concept was definitely more realistic than a cave. Houston, Dallas, San Antonio and Austin, huge cities with millions of residents, were all within reachable distance.

He'd spent more time in Houston more than any of the others – knew its basic layout. Maria lived there, and he'd visited the city several times to spend time with Anthony.

The thought of his son tore at Dusty's heart. Eventually the boy would learn of his father's actions. He wished there was some way to let him know the truth. Resolving to accomplish such a feat as soon as his own survival was assured, Dusty pushed the love of his son aside. He needed to focus.

Again addressing the weapon, "So Houston it is. I know you've never been there – it will be like a vacation for you. We'll fly in at night… land in one of the fringe airstrips. We'll walk into the edge of town and find a hotel. We'll hole up there for a while, maybe see if we can get in touch with Mitch."

Having a plan made him feel better, despite the rail gun not providing its opinion, good or bad. Dusty stood, finished his water, and then proceeded to inspect his airplane.

Rambling around the Thrush, he noticed a few nicks and scrapes in the paint that hadn't been there when he'd left West Texas just before first light. The damage to his pride and joy stirred more anger, sure the military jets firing at him were the culprits.

Inspecting the tail section gave him an idea. Airplanes were all painted with a unique tail number. Like a VIN number for an automobile, each plane received a set of federally registered digits that stayed with it for life. Everything involved that tail number. Boats had names; cars had VINs; and homes had addresses. Planes had their TNs.

If Dusty's plan to park the plane at a small Houston airport had any chance of success, he would need to buy some time by keeping his tail number off the hot sheets of wanted or stolen aircraft. He reached for the small toolbox he kept under the seat, and sure enough, he discovered a roll of black tape and a razor knife. Carefully balancing on the airframe, he modified a "3" to look like an "8," and then changed a "5" to a "6."

The disguise wouldn't stand a close inspection, but given the speed his life seemed to be moving as of late, it might make a difference. After all, there weren't that many canary yellow Thrush Commanders roaming the skies of Texas.

He checked his reference guide and decided on David Wayne Hooks field, north of suburban Houston – just east of Tomball, Texas as his destination. The field was large enough that a new plane wouldn't be noticed right off, yet small enough that the tower wasn't manned at night. He could hike into Houston from there.

Again scanning around his hideout, Dusty estimated he had a little over an hour before sunset. The finalization of his course filled him with calm – enough so that sleep might actually be a possibility. Setting his watch alarm, he stretched out on the wing, the rolled up hoodie cradling his head like a pillow. Ten minutes later the barn was filled with the deep, rhythmic breathing of the exhausted fugitive.

Day 3 - Night

Mitch was beginning to *seriously* dislike Special Agent Monroe. Not only had the man ordered his arrest, but now insisted on asking the same stupid questions over and over again. The interrogation technique was wasted on the academic. The windowless, isolated room, complete with the television cop show, two-way mirror along one wall, was designed to be boring. He was sure the architect had been instructed that the lack of visual distractions would eventually weaken the resolve of the typical human. Mitch wasn't typical.

Even the seating was carefully calculated for eliciting confessions. Agent Monroe's perch was well padded, with armrests and lumbar support. Mitch's chair was hard plastic with only a small backrest – deliberately engineered at a bad angle. The house held the advantage - utilized all the odds.

Monroe was an experienced interrogator, his questions carefully worded with slender nuances and easily misinterpreted innuendo. None of it worked on the mind of the professor.

Mitch came into the room armed with the most potent weapon any suspect could possess. He believed in a cause and was convinced his position was the right one. His superior intellect, nearly flawless memory, and passion for his brother's well-being made the professor a difficult nut to crack.

Monroe was nothing, if not relentless. He believed in his own cause, had faith in his own capabilities. The two personalities clashed in heated exchanges, both experiencing heightened levels of emotion.

"I want to know the name of your visitor, Professor. If, as you insist, no law has been broken, what is the harm in providing his identity?"

Sighing, Mitch responded. "I keep telling you, sir. You don't want to know. This subject is above your pay grade, with an impact to national security far beyond anything you can imagine. Let me call Washington and speak to the Secretary of Energy. Give me that courtesy, and you'll thank me later."

Monroe leaned back in his seat, an expression of disbelief on his face. "I'm not going to let you call anyone, Doctor. At least not until you provide me with some justification."

There wasn't any question asked of him, so Mitch didn't respond. The pause was interrupted by Monroe's cell phone.

Taking the call right in front of his prisoner was another sign of the FBI man's growing frustration. Mitch listened to one side of the conversation.

"He did what?"

"Both of them?"

"How could he have just disappeared?"

Monroe ended the call with a disgruntled, "Yes, sir," and disconnected the call.

Spinning around and leaning across the table, Monroe's angry, red face stopped only a few inches away from Mitch. His voice grew low and mean. "Your mystery acquaintance just shot down two F-16 fighters, Doctor. Nothing illegal? No laws being broken? Bullshit. There's been an air battle some 70 miles west of here, sir. The United States of America has lost two warplanes. I want to know what the fuck is going on, and I want to know *now*."

The news shocked Mitch – his reaction causing his first blunder of the session. "Is Dusty okay?"

"Dusty?" Monroe repeated. "Where have I heard that name... your brother? Your file says you have a brother who goes by the alias of 'Dusty.' You've been protecting your brother all this time?"

The agent didn't wait on Mitch to answer. Turning to the supposed mirror, he ordered, "I want the file on the good doctor's brother. Compare the surveillance photos to his driver's license. I want to know everything about this man – yesterday."

Smug with his victory, Monroe couldn't help but rub it in Mitch's face. "Thank you, Doctor. You've been most helpful." And with that, the agent left the room, leaving Mitch alone to curse his outburst.

Since all of his personal belongings had been removed during the booking process, he couldn't tell how long they left him sitting in the room, but it was a significant amount of time. Unlike most occupants of the facility, Mitch welcomed the opportunity to contemplate.

When a burly police sergeant finally came to retrieve him, Mitch felt a small flame of hope that he would be set free now that the FBI had the answer to their most pressing question. Instead, he was escorted to a small holding cell, and again found himself without company.

~  ~

Monroe left the police headquarters and made for the lab. Dean Floss and two FBI technicians were at the facility pouring over the evidence left behind.

Agent Shultz was also present, greeting his boss with a curt nod.

"What's the latest?" Monroe asked the local agent.

"Not good, sir. The dean has spent most of the time verifying that the lab's equipment isn't malfunctioning. Both he, and the techs you flew up from Houston, don't believe the video evidence left behind. After you left with Weathers, Dean Floss began to change his mind... retract some of what he told us before. Someone actually suggested that were it not for the damaged tube and NORAD's report, they would think the entire episode was nothing more than an elaborate hoax."

Monroe's brow furled, "But *there is* the damaged tube and the magnetic wave."

"Yes, sir. From what I can understand, they've spent just as much time debating over how that could have been staged as actually examining the evidence."

Shultz heard his boss mutter, "Bullshit," under his breath and then he stepped off to address the three-man technical team.

"Dean Floss, can you give me an update, please?" the lead agent asked with a menacing tone.

Being in charge of one of the nation's most advanced schools, Floss wasn't used to being addressed in such a tone, especially in a lab, most certainly in his *own* lab.

"As I told you before, Agent Monroe, I'll provide a detailed report of my findings as soon as possible. As of this moment, I'm still uncertain of what happened here."

Monroe bore in on the academic, his posture bullying the smaller man. "Doctor, I'm beginning to get a bad feeling about *you* and *your* department. I'm being told that an enormous amount of energy was unleashed in this facility – a facility under *your* direct control. The Air Force validates that fact. I've got one of *your* employees under arrest and refusing to corporate with an ongoing federal investigation. Now, you're stalling. Forgive my imagination, sir, but I'm beginning to think

I've stumbled upon a nest of conspirators plotting against my government."

Floss wasn't easily intimidated. Waving off the overbearing man, he replied, "That's ridiculous. The reputation of my school is flawless, sir. My people have the highest civilian security clearances available. We've worked with the US government on so many projects, I've lost count. Your theory is way, way off base – completely unsubstantiated."

"Really?" replied Monroe. "I don't think so. This wouldn't be the first radical plot hatched in the bowels of a university, Doctor." To emphasize his point, he removed his cell and tapped the screen. When the call connected, he looked Floss directly in the eye while speaking into the device. "I need the file on Dr. Martin Floss, College Station, Texas, please. Forward the electronic image to my phone."

Monroe's shadowy threat didn't have the desired impact on the dean. Instead of cowering, the older man crossed his arms in defiance, a look of determined stubbornness settling on his face. The rebellion wasn't lost on the FBI agent. *He'll come around after he thinks about it a little more*, pronounced Monroe.

Circumventing Floss, Monroe moved past and began speaking in low voices with the bureau's own technicians. "Please tell me you've made some progress," he began.

"Not much, sir. We have multiple videos, one of which shows a technically impossible reading of velocity. Dr. Floss agrees with that assessment, but can't find any bug in the hardware or software. Other than that, there's not much here."

"Why is this velocity reading so impossible?"

"Because it indicates an object moving at close to the speed of light, which takes infinite energy. There is no power source in, or available to this lab that would even come close to providing that."

"Could Durham Weathers have taken the power source with him?"

The technician laughed out loud, muffling the outburst when a scowl crossed the senior agent's face. "Sorry," he fumbled, "I thought you were joking. Every nuclear power plant on the earth, combined, couldn't generate nearly enough power to achieve the results indicated on the video. If our fugitive has such a device on his person, you might as well give up your chase, sir. He's carrying around as much energy as a billion stars in his pocket."

Shaking his head, Monroe pointed toward the ballistic tube. "Then what caused that damage?"

"That is unknown as well. We have two pieces of a puzzle here, sir. The pieces don't match. It took a lot of force to damage the tube, but if the video readings are accurate, that tube should be a pile of dust. So would the wall behind it and half of the continent between here and Atlanta. That's why I've allowed the good professor to run his diagnostics – the pieces of the puzzle don't fit together. Something's wrong."

"What if I told you two F-16 fighters were just shot down not far from here? They went down at the same time the Air Force detected an almost identical magnetic pulse to the one generated in this lab."

The tech whistled, his eyes widening. "I can believe it, given the damage to the tube. What I can't explain... what no one can explain... is how. It's just not physically possible, sir. I will say this, whatever is causing these events is completely unknown to our physical sciences. I would advise caution, sir. The power of this device seems practically unlimited and is already housed in a weapon."

Without further comment, Monroe spun on his heels and exited the lab, managing to throw both Shultz and Floss a harsh glance on the way to the door.

~  ~

The temperature outside was beginning to drop, the evening holding the promise of a comfortable, cool Texas night. The combination of air and walk helped cool Monroe off as well. By the time he'd strolled back to campus police headquarters, his mood was almost civil.

As he entered the building, his technician's words kept reverberating through his head. *Extreme caution. Unlimited power.* And then the professor's advice joined in. *Above your pay grade.*

Professor Weathers was yet again the object of Monroe's focus – this time the senior FBI agent seeing fit to visit the prisoner's tiny cell.

"You have repeatedly told me that the information I seek is above my pay grade, or similar words. Tell me who commands a position 'high enough' to be trusted with your information?"

Now we're getting somewhere, thought Mitch. "Dr. Witherspoon – the Secretary of Energy."

Monroe didn't even try to hide the smirk, "Come on, doctor, be serious. Put yourself in my shoes. I call the Department of Energy and ask for the Secretary. What am I supposed to tell them when they ask why? How am I supposed to justify the request?"

It was Mitch's turn to smirk. "You don't have to call him, Agent Monroe. He was my post-graduate sponsor and is the godfather of my children. He'll take the call on my name alone."

Mitch watched his nemesis carefully, secretly hoping for some sort of embarrassment or backpedaling.

He received no such gratification from the name drop. Instead, Monroe signaled a nearby policeman to open the cell, and then calmly waved for the professor to follow.

The two men walked to a semi-empty office, Mitch getting the impression it was Monroe's temporary workspace while he was visiting. Again without a word, the agent pointed to the telephone sitting on the desk and said, "Be my guest."

"Actually, sir, it would be easier if I could use my cell phone. I have the number stored in my contacts."

Nodding, Monroe stuck his head outside the door and ordered Mitch's personal effects be brought to his office. Five minutes later there was a soft knock on the door, and then a uniformed sleeve handed Monroe a large plastic bag.

Mitch dialed the Washington number, a voicemail system answering the call after four rings. "Please leave a message for Henry Witherspoon after the tone," sounded from Mitch's speaker.

After the beep, Mitch said, "Dr. Witherspoon, this is Mitch Weathers. I hope you and Paula are both doing well. Sir, I need your help desperately... an emergency. Please return this message, any time day or night as soon as possible. Thank you."

Monroe was impressed. Most of the civilians, suspects and criminals he worked with on a daily basis exaggerated their connections. "Okay, Mr. Weathers, the answer to this next question determines if you sleep here or at home tonight."

"Okay."

"What would happen to me if I did know your deep, dark secret?"

Mitch considered his words before replying. "You might become corrupted, Agent Monroe. Or someone above you would succumb to the temptation and have you, or anyone else who knew the secret eliminated. I'd hate to see people start disappearing simply because of what they know. I wish I didn't know. Look at what's happened to me since I found out just a few hours ago."

The answer seemed to surprise the senior agent. Thumping a pencil on his desk for a moment, he apparently settled on a course of action. "Go home, Professor Weathers. One condition – if anyone tries to contact you regarding this case, I'm to be informed immediately. Anyone. Do we have an agreement?"

"Does anyone include my brother?"

"Yes… probably the most important person on the list."

"Then we don't have an agreement, sir. I'll not turn on my brother. Lock me away forever, but he's my blood."

Smiling, Monroe nodded. "Good. I think that's the first time you've been absolutely honest with me. Go home, Weathers – with the condition that I'll know about anyone but Dusty contacting you."

Mitch rose to leave, but hesitated at the door. Turning back, he said, "I have an important suggestion for you, sir. You've caused quite the ruckus here on campus. I would strongly suggest you create some sort of cover story. Despite its size, the campus is a close society. People talk. I'm sure the last thing you want is a bunch of conspiracy junkies roaming around looking for a government cover up of some rumored super weapon."

The FBI man pondered Mitch's statement for a bit, and then asked, "What would you suggest, Doctor?"

"A bomb threat… nothing found… false alarm."

"That's not a bad idea. Not bad at all. Thank you, Doctor."

Dusty waited until there was just enough light to safely take off. While illumination wasn't a prerequisite for flying, he was in an unfamiliar area and didn't feel like there was any advantage in waiting.

He'd studied the charts, entered the waypoints into the GPS, and double-checked the aircraft. It was time to leave the secure surroundings of the barn and head to the fourth largest city in the country. Hopefully he could lose himself in the vast humanity residing there.

Opening the barn doors, he carefully taxied the Thrush out into the field. There wasn't any breeze, a fact confirmed by a telling glance at the closest line of trees. The takeoff went smoothly, and in a few minutes, he was 1,000 feet above the remote Texas countryside with just enough remaining light to make out the occasional feature here and there.

Flying at night was a different experience. The rods and cones in the human eye didn't relay as much depth perception in low light as during the day. Vertigo was far more common, with stories of pilots flying their planes right into the ground while thinking they were maintain a safe altitude. It was a sobering thought.

Dusty knew from his charts that the only obstacles he had to worry about were radio towers. He'd carefully plotted a course that would avoid them.

Even at such a low height, he could see for a considerable distance. Lights twinkled in the cooling atmosphere, some clusters of illuminations indicating small towns or villages. Other, more distant examples were distorted with color – a horizon to horizon display of Christmas decorations if he used his imagination.

He was less than an hour's flying to from his destination, and the miles passed quickly. Before long, the sky ahead began to glow a pale yellow, the effect growing more intense as he flew south. Houston's nightglow was enormous, almost as bright as a false dawn. It made sense to Dusty. After all, the city measured over 70 miles wide and 50 miles deep.

The GPS indicated he was getting close to Texas Highway 290, which according to the map was a four-lane freeway close to the metropolis. Right on time, he detected the almost solid line of white car lights heading north, a similar trail of red taillights heading south.

The scene was distracting, his mind playing airborne trivia instead of staying tuned and tight on his instruments and controls. Each unusual ground formation or cluster commanded his attention, curiosity consuming him with the vague images his eyes registered. It was one reason why flying at night was dangerous.

The next identifiable landmark was another highway, this one Texas 249. Dusty crossed the lesser-used road right on schedule, only a few miles from the destination airport.

He got lucky three miles out. Detecting the blinking lights of another aircraft, Dusty first made sure that he wasn't on a collision course. That potential disaster eliminated, it then occurred to him that the other plane appeared to be lining up to land at Hooks. He decided to follow, hoping the other guy had more experience with the facility.

Not only did the other plane have more experience, it also had access to the remote lighting system. This new feature allowed an incoming aircraft to radio a specific code to a computer, which in turn illuminated the runway lights. This good fortune improved Dusty's mood enormously.

Wheels-down was smooth. Looking at the larger than anticipated facility out his cockpit glass, Dusty began scanning for a good place to hide the Thrush in plain sight. He didn't have to look for long.

The sign above the large, metal-sided building read, "North Side Aviation and Storage." In front of the main building, two rows of private planes stretched off into the distance.

The Thrush fit nicely in an open spot about a football field's length away from the office. It wasn't unusual for a visiting aircraft to use the facilities without permission. Normally, the pilot would call or stop by in the morning and pay for the parking, fuel or any other service needed. With any luck, the Thrush wouldn't be noticed until he had put a lot of distance between himself and the plane.

As he emptied his belongings from the cockpit, a dark sadness came over him. He knew this was probably the last time he would see his old girl – at least for a very long time. Despite being a wanted man and feeling the urge to move out, he walked around the plane one last time – his throat tight and eyes moist.

Shaking it off, Dusty headed off on foot toward the edge of the airfield. He knew from the maps that a well-traveled roadway ran north and south along the airport grounds. He intended to use it as a guide.

Three hours later, Dusty had barely managed to travel five miles into Houston. Completely underestimating how difficult it was to follow the road while staying off it, he'd struggled with every fence, subdivision, ditch, and creek.

Wet, sweaty, exhausted, and hungry, he finally found himself in an urban area dense enough where he could walk along the sidewalk and not draw attention to himself. Cars zipped along the thoroughfare, paying him no heed. He'd hiked another mile before a neon sign flashing "Vacancy" drew his eye.

At the late hour, the lobby was locked. The clerk, summoned by the door side buzzer, gave Dusty a hard look before letting him in. When he saw his reflection in the mirror, he understood why. Muddy boots, a small tear in his jeans, and a mismatch of clothing wasn't indicative of his normal personal presentation.

"Do you still have a vacancy, sir?"

"Yes, it's $80 a night with tax."

"Okay, sign me up."

"Could I see your ID, please?"

The question froze the fugitive. While his driver's license was still inside his wallet, he didn't know how sophisticated the law enforcement computer systems were. Would they be immediately alerted if his real name went on the register?

"My wallet's been stolen, sir. That's why I'm here in the middle of the night. I stopped down the street to eat, and when I came out, my car had been broken into and my billfold was gone."

The man behind the counter seemed to ponder Dusty's fake predicament. As an afterthought, the West Texan pulled out his significant wad of cash. "Fortunately, I hadn't left my money in the car, or I'd really be screwed," he offered.

"Eighty dollars for one night," the man repeated while sliding a form across the counter. His intent was clearly for Dusty to fill it out.

Again, he hesitated. The hotel wanted his name, address, phone number and other information. Picking up the pen, he decided to become George Dunlap, the high school shop teacher's name the only one he could conjure up.

Ten minutes later, Dusty was inserting a magnetic key card and opening the door to the "mini-suite." Setting down the backpack, he explored his new residence. "Sure beats sleeping in the barn," he mumbled. In reality, it wasn't a bad place to hole up for a few days. There was a small kitchenette, queen size bed, and free cable TV. What more could any outlaw need?

A shower was the first order of business, the small bottles of shampoo helping eliminate the layer of grit, stress induced sweat, and nervous grime that covered his body. Wrapped in a towel with the rail gun lying next to him, Dusty fell asleep without even pulling back the bedspread.

Day 4

He woke up not knowing where he was for a moment. Gingerly rolling off the bed, Dusty made for the windows, partially curious to see if the parking lot were full of police cars, mostly wondering what his surroundings looked like in the daylight.

There were no police cars, the weather looked hot, and he was smack-dab in the middle of an urban shopping area. The view offered no surprises.

He'd noted that a free breakfast was offered in the lobby, and after verifying he could still make the cut-off, he dressed quickly and proceeded on a determined quest for gratis coffee.

An orange, two cups of java, and a bowl of cereal accompanied him back to the room – the food energy renewing a positive outlook on the day. As he savored each bite, he began scribbling a "to do" list on the free hotel stationery, the cheap pen protesting actual use.

While his A&M pack fit in well within the backdrop of College Station, here it might be more obvious for an older man to carry such an item. Besides, it wasn't big enough for a criminal who was required to carry all of his belongings everywhere he went.

He also needed spare clothing, including underwear and socks. Adding food, instant coffee, a razor, toothbrush and other hygiene products to his list, Dusty felt ready to go shopping. The problem was where to go and how to get there. Walking along the street after dark was one level of risk, doing so in broad daylight yet another.

Staring out the window in an effort to gauge the neighborhood, he saw a solution to part of his problem. A large, brightly painted, metro bus was unloading passengers just a block away. With the transportation issue resolved, the next question was where he could locate the commodity items on his list.

The older woman working the lobby-clerk position that morning provided the answer. Down the road, less than two miles, was a huge shopping mall. The bus line stopped right in front.

One dollar and 20 minutes later, Dusty climbed down from the public transportation and began eyeing the plethora of stores, shops, and restaurants within easy walking distance. Not far away he spied an enormous building, a sign over the door advertising "Atlas Sports and Outdoors."

He soon found himself inside the biggest sporting goods store he'd ever seen. Aisle after aisle filled with clothing, hunting, camping, and shooting supplies that seemed to stretch out forever. Smiling, Dusty thought, *I can spend the entire day in here, and no one would ever find me. I might just move in permanently.*

As he stepped forward, an alarm went off, the sudden alert causing Dusty to freeze mid-step. A smiling young lady approached and asked, "Excuse me, sir, but are you carrying a firearm by any chance?"

He started to lie, but then saw a sign declaring all firearms must be unloaded and checked at the courtesy counter. It made sense, given the facility claimed to offer the services of an onsite gunsmith, as well as trade-ins.

"I'm sorry, but yes, I have a rifle I want appraised in my pack."

"No problem," she chimed. "Let me put a tag on it."

Dusty unzipped the backpack, exposing the rail gun's stock. If the girl noticed anything unusual about the weapon, she didn't comment. Wrapping a lime green piece of tape around the grip, she nodded and said,

"Thanks for shopping at Atlas. If there's something I can help you find, please let me know."

Wait till the boys back in Fort Davis get a load of this, he mused. *A big city store that welcomes a man carrying a rifle. No one will believe me.*

Dusty located everything on his list, and then some. There were so many backpacks on display, he had a hard time making a choice. The camping section offered freeze-dried everything, including stew, bacon and eggs, and even blueberry pie. He also picked up an assortment of hygiene items, intentionally designed to be used on extended outdoor adventures. He even discovered pintsized containers full of laundry soap, the diminutive packets usable in a hotel sink if he needed to hand wash his duds.

Clothing wasn't an issue either. Rack after rack of every imaginable type, brand, and color of active wear was available for purchase. The quality was high, as were the prices, but he didn't care. It would be good to have a change of underwear and fresh socks.

As he meandered up and down the aisles, he came across a display of cell phones that boldly advertised "no contract." Mobile phones were essentially useless in Fort Davis, the mountain-blocked reception spotty at best. But here... could he use one of these devices to contact Mitch?

A young man wearing a store name tag offered a nicely toned, "Finding everything, sir?"

"My wallet was stolen a few days ago," Dusty began. "My cell phone, too. Do I need any sort of identification to use these phones?"

"No, sir. You can buy one and use it almost immediately without any ID or credit card. The purchase price includes a pre-loaded number of minutes."

Anonymous calling, reasoned Dusty. *I bet these would give those television detectives fits. How would the cops trace calls?* Living in a remote area of West Texas, Dusty had never bought a cell phone. Not only did the mountains interfere with the signals, Fort Davis was not a large enough community to warrant its own tower system. He just didn't have the need for such a device, especially since it would only function part-time at best.

But now his location and needs had changed. Thinking of calling his brother after things had settled down, he selected the most user friendly-looking model and threw it in his shopping buggy.

Wandering into the firearms section, a look of enchantment soon covered his face. It wasn't the seemingly endless row of rifles and pistols along the back wall — he'd seen most of those before. Nor was it the tremendous assortment of ammunition. Dusty was enthralled by the accessories. The internet had shown him pictures of many of the cleaners, optics, slings and other items — but to see them in person! He slowly pushed his cart through each aisle — reading practically every label and pitch.

A large, glass display case held special interest for the gunsmith. Full of optics, lasers, battle sights and other aiming aids, he dedicated additional time to browsing the various options. He'd wanted to mount some sort of optic on the rail gun, but didn't have anything suitable in his gun safe at home. Besides, up until a couple of days ago, mounting a scope on the nonfunctional gun was as useless as a politician claiming he wanted to help. It might look good, but no benefit would be gained.

Before he rolled the buggy past the display case, a nice, high-powered scope was riding in the cart along with his other essentials.

Looking at his watch, Dusty realized he'd been in the store several hours. Unsure of how long the buses ran, he decided he'd had enough fun. Besides, he could always come back.

He paid cash at the checkout line, his money roll significantly diminished by the scope. Still, he had over $2,000 dollars stuffed in his shirt and jeans pockets, a little more hidden in the fold of his boot.

He waited almost 20 minutes for the return trip bus to arrive, spending most of his time looking away from the street in case a law enforcement officer was passing by. An hour after boarding the public transportation, he was back in his room unwrapping, sorting and packing his gear. With his dirty clothing soaking in the bathtub, he sat about testing the small kitchen. The beef stew smelled reasonable, the instant coffee better than nothing.

~  ~

The electric golf cart hummed down the pavement at Northside Aviation and Storage. The retired pilot who managed the place advanced slowly, the creeping pace necessary so he could check off tail numbers using the clipboard resting in the seat beside him.

The yellow Thrush caught his eye, the beautiful plane unusual in both color and model. "You're new," he mumbled to the aircraft. "What a pretty lady you are."

Looking at his watch, he figured he had a moment to inspect the new arrival, his love of all things that flew as passionate as the first time he saw an aircraft 70 years ago.

The old Rockwell was a true classic, her stout frame and extra wide wings making her a workhorse of the barnstorming trade. She was a blue collar aircraft – strong and proud, able to earn her keep.

Returning to the cart, he squinted at the tail number and noticed something odd. Sliding out of the seat, he moved closer to inspect and realized someone had altered the numbers. To the manager, there were few sins more egregious than stealing a plane. He pulled the cell phone from his pocket and dialed the police.

"We've found his plane," announced Shultz. "It was discovered on the north side of Houston at a small airport about 30 minutes ago. The engine was cold. No sign of the pilot."

"Houston?" questioned Monroe. Pulling a file from the stack on his desk, he flipped through a few pages and then stabbed the paper with his finger. "His ex-wife lives in Houston. I bet he's gone to her for help."

The lead FBI man looked at his watch, quickly making up his mind. "Let's head to Houston, Tommy. I'll pack everything up here while you run home and throw a change of clothes in a bag. Obviously, the trail leads to the Bayou City."

The FBI helicopter landed at Hooks, not far from the now besieged Thrush. Two black SUVs sat nearby, bureau personnel fingerprinting, photographing, and inspecting Dusty's now-seized airplane. Shultz and Monroe exited the copter, strolling toward the agent running the airport investigation.

"We know his flight history now," relayed one of the techs. "He left the waypoints and route history in the GPS. I can tell you when and where this guy has been going back several months."

"Can you sum it all up and have it on my desk by tomorrow morning?" Monroe asked.

"Yes, sir. You'll have that and anything else we uncover first thing."

After assuring himself that there was little more to be garnered at the airport, Monroe ordered their driver to Maria Weathers' home address. Two additional agents from the sizable Houston office had already verified the suspect's ex-wife was home.

~ ~

Maria was reviewing an offer when the doorbell rang. Puzzled by the interruption, she pulled a .40 caliber M&P pistol from her purse and then made for the front door. Peeking out the security hole, she saw two men, wearing suits, on the stoop. "There's no soliciting in this community, guys. Didn't you see the sign at the gate?"

"FBI, Miss Weathers."

Frowning, she replied, "Sure ya are, slick. You both better skedaddle because I'm calling security."

"Miss Weathers, the guard at the gate will be happy to verify our credentials. I can call him if you wish."

Maria examined the two men again, this time the one in front was holding up a badge. Cautiously opening the door a crack, she inspected his ID. Still unsure, she remarked, "Anyone can buy one of those off the internet, pal. I'm not convinced."

Movement from behind the two men drew her attention, a uniformed Houston constable approaching her door from the sidewalk. "Miss Weathers, you probably don't remember, but you sold me and the missus our home two years ago."

"Officer Gibson, how is… Nancy?"

"You do remember," he said with a smile. "She's fine, ma'am. You can rest assured that these two gentlemen are indeed federal officers, Miss Weathers."

Opening the door, Maria waved the two men inside, the appearance of her pistol causing them a slight discomfort. "You'll pardon my caution, fellas, but I live alone. A girl can't be too careful these days."

After returning the handgun to her bag, Maria offered her two visitors something to drink. Both declined.

Monroe began, "Miss Weathers, when was the last time you saw your husband?"

"Dusty?" She replied, "Dusty is my ex-husband. I've not talked to him for at least six months. Why? Is he okay?"

"So you haven't seen or heard from him... zero correspondence or contact in over six months?"

"That's what I just said. Am I stuttering or something? So what's going on with Dusty?"

"Ma'am, your ex-husband is a person of interest in an ongoing investigation. We know he's in the Houston area, and thought he might have contacted you for help."

Her attitude was dismissive. "Dusty's in Houston? Are you sure?" she smirked. "Doesn't sound much like him. He hates big cities."

The two FBI agents ignored her comment. Shultz continued, "Ma'am, are you aware of any anti-government organizations your ex-husband is associated with, or is a member of?"

Maria snorted, "Dusty? Anti-government? Look here, I don't know who you're looking for, but the man I was married to was as patriotic as anyone I know."

Monroe took his turn at the questioning. "Are you aware of any event or change in his life that would have turned him against the United States of America?"

Realizing the two men standing in her house were actually serious, Maria starting getting angry. "No. As a matter of fact, my ex was a political agnostic – he didn't vote for any specific party, but rather always judged the man. I've never seen even the smallest hint of rebellion in him. He's an honorable man."

Monroe handed over his card, "If he attempts to contact you via any method, please call us immediately. I must warn you, ma'am, he's to be considered armed and dangerous. Don't meet him – call us."

Maria's tone became indignant, "Armed and dangerous? Dusty? Are you sure you're looking for the same Durham Weathers? He's one of the white hats, Agent Monroe."

"Yes, Miss. Weathers, we're sure."

Day 5

Dusty wanted fresh fruit and a higher quality of sustenance. The mobility and compact storage of the camping fare had been attractive to a nervous man on the run. Now that he'd calmed down, the realization that he was effectively a shut-in began to play on his mind. *If I'm going to be holed up in this little room,* he reasoned, *I might as well sample a bit of the local cuisine.*

Determined to find a grocery store, he left the suite and made for the bus stop. Waiting on the elevator, it occurred to him that he didn't have a clue which direction to take the bus. The lobby-clerk had been so helpful before, her knowledge of the area saving him a lot of time. He'd stop and ask, sure that she could point him in the right direction.

Dusty found the woman on the telephone, so he idled around the small lobby, waiting his turn. There was a lounge area next to the front desk – two vinyl covered chairs, a couch and television, a courtesy for weary travelers. He wandered over, not wanting to appear as though he was eavesdropping on the clerk's call.

Browsing a display of pamphlets advertising tourist destinations in the area, the image on the television screen drew his eye. What he saw made him inhale sharply, his body freezing stiff.

The local news station was displaying his picture – an image he recognized from his driver's license. The caption beneath his photo read, "FBI SEEKS FUGITIVE, THOUGHT TO BE IN THE HOUSTON AREA."

They had found the Thrush.

His first reaction was to turn and look at the clerk – to see if she was watching the broadcast. It was a mistake, as his proximity to the television gave her a side-by-side comparison of the photo and his face. His chest tightened as her smile faded, eyes darting between him and the screen.

There was no question that she recognized him. The clerk turned away, the tone of her voice making it apparent she was trying to end the call as quickly as possible. Dusty couldn't think of any alternative but to casually stroll from her sight and then bolt for the elevator.

He'd taken along the essentials in his new pack, the gun and a few bottles of water. Some inner-voice told him to get his clothing and other items and get the hell out of Dodge.

Fumbling with the room key, he rushed inside the suite and began throwing what he could inside the pack. The damp clothes were left behind, food and extra water stuffed inside along with his new duds. His departure was delayed by a few quick glances out the window, his imagination conjuring up visions of every policeman in Houston swarming into the hotel's parking lot. Finally he was ready and out the door.

He took the stairs, hopping down the fire escape steps two at a time. The emergency exit led to a rear door, and when he pushed it open, an alarm sounded. Already peaking with adrenaline, the loud klaxon spiked both his energy and anger.

Stepping out into the back parking lot, Dusty glanced right and left in order to determine his most likely path of escape. The left was eliminated immediately – a large, unclimbable privacy fence separating the hotel from its neighbors on that side.

To the right was a fast food restaurant, and for a moment, he was tempted to casually walk over and order a hamburger. He could sit and watch the police waste their time swarming over the now empty hotel. In his mind, distance equaled freedom, so he decided against that option.

Briskly moving along the back of the building, Dusty wanted to glance around the corner and see what was across the street. Perhaps he could make it that far before the police arrived... perhaps that side would provide a better alternative.

As he poked around the corner to scout, the first vision that met his eye was the flashing blue strobe of a police car, slowing to enter the hotel property. Too late.

Desperate, Dusty again scanned right and left, his only option an empty field directly behind the hotel. He ran for the open spaces.

The knee-high weeds weren't dense enough to drop and hide, but thick enough to make running difficult. The weight of his pack, uneven terrain, and boots that had never been intended for a track meet hindered his speed over ground.

The area he was crossing was undeveloped for a reason. High voltage electrical lines sagged above his head, supported by huge steel towers stretching off into the distance. Slowing to a brisk walk, Dusty made for what looked like an industrial park across the empty spaces. He could see warehouse-like loading docks sprinkled with stacks of pallets and large green dumpsters in the distance. The complex looked to be quite large – a thousand places to hide.

Chancing a glance over his shoulder, Dusty noticed the first police car roll to a stop in the back lot. The officer was soon joined by three other cars, their flashing strobes reflecting off the back of the hotel making it appear as though it belonged on the Las Vegas strip.

Dusty again tried to run, but the effort was clumsy. If he fell, or twisted an ankle, it would be one of the shortest pursuits in history. The police officers, on the other hand, didn't hesitate. Shouting orders for him to halt, they began running at full speed.

He wasn't going to outrun them. That became clear less than 20 steps later. He also wasn't going to out shoot them. The rail gun required some time to recharge its capacitors between shots. In another few moments, the faster officer would be within the range of his sidearm, and that would be the end – arrest or death.

One last desperate glance – an effort to figure another way out – brought an idea into his head. Without breaking stride, he pulled off the backpack and removed the rail gun.

Three steps later, it was assembled. Two more, and the green LED glowed in the morning sun. He almost dropped the ball bearing, but caught it mid-air and managed to load the weapon.

Dusty's thoughts centered on warning the cops. He knew they would start shooting if he pointed the weapon directly at them, but if they realized the power of the rail gun, they might not continue the chase. He looked around for something or someplace to fire the warning shot, the biggest target in the area drawing his attention.

With the laser, aiming was easy. He centered the red dot on the leg of nearest tower and pulled the trigger.

In a carefully timed sequence, the Taser-scavenged ultra-capacitors dumped 50,000 volts of electricity into the rings of spinning magnets. One by one, the vortex of magnetic fields pulled and then pushed the ball bearing.

A thunderclap rolled across north Houston, the sound seemingly out of place given the cloudless sky. The black line flashed, more of a shadow in the bright light than a clear vision, its path slicing through the green-painted steel of the tower's thick leg. A large section of the support simply vanished.

Nothing happened for a moment. Gravity took its time, appearing to be surprised by the sudden availability of a new victim.

A loud groan filled the air – the tortured metal of the remaining supports protesting like a great, wounded beast. Popping noises louder than gunshots followed, rivets and welds exploding under the strain. The 150-foot behemoth of structural steel began to topple.

Dusty and the police officers wisely ran for their lives, but in opposite directions.

The ground vibrated as several hundred tons slammed into the field. Sparks flew and high-tension cables the size of a man's wrist snapped like twine. A cloud of dust rose into the air, soon joined by puffs of black smoke from the burning grass. Blue arks of electrical discharge sliced the air, miniature bolts of lightning dancing across the ground.

The effect was as if someone had built an electrified wall between Dusty and the pursuing lawmen. The crumpled steel, downed power lines, and burning foliage created a barrier that the stunned officers refused to cross.

Dusty ran as fast as he could ever remember. Faster than when he was chased by an angered swarm of hornets after bumbling upon their nest - faster than when he sought the end zone for a game-winning touchdown, a string of pursuing defensive backs desperately trying to deny the quest. His legs, pumping with all determination, carried him across the field and onto pavement.

He spied the open door of a loading bay, his momentum allowing an easy scale of the waist-high threshold. Pausing for just a moment to gather his wits and air, he found himself in an empty warehouse –

scraps of cardboard and nylon packing ribbon scattered around an unmanned forklift.

The sound of what seemed like a hundred sirens converging on the area was overridden – a nearby diesel engine revving with a throaty rumble. On the other side of the facility, a delivery truck was pulling away from the dock, its roll-up back door open and inviting. Again, he was running.

Every fiber of his legs screamed with exertion as he leaped for the back of the truck, the distance between the dock and the departing vehicle increasing rapidly. He felt weightlessness, forward momentum… and then his foot made contact with the lip, his overstretched body losing its balance and slamming into a pile of wooden pallets stacked inside the cargo hold.

Dusty didn't notice the pain at first. Scrambling to hide, his attention was focused out the back of the truck, fully expecting to see an ocean of blue lights swarming behind his ride, chasing him in hot pursuit. None appeared. The rig left the industrial complex, accelerating away from the scene of Dusty's crime, the steady drone of its diesel engine interrupted only by the shifting of gears.

Just as he was beginning to feel a sense of relief over having escaped, waves of nausea-inducing pain began raking his torso. A warm, sticky sensation prompted him to pull up his shirt and examine his abdomen. The splintered edge of a pallet had sliced a gash across his mid-section almost three inches in length, gouging out a trench of flesh as thick and deep as his thumb. While the pain was becoming intense, it was the blood loss that posed the most immediate danger.

He found his pack and dug out a spare, then struggled to remove the torn, bloody shirt from his shoulders. Rolling up the now ruined flannel, he covered the wound and pressed as best he could while pulling on a clean tee.

The truck shifted gears, slowing down to exit the freeway and then a short time later turning into what Dusty could tell was a gas station. Listening intently from his hide, the smell and noise indicated his chauffer was topping off the limousine's diesel.

I hope he's not filling this thing up because he's going on a long trip, Dusty prayed. Looking down at his wound, he whispered, "Shit, I could bleed to death back here before he stops again."

The sound of the truck's restarted engine added to his dismay, a view of the gas pumps appearing out the rear as the vehicle pulled away. Instead of turning back for the road beyond, the driver soon braked again, slowly backing in between two over-the-road semis. *It must be time for breakfast*, Dusty realized. The engine went silent, and then the cab door opened and slammed shut.

He waited for the driver's head to appear around the corner, worried the man wouldn't leave his cargo door open while at the truck stop. Evidently, he wasn't worried about the old pallets and packing blankets.

Dusty waited, the burning in his torso growing more intense now that he had nothing else to focus on. *It's now or never*, he realized, summoning up the strength to stand and move to the rear of the hold. He folded the gun's stock and stuffed it into his pack. Gingerly climbing down, he pretended to study the tires for a moment – hoping any prying eyes would think he was the driver or co-pilot.

He held the backpack in front of the wound, hiding the blood that was already soaking through his bandage-roll and staining his fresh shirt. Walking was pure torture, staying upright to avoid attention requiring every ounce of grit he could muster.

At the entrance to the busy truck stop, he noticed a small newspaper box stuffed with flyers for local real estate brokers. A familiar face smiled up at the injured man. There on the front page was his ex-wife, Maria.

After snatching up a paper, he made for the restroom, finally exhaling as he locked the stall door. *Refuge with a throne and the image of his ex-wife*, he mused. *What more could a man ask for?*

Hanging the ever-heavier pack on the door's hook, he set about working on his wound. The red-soaked bandage-shirt was disposed of in the trash container, a wad of paper towels selected as a substitute. He was incredibly thirsty, downing an entire bottle of water in just a few swallows.

He couldn't think of a way out. Walking was out of the question, hitchhiking posed the risk that someone would recognize him from the news reports. He could try and make it back to the truck that had delivered him here, but there was no way to know where it was going or how long it would take to get there. The arrival of a headache, followed shortly thereafter by a cold sweat made the situation even more dire.

All the while, Maria's smiling face seemed to mock him. Those beautiful brown eyes had warmed his soul since the first time he'd met her; now their gaze felt belittling.

Stop it! He chided himself. *Maria holds no ill will against you. The marriage didn't work for her, but at least you took the high road as it ended. Call her.*

His room-stall started spinning. Closing his eyes made it worse. He reached for the no contract phone inside the pack and dialed the number listed on the brochure.

"Champion Properties," a friendly sounding voice answered.

"Hello," he mumbled. "Is Maria in?"

"I'm sorry, but Ms. Weathers is out of the office right now. She'll be checking her messages throughout the day. Could I let her know you called?"

Dusty hadn't expected this. He didn't want to get Maria in trouble, but on the other hand, he was desperate. A lie popped into his head.

"Yes… yes, please do. My name is Clarence Turner, and I'm calling from Midland Station. I'm relocating to Houston next month, and Ms. Weathers was recommended by a mutual friend, Tina Rodriguez. I'm only going to be in town for a short time, could you ask her to hurry?"

"Sure, Mr. Turner. I'll let her know as soon as she calls in."

Dusty left the number to his phone and ended the call. Clarence Turner was Maria's father's name, Midland her hometown. Tina had been her best friend in high school.

Time passed slowly in the stall. The pain, loss of blood, and confinement all combined to make it seem like days before the cheap, little phone began to ring.

"Maria?"

"Yes, Dusty. The message was cute. Are you all right? Do you know the FBI was at my house?"

He interrupted her, "Maria, I'm hurt… hurt pretty badly. I've lost so much blood; it feels like I'm going into shock."

The voice on the other end changed, the words laced with concern. "Where are you? I'll come get you right now."

"I'm at a truck stop. I don't know where though. It's called The Gulf Station. You'll have to look up the address. I'm in the men's room, hiding."

She didn't hesitate, "Stay right there. Hang on. I'm on my way."

Dusty finished the last bottle of water, his thirst unquenchable. Knowing that help was on the way improved his mental condition. He had hope... an out... a chance at escape.

He gently used another handful of paper towels to redress his wound, the blood flow about the same. He killed some time rearranging the pack, and making ready to leave once Maria arrived. He was weak, dizzy, and constantly feeling like he needed to vomit. The pounding in his head was relentless.

Twice he started to call her back, illogical visions forming in his mind. At one point, he was sure she'd forgotten, a minute later convinced she changed her mind and decided not to come. Each bout of paranoia grew stronger, more difficult to fight off. He then began to worry he was going insane.

A voice called out, a hint of humor in the tone. "Clarence Turner, your wife is here looking for ya. She doesn't look happy."

He almost ignored the use of the fake name, the pain and thunder in his head making reasoning difficult.

He managed to stand and unlock the stall, his legs wobbly and weak. A few difficult steps, and then he was looking at Maria, concern painted on her face.

"If you bleed all over my car seats, I'll be pissed."

Somehow, she managed to get him into her car, the smell of leather and her favorite musk permeating the interior. He fell asleep before they had exited the lot.

He dreamed about being irate with her. She was pushing him along, encouraging him to walk into some strange place. He didn't want to go, the car's seat comfortable and safe, the smell of her reminding him of cool spring mornings in their bed. The dream continued, his beautiful Maria becoming angry, insistent that he enter the new place, pulling on him physically while chiding him mentally.

Tim Crawford gradually worked his way around the perimeter of law enforcement personnel behind the hotel. He recognized one of the cops, the officer obviously bored with the task of keeping a throng of curious onlookers well away from the site.

Making sure his press ID wasn't visible, Tim made his way over to his acquaintance and smiled. "What's going on, McCormick?"

"Move on, Crawford. I don't want anyone to see me talking to you right now."

Taken aback by the rude response, the reporter from the *Houston Post* feigned hurt feelings. "Jezzz McCormick, what the hell did I ever do to you?"

"Nothing that I know of, and I want to keep it that way. There's a busload of feds crawling around here, and that makes my captain nervous. Shit rolls downhill, and I don't want to be at the bottom of an avalanche."

The reporter snorted, dismissing the less than talkative cop with a wave. "Whatever."

Crawford considered joining the gaggle of other reporters, most of the on-scene press from the local news channels. Their fancy vans, bright lights, and handheld cameras had been herded into a corner of the hotel's parking lot, a thick wall of police between them and the downed tower.

Judging the isolated press pool as the last place he'd gather any real information, he continued to casually saunter through the field, at least as close as the authorities would let him. That was close enough to be in awe of the disaster.

On an average day, the high-voltage towers were overlooked by the average citizen. When standing upright, they didn't attract attention like a building of the same stature. People drove and jogged and walked their cocker spaniels past them every day, hardly giving the critical structures a second glance.

That all changed when the tower fell. The length of crumpled steel lattice looked like the spine of a slain giant, felled after a ferocious battle. The thick cables, randomly strung along the ground and draped over the crumbled metal, resembled the great beast's entrails. Dark patches of burned grass were the bloodstains – scarred soil where the life had drained from the titan. The entire scene had a melancholy feel, the carcass of a mighty warrior surrounded by an army of human ants.

Being naturally nosey made Crawford a good reporter. That unrelenting curiosity, combined with a higher than average IQ, propelled him to the rank of journalist. An innate distrust of his fellow man garnered him rewards and accolades, and at that moment, he smelled a story hidden in the mundane explanation provided by the authorities. *Failed structural integrity my ass*, he determined, staring at the fallen monstrosity.

The first piece of visual evidence of a cover up was the plow mark. Looking to the reporter's eye like some sort of odd crop circle taken from a photo shopped tabloid picture, a gash in the field started 50 yards away from where the tower had stood and followed a perfectly straight line to the now-mangled base.

There wasn't any fallen debris close to the trench, and the grass was flattened on each side. Something had ripped through the field on its way to the tower – a meteorite or projectile of some kind. He'd seen similar scars in the earth while working in Iraq, furrows of tilled, desert sand left after American tanks had fired their massive cannons. Yet there was no tank or anything else that would explain the damage.

Crawford pulled his smart phone, tapping the screen a few times until he found the weather. Three days ago, a thunderstorm had rolled through north Houston, the highest recorded wind speed reaching 38 mph, from the west. The tower had fallen as if it were pushed from the southeast. If the story were to be believed, wouldn't the failure have occurred during the storm? The last few days had been calm.

The most suspicious aspect of the entire affair was the presence of the feds. As McCormick had stated, the place was thick with them. Sure, the tower was a major hit to the north side's infrastructure, some 350,000 people now without electricity. Sure, it was possible such an incident might provide the federal boys a chance to get out of the office on a slow day. But it had taken him two hours to arrive, snarled in gridlock due to the powerless, non-functioning traffic signals. Guessing that the tower had fallen three hours ago, he asked himself how long would it take the FBI to figure out this wasn't a terrorist attack and leave. They sure seemed to have officially labeled the cause very, very quickly – unless they already knew.

Pulling out his digital camera, the reporter snapped a few pictures from the best angle. Visual extravagance was the realm of broadcast news; his story would be told mostly with words.

While he zoomed in on the base, movement caught his attention. Two men wearing Houston Power and Light hardhats were strolling over to speak with what appeared to be an FBI agent. After about five minutes of animated pointing and uncomfortable body language later, the electric company workers headed for the parking lot. Crawford moved to follow.

They were just closing the trunk lid of the white Ford sedan, complete with HL&P logo, when Crawford accosted them. "Excuse me guys," he said, flashing his press ID, "I was wondering if I might ask you a couple of questions?"

"Sorry," the older one replied, holding up his hand, "you need to speak with law enforcement. We have no comment."

"Okay," Tim replied, a sense of disappointment in his voice. "If you want your company to take the heat for this, that's up to you. My editor is good to go with the lack of maintenance angle."

"What do you mean, 'lack of maintenance?'" responded the younger guy, despite the harsh look from his partner, "There wasn't a lack of maintenance on shit."

Crawford shrugged his shoulders, "That's not what the FBI is telling me off the record. Word is, the tower hadn't been properly inspected or maintained, and that's why it went down."

The older man stiffened his spine, flashing Crawford an annoyed look. "Bullshit. Pure, unadulterated cow droppings. Metal fatigue, poor maintenance, or nothing else I know of had shit to do with that tower coming down. We don't know what kicked it over, but sure as God made little green apples, HL&P had nothing to do with it."

"How do you know?"

The younger guy stepped forward and lowered his voice, "Off the record, okay? I've never seen anything like it. The steel in that support is four inches thick. An entire section is just missing... gone. Now, I've used just about every technology out there to cut steel. Saws, lasers, plasma torches, you name it. Nothing can slice metal and leave a smooth edge like that... nothing. We examined it at a microscopic level, and there wasn't any fatigue. It was like someone just snapped his fingers, and the metal wasn't there anymore."

"How... is there... what could do that?" Crawford asked, trying to piece it all together.

Shaking his head, the older man opened the car door, signaling his coworker to do the same. They had already said too much. "Nothing Mister, nothing of this world."

~  ~

Grace pumped the soap dispenser, wringing the yard dirt off her hands at the kitchen sink. As she rinsed them under the tap, her gaze focused out the window, happy with the placement of the new flowerbed. When it bloomed in a few weeks, she'd have a lovely splash of color to make washing the dishes less of a chore.

She'd just reached for the dish towel when the phone mounted nearby rang. *Durham?* She hoped, hurrying with the drying and reaching for the receiver.

"Hello."

"Ms. Kennedy, this is Eva Barns," sounded a distressed voice. "I'm sorry to bother you, but I don't know where else to turn."

"What's the matter, Eva?"

"The police were just here and arrested Hank," the woman sniffled, "They said he was conspiring against the government of the United States of America."

Grace was sure she had understood the distraught message; however, the caller's suppressed tears made it difficult to know for certain what was going on. "Eva, now settle down, everything will be all right," she said in as soothing a voice as she could muster. "Can you tell me who arrested Hank?"

"They were from El Paso. Some wore jackets that said they were from the FBI, others had coats with 'ATF' embroidered across the back. They searched our house and wouldn't let me call anybody for help. They handcuffed Hank and walked him out to a car like he was a common criminal, Ms. Kennedy."

Grace was taking it all in, the mention of ATF, or Alcohol, Tobacco and Firearms, raising the bar of seriousness. "Okay, Eva, let me get dressed, and I'll be right over."

Twenty minutes later, Grace pulled into the driveway, her arrival anticipated by Eva pacing anxiously on the front porch. "I don't want to go in there," the distraught woman announced. "It's like my home has been violated."

The woman was terrified, clutching a wrinkled handkerchief and seemingly unable to focus on anything for more than a few seconds at a time. Guiding her to a wooden swing, Grace gradually settled Eva down, interlacing soothing reassurances with the occasional question. The story that unfolded didn't make any sense, and that fact concerned Ms. Kennedy more than anything.

Eva claimed the FBI men kept harking on Hank, pressing him over a recent visit to Dusty's gunsmith shop. Over and over again, Eva had listened to her husband deny any wrongdoing. "What's so terrible, Ms. Kennedy, is that I know he wasn't telling the truth. A woman learns those things after so many years of marriage, I guess. I've never known Hank to act like that."

Grace studied the woman carefully, the attorney inside of her unable to place blind trust in anyone. Eva appeared to be telling everything she knew about the situation. "What else did they ask him about, Eva?"

"That was all I heard. Dusty this and Dusty that... they kept asking Hank about some invention and how Dusty's workshop got damaged. For a little while, I thought they had come to the wrong address. I even told the one young man that Dusty Weathers lived down the road, but he ignored me."

Evidently, the FBI's lead agent didn't buy Hank's story either and arrested the man. They had hauled him off three hours ago, a pale, handcuffed Hank peering at his wife out the back window of a government SUV, a tear running down his cheek.

"Eva, let's go down to the courthouse and find out what's going on. If we hurry, we might be able to see Hank before they transport him elsewhere."

Wiping her eyes with the handkerchief, Eva nodded. Fortifying herself after a horror-filled glance toward the door, she managed to go inside to gather her things.

As they drove to Fort Davis, Grace warned Eva that she wasn't a criminal attorney. "But you're the only lawyer I know," Eva had responded.

The two women arrived at the Jeff Davis County Courthouse a few minutes later. The old building served as both the county seat and the county jail, a few small cells in the basement. In reality, there wasn't much crime in the area, and most of the time the small facility was empty.

As they parked, Grace pointed out several black SUVs and basic, factory equipped government sedans. "I think we may have gotten here in time, Eva. It doesn't look like the federal officers have left yet."

The two women trotted up the limestone steps and pushed open a heavy, frosted glass door. They were met with the smell of old wood and floor wax. The main entrance led to an atrium of sorts, rings of offices bordering the open space. As they headed for the sheriff's portion of the building, their footsteps echoed off the marble floor, the sound ominous as it bounced through the otherwise empty building.

The tranquil atmosphere was broken as Grace opened the door to the sheriff's office, a wall of voices and other activity greeting the two visitors. As the two women entered the lobby, everyone stopped to look up, the attention making their entrance even more difficult.

Sheriff Clay was standing nearby, talking to a uniformed deputy and reading a report at the same time. Looking up, the local lawman interrupted his conversation and approached the two women.

Nodding, he said, "Mrs. Barns, Ms. Kennedy."

"Good afternoon, Sheriff. We're here to see Hank Barns. Eva has asked me to represent her husband."

The local officer's nervous shifting made it obvious he was unhappy with the situation. "Yes, ma'am. If Hank was my prisoner, there wouldn't be any issue. Unfortunately, he's not. He's technically under federal jurisdiction."

Eva stepped closer to the man, her finger pointing at his chest. "Jefferson Thomas Clay, you know good and well my husband is an honorable, law abiding citizen. You've known him all your life, young man. You should be embarrassed this has happened, and let him out of this jail immediately. I was your Sunday School teacher. Hank was your little league coach, and even counted the votes the night you were elected to office. What has happened to law and order, common sense and good manners in this county?"

Sheriff Clay flushed red, obviously feeling uneasy. Before he could comment, a young man Grace had never seen before appeared at the sheriff's side. "Is there a problem?"

"Ladies, this is Special Prosecutor Beckman, from the Department of Justice office over in El Paso. Mr. Beckman, this is Grace Kennedy, a local attorney, and of course, you've met Mrs. Barns."

The smug young man didn't acknowledge either woman, an intolerable display of rude behavior in rural Texas.

Grace didn't let the silence hang in the air long. "I'd like to see my client, Mr. Beckman."

"I'm afraid that's not possible."

"He has the right to representation, sir. I'm an officer of the court and demand that my client's right to an attorney be acknowledged."

Grace had seen Beckman's type before. Young, self-centered, and with an ego the size of a football stadium, they were always convinced that they were smarter and better prepared than the person across the table. She loved it when they underestimated her.

"We've arrested Mr. Barns under Section Eight of the Patriot Act. His due process is suspended," replied the cocky DOJ lawyer.

He thinks I'm some country-bumpkin attorney, reasoned Grace.

"Mr. Beckman, Hank Barns is a citizen of the United States. Section eight doesn't apply to US nationals. I demand to see my client."

Grace's knowledge of the terrorist law seemed to surprise the federal prosecutor, but he still didn't give ground.

"Technically, the Supreme Court hasn't offered an opinion on that issue, as of yet. Until that time, the attorney general has an established policy that all sections of the act do indeed apply to US citizens suspected of collaborating with foreign terrorists, or plotting acts of domestic terrorism against the United States."

Grace shook her head, looking at Sheriff Clay for support. "That's preposterous, sir. Hank Barns is as much a terrorist as my left shoe. Why is DOJ doing this? What possible reason could they have to believe this man is anything but a law abiding individual?"

The federal lawyer ignored Grace's question and referred to his watch. Turning his back to the women, he yelled to another man across the room. "Let's get everyone loaded up. We're done here."

Turning back to face Grace, he said, "You can take up any issues you have with the federal magistrate in Houston. Mr. Barns will be arraigned there in two days."

And with that, the man pivoted and began issuing orders to his underlings.

Grace was shocked. While she wasn't technically a criminal attorney, she'd wandered into that area as part of her practice. The arrogance and lack of respect for the basic legal rights demonstrated by the Department of Justice was unheard of – an abomination.

Anger started welling up inside of her. The injustice of the entire episode boiling her blood. Her legal mind immediately started inventorying her options. She could think of a variety of ways to counteract the federal government's heavy-handed actions, those ranging from calling a press conference to contacting various elected officials. She'd even served as head of the campaign funding committee of a currently serving US senator.

None of that was going to happen in Fort Davis, however. She needed the press, legal resources and a host of other assets to fight for Hank.

Keeping her face emotionless, she turned to Eva and announced, "Let's go get some things packed, Eva. We're heading to Houston."

His modest desk was surrounded by curious onlookers, all them peering over Crawford's shoulder at the photographs he'd taken of the fallen tower. The newsroom was abuzz with excitement, the story a welcome diversion from the normal local events. One by one the staff members cast their votes on which picture should adorn the morning's front page. No one counted the ballots because the polling didn't matter. The editor would choose, and his vote trumped all.

Crawford politely acknowledged the compliments, caring little for everyone's opinion of his skills with a camera. His focus was on his prose and the mystery surrounding the collapse.

Despite being "old media," the *Post* maintained significant research capabilities, including every known publically accessible database, and a small number that were supposed to be entered by only a select few. Reams of microfiche images were also at his disposal, and of course, the internet.

His award winning reporting was due to a simple secret. He followed stories using deductive reasoning and logic, not emotion. On the occasions when he'd been invited to speak at journalistic events, his advice to the young had always been to ignore the bright, shiny objects and concentrate of the dark side of human nature. That's where the story was; that's where the truth would most likely surface.

He also didn't believe in unassociated events. The tower didn't collapse on its own. Something led to its failure, perhaps an entire string of prerequisite actions.

He started his search three days prior, looking through news stories, legal notices, and other related information. He gave law enforcement activity top priority, still curious why the feds were crawling all over the scene.

His inquiries resulted in three significant stories. The first was the bomb threat up in College Station. There was film footage out of a Dallas station that showed a government helicopter taking off in the background. He was reasonably sure that aircraft belonged to the FBI in Houston, but presumed the event unrelated.

The second was the loss of two Texas Air National Guard Falcon aircraft the same day. While the NTSB hadn't offered an official explanation, most aviation experts believed the craft had "touched" mid-air, resulting in both planes going down. This story, like the bomb threat, didn't seem to tie in.

The third odd occurrence was the public service bulletin, the one asking for information leading to the arrest of one Mr. Durham Weathers. The reporter knew it wasn't all that common for the local police to make such a request, perhaps three or four times a month was the norm. What was different about this latest "wanted fugitive" effort was the source. The photograph distributed to the various press outlets was from an FBI file, the watermark at the bottom of the grainy picture making the connection obvious.

The FBI office in Houston was huge, handling dozens, if not hundreds, of ongoing investigations at the same time. Connecting those dots would be difficult, if not impossible.

Crawford then began to study the various emergency calls surrounding the collapse of the tower. The police hadn't released the 911 tapes, yet. He made a note to have his paper press hard for the actual recordings. While that critical information wasn't available, there was something almost as good.

The *Post* had police scanners monitoring all law enforcement frequencies. These conversations were digitalized and then converted into searchable text. He started with something simple – the address of the hotel.

As the results rolled across his computer monitor, Crawford's brow wrinkled in confusion. There had been a dispatch call to the hotel 15 minutes before the first report of the downed tower. The dispatcher's initial broadcast indicating the police code 10-91, or units responding to pick up suspect. This had been followed a few minutes later by a 10-80, or "in pursuit."

Crawford double checked the address and times – there was no mistake, the police were already at the hotel when the tower fell. *What were they doing there?*

The connection came next. The public service bulleting – the wanted man. Someone had called in… Durham Weathers was staying at that hotel, and that's why the police rolled before the tower fell. Tim changed the search parameters, concentrating his inquiry on the fugitive.

Again, the computer's brain did its work, and data began scrolling down the monitor. Fort Davis, Texas. Property tax receipts for 320 acres in Jeff Davis County. Gunsmith certification. Private pilot's license and an old ad for crop dusting services….

The reference to crop dusting rang familiar to the reporter. He began reversing his search, sure he'd seen the term in the last 30 minutes. There it was! The police dispatch call records… David Wayne Hooks – possible stolen airplane. A Thrush Commander *crop duster* with an altered tail number.

Crawford leaned back in his chair and summarized what he knew. One Mr. Durham Weathers had altered the tail numbers on his aircraft and flown into Hooks. Somehow, he made it to the hotel. The aircraft had been discovered, so the FBI suspected he was in Houston. The local media had plastered Mr. Weathers' face all over town, and someone recognized him and called the cops to the hotel.

The reporter invested a serious amount of mental energy trying to piece together what had happened to the tower, and what Weathers had to do with it. Every avenue of deduction was a dead end. Frustrated with the effort, he decided to work backwards from his last known fact. The Thrush, altered, at Hooks.

Clearly, Weathers had known he was wanted by the authorities while still at Hooks. Why else would he change the identification of his plane? So where had he come from?

The journalist searched the few available records for Fort Davis, the small town's police blotter and newspaper providing zero input. By accident, he forgot to enter the fugitive's first name on the next search, pulling up a long list of references to the name "Weathers."

Grunting at his mistake, he began to re-enter the query when one of the listings caught his attention. An arrest of one Dr. Mitchell Weathers, in College Station, the same day as the bomb threat. Four clicks of the keyboard later, Crawford's heart began to race. Mitchell Weathers was originally from Fort Davis, probably related to the fugitive.

He stood now, staring at the screen on his desk. He knew there was a connection, the parts starting to mesh like a set of perfectly matched gears. His analysis was interrupted by his boss.

"What's up, Tim?"

"Boss, I'm onto something really, really interesting here. There's a trail of seemingly unrelated events leading to that mysterious tower coming down, which didn't have a damn thing to do with metal fatigue. I need to take a road trip."

"A road trip? Shit! I was told all these expensive do-dad computer research things would save the paper money on travel. What happened to that?"

"It's only to College Station, boss. I'll even drive my own car. Just a few days. I think I'll hand you one of the biggest stories the paper has ever printed when I get back."

The editor rubbed his chin, finally nodding. "Okay, Tim, but don't hit me with a huge bar tab on your expense report. And keep in touch."

Day 6

Dusty opened his eyes, and for a moment believed he'd been captured and sentenced to life in a prison with an "Easter wonderland explosion" decorating theme. A devilish design, his cell was guaranteed to torture the typical male prisoner for eternity.

Splashes of pastel yellows and blues filled his blurry vision, the spring holiday hues encompassing everything from the comforter covering his prone body, to the pillowcase supporting his weary head. The wallpaper depicted colonies of rabbits sporting annoyingly unfashionable spring bonnets, delivering baskets overflowing with brightly colored eggs. Flowers sprouted throughout the landscape but were especially thickly woven into the white picket fence that anchored the design. He wondered if the guards had confiscated his belt, and if not, was the leather strap long enough to stretch a neck – his neck.

Still, the mattress was comfortable for a penitentiary. That soft, billowy feeling beneath him evaporated when he tried to shift his bed-weary frame. Sharp pains reminded him of his recent encounter with the stack of pallets, and then the rest of his recent history flooded his short-term memory.

Despite the stabbing pains running up his torso, his first thought was of the rail gun. The backpack, complete with super weapon, was leaning against the wall nearby. That anxiety dismissed, he decided to take advantage of being propped on one elbow and studied his surroundings in detail.

On the nightstand was a pitcher of orange juice, a small tumbler, and a note. It read:

Dusty,

You're in a client's home that I'm getting ready to list on the market. The owners have been transferred overseas and won't return. Don't make a mess.

If you bleed on anything, you will have to pay for it. Don't make a mess.

Drink this orange juice. You've lost a lot of blood and probably feel like shit. There's aspirin in the bathroom. Don't make a mess.

Maria

He had to smile at her prose, the mixture of caring and scolding, a facet of her personality he'd grown to love.

He decided to follow her advice, pouring a glass of the lukewarm OJ and draining it in a few gulps. The effort was exhausting. His next feeble move was to examine his wound, but the exertion of pulling back the covers and raising his shirt was pointless. A heavy bandage was wrapped around his mid-section, the bulge of a thick compress covering the wounded area beneath. It was such a thorough job, he decided it might be unwise to rework Florence Nightingale's apparent handiwork.

His body announced it was finished with the day's activities, weakness and exhaustion the message in spades. Lying back, his last thought before going to sleep was of Maria. *Did she still love him?*

Patty answered the phone with her usual cheery voice, Maria half-listening because she'd forgotten to close the door.

The entire day had been a waste, much of the north side of Houston without power, customers canceling appointments by the handful. Warnings were on the radio and television – don't drive unless it's absolutely necessary. Despite everyone knowing the streets would be chaos without electric traffic signals, the helicopter news cameras showed endless video footage of the gridlock.

Patty didn't bother with the intercom, choosing instead to appear at the door. "There's an Eva Barns on line one. She says you are an old friend from Fort Davis, and she has an emergency."

Maria tilted her head, the name from the past completely unexpected. *What was this*, she questioned, *old home week?*

Reaching for the receiver, she forced friendliness into her tone. "Eva! Why Eva Barns, how are you?"

"Hi Maria, I'm so sorry to bother you, but I don't know who else to turn to. Hank's been arrested, and his court appearance is in Houston. I'm on my way to your city right now, and I was wondering if you could make a recommendation on where I could stay. Hank and I aren't exactly wealthy people, you know, and… well… I thought you might be able to recommend someplace safe and reasonable."

Memories of her past life came flooding into Maria's mind. Eva, such a kind and caring soul, taking care of the house after Anthony had been born. Eva bringing over home cooked meals when Maria had sprained her ankle, and Dusty was off in Oklahoma spraying crops. Eva – always there and never asking for anything in return.

"Eva Barns, how dare you ask such a question? You will stay at my home for as long as you need, and I won't hear another word to the contrary."

"That's so kind of you, really it is. But I don't want to bother you, and I've got my attorney with me. Her name is Grace Kennedy, and she's helping me get this straightened out."

The name caused the real estate broker's interest to peak, her son relaying the dinner he had shared with his father and a nice lady named Grace who had recently moved to town.

"Is Grace from Fort Davis?"

"Why, yes. Yes, she is."

"Well then," announced Maria, "she's like family. I've got plenty of room, too much really. I demand both of you stay at my place until this is all straightened out."

"Are you sure, Maria?"

"Oh, believe me, Eva. I wouldn't have it any other way. Now, grab a pencil, Eva. I'll give you the address and my cell number."

After hanging up the call, she sat and pondered what possible trouble Hank could have gotten into. Surely, it had something to do with Dusty's recent endeavors – the two men being as close as they were. Having the chance to repay Eva's kindness over the years made her feel better about the day. Besides, she wanted to meet this woman who turned her ex-husband's head.

After checking into his hotel, Tim Crawford decided to visit the section of the campus where the bomb threat of a few days ago had occurred. He toured around several large facilities, including Anderson Hall and the administration building for the science department.

He had downloaded several pictures onto his pad computer, the visual references making it easier to navigate around the vicinity. After the familiarization tour, he headed for the campus newspaper's office and a scheduled meeting with the student-reporter who had written the paper's article covering the event.

The *Battalion* advertised itself as "The Student Voice of Texas A&M since 1893." Crawford entered the paper's modest offices where he was greeted by a friendly, young woman working the main phone. He introduced himself, explaining he had an appointment with Miss Wendy Hardin.

Much to Crawford's surprise, the girl at the desk responded, "I've read a lot of your work, Mr. Crawford. The piece you did on the corruption at the Port of Houston was a classic."

"Why, thank you."

Nodding, she turned and yelled over the tops of the cubical, "Wendy, Mr. Crawford is here."

The top of a blonde head appeared two rows back, Crawford following the girl's progress as she approached.

Wendy wasn't what the reporter had expected – not at all. *Stereotyping*, he admitted. *It never pays.* Rather than a mousey journalism major with thick glasses and stringy hair, Tim was greeted by a very attractive co-ed with blonde curls, green eyes, and an extremely robust figure – at least the top half was robust.

Forcing his eyes to remain above the girl's shoulders, he accepted her invitation to return to her cubicle. Proper social amenities exchanged, he settled into the guest chair. That was when Crawford received his second surprise of the visit.

"That bomb scare was pure bullshit," the young co-ed began. "I know it was because they didn't even bother with the hazardous materials unit. If there really had been any threat of a bomb, they would have called in the guys with the padded suits and oxygen masks, but they never did."

Brains and beauty, Tim mused. Trying to play the role of the sage, old newshound, he prodded, "Did you ask any of the authorities about your suspicions?"

"I tried. The local dudes were all tightlipped. I couldn't even get close to the federal guys. I did, however, manage to gather a *little* information." She cleared her throat before continuing, "Just not in any academically endorsed manner, if you catch my drift," she finished.

"Oh?"

After looking over her shoulder to make sure no one was watching, Wendy punched a few keys and then pointed to the screen. "I know one of the campus cops. I went to see him, really to dig around, and saw this image on one of the computer screens. I snapped this with my cell phone while my friend was checking out my assets. It's amazing what a low cut top can do sometimes to champion truth, justice, and the American way," she smiled.

"They let you in the station while a bomb threat was going on? That's some pretty good access."

Grinning, Wendy leaned back in her chair, providing better vantage to admire her impressive figure. "Yeah, well, this cop has made no secret that he wants in my pants pretty badly. Besides, a girl has got to use her God-given assets in a cutthroat business like this. I have noticed that when you're equipped with a pair of these," she declared, gesturing toward her ample chest, "men seem to become distracted. They're a great tool to prompt conversation," the young girl teased.

Crawford had to laugh at the girl's honesty. He also acknowledged that she was wise beyond her years, making a note to invite her down to Houston to interview when she graduated.

Turning to study the photograph, he couldn't make out exactly what the image was. Wendy, evidently noting the puzzled look on his face, offered to help. Pointing at the screen, she said, "It's a rifle or some sort of gun. You can see the outline of the barrel here, the stock back on this side."

With her help, Crawford could indeed make out the shape of a rifle. "Have you asked anyone to clean up this image?"

"No. Until you called, I wasn't sure what I would do with it, and while I know some serious computer nerds here on campus, I didn't want the word spreading around that I took this pic. Besides, those guys creep me out."

"No problem," Crawford offered, "we've got some techs down at the *Post* who might be able to enhance this image."

Tim began to explain his suspicions, but Wendy stopped him with a finger to her lips. Leaning forward, she whispered, "This is a very competitive environment around here. Why don't we go get some coffee and talk in private?"

Before long, the duo of reporters was strolling across the campus, heading for a place Wendy called "the Barn." As they walked, Tim started at the beginning of what he knew and proceeded through the timeline, Wendy listening intently to every word.

"That all makes sense," she commented as they entered the Java Barn.

After ordering the beverages, they found an empty corner table that afforded some privacy. "You know they arrested Dr. Mitchell right here at the Barn, don't you?"

"No, I didn't know that. He was drinking coffee?"

"Yup. One of the guys that works here told me that two policeman came in with a picture of the professor, asking if anyone had seen him. Dr. Weathers was sitting right here at this very table, according to my source."

Crawford chuckled at her use of the term. "We need more facts to back up this wild and wooly tale. Do you know where Professor Weathers might be? I'd like to interview him."

"I know he's out of jail. Sandy, the girl at the reception desk, saw him yesterday. From what I hear, he's keeping a low profile. We might find him at his office."

"Do you know where that is?"

"Yup. I can take you there."

Sipping his brew, Tim made up his mind. "Wendy, let's do this story together – equally shared byline. We'll release it in both papers at the same time."

"Really? That would sure help my grade," the girl replied with a smile.

After finishing the outline, the two reporters left the Java Barn, the College of Science administration building their destination. The lobby directory pointed them to the second floor where they soon found Professor Weathers' office.

Mitch was sitting at his desk, rearranging his schedule. It was the summer semester, and his class load was light. Finding replacements wasn't proving difficult. A light knock at the door drew his attention, a middle-aged man and student-aged girl standing in his threshold. *A student in grade trouble and her father*, immediately came to mind.

"Hello, may I help you?" the professor asked.

The man produced a business card, handing it to Mitch across the desk. "Professor Weathers, I'm Tim Crawford from the *Houston Post,* this is my associate, Wendy Hardin from the *Battalion*. We'd like to ask you a few questions, sir."

Mitch's facial expression flashed surprise, mostly at his misread of the visitor's intent. That reaction was immediately replaced by fear. *Agent Monroe would shanghai his ass back into a cell over this.*

"I'm... I'm sorry, but I'm incredibly busy at the moment. I'd be happy to conduct an interview later, if we could schedule a time... say next week?"

He's scared, Crawford realized. *He's almost terrified. I wonder why.*

Clearing his throat, the *Post* reporter decided to go for the kill with the first question and avoid giving the man across from him time to recover from his anxiety. "I apologize for dropping in unannounced, sir, but this story is moving very quickly. I'd like to ask about your brother, Durham, and this device that's causing all the headlines."

Crawford studied his victim's reaction carefully. He'd interviewed thousands of different people during his tenure as a newsman and felt like his ability to interpret someone's body language was as close to scientific as you could get. What he saw on the professor's face was fear being replaced with horror. Pure, unmasked, soul-deep horror.

Stuttering, Mitch replied, "I, I don't know what you're referring to, Mr. Crawford."

Shaking his head, Crawford bluffed. "Oh, come on, Doctor. We know about Durham's flight from College Station. We know about the military jets. We know he was in Houston when...."

Mitch interrupted, his words confirming Tim's suspicions. "How do you know...." The professor caught himself – too late. Tim had his confirmation.

"We have our sources, Dr. Weathers. We know all the facts from the government's angle. I'd like to know the other side of the story before we go to press."

Professor Weathers clammed up, but Crawford didn't care. Those four little words, "How do you know," told him everything he needed. It all fell into place as Mitch was asking them to leave.

On the way out of the building, Wendy commented, "Well, we didn't get much there. Sorry."

"But we did, Wendy. We got everything we needed. When I mentioned his brother's escapades, he didn't reply with 'What are you talking about,' or 'That's not what happened.' No, he was terrified we already knew. We did good."

"So you're going to count that as a confirmation? That's a stretch if you ask me."

Crawford held the door open for his associate and replied, "Your name is going to be on the byline, Wendy. If you don't believe the article is accurate, then we won't publish it."

Stopping, the girl peered at Crawford before responding, "I never said that. Let's go get it written up, and then we'll see if we agree."

Fifteen minutes later, they were back at the Java Barn, fingers flying over Tim's keyboard.

~ ~

Mitch sat at his desk, stunned. He held the business card from the obnoxious reporter in his hand, the sweat from his palm already discoloring one edge. He played the upcoming conversation with Monroe over and over in his head, almost as many times as he debated whether to even call. That decision was made when he realized the FBI probably had his office bugged.

Finally, he pulled his cell phone out and tapped the Houston number.

"Monroe."

"Agent Monroe, this is Mitch Weathers. I'm honoring my word by notifying you I had two visitors this morning. Both were reporters, both know a shocking amount of facts concerning recent events."

"Go on."

"I didn't tell them anything, but one Mr. Timothy Crawford from the *Houston Post* sat here in my office and recited quite a bit of yesterday's activities. Claimed he had government sources and wanted my side of the story. He knows about Dusty, the military jets, and the rail gun."

"What? How could he…. Are you sure you didn't spill the beans, Doctor?"

Mitch lied, a little. "I swear it, sir. I said nothing."

"This is disturbing. It looks as if your idea to promote a bomb threat didn't work."

Mitch pulled the phone away from his ear, looking at the device as if it had generated the insult. He said, "Or you didn't implement it very well. Besides, the reporter claimed to have a government source."

The man on the other end of the conversation didn't respond for a minute. Finally, "What paper was the other reporter from?"

"I can't remember. I think he said where she worked, but I was a little taken aback and can't recall."

"This is unfortunate. One paper, we might be able to influence the leak. Two papers present a more complex issue."

I bet it does, pondered Mitch. "I've honored our agreement, Agent Monroe. Is there anything else you need to know?"

"No. I hope you receive a call back from Secretary Witherspoon today. We're getting close to your brother, and I doubt he'll surrender peacefully."

"What is the cutoff for your deadline?" Wendy asked.

Crawford smirked at the junior reporter over his cup of coffee, "For this story, they'll hold the edition. What do you think?"

"I think we're done. My editor is going to throw a fit over the amount of speculation. He's an old fuddy-duddy when it comes to hard, verified facts, but if the *Post* is running it, he'll bend the rules."

Tim held a single finger high above the keyboard and mumbled, "Fire away." He pressed the command to send the email, and then grinned at Wendy. "This calls for a celebration. How about I buy dinner?"

The younger girl was skeptical, "Your boss hasn't agreed to publish the article yet. Isn't it a bit pre-mature to celebrate?"

"He will. Trust me. He will."

The two newshounds were just finishing their coffee when Crawford's cell phone rang. Glancing at the caller ID and then his partner, he mouthed, "My editor – right on time," and answered the call.

"What's up, boss?"

"Crawford," boomed the gruff voice through the tiny speaker, "What is this pile of shit you've dumped in my inbox?"

"I think it's the best piece I've ever written. Is there a problem?"

"I'm not sure you understand, son. We are running a newspaper here, not some supermarket tabloid. You might as well claim this gun you're talking about was left on this planet by aliens."

Tim looked at a concerned Wendy and winked. Covering the phone's mic, he whispered, "He always does this. He likes the article, I can tell."

Wendy was skeptical.

"Look, boss, most everything in that piece I can back up, and the part that is conjecture is clearly identified. Most of it is already public knowledge anyway."

A loud grunt came from Houston, followed by, "How you've cleverly packaged this supposedly clear conjecture is what I'm the most worried about, Tim. You should have been a lawyer. Nine out of ten people will read this, and believe it's all the gospel truth."

"Actually, I'm very sure it is all true. Besides, the main point of the piece is for the government to come clean and tell us what they know. After all, if there is a madman running around with a weapon that powerful, the public has a right to know."

Again, a long period passed before any response, Crawford visualizing the editor rubbing his temple from the headache the reporter just delivered. "Okay, we'll splash it on page one tomorrow. Heaven help us all."

"Thanks, boss."

Tim ended the call and then high-fived Wendy, both reporters beaming with excitement. "Now, he said, let's call your editor and then grab a bite."

Mitch was so lost in thought, the ring of his cell caused him to flinch. An unknown caller ID flashed on the screen.

"Mitch, it's Henry Witherspoon. I received your message. What the hell is going on down at A&M?"

"Dr. Witherspoon, thank you so much for calling, sir. I was beginning to think I was poison."

"That's ridiculous, Mitch. You know I have the highest regard for you and your team."

The Secretary of Energy remained silent while Mitch explained the situation. During the conversation, he emailed some of the video proof of his claims to a private account of his former professor.

"In summary, sir, you can understand the reason why I've pulled you into this conundrum."

Witherspoon was quiet for a moment, obviously digesting Mitch's core dump. "This is extraordinary – almost unbelievable. If this information was coming from anyone but you and Floss, I'd never believe it."

"I was there, sir, and I still find myself questioning a million things about the entire episode."

"If this data is accurate, we have the opportunity to channel infinite energy. It's a fork in the road. We can go the right direction and utilize this for the benefit of humankind – or the wrong path that results in ultimate destruction. I get it. You were wise to try and keep this under wraps, Mitch. The whole thing reminds me of Einstein's quote about the atom."

Mitch chuckled at the analogy. Well acquainted with the agony of his hero, the professor's mind extracted the famous quote from its archived recesses. *'The release of atom power has changed everything except our way of thinking...the solution to this problem lies in the heart of mankind. If only I had known, I should have become a watchmaker,' Einstein had ruminated.* The agony suffered by the genius over his theories leading to the development of the atom bomb was well documented in the scientific community. "I think my brother would say being a gunsmith is just as noble as a watchmaker, sir."

"I think I would like your brother. Let's hope I get to meet him one day soon. In the meantime, I'll get a meeting scheduled with the president to discuss this discovery. My office doesn't carry a lot of political weight in Washington, so it might be a bit before I can gain access to the castle, but I promise you I will. The Commander in Chief has a lot on his plate at the moment. I'll do my best."

Day 7

The folded copy of the *Post* hit the table with about as much force as a newspaper could. More noise than kinetic energy, only two of the FBI personnel seated around the conference table flinched. The paper scooted across the table, the bold headline reading, "God's Gun Loose in Houston," clearly visible.

"God's gun," hissed Monroe. "How do they dream this stuff up?"

No one answered, a signal for the lead agent to continue his rant. "If I find out who the leak is, he or she will be spending quality time with many of the criminals we've put behind bars. I hope he gets a cellmate named Bubba, and I hope the resident jailbird finds our snitch attractive."

The crude threat hung in the air for a moment, Monroe venting frustration that went beyond the article. He continued, "Our fugitive has gone down a rabbit hole. We've not had any contact since the police witnessed him knock down the towers. He's obviously getting help from someone in this town."

"It's not his ex-wife," offered a younger agent at the end of the table. "She's a difficult surveillance, for sure, but I'm convinced there's been no contact. We've got her office, home, and car covered. Her cell, office, and home phones are all wired. She moves around a lot, showing houses and meeting clients, but we've seen zero evidence of Mr. Weathers."

Monroe processed the report, finally offering, "What about turning on the microphone on her smart phone?"

The man in charge of Maria's detail looked down. "DOJ messed up on the warrant. They didn't get that included in the paperwork."

"Well do it anyway!" shouted Monroe. "If a case is eventually brought against either of them, we can always implement parallel construction afterwards."

Broaching the subject of parallel construction added a layer of stress to the members of Monroe's team. While commonly used against drug dealers, international syndicates, and organized crime, the order to use the questionable method against a United States citizen wasn't very common. While the concept was simple, the ramifications were not. If evidence was gathered via an illegal act, it wasn't admissible in a court of law. What Monroe was suggesting involved creating a false, but seemingly legal trail, so prosecutors could use the ill-gotten gains against a defendant. It was lying. Perjury.

"Is there a problem here, people?" Monroe asked, scanning from face to face around the table. "Just in case some of you missed it, let me catch you up on current events. Our suspect has engaged and destroyed two, fully armed, military interceptors. He is responsible for untold financial damage to the citizens of north Houston. We have businesses without power, homes without water, and roads that are impassable. Millions and millions of dollars lost. Can anyone here support an argument that extreme measures aren't warranted?"

No one offered any such support.

"I didn't think so. I'm tempted to haul Maria Weathers in, regardless of what our surveillance says. I think she's waist deep in this."

Agent Shultz, now on temporary assignment to the Houston office, finally spoke up. "I wouldn't recommend that, sir. She's a known public figure and very well connected. Besides, given how most divorced people feel about each other, you might actually be doing Weathers a favor."

Shultz's logic broke the tension in the room, a few chuckles here and there.

Monroe saw no humor in the response. "This bureau doesn't avoid making arrests because of wealth or fame. The only reason I'm not bringing her in is because if she is helping Weathers, she'll mess up, and we'll catch them both. If she's sitting in a detention cell, he can't contact her."

Shultz didn't like being scolded, but let it pass. "Sir, we're now tied into the NSA's facial recognition systems with a dedicated fiber optic pipe. Every police cruiser's dash cam, every traffic camera, every tollbooth… hell, every camera in the city is being fed into the system. We're scanning over 10 million faces an hour. If he's walking or driving around Houston, we'll find him eventually."

Another agent chimed in, "We also have two Mark IV Predator drones on constant orbit above the city. They are feeding into the spook's system as well. We're scanning everyone from the homeless under overpasses to the parking lots of grocery stores. He'll look up eventually."

Satisfied with the scale of the dragnet, Monroe dismissed the meeting.

~ ~

Maria heard the car's engine outside, a signal Eva and her lawyer had arrived. Checking herself in the hallway mirror, she was at the door before her guests could ring the bell.

"Eva!" Maria greeted, hugging her old friend straight away. After the embrace, she held the older woman by the shoulders at arm's length and stated, "You haven't aged a day!"

The host's attention then turned to Grace, a sweeping glance informing the ex-wife that the new girlfriend was indeed an attractive woman, smartly dressed with engaging eyes. Maria was sure she had just been assessed as well.

The two guests pulled small suitcases, the wheels rolling noisily along the marble entrance to Maria's grand foyer. The visitors entered wide-eyed and inhaling sharply, compliments like, "Oh this is beautiful," and "Isn't this just gorgeous," filling the air.

After being shown to their guest rooms and given a chance to freshen up, the three women reassembled in the kitchen. Maria and Grace deciding on wine, Eva opting for decaf coffee.

The granite countertops, room-dividing bar, and plush stools always seemed to be the natural place for social clustering in the home. Despite the huge sectional sofa in the nearby family room and a formal living room with dimensions just slightly smaller than a high school gymnasium, people always gravitated toward the kitchen. This evening was no exception, and Maria had already prepared a tray of cheese, crackers, and various finger breads for her visitors.

Both Maria and Grace were extremely curious about each other, both determined not to let it show. Despite Dusty being a shared point of reference for both women, each understood that Eva was the one in need, her husband in peril.

"The police kept asking Hank about his last visit to Dusty's workshop. Over and over again, they kept repeating the same questions. It was like Hank and Dusty were drug dealers… or worse," Eva fretted.

"I heard on the radio that the police suspected Dusty was in Houston. I assume they've been by to speak with you, Maria." Grace probed.

"Yes, the FBI sent two men here to question me. I found their way of thinking just plain silly. What man on the run goes to his ex-wife for help?"

Eva started to protest, "Now, Maria, we both know that you and Dusty…" but Maria held up a finger to her lips. Quickly snatching up a piece of paper, she wrote, "The FBI has my house bugged, I'm sure. Please don't say anything."

Both visitors nodded as their host spun the paper around so they could see her note.

"Anyway," Maria continued, winking at her guests, "They've been following me everywhere. What a waste of the taxpayers' money."

Grace nodded, "This entire endeavor is a waste of money. You should have seen the number of government men in Fort Davis. It was as if the town were invaded. And for what? Hank? No offense, Eva, but Hank's not exactly a dangerous man."

Snorting, Maria added, "I bet that entire berg is up in arms over this. The scandal of it all," she mocked, rolling her eyes. "That's one of the reasons why I had to leave. I just couldn't handle everyone knowing everyone else's business."

Grace countered, "I'm just the opposite. I had to get out of Dallas and find a simpler place – a slower pace."

"I bet you stirred the rumor pot when you first arrived in Fort Davis," Maria ventured.

The lawyer nodded, her eyes focused on nothing as she recalled her first few months in a new town. "It was difficult at first, but I'm glad I did. You know, Dusty, Hank, and Eva were all so kind to me – helped smooth the transition."

Maria studied Grace, deciding she actually liked the woman. There was nothing competitive about her, despite her education and financial success. She actually found herself visualizing her guest and her ex-husband as a couple. They would be good for each other.

Eva excused herself, heading off to the powder room. After she was gone, Maria grabbed the notepad and scribbled, "Dusty Is okay. He's safe for the moment."

The smile that flashed across Grace's face said it all. *She does feel for Dusty… beyond any attorney-client bullshit*, concluded Maria. *I wonder what Dusty thinks of her?*

It occurred to Maria that Grace might not have seen the day's newspaper article. Eva was just returning when, holding a finger to her lips, Maria slid the paper in front of her two guests. Both women read in silence with Grace finishing first, her mannerisms mimicking someone who had just figured out a complex puzzle.

Eva's reaction was completely different, sitting quietly with a far off gaze. Taking the nearby notepad, she scribbled, "Can this be true?"

Both Grace and Maria nodded, neither woman realizing the effect on Hank's wife. "I'm scared for Hank," she whispered. "I had no idea he was involved in anything. I don't think he had any concept of what was going on."

Grace chose her words carefully, always conscious of someone listening in. Taking Eva's hand, she soothed, "Your husband didn't do anything wrong, Eva. I'm sure of that. I think the government is making a mountain out of a molehill because of paranoia over terrorism. Besides, all these cops have to justify their existence somehow. We'll get it straightened out at the hearing."

That compassion was genuine, observed Maria. *She honestly does care, and in the end, that's all that really matters.*

With Dusty resting just over a mile away, he had no idea how lucky a man he was. There was no way he could know or understand that his ex-wife had just given her seal of approval to the new woman in his life.

~ ~

Four blocks away, an FBI agent yawned and adjusted his earpiece. He'd been watching and listening to Maria's home for nine straight hours, virtually trapped in the small, unmarked sedan. His relief had a sick kid and would be a few hours late.

Stretching stiffly, he cursed the men who had ordered him to spend such a lengthy period sitting in a seat that wasn't designed for extended stints of stationary work.

He wondered if the "good old days," when surveillance was conducted from the back of a panel van, wasn't a better idea. *At least you could stretch your legs*, he reasoned. The few men left at the bureau who had actually worked with such equipment claimed otherwise, telling stories of constant sweating due to the heat generated by the radios and electronic equipment.

Long gone were the days of entry teams burglarizing a suspect's home, planting electronic eavesdropping devices at key locations while others disguised as utility repairmen twisted wires on utility poles and switch boxes. Now, entering a residence was completely unnecessary.

The agent looked down at his pad computer, switching microphones with a simple tap on the screen. The listening devices were actually outside Maria's home. Four tiny, fly-sized buttons were in place on strategic windows, fired from over 50 feet away by a special air-powered pistol. Coated with a layer of super-sticky gelatin, the devices could send both video and audio data and would remain in place for 40 hours. After that, they would fall harmlessly to the ground, eventually dissolving into nothingness.

The sticky bugs weren't the only technology keeping an eye on Dusty's ex-wife. With a mere tap on the screen, the agent could turn on the microphone of any smart phone inside the residence, listening and recording conversations without the phone's owner having the slightest hint. This particular suspect kept her cell phone inside her purse, he noted. Despite the high-end model, he couldn't hear anything but muffled tones through that channel.

The webcam of any laptop computer could be switched on remotely as well. He'd briefly enjoyed the view of Maria checking her email this morning, her sheer nightgown enhancing the experience. He had already browsed her messages before she had even switched on the coffeepot and knew she didn't have anything worthy of scrutiny. Now, that window into her world provided nothing via that channel but a darkened view of Maria's office, a high-back desk chair and bookshelf filling the screen.

The images generated by any home security system could be hijacked and stored on the FBI's computers as well. Despite its size and affluence, the owner of this home hadn't installed a video system. While the agent could also easily tap into baby monitors, there were no infants at the residence.

Even the bureau's vehicle was radically advanced compared to the heavy, obvious vans of just a few years ago. The FBI realized bad guys weren't completely stupid, often searching a neighborhood's streets before conducting their nefarious activities.

The sedan was equipped with what the tech called "curtains," or thin vinyl window coverings that were printed with an image that mimicked the interior of the car – an empty, harmless car that couldn't possibly contain law enforcement personnel or equipment. The agent could see out just fine, but anyone driving or walking past his unit would notice an empty, non-descript Ford. Even the extra antenna, required by the high-powered transceiver in the trunk, was embedded in the glass of the rear window, disguised as a defroster.

This stakeout had its issues, unique little quirks that degraded what could be ascertained. The placement of the sticky bugs had been imperfect, the scouts believing the primary social areas of Maria's home would be the den or formal living room. This evening's gathering had proven the kitchen was the hot spot, and they didn't have video focused there – a situation that would require another two bugs being deployed to different windows of the residence.

The video wasn't the only issue. One sticky bug, at the rear of the home, wasn't transmitting properly due to interference from the pool pump. The agent snorted at the thought, wondering if he shouldn't give the owner a heads up that her pump was about to go bad.

Not my problem, he decided, and returned his attention to the conversation in Maria's kitchen, which unfortunately for the bored agent, had progressed to the latest gossip from Fort Davis, Texas.

Day 8

The rain actually cheered Maria, the cooler weather providing both a wardrobe opportunity and a fair chance at visiting Dusty unobserved.

Following her normal morning routine, the first order of business, after coffee and email, was to check in with Paula. Normally, the two co-workers would exchange a brief phone call or text message, but today Maria called her assistant via Skype and used the video option, all but sure the FBI would be listening.

Somewhat surprised, Paula answered, her image appearing on Maria's display.

"Well good morning, boss. Why are you using Skype?"

"I don't know," Maria lied. "I've been fooling with this for a while and wanted to test my skills."

"Ahhhh… well, no messages this morning. I think it's going to be a slow day with the weather."

"Okay… I'll be in shortly. Bye."

After disconnecting the call, Maria sat back in her chair and sighed. Paula was wearing a dark blue blouse and white khaki slacks. She had a very similar outfit in her closet.

Paula was a strawberry blonde, Maria raven haired with a longer cut. A hat was the answer, and Maria had plenty of those.

Forty-five minutes later, Maria backed her car from the garage, making a point to stop at the end of the driveway. Sporting a fire red umbrella, she pretended to check her tires, walking around and kicking all four as if the vehicle were handling funny.

After faking the imaginary flat, she proceeded to the office as normal, a slight tingly feeling surging through her body at the excitement of her secret mission. She spent the time in traffic recalling every spy novel she'd ever read.

Paula, as usual, had also run from the parking lot to the office under the protection of a blue bumbershoot. Maria smiled as she shook the raindrops from her canopy and placed it beside Paula's at the door. Her grin widened when she saw her assistant's jacket was made from the same navy linen as her own.

"I see you got the memo on the dress code today," Paula observed, nodding at her boss's outfit.

Maria cringed at the comment, hoping the cops didn't have the office bugged. She responded with a smile and spread arms, the gesture meant to say, "Oh, well, what can you do."

An hour passed, the real estate office slower than usual, just as Paula had predicted. Taking a deep breath, Maria initiated her plan.

Her first step was to borrow Paula's car, but how to ask using a method that wouldn't be recognized by the cops? She decided on a trip to the ladies room, and after fiddling around for the appropriate amount of time, reached up and unscrewed two of the light bulbs above the vanity.

"Paula, could you come here for a second?" she called.

Frowning, her assistant rolled back her chair and walked back to the private facility. As soon as Paula was inside the small space, Maria reached down and flushed the head, acting as if she'd forgotten to do so. With the sound of the running water in the background, the boss asked, "Do we have any spare bulbs? These keep burning out all the time."

"No, I used the last one in the supply closet two weeks ago. Do you want me to run and get some?"

"Naw, I've got to run a few errands anyway. I want to pick up some extra groceries for my houseguests. Can I borrow your car? I think mine has a low tire, and your SUV holds more than my Mercedes."

"Sure, you know I love driving your car anyway."

The toilet stopped running at the same time as the conversation ended. Maria hoped it was enough. After all, radios and running water always defeated bugs in the spy novels.

Maria pretended to be busy until the phone rang. Knowing Paula would be on this call for a while, Maria went to the reception area and dropped her keys on the busy girl's desk. Flashing a thumbs up, the assistant dug in her purse and produced her own key ring.

Maria pulled a hat from her jacket pocket, a plain skullcap that she'd worn once for a Halloween costume. Grabbing Paula's blue umbrella, she opened the unit and dashed for the parking lot.

Unlocking the SUV, she was proud of how little she'd exposed of her face while entering the driver's seat, and was pulling out of the lot a few moments later.

Leaving her cell and purse back at the office, Maria had nothing more than her billfold stuffed inside one of the jacket's pockets. Again, thankful for the weather, she began to drive around north Houston, trying desperately to see if anyone were following her.

Twenty minutes later and having seen no clues of pursuit, she pulled into a grocery store and hurried through the aisles buying basic foodstuffs for her injured ex-husband. She paid cash, not wanting any records showing on her normally well-used debit card.

The home where she had Dusty tucked away was at the end of a single-street, gated subdivision. The neighborhood was very affluent, homeowners using massive 4 and 5-car garages fronted with estate-style driveways. It was rare to see any car on the street, and today Maria was relieved to see empty curbs all the way back to the hideout.

She found Dusty asleep, the beaker of orange juice empty.

"Wakie, Wakie, eggs and bakie," she said softly.

"I don't smell any bacon," he mumbled back.

The covers rustled, his head appearing from under a fold, one eye open. "What day is it?"

"You've been here a little less than 48 hours. I bet you're hungry."

Yawning, he had to agree. "You're right, I'm starving."

Maria moved her hands to her hips, jutting out her jaw. "Of course I'm right. Don't tell me you've forgotten that I'm always right. Has it been that long?"

"Yes, ma'am," he pretended, sarcasm thick in his tone.

Maria laughed, happy with her false victory. "Let's get your lazy ass out of bed, cowboy. While you take a shower, I'll fix you something to eat."

Nodding, Dusty pulled back the covers and managed to perch on the edge of the mattress with only one moan and two grimaces. After helping him stand, Maria unwrapped the first layer of bandages, anxious to see the results of her doctoring.

The wound looked healthy and pink, four butterfly bandages holding the folds of skin together. "I didn't think you wanted my taking you to the emergency room for staples, so I used these bandages. Do you remember using them the time Anthony fell off those rocks? We were on vacation, and there wasn't a hospital for 80 miles? That guy that helped us... the army medic... he showed me how to do this."

"I remember that guy," Dusty said, "That was a nasty cut on the boy's leg. As I recall, the Good Samaritan was hiking and heard Anthony crying."

Maria laughed at the memory. "I was so scared. I'll never forget how calm and cool you were. I was losing my mind thinking our son was going to bleed to death."

Dusty examined his torso and said, "The cut is mostly scabbed over. I don't think it will hurt to get it wet. A shower sounds good about now."

"It might sting a little, but I think you're safe. I'll coat it in antibiotic crème after, like I did the other night. You've lost a ton of blood, so it's probably going to be a few days before you're back up and about."

Dusty frowned, something troubling him. "Maria, are you sure you're not going to get in trouble by helping me?"

Guiding her ex to the bathroom, she recounted a quick summary of the last few days. Dusty didn't comment, just listening with his normal intensity. After she was sure he wasn't going to collapse or fall while bathing, she made for the kitchen to deliver on the promised home cooked meal.

"Damn he looks good," she mumbled on the way. "How do men do that? I spend two hours a day in the gym and still don't like how I look naked. He looks better than he did when we were 25 years old."

Shaking her head, she set about scrambling four eggs and frying a pound of bacon.

A short time later, he appeared wrapped in a towel. Maria sat watching him wolf down the meal, which he washed down with an entire quart of orange juice. "You need to keep growing the beard, it looks good on you."

Dusty smirked, "I was going to shave, but there isn't a razor. I forgot mine when I left my hotel in a hurry."

"So, are you feeling strong enough for some bad news?"

Wiping his face with the napkin, he nodded.

Maria took the folded newspaper and placed it in front of him, watching his reaction carefully.

He quickly scanned the article titled "God's Gun" the first time, raising his eyebrows once and grunting twice. He read it carefully the second time, never making a sound.

"This reporter got it mostly right," he commented calmly, the reaction taking Maria completely by surprise.

"*He got it mostly right?* Is that what you just said?" She replied with a raised voice. "What the hell is going on Durham Anthony Weathers? Since when do you go around shooting down airplanes and blowing up public utility towers?"

Looking at her with a deadpan expression, he responded. "You're the one who said Fort Davis was too boring, my dear. It was you who had to leave or, how did you put it, you'd go insane from the riot of quiet. I decided you were right. I thought I'd spice up my life a little... step over to the wild side."

"Bullshit! Now tell me what really happened."

Pointing to the paper, he replied, "Like I said, he got it mostly right."

"How did you create this super... crazy... thing? Where did it come from?"

Dusty began filling in the blanks, telling Maria everything.

After he finished, she commented, "So that's why they arrested Hank."

"What? Who arrested Hank?"

"The FBI and ATF from what I hear. Eva and Grace are staying at my place, waiting on Hank's hearing tomorrow at the courthouse."

"Grace? Grace is in Houston?"

A sly smile crossed Maria's face, her expression relaying joy over Dusty having exposed his feelings. "So you *do* have a thing for her? I was beginning to wonder if you had turned gay or something. She's a good looking woman."

"Maria!"

"Well... I never hear of you dating anybody. It's good to know you're still interested in women, Dusty. I don't want to walk through life thinking I neutered the Bull of Jeff Davis County."

"Maria! Now hold on just a minute," he managed, but she was on a roll.

"Now Dusty, I know that there are lots of gay cowboys. They even have their own movie. It's nothing to be ashamed of. You should...."

He moved with the speed of a pouncing lion, lifting her effortlessly. Before she could inhale, she was on the couch, his face an inch above hers – their lips almost touching. His bare chest pressed into her breasts, firm and powerful, she could feel the strength of his muscles flexing beneath warm skin.

Without her eyes ever leaving his, she put on a halfhearted struggle, only managing to spread her legs. His weight shifted, now pressing down on the inside of her thighs. His towel had fallen away, and she could feel his heat. Her own body took over, reacting with a will of its own... an animal without conscience or control. Right or wrong didn't matter. Old or new had no meaning. She could feel the need building. Moist hotness began spreading through her, desire about to lose control.

Her arms were pinned against the sofa, his powerful embrace like two bands of steel enveloping her soul... holding her tight... pulling her closer. She knew if she didn't stop this soon, he'd reach a point of no return, taking her for his pleasure, using her body to satisfy his needs.

It's not right, her mind protested. *Don't succumb to the lust,* she thought. *You're only going to open old wounds*, she reasoned. *Stop him now.*

"Dusty, stop. You've proven your point – I don't think you're gay," she offered, hoping to give him an out.

For a moment, she thought she had waited too long. He didn't move, or smile... his eyes never left hers. Part of her wanted it to be so, ached for him to use her for whatever he wanted. She considered a struggle, to break the trance, but she knew it would be fruitless. She was only a butterfly, gentle elegance and delicate beauty. He was the oak tree, solid, stout and unyielding. He probably wouldn't even notice any protest on her part.

He blinked once... twice... and then averted his gaze. The spell had been broken. Exhaling, he pushed off of her, quickly bending for the towel and covering himself.

"I'm so sorry, Dusty," Maria offered, her tone sincere. "I shouldn't have teased you about Grace. I actually like her. You're a good man Durham Anthony Weathers, you deserve someone like her."

Despite the dark tan and complexion of a man who spent a lot of time outdoors, the flush on Dusty's cheeks was obvious. "She's a good friend and excellent lawyer, Maria. It's not gone any further than that – yet."

He then changed the subject, erasing the last sexually charged particle from the air. "What is this about Hank? Why could they possibly arrest him? What are the charges?"

She explained it all to him, including what she'd learned that night before at her house. The impact on her ex was obvious, his temper starting to churn.

"That's bullshit and horse feathers," he growled in a low, mean voice. "They're just doing this to draw me in. Hank didn't do anything wrong."

Maria looked at her watch, slightly taken aback by the time. "Look, I've got to get back to the office before the cops figure out it wasn't Paula that left. You've got food, antibiotic crème, and plenty of shampoo. You lay low, and I'll come back when I can."

Nodding, Dusty looked his ex in the eye and said, "Thank you, Maria. I owe ya for all this."

"We'll see how you feel about that when you get my bill." she replied, and then left him alone.

~ ~

Sergei Primakov pulled the two sheets of typewritten Slavic text from the paperclip, exposing an original copy of the American newspaper article. He preferred to read the native English because he'd seen inaccurate translations in the past. It wasn't unusual for the Russian language experts employed by his agency to miss sarcasm and innuendo, errors that could lead to a whole host of issues later on. Besides, his English was perfect, and he wanted to keep it that way.

There weren't any hidden meanings in the article titled, "God's Gun." Nor could the director of the Russian Foreign Intelligence Service (Sluzhba Vneshney Razvedki, or SVR) find any humor within.

Rising from his chair, one of the most powerful men in Russia moved to the window of his expansive office, his empty gaze lost somewhere over the Yasenevo District of southwest Moscow. The bright sunshine of the day didn't match the director's mood, his thoughts troubled with the news from America.

Primakov had originally been recruited into the old KGB. A child of the communist regime, his academic performance and physical abilities had made the young Sergei a prime candidate for recruitment into the world famous spy agency.

When communism had fallen, Sergei hadn't been high enough in the ranks to be automatically targeted for removal. Things began to change rapidly as the country accelerated toward democracy, and those at his level who couldn't adapt were bypassed by the more flexible, nimble thinking individuals. Primakov had seen the opportunity and run with it - his specialty, American capitalism, giving him a leg up on his inter-agency competitors.

Sergei had understood early on that the game was changing. No longer were military secrets and strategic analysis the most valuable intelligence for his country. The Motherland now required industrial secrets, manufacturing capabilities, and free market analysis. The projected battlefields of central Europe had been replaced by global export markets. Combat power and combined arms capabilities were superseded by currency manipulation and world commodity exchanges.

While his SVR still monitored the world's military apparatus, the emphasis of the organization was now economic, and that's why the American farmer's invention troubled him so deeply.

The Russian economy depended on the export of arms. After the embarrassing setbacks dealt to his country's weapons system by the American Army's invasion of Iraq, the market for Russian arms had gradually recovered over time. During this period, billions of rubles had been lost to his countrymen, a result of the

US thrashing issued to Saddam's forces and their Russian weapons. The Motherland's armament industry had been reduced to a second-rate player, severe discounts required to sell anything. It had taken ten years and a significant investment to recover.

In a way, he reconciled, *this has always been the status quo*. Sergei recalled how the Americans had outspent the former Soviet regime and basically bankrupted his country. Western newspapers had referred to the contest as the "arms race." In reality, it wasn't merely a game of numbers – a competition over quantity of missiles, submarines, and tanks. There was also a game within a game – economic obsolescence.

Sergei couldn't recall how many times a super-expensive weapon was rendered obsolete by a cheap countermove from the other side. He remembered the MIG-23 aircraft, a product requiring an investment in research and development that had cost millions of rubles.

A month after the first squadrons were being equipped with the extraordinarily expensive warplane, the Americans demonstrated the first shoulder fired, ground to air, anti-aircraft missile. The MIG, costing 35 million rubles each, had been rendered obsolete by a missile costing less than $2,000 per copy.

Both sides had continued these leapfrogs of technology for over 40 years. The Americans won because they had deeper pockets, better leadership, and more motivated engineers. The communists had fallen, leaving Sergei's beloved Motherland in disarray.

The ongoing contest had cost more than a change of government. Russia was left with a rusting industrial complex, millions of obsolete weapons, and a bruised national pride. The export of arms had been a key factor in the road to recovery.

Now, a previously unknown farmer from Texas was again threatening to destroy an industry built with the sweat and sacrifice of millions of Russian workers.

Primakov was familiar with the concept of magnetically launched projectiles. He had read the extensive file created years ago during the Cold War. The then-Soviet scientists had deemed the technology too problematic to pursue. Portable energy sources, battlefield detection, and numerous other issues had led to the abandonment of the project.

Even when the US Navy had continued to develop the technology, it was thought to have limited use in the Soviet armed forces. Now, some peasant farmer had surprised the world with an invention that seemed to prove the world's most brilliant engineers wrong.

It wasn't that the SVR's director worried about a cowboy showing up at the Kremlin and demanding to rule Mother Russia. No, the primary issue was the obsolescence of sophisticated weapons of war... weapons critical to his country's economy and worldwide respect.

How effective would a tank costing 78 million rubles be when a single soldier firing a rail gun could split the hull in half? Who would purchase a multi-million dollar anti-air defense system when one rebel with a rail gun could obliterate an entire air force with a few shots?

It was troubling, and Sergei needed to sort it out.

Moving back to his desk, he checked the calendar resting on the polished oak surface. Smiling for the first time that morning, he hit the intercom and instructed, "Please clear my calendar for this afternoon and have my car brought around to the east entrance immediately."

"Yes, Director."

A few minutes later, and much to the chagrin of his security detail, Primakov was racing away from the headquarters building, the director wrapped in a steel gray Mercedes Benz SL63 two-seater.

He'd discovered the road not long ago, a rare, lightly traveled lane on the outskirts of his country's largest city. Recently resurfaced, the glass smooth track had yet to experience the harsh Russian winter, and Sergei reveled in pushing the limits of the fast German sports car. It was a glutinous self-indulgence, the only one his tightly disciplined lifestyle would afford.

Something about the freedom of driving touched his soul, controlling the powerful machine seemed to clear his mind. *I wonder if the American farmer feels the same sensation when he fires his super weapon*, he pondered. *I wonder if it clears his mind to control such a powerful beast.*

The thought refocused the intelligent man, his logical mind shifting gears as smoothly as the car that carried him through the countryside. Changing mental tracks from concern over Mother Russia's future to a more selfish reasoning, Sergei began to picture himself possessing the weapon. What would it mean? What could he accomplish?

The growl of the German V8 was a symphony to his ears as he flattened out of a banked curve and accelerated down a straight section of the road. The embrace of the leather seat felt like the welcoming arms of a beautiful woman as the car passed 180 kilometers per hour and continued to climb.

I need to control that weapon, he realized. *Not for my country, but for me.* He could right so many wrongs with such power.

Sergei's mind began to perform its finest art – planning. As the German road machine flew through the Russian farmlands, he set forth timetables, reviewed personnel lists, and established deliverables. Once the outline and schedule was complete, he then concentrated on the sales pitch to his superiors. Even the mighty SVR had its boundaries and budgetary limits.

His presentation would be simple and believable – mainly because it was true, for the most part. He would obtain their support because he wanted to save Russia's arms industry from this economy- destroying technology loose on the American streets. He would find and take the weapon before the American authorities gained control of the device.

A thin smile crossed his lips, the first one of the day that wasn't attributed to the car. He would use the significant power of his agency to obtain the rail gun, and then he would control Mother Russia, turning it into a fine tuned machine of power – just like his Mercedes.

Why stop at Russia, he reasoned. *Why not the world?*

Day 9

The security procedures seemed deliberately slow and invasive, delaying Grace and Eva's arrival at the judge's private chambers. Not only had the repeated scanning, pat downs and questioning been excessive, the two women felt like they were being held back intentionally.

If the process had been purposely designed to stall Grace's arrival, it worked. Barely entering the quiet confines of the Federal Magistrate before the scheduled time, she hadn't had time to visit with her client or review any last minute preparations. The morning's events caused her building anger to fester a few degrees higher.

A young Department of Justice prosecutor entered the chambers shortly afterwards. He glanced at Eva and immediately hissed, "She can't be here."

"She is the defendant's wife; she most certainly can be here," responded an already pissed Grace.

"You're out of your league here, Ms. Kennedy. This isn't some hearing over patent infringement or copyright law. This is a matter of national security being prosecuted under the Patriot Act. I'm giving Mr. Barns a huge benefit by even agreeing to this arraignment at all. I don't have to, you know. There's no due process required for domestic terrorists."

"And where might my client be, young man? I want to speak with him before this circus begins."

"The suspect is locked up in a federal holding facility and is in good health. He is being treated as a prisoner of war."

Before Grace could respond, the judge entered the room. All the attendees automatically stood, quickly waved back to their seats by the salt and pepper haired man wearing a smartly tailored business suit and carrying a fine leather attaché case.

As the magistrate settled into his seat, the DOJ lawyer spouted, "Your honor, I must request that Eva Barns be removed from chambers. This is a national security matter where sensitive information may be disclosed. Mrs. Barnes has no clearance, nor does she have any standing before the court."

An annoyed look flashed on the judge's face, a hint of distaste showing before his stoic expression returned. He looked at Grace and said, "Ms. Kennedy?"

"Your honor, I don't possess any sensitive information, only the DOJ is in possession of such material. Given that, I would offer that the prosecutor is in control of what is disclosed and what isn't. If he feels the need to reveal any information relating to national security, then Mrs. Barns could be excused from these chambers at that time."

Nodding, the judge replied, "Sounds fair enough. Let's get started. Please read the state's charges, Mr. Haskins."

Pulling a single sheet of paper from his briefcase, the DOJ lawyer began. "The Department of Justice, under the powers granted by the Patriot Act of 2001, does hereby charge Mr. Henry Wilson Barns as follows. One count of conspiracy to commit an act of violence against the sovereign government of the United States of America, said conspiracy having the intent and forethought to damage, render ineffective, or corrupt the government's ability to enforce rule of law. One count of participating in the development of a weapon of mass destruction, as a violation of the National Firearms Act of 1968. Two counts of hindering a felony investigation, three counts of withholding information from federal law enforcement officers."

After scanning the papers offered by the DOJ attorney, the judge turned to Grace. "Ms. Kennedy?"

"Your honor, this is an abomination of justice, a clear violation of my client's constitutional rights. Furthermore, the state is intentionally withholding evidence directly associated with my client's defense. The DOJ is completely out of line here. There is no indication of any conspiracy against the government, any intent of wrongdoing, and it is an extreme overreach to even propose a single illegal act by Mr. Barns."

Without waiting on the judge's response, the special prosecutor handed the judge a stack of papers. "These documents are the transposed statements from recorded interviews with Mr. Barns on the night of his arrest. You will see that he clearly admits knowing one Mr. Durham Weathers had built a device using components from both Russia and China, foreign powers with known hostilities and radical terrorist elements opposed to the United States. Furthermore, Mr. Barns fully confesses to witnessing the test firing of a weapon of mass destruction, yet didn't alert the proper authorities on the night in question."

Grace hadn't seen Hank's statements, another violation of her client's privilege. She decided to play it by ear. "Mr. Barns had no way of knowing this weapon's capabilities. The parts referred to in the state's complaint aren't banned or restricted for import. If the DOJ is going to imprison everyone who possesses imported goods from Russia or China, then surely every US citizen will be incarcerated, your honor. There was never any discussion between Mr. Weathers and Mr. Barns involving intent to use the weapon against the United States, or anyone else for that matter. As a matter of fact, Mr. Barns was informed that the inventor of the device was going to travel to Texas A&M University in order to have it examined by an expert. Where is the conspiracy here, your honor?"

The magistrate seemed to ponder Grace's argument, finally turning to the man from Justice and raising his eyebrows.

Haskins considered his words carefully. "Your honor, we can prove that this device was used in a direct attack against two warplanes of the United States Air Force. Furthermore, we can prove that the same device was used to avoid pursuit by law enforcement officers and is directly responsible for the felled high-tension towers in north Houston just a few days ago. Mr. Barns should have contacted the authorities immediately after the discovery of the weapon. He did not. Not even after repeated national news stories did he volunteer the facts in his possession. We have a solid, provable foundation for these charges, your honor."

Grace sensed she was losing. With the spin of events being delivered to the judge, she felt like she was swimming against a tide of logic. She decided to at least salvage enough to give Hank a fighting chance.

"Regardless of this supposed evidence, I pray your honor will at least grant my client the right to a proper, legal process. We've been denied numerous constitutional protections and been shown no evidence before this hearing. Even the warrants have been sealed and unavailable to counsel. My client can prove his innocence, your honor, if we are allowed due process of law."

Haskins started to counter, but the judge held up both hands to silence the two attorneys. "I think I understand what is going on here. Ms. Kennedy, I'll give you 24 hours to deliver a written rebuttal to the state's position on this matter, after which, I will rule within another 24 hours. Until then, I'm ordering Mr. Barns be given access to his counsel and for the state to make available the documents delivered to me today. This hearing is over."

The judge promptly rose and left, leaving the two combatants and Eva staring at each other. Haskins wasn't pleased. "I'll fight you every step of the way on this, Kennedy. We're tired of these domestic lunatics using every little loophole in the law to avoid justice."

Grunting, Grace stared at the younger man straight in the eye. "These little loopholes you reference are how our system of justice works. All we ask is a fair trial and adherence to my client's constitutional rights. I'm sure the American people won't be pleased to know their government has decided to mimic Nazi Germany when it comes to how it treats its own citizens, complete with trumped up charges and false crimes."

Tilting his head, the man from Justice asked, "Are you threatening to go to the press on this, Ms. Kennedy?"

"I most certainly will do that, and any other legal step within my power to protect the rights of Mr. Barns, sir."

Without another word, the government lawyer rose and left the room. Grace heard sniffing sounds from behind her, turning to find Eva in tears. "Why?" the terrified woman wailed. "Why are they doing this to Hank? He's a good man, not a criminal."

~ ~

Eva and Grace's exit from the courthouse didn't take nearly as long as their entrance. Stepping down the front steps of the monolithic building, two men in suits suddenly blocked their way.

Flashing a badge, the older man barked, "Grace Kennedy?"

"Yes, what's the problem?"

"I have a warrant for your arrest."

With that, a female agent stepped closer and pulled Grace's hands behind her back after removing the attorney's purse.

"What the hell are you doing? I'm an officer of the court and...."

"The charge is espionage. More specifically, you are accused of threatening to leak classified information to public sources. Special Prosecutor Haskins just swore out the warrant, not five minutes ago."

"Grace?" Eva's shaky voice sounded behind her. "What's going on?"

"They are arresting me because I threatened to go to the press, Eva. It will be okay. Call Maria, and see if she can come down here and pick you up. I'll be okay."

Eva began fumbling for her phone, pausing as the two FBI agents escorted Grace back inside the building. She somehow managed to dial her cell, explaining to her host what had just happened.

"I'll be there in 40 minutes, Eva. Stay put," Maria promised.

Secretary Witherspoon entered the Oval Office with an attitude. Despite his repeated calls to the White House, it had taken days, not hours for the Commander in Chief to finally see him. It wasn't a positive sign.

"Henry," opened the president, "Let's sit on the couches and be comfortable."

Walking toward the sofas, Witherspoon intentionally stepped around the Presidental Seal woven into the carpet. Somehow, in the acidedimic's mind, stepping on the emblem was disrespectful to the office. He cringed when the president didn't do the same.

The two men sat on opposite sides, facing each other across a tasteful coffee table adorned with a heaping bowl of apples. The Secretary of Energy was curious if they were real, but decided not to waste his boss's valueable time exchanging social amenities.

"Sir, I appreciate your seeing me. I feel this matter is most urgent."

"I've read the brief you sent over. I also received a face to face update from the Secretary of Homeland Security and the Department of Defense. I must say, this is all a bit confusing."

"Confusing, sir?"

The president crossed his legs, folding his hands over his knee. "I'm hearing different opinions from my staff, and while that's not unusal, I rarely see such a wide differential as the briefs I have received on this situation."

"Mr. President, I believe the discovery at A&M, if validated, could be the greatest single breakthrough in the history of our species. I also feel strongly that abusing the technology could lead to the end of our race, if not the entire planet. That's why I've been so persistent in my requests to speak with you."

Nodding, the chief executive responded, appearing to choose his words carefully. "I understand your concern, but species-ending technology isn't exactly new, Henry. You probably noticed that Air Force officer outside. He's carrying the launch codes for our nuclear arsenal. I have stealth bombers, intercontintental ballistic missiles and a fleet of submarines at my disposal. I, and a few other world leaders, could end man's existence at any time. I'm struggling to see the difference."

The ex-professor rubbed his chin. "Sir, there are several hundred people involved in the construction, deployment, and maintenance of those weapons. Any unjustified, unwarranted mass launch would be difficult for even you to initiate. Your forces are going to wonder why - question their orders - perhaps even move to stop you if they believe you are insane."

Frowning at the suggestion, "Go on."

"This weapon is different. One man supposedly built it; one man can supposedly deploy it. If what we know so far is true, he didn't have access to any special equipment or manufacturing capabilities. A simple gunsmith's workshop being all that was required. That's the difference, sir. That is what is so troubling. If this technology is viable, then practically anyone can build a weapon far more powerful than a nuclear device."

"So why doesn't he just turn himself in and let us handle the technology like we've taken care of our nuclear arsenal since 1945?"

"I can't speak for the inventor, sir. I believe his argument to your proposal would be that nuclear proliferation is a serious issue, what with all the headlines about Iran and North Korea. I'm sure he's realized that the more people who know how his device functions, the more leaks are going to occur. Virtually everyone is aware of the nightmare scenario of the suitcase nuclear bomb. How long would it be before a zealous, radical individual built his own rail gun and wasn't afraid to use it?"

The president waved him off, "I've heard the argument, Henry, but I'm not convinced. I've been told by several scientists that the stories surrounding the event at A&M have to be greatly exaggerated. Over and over again, I'm told that the entire story is impossible from several different aspects. I'm receiving input from State that it's impossible that one man could have designed and built such a weapon. Many are suspicious of foreign influences – perhaps even outsiders controlling the inventor."

"Sir, there have been numerous incidents of basement inventors making discoveries that have rocked the academic world. Skepticism ran rampant with them as well."

The president sighed, his eyes drifting off while he digested Witherspoon's last comment. "Henry," he finally began, "I'll abide by your recommendation and set up a blue ribbon panel to analyze how this newfound wizardry can be implemented and controlled. I'll handle this quietly, without fanfare or political exposure. But I have to warn you, it won't happen quickly. I'm not going to drop everything and rush around like a madman to solve an issue I'm not 100% sure exists. I want you to lead the effort. Put a list of the people you think should be involved on my desk, and I'll get the ball rolling. That's the best I can do."

Smiling with the small victory, Witherspoon couldn't help but try for just a little more. "Thank you, Mr. President. Is there any chance you could call off the law enforcement dogs? They are chasing the inventor, and I actually fear they'll catch up to him. Bad things could happen if that comes to fruition, sir."

"No. I won't do that, Henry, and here's why. If the others are correct, if we have a criminal situation on our hands, then I would be doing a disservice to the American people if I stopped law enforcement from performing their duties. I can just see *The New York Times* headline if such a thing were to occur. The scandal would destroy my administration. Form your commission, but in the meantime, I have to enforce the law."

Secretary Witherspoon was visibly disappointed. Looking down at the presidential seal, he said, "I hope you're right, and I'm wrong, Mr. President. I sincerely do."

Day 11

Maria pulled her disappearing act again. This time it was her housekeeper who provided the car and alternate persona.

Dusty was up and about when she finally made it to the hideout, burning with the news of Grace's arrest, but unable to safely visit her ex for two days.

His reaction was predictable, a storm brewing behind his normally friendly eyes. Maria watched the anger spread, almost predicting his slightly faster breathing and then erect, stiff spine. There was no final explosion, however. Just like when they were married, the man had always been able to hold his temper, if just by a thread.

"They're doing this to pull me in," he stated. "They're sending me a message to surrender."

"I've got to admit," she responded. "I've never seen or heard of anything like this. You read all of those conspiracy blogs and stories on the internet and dismiss them as the rants of crazy people. Now, I'm feeling a little insanity myself."

Dusty paced around the kitchen for a bit, thumbs hooked in his pockets and head down. He looked up at her and said, "I can't let my friends rot in jail, Maria. Not when I know they're innocent."

"So you are thinking of turning yourself in?"

"It's not me they want – it's that gun. I've thought about destroying it and then handing myself over, but that would probably result in them locking me away in some dungeon and being interrogated until I die. They'd never let me out – I might blab to the press or write a book or something."

"What if you hid the gun and then surrendered? You can use the weapon's location as a bargaining chip."

Dusty grinned and then shook his head. "I've pondered that route as well. To be honest, I'm too scared to do that."

Maria didn't follow, her expression making it clear that she wanted Dusty to expand.

"I would be completely at their mercy. They could use drugs, waterboarding – all kinds of ways to get me to talk. Again, after they had their hands on the technology, I'd never see the light of day again."

Maria started to protest his thinking, the words "Our government would never do something like that," coming out of her throat before Dusty's raised eyebrows stopped her cold. A sheepish look came over her face when she realized how silly she sounded.

"So what do you want to do?" she finally asked.

"I think it's ridiculous that I'm sitting here, hiding like some sort of bank robber, when I'm in possession of what be the world's most powerful weapon. They want me so badly because they're scared of the gun. Maybe I should give them good reason to be frightened."

Tilting her head, Maria asked, "So you would commit a crime because you're not a criminal?"

Dusty shook his head, "The FBI appears to have lost all restraint. They've been the big kid on the block for a long, long time. They must feel pretty cocky… unchallengeable. Perhaps someone should challenge them, and the courts don't appear to be the place to do it anymore."

"You can't shoot the entire FBI with that gun, Dusty."

"I know, but I can send a message. Any chance you could go shopping for me? I need some stuff."

Rolling her eyes, Maria started to question her ex, but the look on his face was concrete. She knew there wouldn't be any answers and worse yet, she knew it was a waste of time trying to change his mind.

"Okay," she sighed, "What do you need?"

Paula looked up from the receptionist desk and smiled as Maria entered the office. After a quick exchange of salutations and phone messages, Maria spoke loud and clear for all to hear.

"Could you do me a huge favor this afternoon?"

"Sure, what's up?"

"Anthony's birthday is coming up, and I need to pick up his present. It's a bicycle and some other gear that would fit easier in the back of your SUV than in my car."

Paula, always eager to get out of the office and do something different, replied, "No problem. Do you want me to take it back to your house?"

The boss pretended to think about her response. "No, he might be coming back this weekend, and I don't want him to find it. How about you drop it off over at the Fitzgerald place? They've already moved to England, and their garage is empty. I don't have it listed yet, so no one would bother the stuff."

"Sounds like a plan," Paula agreed.

"I'll write down all the items I want, and of course give you my debit card."

Disappearing into her office, Maria emerged a short time later with an extensive list. "I went ahead and put a few other stops on here, if you don't mind."

Scanning the paper, the assistant whistled and then looked at her watch. "Okay, I'd better get going. You know my birthday's coming up soon, too. I wish my mom was so generous."

"I'll hold down the fort while you're gone," Maria promised, a slight grin on her face.

~ ~

Dusty heard the car pull in the driveway, just as Maria had predicted. He'd already toured the house once, just to make sure he hadn't left any tracks.

The closet was dark and small, but he didn't mind as he listened to the garage door open and then the sounds of someone making several trips to unload.

Again, he listened to the sound of the garage door going down this time, followed by footsteps in the house and finally the front door opening and closing. He exhaled as the car started, the engine fading into the distance. He gave Maria's assistant five more minutes, in case the woman discovered she'd forgotten something. After that margin of safety had passed, he carefully made his way to the garage to inspect the delivery.

Ten minutes later, he grunted with satisfaction, surveying the pile of boxes, bags, and packages lying on the garage floor. Maria had sourced every single item on his list and thrown in a few extras to boot.

Job one was to find the tool kit included on his list. After that, he'd have a full afternoon of assembly.

Day 13

The conference room table was filled with half-empty cups of coffee, a few bottles of water and two snack wrappers from the machine in the break room.

Special Agent in Charge Monroe looked up from the pile of status reports, his preference of receiving paper copies a widely known annoyance throughout the office. "I can't believe Weathers has simply disappeared from the surface of the earth," he began. "Yet, I know we're doing everything in our power to find him. Any additional suggestions?"

"The hit is going to come from a video camera in all likelihood," commented Shultz. "He doesn't have any credit cards and he's smart enough not to show his driver's license. He's going to look into a camera at some point in time, and then at least we'll know what part of town he's in."

Nodding his agreement, Monroe looked down the table at his head technician. "What's the turnaround time from the NSA at the moment?"

We have a quad-pipe of dedicated fiber optic running at full speed between our data center and Fort Mead. They're processing the facial recognition stream on about a two-hour average – give or take."

Shultz whistled, "Two hours? How many images are they receiving per second?"

The tech, clearly proud of the geeky capabilities, responded with a smile. "We have 1,800 traffic cameras, 10,000 police dash cams, and over 240,000 private security video feeds that we're processing. It is just over a terabyte per second."

"And they're back to us with potential hits in two hours? I remember when it used to take longer than that to get a match on a fingerprint."

Nodding, the computer guru continued. "They run an eight-point facial recognition algorithm on every face that shows on one of those cameras. That's after they clean up the grainy and out of focus pics."

"Amazing," was Shultz's only response. Monroe, however, wasn't impressed.

"One of my biggest fears is that all this technology is going to make everyone think they can sit around on their asses and wait on the computers to catch the bad guys. Good old-fashioned hard work is what puts more criminals behind bars, not computer chips and megabytes of whatever."

Before anyone could comment, the door burst open, and a woman's head appeared in the opening. Her voice was high pitched from excitement. "He's on line two."

Monroe, upset by the interruption, replied in a growl, "Who is on line two?"

"Durham Weathers, sir."

The head agent's initial reaction was as if he didn't understand what the female agent was saying. Frowning, he glanced at the cream-colored phone on the table top, his eyes seeming to focus on the blinking light labeled "Line 2."

Inhaling deeply, Monroe reached for the phone and punched the button. "Agent Monroe speaking."

"Agent Monroe, this is Dusty Weathers. I understand you're looking for me," answered a cheery voice with a strong, Texas accent.

Before responding, Monroe looked up at the tech and mouthed the words, "Is this being traced?"

"Automatically," came the whispered response.

"Mr. Weathers, you are correct. Several thousand of my colleagues and I would very much like to speak with you. Why don't you turn yourself in and get it over with?"

Laughing, Dusty replied, "I'm afraid I'm not going to make it that easy on you. As a matter of fact, if things don't change, I'm going to make it more difficult on you, sir."

"Are you threatening a Federal agent, Mr. Weathers?"

"I'm threatening *all* of them, Mr. Monroe. But this sounds so harsh, so antagonistic. The purpose of my call was actually to make you an offer that I feel is a fair compromise."

Monroe rubbed his chin, clearly wondering where the conversation was going. "I will inform you that the government of the United States does not negotiate with terrorists, Mr. Weathers. With that being said, I'll be happy to listen to your offer if it will make you feel better."

Again, a relaxed, genuine chuckle came from the other end of the call. "Very well, sir. Here's my offer, the president will grant a pardon for all of my friends and family associated with my invention. That includes Hank, Grace, Mitch and anyone else you might choose to arrest in order to piss me off. In exchange for this pardon, I will destroy the rail gun and end this entire thing."

It was Monroe's turn to laugh, somehow the agent's expression didn't seem so relaxed. "I'm not even going to bother, sir. We would have no way of knowing you actually destroyed the device, and besides, you've already committed acts of terrorism against your country. Acts for which you must pay with your freedom, perhaps your life."

Monroe's response shocked Shultz, the junior agent's face showing surprise at the harshness and inflexible position. Looking around, he saw several others agreed with his assessment.

The other end of the line was silent for some time. When Dusty did speak again, his tone was low and cold. "I predicted that would be your response, sir. I thought my guilt was a foregone conclusion. Are you near the east side of the building, Agent Monroe?"

"No, and what does my location have to do with your surrender?"

"I'll give you one minute to find a window with a view looking east. I think you'll want to see this," and the line went dead.

All the agents in the FBI conference room seemed to rise from their chairs at once. After a dirty look from Monroe, the meeting attendees filed out calmly, all of them crossing the hall and finding any empty space to peer outside.

Shultz maintained the wherewithal to turn on his smart phone's video camera while the technician was calling to his lab, trying desperately to get someone with a digital video unit pointed east. He was too late.

Dusty smiled when the green LED glowed bright. He turned on the aiming laser and then pushed in his earplug. The power setting was at 10%.

Bracing against the window frame, he peered through the scope and found the small red dot of his laser illuminating the fender of the closest black SUV. He was on the fourth floor of an under-construction office complex six blocks away from the target, the first shift of workers not scheduled to arrive for another half hour.

Mindful of his promise to wait one minute, he glanced at his watch and scanned the area around his target one last time, hoping to avoid collateral damage. The top floor of the 3-story garage next to the federal building filled the view of the powerful optic. Two rows of neatly parked, government-issue, black SUVs rounded out the image.

Why the vehicles were exposed on the roof of the structure was anybody's guess. Dusty assumed that the employees wanted to keep their personal cars in the shade provided by the lower floors – to hell with the taxpayer's money. Maybe he was being harsh – maybe they parked the law enforcement vehicles as high as possible for security.

Shrugging his shoulders to dismiss the question, Dusty again checked his watch – it was time.

He centered the glimmering red circle of the laser and pulled the trigger.

The ball bearing changed state before exiting the gun, the friction of the air causing the hardened steel to melt before clearing the last ring of magnets. Despite being a jet of molten metal, the magnetic properties of the missile didn't change, and the rivulet of liquid shot forth still suspended in the rail's magnetic field.

Four feet after leaving the gun, the molten stream began igniting the oxygen in the air, the net effect similar to an arch of plasma racing toward the target at over 20,000 feet per second.

Like the conversation piece often called "Newton's Cradle," the sub-atomic particles of the atmospheric gases began to slam into one another, just like the steel balls hanging from the desktop toy. The aiming laser had excited the air just enough for the exploding chain of protons to follow its path, accelerating with every collision and following the path of least resistance.

At this point of the discharge, known particle physics ceased to apply. Billions of protons began splitting, each release of energy adding to the freight train of energy following the red laser. The speed kept increasing until the universe had to defend itself from the ultimate catastrophe of infinite mass.

A door opened into another dimension, the gap in both time and space expanded at the speed of light. It wasn't a wide doorway, no larger than an inch in diameter, but the energy released was immense.

From the sixth floor of the federal building, it looked as if the roof of the parking garage below shuddered. Then complete bedlam broke loose. The black metal bodies looked as if they were being crushed by a giant, invisible hand, bending and mauling right before the on-looking FBI agents' eyes. And then the detonations began.

Scraps of flaming metal erupted skyward, closely pursued by rolling balls of black smoke. Blizzards of exploding shards of glass flew in all directions, the glint off the morning sun creating the impression of an early morning frost.

The blast wave hit next.

Like a gigantic clap of thunder, the rail's crack echoed through the glass and steel canyons of downtown Houston. For several blocks in every direction, windows were swept with a wave of air moving at over 700 miles per hour – almost ten times the speed of hurricane-force winds.

Dusty hadn't counted on the impact of the wave, a look of horror crossing his face as he watched spider webs of glass replace the shiny, clear windows in nearby buildings.

The fast moving wall of air raised dust and debris from rooftops and sidewalks, a few pedestrians knocked to the ground.

Dusty shook himself out of the hypnotic state, feeling like a motorist rubbernecking at a roadside accident. He forced his eyes away from the damage. He had to move, and move quickly.

Breaking down the weapon, he stuffed it into his pack and casually walked to the stairwell, listening for footsteps at each landing until he exited at street level. He then strolled with purpose through the construction site, squeezing through the chain-link gate and out onto the sidewalk.

The few people who were on the street didn't notice the man leaving the construction zone – their attention focused on the huge ball of smoke rising from the FBI's parking garage.

Two blocks later, Dusty entered a coffee shop and ordered a large cup of blonde roast – with room for crème.

Everyone instinctively flinched on the sixth floor of the federal building, the flash of the explosions below causing the witnesses to turn away. The windows rattling with the impact of the blast wave prompted several people to scurry back.

Monroe recovered first, the experienced man turned and then began shouting, "Where is he? Where is my trace?"

The tech, standing nearby, checked his smart phone and answered, "Got him! He's at 500 McKinney Street."

"That's only a few blocks away," someone added.

"Let's go! I want my team there now! Someone call Houston SWAT, and HPD – I want that area with a ring of steel around it in three minutes!"

The elevator car filled to capacity after opening, anxious agents crowding inside for a ride to street level. A minute later Monroe's team hustled through the lobby and onto the sidewalk, all of them running at full speed toward the nearby street where they hoped to find the man who had just attacked them.

Like a television drama's chase scene, the team raced through the streets, badges in the air and screaming for pedestrians to get out of the way. Dozens of sirens began wailing in the distance, all apparently heading in the same direction.

As Monroe rounded a corner one block away from the address, he paused for just a moment to look back at the now flame-engulfed roof of the garage. He realized that there wasn't a clear shot from this direction – no way could a weapon have been aimed from here. He began to get a sick feeling in the pit of his stomach.

As the agents converged, they realized the address where Dusty's call had originated was the Houston Public Library. The fact that a spacious public building was their destination slowed the team's pace – frustration filling their faces.

The first police cruisers began arriving at the same time. Monroe with his gold shield exposed, began shouting orders at the first officers on the scene. He wanted a perimeter surrounding the library, and he didn't want anyone exiting the building.

A police captain soon appeared, taking over for Monroe, the FBI man's plain clothes and shouted orders confusing to the first wave of cops. It wasn't five minutes before the first SWAT van screeched to a halt directly in front of the structure, the eight-member team flowing out the back in full combat regalia. That vehicle was soon joined by two of its siblings, rapidly discharging its cargo of specially trained officers.

After a significant number of uniformed lawmen had arrived, Monroe pulled his people back and let HPD do its job. With his team gathered on the front steps, he watched with anticipation, hoping to see Durham Weathers led from the building in handcuffs.

Dusty stood with all of the other coffee shop patrons, staring out the window at the spectacle of excitement. Like everyone else, he pointed, oohed and awed, commenting on the seemingly endless waves of flashing lights and sirens converging on the area.

Waiting for what seemed like an eternity, he finally decided enough time had passed, calmly reaching down for his pack and exiting the shop.

The sidewalk was ringed with businessmen, shoppers, and office workers who stood gawking, their attention focused on the library. Gently probing his way through the thick crowd, he entered an older office building and climbed the mosaic-patterned marble stairs to the men's room directly off the second floor landing.

He pushed open the ancient maple door and searched the interior, relieved to find the three stalls and urinals all unoccupied. He pulled a cardboard sign from his pack, the bold letters declaring the facility "Out of Order – Overflowing," and hung it on the door. He threw the lock, just to be sure.

A small, high window adorned the outer wall of the room, the natural sunlight passing through the smoked glass that was a clear indicator of the building's age. Dusty slowly cranked the glass open, the effort exposing a view of the street below, leading to the library four short blocks away.

He assembled the rail gun, quickly snapping the stock to the primary body of the weapon. Again, the green LED glowed bright and steady. The ball bearing filled the chamber, soon followed by foam plugs filling his ears.

He turned down the power, still shaken by visions of imploding windows – the glass possibly blinding innocent office workers who happened to be in the wrong place. His anger was at the government, his desire to issue punishment limited strictly to that entity... that symbol of authority that had taken away his friend's freedom. The small red letters read 5%.

Keeping the muzzle end well back from the edge, he began to scout the scene below, considering a suitable target. The SWAT vans, all lined up at the curb in front of the library, caught his attention. He couldn't detect anyone nearby, the closest policeman across the street, trying to keep the crowd at a safe distance.

He switched on the laser, aimed the dot at the back of the nearest van, and pulled the trigger.

Even at the reduced power, thunder rolled through the crowded streets. The nearest van shook for a microsecond, the steel of its frame expanding and then contracting. Like dominos falling down a line, the next three vehicles performed the same dance – and then all four exploded with tremendous force. The rear van was launched into the air, flipping end over end and landing on one of its twins. Tires, glass and sheet metal rose into the air while boiling yellow flames of ignited gasoline spread from the destruction.

Police officers up and down the line ducked for cover, many of them taking a few seconds to realize they were under attack. Some stood stunned, momentarily mesmerized by the burning mass on the street – the concept that anyone would attack them while they were deployed in such force completely foreign to their reasoning.

The roaring discharge echoed through the streets, hurting Dusty's ears despite the protection of the plugs. The carnage of screaming, tortured metal was soon replaced by the shouts and despair of terrified humans as the mass surrounding the library scattered in panic.

All of it was lost on Dusty. He had ducked immediately after the shot, rapidly breaking down the rail gun and stuffing it in his pack. He moved with purpose toward the door, plucking the sign from the exterior and walking briskly to the rear exit of the complex.

Less than a minute after his second shot of the day, Dusty was stepping through a back alley, quickly putting distance between himself and the bedlam he'd left behind.

~ ~

Monroe's team was less than 100 yards away from the impact point of Dusty's shot. A few of the FBI agents were knocked to the ground, the others going prone as a reaction. It was actually several minutes before everyone began to accept that the attack was over. Slowly, cautiously, heads began to appear around cover – tentatively exposing themselves as if expecting another shot. Many officers had their weapons drawn, scanning the surrounding facades for any sign of the shooter.

As the agents recovered their wits, Monroe surveyed his team, checking on his people. After verifying everyone was unhurt, he immediately went to help the police officers who had been bowled over by the shockwave. It was a miracle that only a few broken bones and burst eardrums appeared to have been inflicted by the brutal ambush.

Monroe wanted revenge, but soon realized there wasn't anyone or anything to receive his rage. Scanning the wreckage of police vans, he couldn't even discern the direction of the shot, let alone give chase to a suspect.

Ambulances, fire trucks, and additional officers soon began to arrive, some of the drivers hesitant to enter what appeared to be a combat zone. The more time that passed the more everyone began to accept that the fight was over. No one had any doubts over who had won.

It was also obvious that the suspect was no longer in the library. Monroe observed his team standing around, helpless to do anything but watch the beehive of activity. He began shepherding his people back to their home building. It wasn't good for morale to watch the wounded being evacuated from the battlefield.

Trekking back to their headquarters, the FBI team was sullen and quiet. The police had cordoned off the area, the normally bustling street quiet with an eerie sense of abandonment. The silence was broken by the jingle of Agent Monroe's cell phone.

Looking at the device as if he expected the devil himself to jump out, Monroe almost didn't answer. He was expecting harsh words from Washington as soon as word of the fiasco reached the nation's capital. His sense of duty forced him to answer.

"Monroe."

"Agent Monroe, Dusty Weathers here. I'm feeling optimistic, hopeful that you are in a better frame of mind to discuss my terms."

"You son of a bitch!" Monroe yelled at the phone. Catching himself, regrouping quickly, the lead FBI man glared at one of his team, mouthing the words, "Trace this call."

"Now, now, sir. Calling a man names isn't wise, especially when he just issued your sorry ass one class-A butt whooping. Now be a good sport and reconsider my previous offer – before I get really pissed."

Monroe's face knotted into a scowl, his imagination conjuring up images of Weathers in his gun sights, hot slugs of lead piercing his body. "I'm not reconsidering anything, you scum. You are a terrorist and a traitor. We're going to hunt you down and kill you – of that you can be sure."

"So I was correct, rule of law in our great country no longer exists. The government executes citizens at will without benefit of juries of their peers. You're convincing me I'm on the right track. Perhaps I should take even stronger action."

The federal agent reached to disconnect the call, but some fiber of his soul was touched by Dusty's words. A quick look ahead at the fire trucks arching streams of water onto the still burning federal garage terminated his hotheaded, vigilante attitude.

"Okay, Weathers. I'll give you my word; we won't shoot you where you stand. I'll wait and watch them stick a needle in your arm after the trial is over."

Again, the man on the other end laughed. "Bump my offer up the ladder, Agent Monroe. Do so quickly. I'm detecting an attitude from you, an official representative of the US government, and it sounds like you're declaring war. If you want war, Mr. Ambassador, I'll give it to you. I might decide to use my little invention on the San Andres fault and accelerate the inevitable slide of California into the sea. How about I take aim at the Indian Point nuclear power plant just 38 miles north of New York City? I could stand in the center of the Washington Mall and fire one shot in both directions. Reconsider, sir. Let's end this before someone gets killed, or I change my mind and decide I want to run the country. I'll be in touch."

Dusty tapped the disconnect button, pulled the battery from the case and crushed the phone under his boot. The now-scrap electronic components were tossed into the back of the trash hauler parked nearby. He strode briskly around the corner and entered the lobby of a bank building, proceeding directly down an escalator into the Houston Tunnel System.

The nation's fourth largest city sat upon an extensive network of pedestrian tunnels, the massive complex stretching throughout most of the downtown area.

Air-conditioned, wide walkways, many over 30 feet wide, connected most of the area's larger skyscrapers. Shops, restaurants, newsstands and even clothing stores lined many of the subterranean passages. The system was popular, workers flowing down from the high-rise offices and cubicles en mass, using the cool venue to avoid walking the hot summer streets or the occasional downpour of rain.

Dusty didn't take the time to browse the stores, nor did he intend to grab a bite. What he did want was distance, and the lack of traffic lights and intersection walk signals made the tunnels the fastest route.

He covered four blocks in little time, riding up an escalator to the marble floor of an oil company headquarters, out through the revolving glass doors and into the street. He jaywalked after noting no law enforcement in the area and entered a parking garage.

In a dark, back corner, he located the equipment stored a few hours earlier and began to change his shirt and shoes.

Five minutes later, a bicycle messenger zoomed out of the facility, his helmet, sunglasses and backpack appearing like any one of the dozens of other such delivery riders prowling the streets. The disguise was rounded out with a slightly soiled white tee shirt, the logo clearly indicating the rider was an employee of the *Monroe Delivery Services*. He had laughed with glee two nights ago when the idea had popped into his mind.

Dusty hadn't ridden in some years; his only practice was zipplng around his hideout's neighborhood. True to the old saying, he hadn't forgotten how to ride a bike.

He headed south, staying in residential neighborhoods and carefully crossing busy intersections. His destination was the Medical Center, a city within the city of Houston, a little over a mile from the site of his attack.

A collection of over 30 hospitals, teaching facilities, labs and research centers, the Medical Center could have been a major metropolitan area all its own. With an impressive prospect of high-rise buildings adding a second skyline to the horizon, the area was densely populated and quite upscale.

It took Dusty only 20 minutes to cover the distance. He had memorized a map of the area, realizing a real messenger wouldn't stop and pull out a street guide. Without delay, he found his destination. Steering the bike into a small adjoining garage, he lowered the kickstand, locked the bike, and then hurried to the front entrance of the Midtown Lofts.

A client of Maria's had a listing in the building, a one-bedroom condo on the third floor. According to his ex, the doctor who owned the unit had "completely priced it out of the market." She assured Dusty that no one would be coming to see the property until she convinced the seller to lower his asking price.

Dusty rode the elevator to the third floor, his backpack riding easily on his hip. He found "312" on the door, and sure enough, a realtor's key-box hung from the knob. He punched in Maria's code, and the little container opened with a clang. The condo's door key was nestled inside.

The place smelled of stale air and inactivity. He opened the balcony's sliding glass door and the bedroom's windows to circulate a breeze. The water worked, as did the air conditioner. It was exactly what he had expected from a dwelling that had been abandoned for almost a year, and he was content with the space.

After overcoming the restlessness of new surroundings, Dusty eventually settled on the couch. His curiosity peaked as he stared at the blank television, his mind speculating what the newscasters were reporting about the attack. On one side, he was worried that he'd taken a human life, the unexpected effect of the shock waves fueling those concerns.

On the other side, he wanted to see if his message had been delivered. His purpose had been to raise awareness and cause people to ask why. Why had this madman attacked Houston? Why had this idiot disrupted everything from my lunch break to my commute home?

The batteries in the remote control were dead, prompting him to operate the television the old-fashioned way. Kneeling in front of the boob tube, he found the power button and was immediately disappointed to see that the cable had been turned off, no doubt an effort by the owner to save money.

It took 15 minutes of fiddling to figure out how to source the TV from the inactive cable connection to the somewhat-workable rabbit ears. He sat back on the floor and sighed, three local channels broadcasting strong enough signals to maintain a clear picture, one of those a Spanish language station.

Still, the local newscasts were all over the story. He was glued to the screen as helicopters provided aerial coverage of the "destruction," while on-street reporters interviewed "survivors."

It was at least 15 minutes before he heard the magic words, "So far, Bruce, local hospitals are reporting 26 people injured, but luckily, no causalities at this time." Dusty grunted, disgusted that the reporter sounded disappointed in the lack of dead bodies.

Next began a parade the law enforcement officers, all of whom offered no comment regarding what had happened or who, if anybody, was responsible. The journalists did their best to draw out the cops, but they wouldn't budge. The lack of official explanations didn't hamper the reporters' speculations, however. Varied opinions were offered that ranged from terrorist bombs to gas main explosions. One fellow even commented that the scene in front of the library looked like the site of a meteor strike.

Finally, a cycle of eyewitness accounts and interviews filled the airwaves. Dusty, having been there, was amazed at the discrepancies vocalized to the on-scene reporters. One woman claimed to have seen several masked gunmen carrying assault rifles, while another recalled seeing utility trucks in the area. One guy was sure it was a dual bombing, much like the Boston Marathon incident some time ago. On and on it went, the faces of ordinary citizens spouting a wide range of fiction and conjecture.

Dusty muted the coverage, leaving the images flashing silently on the screen. Sitting back and exhaling, he wondered how long it would be before there was official word that today's events were indeed an attack.

How long before his image was displayed on every news broadcast in the country? He actually wanted the coverage – the attention. It was critical to his plan.

Dusty hoped his message would resonate with the American public. He wanted people to seek an understanding of his actions to question his motive. Once they did, he'd be happy to answer, and hopefully, Hank and Grace would go free. Even more importantly, he prayed his government would reform – returning to the principles that had made the nation so great.

"You pissed him off, boss. You did it on purpose, and I think we've all learned something from the experience," Shultz blurted out, no longer able to contain his opinion.

The junior agent's timing wasn't impeccable by any sense. Since the attacks four hours ago, Monroe's phone had rung constantly, the callers including the director, both Texas senators, and a host of representatives. The governor and mayor had added their voices as well.

The head of the Houston office didn't have the energy to explode at his subordinate. While most of his conversations had been positive, there had been a few heated words. Many of the elected officials seemed genuinely concerned, asking if he had enough resources at his disposal, what kind of assistance he and the Houston office might need. On the surface, it all seemed so positive – supportive.

Monroe knew better. The politicians were already calling news conferences, boasting of their involvement, bragging of their support and concerns for the people of Houston, vowing to get to the bottom of whatever had happened. *How illogical*, concluded Monroe. *How can you promise to fix something when you don't know what occurred in the first place?*

"And what would you have me do, Tommy? Negotiate with a terrorist? Violate 30 years of bureau policy? Release prisoners just because some guy called and threatened us?"

Shaking his head, Shultz calmly replied, "No, sir, that's not my point. I would suggest we bring in the bureau's hostage negotiators – trained psychologists and other experts to handle Mr. Weathers the next time we have contact with him. You tried brute force, and he responded in kind. It's clear that method isn't going to work; the man won't be intimidated."

Monroe seemed to consider the younger man's advice. "Why should we treat this man any differently than a bomber? If we had a guy running around planting C4, he could do the same damage. Would you be recommending that we negotiate with such a person?"

"What about the airplanes, boss?"

"The final report isn't in from the NTSB. We don't know if those jets bumped each other, if there was mechanical error, or if the pilots just freaked out as a side effect of Weathers shooting at them. I do not doubt that the guy has a powerful weapon, I'm just saying it's *not* God's gun."

Shultz didn't hesitate, "I've read the interrogation transcripts and all of the interviews. I think Weathers is a West Texas gunsmith who stumbled onto something by accident. He did what any of us would do. He sought the expertise of a family member or trusted friend. I've not seen one iota of evidence to support the bureau's official position that the guy is a terrorist, or that he is under the influence of foreign powers."

"I must disagree, Tom. The average US citizen doesn't shoot at warplanes. We know he did because the satellites picked up the pulse. The average West Texas cowboy doesn't knock down high-voltage towers or run from police. For sure, our fellow Americans don't make a habit of launching an attack against a federal facility followed by a premeditated attack against law enforcement."

Shultz sighed, appearing to hesitate over his response. Finally, he announced, "I think we're going to see a lot more of this type of pushback. The Patriot Act, NSA scandals, public disclosure of our monitoring techniques and that mess at the IRS are all contributing to a growing distrust of our government... us. If I put myself into Weather's head, and I had such a device as his brother claims, I would think twice about turning it over to our government."

Monroe rolled his eyes. "I've heard this abuse of power argument over and over again. We don't set the rules, Tom; the lawmakers do. I'm given a set of tools to use, and I implement them to the best of my ability. I, for one, am glad we are given these liberties. I'm fighting drug cartels that have a larger budget than most countries. They use sophisticated technology, advanced banking and accounting methods and play the corporate game better than most of the Fortune 500. We are fighting terrorist cells and jihadist movements that are as motivated as any Special Forces military unit, and almost as deadly. I've got organized crime syndicates from the Far East that make the Italians look like Boy Scouts. I've not even mentioned foreign intelligence services spying on our manufacturing, a spike in cybercrime that is more than concerning. I could go on and on, and you know it. I need every tool I can get – and then some."

"I agree with that sentiment, sir. I'm just pointing out that many of our fellow citizens think we're infringing on their rights."

Nodding, Monroe replied, "On Monday they run around screaming, 'Protect us from terrorists and thugs,' then on Tuesday the marchers in the streets are calling us Nazis. The public is manipulated and fickle, Tom. If they don't like how we are doing things, then they need to take the legal actions granted to every citizen. Vote, pressure representatives, and become involved in the process, not shoot super weapons at government aircraft and vehicles."

"Aren't we citizens too, sir? Don't we hold some responsibility in defining what's right and wrong?"

Shultz's point entered territory that his boss wasn't willing to navigate, the entire discussion leading towards the slippery slope of "Just doing my job," and "I was only following orders." Both men knew it, but the senior agent wasn't in the mood to deliberate the underlying, ethical quandaries that had evolved in law enforcement. Monroe rubbed his temples with both hands. "Do I need to reassign you, Tom? It's sounding like your heart isn't in this one anymore."

"That's up to you, sir. It's my job as your second to propose alternative theories and play devil's advocate. If you don't feel like I'm meeting my obligations, then you should reassign me."

Shaking his head, the Agent in Charge grinned. "No, I don't see the need - yet. Forgive me, but right now I'm exhausted and frustrated."

Shultz's reply was interrupted by Monroe's desk phone ringing. Glancing at the caller ID, he answered the call with a gruffer than normal "Monroe."

Shultz sat listening to a series of "Uh huhs," "I sees," the short responses accented with the occasional Okay." The call ended quickly.

Peering across the desk, the senior agent announced, "They've finally figured out how he placed the call without being in the library at the time. The tech is on the way up."

A few minutes later, a soft rap sounded on the office door, immediately answered with a, "Come in." The two agents were fascinated as the FBI technician carried in a tower computer, complete with a cell phone duck taped to the back of the cabinet.

"He must have set this up ahead of time. The computer was logged into an internet-based voice system, commonly used to make free phone calls to others over the web. The cell phone was attached to the computer's modem, configured to automatically answer when the cell rang. I was quite surprised to find they still made computers with dial-up modems, but then I learned that the models in the library are a few years old. Most people don't even know how a modem works, let alone how to configure it."

Shultz scratched his head, "So Weathers went into the library and set this up, and then left?"

"Yes. He knew the cell number of the unit attached to the computer and could dial it from anywhere. A simple DOS script was then used to have the computer's modem call this office. Simple, easy, and very clever. It is also incredibly old school. Most hackers today don't even know DOS script exists – 1990s technology."

"So can we trace what cell number dialed the one in the library?" asked Monroe.

"Already done," replied the tech. "From the triangulation of the cell towers, we have a generalized local about 6 blocks away from the garage. That number then made a second call to your cell, Agent Monroe. The suspect had moved closer to the vicinity of the second attack. The signal ended four seconds after he ended the second call with you."

"I'll bet my next pay check that second phone ended up down the sewer or in a dumpster somewhere," commented Shultz.

"There is a bit of good news. We have a new picture of the suspect. My lab guys cleaned it up," added the tech as he held up an 8x10 image of a man sporting a thin beard. Both Monroe and Shultz recognized it as Durham Weathers immediately.

After thanking the technician for his report, Monroe closed the door behind the man. Turning back to Shultz, he said, "Weren't you just commenting that you didn't think a simple-minded West Texas gunsmith could be a criminal mastermind? Didn't I just hear you spouting off about how our high-tech devices were intruding on American civil liberties? Ironic, isn't it? We use technology; the bad guys use technology. It's like an arms race between us and the criminals."

Dusty checked the local news after a hot shower had relaxed him enough to nap for a few minutes. The authorities still hadn't released his name or tied the events downtown to any sort of human cause.

He needed supplies, clothing and most important of all — coffee. Even the shower had made his lack of necessities obvious — no towels, soap, or shampoo. Toothpaste was out of the question, the toilet paper roll, fortunately, was still operable.

The messenger carrier Maria had secured for him wasn't big enough to pack everything he needed. A bag of jerky, bottle of water, two no-contract cell phones, his hat, and the rail gun had filled the small satchel.

His cash situation was pretty good. He had left Fort Davis with about $4,000 and spent half of that his first day on the run. Maria had managed to refurbish his kitty, emptying her petty cash drawer at the office and withdrawing a few extra dollars on each trip to the ATM. He was sitting with close to 5K of greenbacks.

Given the cops weren't splashing his face all over the local media, he decided now was as good a time as any to go shopping. One of his biggest concerns with this morning's movements all over downtown Houston was that a camera would catch a clear picture of his new look. With less than two weeks of growth, his beard was by no means full, but thick enough to break up the outline of his face.

The sun was fading in the west, and the lack of natural light would provide a tiny bit of cover. It was time to go.

Loading his meager supplies into the messenger bag, he exited the condo as quietly as possible – just in case nosey neighbors could hear his activity in their own units. He decided to descend the stairs, despite his legs being a little sore from the bike ride. *I would have stepped up my work out if I had seen this coming,* he thought. *I hope I don't have to run anywhere.*

Exiting the building, Dusty remembered seeing a corner convenience store on his ride into the area. With the small shop as his target, he began walking away from his newest hideout, eyes scanning for approaching police cars or anyone paying him too much attention.

Unnoticed on the trip in, a large, "one-stop shop" pharmacy was right across the street from his original target. He decided the national chain outlet might satisfy more of his list, so he entered the store.

Dusty was amazed at the variety in the place. Not only was it a drugstore, it carried almost as many groceries as the IGA back in Fort Davis. Walking through the almost deserted establishment, he found aisles of toys, some clothing, and even full sections of beauty products.

Never one to spend a lot of time shopping, he had made a list of essential items which took several orbits to procure. While he was browsing the shampoo section, an end-cap advertisement caught his attention. The advertisement displayed pictures of a man with gray hair before, and dark, wavy locks after use of the indicated product. Of course, the beautiful model was hanging on the gent's arm after his hair was darker. *I wonder if he won the lottery in between*, Dusty mused. Still, the poster gave him an idea, and a bottle of the comb-through hair coloring landed in his basket.

Plastic spoons and forks, paper plates, garbage bags, and seemingly everything else required by a human being on the lam flew into the basket. It became so full; he ended up exchanging it for a four-wheel buggy at the front of the store.

As he began to wheel away the larger cart, he glanced out the front doors and saw a police cruiser turning into the parking lot.

There was no way Dusty could make the exit without drawing suspicion. His initial thought was that the bored looking cashier had called him in, but the uninterested woman was restocking the film behind the counter, completely oblivious to his presence.

Maybe they sell doughnuts here, he thought, quickly heading for the back of the store. He searched for a rear exit as he retreated, finally spotting the sign in a far corner.

Positing himself along the fingernail polish aisle, Dusty felt semi-hidden but still maintained a clear view of the front door. He was less than 20 feet from the exit – if it came to that.

The automatic front door opened, admitting a middle-aged uniformed HPD officer who was more than a little overweight. Casually smiling, he made for the cashier without even glancing back into the retail section of the store. "Hi ya Brenda, how's things?"

"Good, good. How are you doing, Mike?"

"Slow night. All the excitement is downtown. Seems like everyone around here is staying at home and watching the news."

"Kinda slow in here tonight, too. One pack of Winston's or two?"

"Just one – I'm trying to cut back gradually."

Dusty watched, relieved as the cashier turned to the rows of multi-colored cigarette packs behind the register. Picking the cop's brand, she spun and began ringing up his purchase. A minute later, the officer left, packing the tobacco against his palm as he exited the building.

Exhaling, Dusty decided he'd bide his time for a while before finishing his checkout, the incident flushing his system with nervous energy. He had also learned a few things from the overheard conversation. First of all, the police had no hint that he'd managed to get out of downtown. That was good. Secondly, and not so great, was the fact that many of the Bayou City's residents were staying off the streets.

On his way to pay for his selections, Dusty passed a small travel section and noticed the bottom shelf held a few different types of packs and duffle bags. He decided on a model just long enough for the rail gun, yet large enough that if he did have to bug out again, he wouldn't have to re-purchase every little thing.

"Looks like you're going camping," commented Brenda as she began emptying his cart.

"My sister is having surgery over at the hospital, and I didn't have time to pack everything before rushing over," he lied.

The woman behind the register seemed okay with his story, never missing a beat.

Dusty was surprised by the three oversized grocery sacks filled by his purchases. Taking one in each arm and squeezing the third in the middle, he realized it wasn't a bad disguise for the walk home, the bags blocking the clear view of his face.

By the time he arrived back at the condo, his arms were burning tired, so taking the elevator was an easy call. He didn't see another soul, only the muffled sound of a television as he walked down the hall toward his unit's door.

Closing the door behind him, the relief surging through his system was two-fold. Dropping the heavy bags on the counter helped his arms and shoulders, the safety of the surrounding walls renewing his confidence.

Putting away his purchases ate more time off the clock, and he was beginning to yawn by the time he'd finished the chore. Heating a Styrofoam cup of water in the microwave for coffee, he turned on the television to check the news.

His timing was spot on, the screen showing an image of a woman behind a podium with several men standing behind her. The caption at the bottom of the image declared the woman to be Houston's mayor. He turned up the sound.

"I want to reassure the citizens of our great city that every effort is being made to bring those responsible for today's attacks to justice. I'll turn the mic over to Chief Maxwell."

And with that, the woman stepped aside, replaced center-stage by an older man in a very elaborate police uniform.

"Thank you, Mayor. This afternoon an unknown number of suspects is believed to have planted several explosive devices at two locations in our city. We are looking for this man, as a person of interest. We believe he was directly associated with the crimes committed today."

The screen flashed to an image of Dusty, a new picture he'd never seen before. It took him a moment, but he eventually figured out it had been taken inside the library. It was a reasonably clear photograph and showed his facial growth quite well.

"Anyone with information concerning the whereabouts of this person should call 911 immediately. Do not approach this man, as he is considered armed and dangerous."

So his worst concerns were realized. They now had a picture of him with the partial beard. *No worries*, he resolved. *I don't like the scratchy thing anyway.*

Seeing the latest image of himself caused a wave of emotion to well up inside. He worried that the cashier at the drugstore would remember him, giving the police a much smaller area to concentrate their search.

Remembering the hair-coloring product, he decided to change his natural toe-headed mop to a darker tone. He'd cut it close, like a military style buzz and of course, shave the beard. It wasn't much, but it was the best he could do at the moment.

Day 15

Dusty woke up to pouring rain outside and a growing sense of cabin fever inside. He'd been holed up in the small condo for two days, the urge to step further than the balcony overridden by the fear of being recognized.

Lying in bed, he felt a pang of discomfort in his core, a hollowness he hadn't felt in years. He was homesick. Feeding on memories of his ranch, the Davis Mountains, and the freedom provided by the Thrush, anger quickly began to override all other emotion. He hadn't done anything wrong; why was he being punished? Was it bad luck? Had he made a mistake somewhere along the line?

His passion began to overwhelm his common sense. Fantasies of revenge filled his mind – daydreams of conquest born of the injustice he was suffering. He would take the rail gun and destroy all of the FBI and anyone else who came up against him. He'd vaporize them all until they realized it was their fault... *their* missteps leading to *their* own demise. He would return freewill to the United States of America.

Where had the trust gone? The question stopped his tirade cold. He initiated an inventory of American presidents, voting thumbs up or down on their worthiness of trust. Lincoln? Of course. FDR? Yes. Kennedy? Maybe. But all of those men were dead before he was born, his only source of confidence being history books and documentaries. When it came to modern day leaders, he found himself giving each and every man a robust thumbs down. There were some great men who had achieved the oval office in his time, but none of them would he trust with the rail gun and its potential to corrupt.

Did he trust himself? Surely he was no stronger morally, possessed no magical immunity to the draw of ultimate power. So why did he feel the world's most potent power source was safer in his hands than in the hands of the leader of the free world? Why did he proceed under the guise that he should be the guardian of such a corrosive thing?

Where had the trust gone? Why wasn't he like the scientists who proudly passed along any knowledge to their government during WWII? He recalled the stories of brilliant men who worked tirelessly with no thoughts of any reward other than victory for their country, names like Oppenheimer and Fermi surfacing though his fog of internal reflections. Those men trusted their leaders. *Why couldn't he?*

Maybe it was time for a common, simple man to take control. Perhaps that is why the good Lord had seen fit to bless him with such power. Perhaps his purpose on earth was only now being revealed. Was his role to begin the revolution? Was his lot in life to take control away from the corrupt and return it to the people? He could rule the US with the rail gun. He could rule the world. He could fix it all.

Dusty sat up on the edge of the bed, checking out the narrow confines of the condo's diminutive space. It sure doesn't look like the emperor's palace to me, he thought. More like a jail cell. He realized it was his confinement that was driving the grandiose thoughts of conquest. *Hank was right. I gotta get out more,* Dusty lightheartedly ruminated. Despite the humorous thought breaking the mega-maniac spell, his mind couldn't shake the fact that he was essentially a prisoner.

Shaking off a growing urge to lash out and strike at what were effectively his captors, he rose for the day and began repeating the same routine.

The first step was to check the street below. Peeking through a narrow slit in the curtains, he looked for anything unusual. He noted a normal amount of automobile traffic and a fair number of umbrellas bobbing along the sidewalks.

That's it! He realized. The bumbershoots provide excellent cover. Maria used the same disguise to come visit me. I can get out of here and at least go for a walk without taking a huge risk.

He finished breakfast and his morning tasks of hygiene, as anxious as a kid on Christmas morning. There was only one issue; he didn't have an umbrella. Returning to the curtain, he decided a newspaper would do the trick until he could find a shop that sold the rainwear. He didn't have a jacket or raincoat, and only one change of clothes, but he didn't care. To breathe air that wasn't contaminated by the four walls of this residence was all he cared about.

Lopping down the stairs two at a time, he stopped in the lobby where he'd seen a pile of plastic-wrapped newspapers delivered for subscribing residents on a daily basis. Stealing one of the bundles, he fashioned a parasol utilizing a combination of plastic and a partially unfolded paper, and then stepped out into the rain.

It wasn't coming down hard, more of a steady drizzle, but Dusty didn't care. He inhaled deeply and began walking, the newspaper held at an angle to hide his face from the street. For a few moments, he worried that moisture might harm the rail gun he'd brought along for his walk. Stopping under the next overhang to check, he found the messenger bag Maria had purchased for him was waterproof – the weapon nice and cozy dry.

Continuing along, he came into an area of small shops and restaurants, the smell of bacon and eggs waffling down the sidewalk. His stomach reminded him that he hadn't enjoyed anyone else's cooking in days, so he changed direction and made for the small greasy spoon, the neon sign out front declaring its name was "The Nook."

Pushing open the door, he stomped the water off his boots on the mat inside and then looked up to the greeting of a gracious, middle-aged woman holding a stack of menus. "Booth, table or at the bar, hun?"

Dusty saw a television above the counter, the local weatherman pointing to a map full of symbols and curvy lines. Despite the change in his hair color and removal of facial hair, he didn't want to be in proximity to the TV if it flashed his picture.

Nodding toward a booth, he followed the greeter and took a seat facing the door. Holding the plastic-fold menu up in front of his face, he ordered and then pretended interest in the eatery's other selections, all the while scanning the other patrons to see if he had been noticed.

He felt like a private eye from some B-grade movie, pretending to read a newspaper while covertly keeping watch on a suspect. Just ignore me... nothing special here... just a guy reading the menu... no need for you to see my face.

Both the breakfast and the coffee were excellent, his meal enjoyed without any pesky interruptions by the police or observant citizens. He paid cash, left a nice tip, and nodded shyly at his waitress on the way outside. The drizzle was still falling, and according to both the meteorologist, and the young lady who waited on him, it was to continue all day.

He walked a short distance further when he spied a secondhand Goodwill store. He was familiar with the charity-based operation from when he and Maria had first married. Back in those financially strapped days, a drive to the Goodwill store in El Paso was the only way they were able to purchase clothing for both of them as well as Mitch. Even then, they had to manage their funds carefully.

Remembering simpler times, Dusty crossed the street and entered the large outlet. This particular store smelled exactly the same as the one in El Paso.

Originally wanting only an umbrella, Dusty decided he was in no hurry and walked the aisles, reminiscing about his early days of marriage. The one woman working at the counter paid no attention to him, her upset voice carrying through the store as she argued with her boyfriend on her cell phone.

He found an overcoat that would fit his shoulders and was the proper length, the unit marked for pennies on the dollar what it would cost new in a men's store. The wide collar could be turned up, adding another layer to his disguise.

He was on his way to the front, bumbershoot and overcoat in hand, when something caught his eye on the toy aisle. Doing a double take, he saw a child's play rifle lying on a shelf. It looked very similar to his rail gun.

Reaching for the pretend firearm, he was amazed at how close the replica was. With a little different paint, a few electrical coils and a spare battery, he'd have trouble telling the difference. Not sure why, he decided to purchase the fake.

He didn't think the woman at the counter even looked at him. Something had gone wrong last night at dinner, and her boyfriend, Nate, was hearing all about it. So was everyone else who entered the shop. *And I thought I was in hot water*, mused Dusty. *I'd hate to be in poor Nate's shoes*.

Taking his purchases around the corner, Dusty ducked into a narrow alley, quickly donned the overcoat, opened the umbrella and slung the sack over his shoulder with the satchel. Delighted with his day so far, he decided to continue his stroll, regardless of the increasing precipitation.

He had progressed two blocks when he caught sight of a familiar logo, the shield and letters spelling out Houston Police, on the door of a passing car. Forcing himself to keep the cruiser in his peripheral vision and avoid looking directly at the cop required all of his discipline. Even more self-control was required when shortly after passing him, the officer signaled he was turning.

Is he circling around for another look? Dusty questioned.

Detouring at a right angle away from the policemen led to a slightly less affluent area, but he was the only person on the sidewalk, the heavy precipitation obviously keeping other pedestrians inside. Almost at the end of the block, Dusty paused, his attention focused on the lot of a small, private, used car dealership. There, parked on the front row, was a 1966 Chevy half-ton pickup – the exact model his father had driven for years.

A quick check of the traffic showed no sign of the patrol car, so he decided to walk onto the lot and have a peek at the old girl. If nothing else, getting off the street would help him relax.

Someone had invested a serious number of hours into restoring the old truck. Wiping the rain from the driver's window, Dusty could see the vinyl upholstery looked new, as did the floorboards and parts of the dash.

The interior reminded him of his childhood, so many hours spent with his dad riding in just such a vehicle.

Walking around and inspecting the body, Dusty could see a few patches here and there – body putty used to fill in areas of rust or damage. The paint job wasn't worthy of a high dollar restoration, but it wasn't terrible either.

"She runs as good as she looks, señor," announced an older Latino man. "My son did the restoration after we picked it up from an auction."

Dusty glanced up at the salesman, the fellow toting a huge umbrella advertising a popular Mexican beer. As he approached, he stuck out his hand and said, "Juan."

"Max," replied Dusty, deciding to use his father's name in honor of the old Chevy.

Juan inserted a key into the driver's side lock and then moved to the front and opened the hood. Dusty met him there where the two men stared down at a clean, plain looking engine. "From a simpler time," noted Dusty.

"Not a computer chip or circuit board in there," replied the salesman. "Simple, rugged and dependable."

Dusty moved to sit behind the wheel, the maneuver requiring the closure of his umbrella. Juan didn't seem to notice the quick glance his customer cast up and down the street before entering the cab. The coast was still clear.

While the outside of the old hauler sparked memories, the interior submerged Dusty into the past. The "three on the tree" shifter, the tarpaper like floor covering, bench seat, and primitive AM radio pulled him back to a simpler, happier time.

Reaching up to touch the shifter on the steering column, he recalled his father's muscular arm working the gears in smooth motions, the manual effort seemingly second nature. The steering wheel was huge compared to modern vehicles, the diameter required due to the lack of power steering. Controlling a truck from this period required both upper body strength and coordination.

The dash was ridiculously simple. A well-worn, chrome slide controlled three environmental settings; vent, heat and defrost. There were no air conditioning, recirculation, or temperature controls. The radio was equipped with only two knobs bookending a row of green digits that indicated frequency. A thin, red post moved right and left to indicate where the unit was tuned. The small window of numbers would fill the cabin with a warm glow of light during nighttime driving.

Citizens of Fort Davis in the early 1970s received only one radio station, and that was often filled with bursts of static. Dusty remembered his father's rapt attention as he listened to announcers rambling on about the price of corn per bushel, pork bellies, and bean futures. The market reports were typically followed by simple country and western music, the serenades often portraying the broken heart of a cowboy recently abandoned by the love of his life.

There weren't any seatbelts, the safety feature not included or required for several years after this model year. The windows were raised and lowered via a manually cranked knob, the main panes of door-glass assisted by smaller vents at the front that were pushed out and whistled if the speed exceeded 30 mph.

Dusty reached up and pulled down the visor, half expecting a foil of chewing tobacco or pack of Marlboro to fall into his lap.

"Start her up," suggested Juan, handing over the keys.

And he did just that.

The engine caught on the first cycle, no blue smoke visible out the single exhaust. Dusty paid attention to the vibrations in the floorboard more than anything else. He thought the engine was in remarkably good shape considering the many miles the vehicle must have travelled.

"Do you want to take her for a spin?" Juan asked, clearly hoping he was wrong about the rain keeping all the customers away.

"Sure," replied Dusty, "Why not."

Returning a short time later with a temporary tag, it occurred to the gunsmith that he might have just uncovered a way to secure transportation. He waited for Juan to get into the passenger seat and then put her in gear.

The Chevy ran fine, its suspension much stiffer than Dusty's current model pickup back home. Steering required work, but was manageable. After a few miles, the two men pulled back into the lot.

"How much?"

"I'll take $3500 for her, señor."

And so the negotiations began. Dusty worked the man down to $2800, and then threw down the final demand. "Okay, friend, I want to have a mechanic I know look her over. I'll leave you $2,000 in cash as a deposit. I'll either bring her back in three days, and you can keep $200 of that for the trouble, or I'll come back in and pay off the rest."

Juan took his time weighing his options. The truck had been on the lot for a few weeks, no one showing the slightest bit of interest. If the guy never returned the unit, he could file an insurance claim and pocket the deposit. If the customer returned the truck, one hundred per day wasn't a bad rental rate.

"Okay, sir. You have a deal. Come on in the office, and we'll fill out the paperwork."

The word "paperwork" caused a knot to form in Dusty's stomach, but he followed the man inside anyway.

"May I see your driver's license, please?"

"My license was stolen a few days ago," Dusty lied as he began counting out $100 bills. "I should have the replacement copy in the mail before long."

Juan, looking greedily at the money, replied, "No problem; many of my customers don't have the necessary documents." And without another word, the salesperson began filling out the numbers for a temporary tag.

Watching the man basically perform an illegal act, Dusty guessed that Juan, and others like him, probably served a huge underground economy. Millions of undocumented workers were said to be in the United States. How did they buy cars, rent apartments, or procure bank accounts without the proper papers and documents? It had never occurred to the West Texan to ask such questions, but now that he was in a similar situation, he thought it was a good time to learn. Juan was providing an important first lesson.

Ten minutes later and 20 Ben Franklin's lighter, Dusty hopped in his new ride and left a smiling Juan in his rearview mirror. He drove for a short period before realizing the gas tank was near empty. Thinking it would be best to keep it full in case he had to make a hasty departure, he found a gas station a few blocks later.

The simple matter of filling his truck with gas initiated a whole new series of problems. First of all, he didn't know if unleaded fuel would harm the old engine. Finding leaded gasoline would be next to impossible.

Next, he considered the question of pumping regular, mid-grade, or premium. He hadn't put anything but regular octane in a car in years. He decided on the premium, just in case. Then he had to pay.

In Fort Davis, a man pumped his gas and then went into the station to settle up. There was a factor of trust involved in the transaction. Here, it was a requirement to enter the station first, pay, and then pump fuel. This was mandatory unless the customer had a credit card - something Dusty didn't believe in, nor could have used even if his wallet had been full of plastic.

To make matters worse, the place was filthy with security cameras. Pulling the bill of his hat low, he sighed and made for the cashier.

Without thinking, he peeled off a $100 bill and then pointed to the old truck. The kid behind the counter nodded and said, "I've got one hundred on pump number 8." Dusty was handed a receipt, and then left to fill his tank.

The truck wouldn't hold $100 worth, the automatic shut-off stopping the flow with a significant amount of change due. He was going to get in the truck and leave, but visions of the clerk chasing after him changed his mind. Simply leaving might draw attention that was unacceptable.

Dusty returned to the store and waited in line for his change. The kid remembered him, looked at the computer-like screen, and counted out the change.

Putting away the money, Dusty looked up and saw a police car pulling into a parking space, the driver navigating it directly into a parking spot between the station's front door and his truck. Holding his breath, he forced himself to walk casually around the cruiser, passing the front bumper just as the policeman opened the door.

He didn't breathe until he reached for the Chevy's door handle, his hands shaking so badly he almost couldn't manage inserting the key. His mind kept waiting for an authoritative voice to shout, "Freeze," or some similar command, but it never happened.

The tingling of fear didn't leave his legs for several blocks. It was another five intersections before he stopped looking in his rearview mirror every few seconds.

Dusty used the condo building's parking garage, finding the reserved spot for his specific unit. Despite the close encounter with the police officer at the gas station, he closed the door behind him, carrying an improved outlook on life alongside his purchases.

~ ~

Tim couldn't see clearly anymore, his eyes strained from working at least 60 hours in the last three days, the pace of local news events not allowing for much sleep. The *Post's* office had been absolute bedlam trying to cover the attacks downtown. Every reporter, staff member, and typesetter had worked around the clock, playing angles, gathering information and putting a unique perspective on Houston's latest newsworthy event.

He called the initial rumors of a natural gas leak as bullshit, talking his editor into not wasting time on any background story and saving the paper some money and face. He had known immediately it was the guy with "God's Gun," his instincts bristling when the first explosions occurred at the federal building.

Despite the unwavering feeling that Weathers was behind the outbreak of violence, his boss wouldn't let him run with the story - at first. The *Post* had taken a lot of criticism, from both the authorities and the general public, over Tim and Wendy's first article. The paper's owners had passed the word down - make certain that speculation didn't run rampant after the explosions.

Then the mayor's press conference had vindicated Crawford. Tomorrow morning's edition of the paper would contain a front page full of "I told you so," coverage, touting the fine reporting and award winning journalism of the rag. Bragging openly about being the first to cover what had become an ongoing, critically important story.

Tim looked at his watch, the small numerals on the face blurring beyond recognition. *It doesn't matter what time it is*, he realized, *it is damn late. I've got to get some sleep... and a shower.*

The air, cooled by the day's rain, felt good against his face as he walked down the steps in front of the newspaper's downtown offices. Despite the rinsing effect of the precipitation, he could still detect the aroma of burnt rubber from the fires, his office only a few blocks away from the library.

He crossed the street and saw Joe was in his normal spot, sleeping soundly on two pieces of cardboard, a shopping cart full of empty water bottles, scraps of clothing, and empty fast food bags nearby. He pulled four bucks out of his pocket and dropped them in the homeless man's lap. It was twice his normal donation, but he'd been working double shifts.

His Ford sedan was on the second floor of the garage. Enjoying the night air, he decided to walk up the ramp instead of taking the elevator. Besides, it always smelled like mold and old urine after a day's rain.

He pulled the keys from his pocket when a voice sounded behind him, the presence startling the hell out of him.

"Mr. Crawford?"

Inhaling and pivoting both at the same time, Tim found the outline of a man in the shadows. "Who's asking?" He decided to act tough.

"My name is Dusty Weathers. I'm the man you wrote about in your paper. Sorry to startle you, I mean you no harm."

Relief flooded through Crawford's bones, the fact that he wasn't going to be instantly assaulted or killed outright stopping the gusher of adrenaline surging through his system. The follow-on realization that he was standing 20 feet away from the most wanted man in the world renewed his agitation, but it was of a different flavor.

"I'm sorry, sir, but I've received about a million prank calls from people claiming to be Durham Weathers since I ran that article. How would I know you're the real McCoy?"

Dusty reached for his wallet, a slight grin passing across his lips when the reporter took a step backwards at his movement. "I'll show you my driver's license. Will that do?"

The West Texan stepped closer, the movement bringing him into the light. He extended Crawford the license, but it was unnecessary. The man's face was as familiar as an old classmate at a high school reunion – the unusual looking weapon slung across his chest all the proof the reporter needed.

"You've shaved the beard and changed your hair color," Tim noted, ignoring the offered ID. "Still, I recognize your face."

Grunting, Dusty returned the card to his wallet, and then his attention to the reporter. "I'm sure a man in your profession has a million questions, Mr. Crawford. I'm a guy with a million answers, but not tonight. You look tired and in need of a good night's rest. I promise not to generate any more news for a few days – unless I'm pressed into doing so again."

"Pressed? Again? I'm not sure I follow, Mr. Weathers."

"The reason why I acted against the cops is because they have taken two of my friends into custody and won't give them a fair hearing or due process of the law. My friends, freeborn Americans, are being treated worse than the prisoners down at the military jail in Cuba. I tried to negotiate with the FBI, but they kept calling me a terrorist and a traitor and wouldn't listen. I hit their garage and the SWAT vans to send a message, both to you and to them."

"To me?" Crawford's voice sounded nervous.

"Yes, to the press. Please keep in mind, sir, that I could have collapsed that federal building. I could have turned the entire structure to dust – everyone inside would have been killed. I didn't. I'm not a murderer, terrorist or traitor. I'm a common man who accidently invented a very powerful gun. Now, my government wants to kill me and take the weapon."

"Have you offered to just turn it over to them?"

"No, and the powers that be aren't too happy about it." Dusty patted the rifle-like device hanging across his chest, and continued. "This is too much for mankind right now, Mr. Crawford. We barely kept from destroying the planet with nuclear weapons, and the destructive power of this technology is several fold beyond splitting atoms. This is small, compact, easy to make and, according to my brother, has the capability to generate virtually unlimited amounts of energy. I judge my fellow man far too immature to handle this right now, and that's why I won't hand it over to my government, or anyone else for that matter."

Pulling the sling over his head, Dusty offered the reporter the rail gun. "Here, hold "God's Gun" for yourself."

Tim hesitated, not sure if the device was being surrendered or if Weathers wanted to give a demonstration. In the end, curiosity got the better of the reporter, and he accepted the weapon.

Crawford had spent a fair amount of time around guns. He'd hunted, shot trap and skeet. After hefting the weight of the piece, he shouldered the rail gun, aiming at distant skyscrapers visible above the half-wall of the garage.

"Whatever you fire at is certain to be destroyed," began Dusty. "It doesn't matter if it's a building, plane or an aircraft carrier, the weapon will pulverize anything. Nothing on this earth can withstand it."

"So I could just pull the trigger, and it would destroy that entire building?"

"Yes, and the one behind it, and the one beyond that if the power is turned up enough."

Crawford believed Dusty. He was also surprised at the lure of the gunsmith's creation. Unlimited power, right there in his hands. Easy to use, unstoppable. His mind began to race with the possibilities, interrupted only by the big cowboy's arm reaching outward, obviously wanting his weapon back.

Tim hesitated, not quite ready to give it up. At first, he told himself that he was simply curious about the technology. Honesty broke through, the reporter finally admitting that the feeling of invincibility was a powerful emotion. To hold such power – right here – in a parking garage. He shook his head to erase the developing fantasy.

"You see my point, don't you sir? It's difficult to hand it back, isn't it?"

After another moment, Crawford did hand it over. He felt a deep sense of loss watching Dusty re-sling the weapon.

The reporter's eyes focused on the gun, stunned at his own reaction to holding such power in his hands. He hadn't considered Weather's side of the story. It had never dawned on him that the now-vilified fugitive might actually be a good guy trying to protect others.

"Mr. Weathers, you'll pardon my skepticism, but how can I know you're telling me the truth? How can I prove what you're saying is accurate?"

Nodding, Dusty replied without hesitation, holding out a small piece of paper. "I was hoping we would get past the invention and around to that question. My story is easy to prove, sir. Find out what is happening to these two people, and you'll see the government's lies begin to unravel. Once you do that, I'll be happy to sit with you and answer all your questions."

Tim accepted the paper, holding it so he could see in the light. There were two handwritten names on the small note, Hank Barns and Grace Kennedy.

Before he could ask another question, the sound of a car engine came from the first floor below. Crawford spun to look at the source, which quickly began fading into the distance going the other direction. When he turned back, Dusty was gone.

"We've got him," came the excited tech's voice through Monroe's phone.

"Weathers?"

"Yes, at a gas station - Medical Center area. He showed up on a cop's dash cam, the NSA's facial recognition system picked it up."

"How long ago?"

"Late this afternoon."

"Fuck! Get me the information, like now!"

A few minutes later, Monroe and Shultz were speeding south in a bureau SUV, the blue strobe lights in the grill helping clear the evening traffic. Two other FBI units were right behind them.

By the time they arrived at the gas station, the parking lot was full of blue lights. HPD's units had arrived first, quickly followed by just about every other cop in the sector. Shultz looked at his boss and said, "Didn't they get the word that Weathers hasn't been here in over eight hours?"

"I think our co-workers in blue want a little payback for Weathers hitting their SWAT team and scaring the shit out of another 100 officers or so. You know police; they don't like their authority being questioned."

The duo of FBI agents split up once inside the facility. Monroe broke off to find a shaken store manager being questioned in the back office by three large officers, while Shultz investigated the store's video system.

Less than an hour later, Shultz found his boss talking to a sleepy clerk who had been rudely awaked by two HPD officers banging on his door and then hauling the lad down to his place of employment. Clearing his throat, the junior FBI man motioned his boss out to the hall.

"Bad news on the store's video system. The cameras covering the pumps are recorded randomly, each island being taped for about a minute and then switching to another. I never saw any image of Weathers at a pump. We have plenty of video of the suspect standing in line, paying cash and then getting his change, but I can't tell you what he was driving, or what the plate number is."

"Shit," commented Monroe, "The clerk doesn't remember either. He recalls the guy paying with cash, but didn't look any further. We can tell by the store receipts it was pump #8, but that's about it."

Shultz rolled his eyes, becoming frustrated by missing such an opportunity. "How much gas did he purchase?"

"About $70 worth, which tells us nothing. There must be two hundred models out there that have 20 gallon tanks, or he could have just been topping off – getting ready to make a run for it."

Monroe paused, thinking about the situation. "What we do know is that he has got to be in this area. We've not picked up a single Predator image, nor have the traffic cameras gotten a hit. That tells me he's hanging around locally. We'll tighten our dragnet to this side of town and focus all the HPD efforts around here."

Nodding, Shultz added, "Is it time to call in the little drones?"

Smiling, Monroe said, "I already have, and I called Washington. We'll have two Hostage Rescue Teams, complete with extra snipers. They'll all be here within 24 hours. Tomorrow, we're going to get serious about finding one Mr. Durham Weathers, and he's not going to escape again."

Shultz whistled, "Calling in the big guns, eh, boss?"

"If we find him, I'm not going to bother approaching. We'll take him out from a distance – before he even knows we're there."

Day 16

The Houstonian was a household name in its hometown, yet few of the Bayou city's residents had ever visited the reclusive retreat.

Despite being located right in the middle of a densely populated section of town, the facility was well hidden from the passing public by its lush 89 acres of landscaping and sub-tropical growth.

Its fame was derived mostly from the fact that presidents, kings, and other heads of state commonly sheltered at the hotel while visiting Houston. Security teams loved the centralized location and restricted visibility, while their VIPs enjoyed the lavish facilities and luxury appointments. The service was second to none. That fact combined with the privacy afforded, made it a unique destination.

The wealthy, non-dignitary class often frequented the property as well, prompting the hotel to be named one of the top 25 finest in the world by more than one travel publication.

Sergei was enjoying breakfast on his balcony, the view of the pool and tennis courts pleasing to his eye. The seemingly non-ending skyline of Houston was visible to the south and east, clusters of high-rise buildings trailing off into the humidity-obscured distance.

Seated next to the director was a stoic man dressed in clothing more suited for the gym than having a meal with one of the most powerful men in his home country. Sergei wasn't insulted, no, quite the contrary. He understood the captain's discipline and near-slave like attitude toward physical fitness, a welcome attribute for a SPETZ team commander.

Western media had romanticized the now famous acronym SPETZNAZ, the term commonly used as the designation of an elite group of fighting men - the Soviet military's equivalent of the American SEALs or Green Berets. While such units did exist, in reality, the name applied to any special group or unit of men. "SPETZ" was literally an abbreviation for the Russian language, "Special Forces."

Many government organizations in the Motherland had SPETZ units. One such group carrying the moniker worked for the Department of the Interior, a special rescue team trained to find lost hikers and vacationers.

Sergei's agency had its own SPETZ units, one of the best commanded by the burly, young officer seated next to him, enjoying a double order of ham and eggs. The SVR's special units were highly trained in two arts, espionage and military tactics.

Their US State Department-approved travel visas included a visit to the Syrian consulate located not more than two miles from where the two Russians were enjoying their meal. Sergei had no intention of even driving by the remote annex of his country's Middle Eastern ally. His purpose in Houston didn't allow for such frivolous expenditures of time.

The plan was simple.

Sergei knew from past experience that the FBI would deploy their Hostage Rescue Teams. His men were very familiar with the bureau's elite units, many of his own personnel having trained together at various schools and courses. After all, the two countries were now "friendly democracies," and past American administrations believed that Russia would benefit from strong rule of law. Why not train their enforcement agencies?

The director also knew that the HRTs would arrive in Houston with a lot of special equipment, most likely at a military airfield. That made their stakeout simple enough, and now three of his team were monitoring the potential landing spots, waiting for the special FBI shooters to arrive.

Once they were on location, Sergei's men would simply follow the HRTs around, waiting on them to deploy against the farmer who had invented the rail gun.

Sergei smiled smugly, happy with his plan. In addition to its simplicity, it was cost-efficient and offered very few risks for himself or his men. He would use the American's resources against them, allowing them to lead the effort until the very last moment. Right when the US authorities relaxed, thinking their mission was over, he would snatch the weapon away and fade into the night. It was brilliant.

As if on cue, the captain's cell phone rang. "Zdrahstuiteh."

Sergei could hear the little voice on the other end, but couldn't make out what was being said.

The captain nodded, replying with a curt "Da," and then disconnecting the phone. He looked at his boss and announced, "Sir, the FBI teams landed at Ellington Field and were transported to a hotel in the Medical Center area. They have deployed two units, supplemented with three long distance marksmen. Our men have taken up observation positions around their quarters and will inform us when they move."

"Good, Captain. That's very welcome news. Could you pass me that beaker of juice?"

Monroe put his car keys in his pocket and proceeded out of the garage. Casually glancing around, he was thankful none of the members of his team were on the sidewalk, a little embarrassed that he was parking his private car somewhere other than the FBI garage that had been attacked.

The two-block walk passed quickly, his later than normal arrival avoiding the heaviest of Houston's traffic. He was only a few steps from the steps of the federal building when a voice sounded nearby.

"Agent Monroe?" A man was suddenly blocking Monroe's path. "Tim Crawford from the *Post*. Would you have time to answer a few questions?"

The FBI man started to wave off the man. "I'm sorry, mister. What did you say your name was?"

"Crawford, sir."

"You're the reporter who wrote the piece about God's Gun – am I right?"

Looking down, almost shyly, Crawford replied. "Yes, sir. That would be me."

"I didn't like your article, Mr. Crawford. I'm afraid you'll have to speak with an official bureau spokesman, I can't comment on an ongoing investigation."

"Dusty Weathers claims you're holding two of his friends on trumped up charges. He also said that he offered a compromise on two different occasions. Are either of those accusations valid, sir?"

The mention of Weather's name froze the FBI agent mid-stride, just as the reporter knew it would. Monroe turned, his face twisted in anger. "Are you saying that you spoke to Durham Weathers and didn't notify law enforcement immediately?"

Tim had been ready for that angle, his response critical to the remainder of the interview. "I had no way of being sure the man who contacted me was actually

Weathers. It was only a short time ago that I verified the man was actually who he claimed to be, and now I'm here – talking to the FBI about what he said."

Monroe's career at the FBI had encompassed numerous encounters with the press. He knew the game as well as Crawford. "As I said, Mr. Crawford, I can't comment on an ongoing investigation."

"I called several people out in Fort Davis, sir. They confirm one Mr. Henry Barns was apprehended a few days ago, by federal officers. They also confirm that one Miss Grace Kennedy is missing, along with Mr. Barn's wife, Eva. The people I spoke with claim that Kennedy and Mrs. Barns were on their way here to Houston, where Mr. Barns was to be arraigned. Yet, I can't find any public court records validating these accounts. Are these people in your custody, Agent Monroe?"

The agent frowned, and then jutted out his chin in defiance. "I can't comment on an on-going investigation."

Crawford shook his head, "The arrest of any US citizen has never been considered confidential information. Furthermore, in my 25 years of reporting, I've never encountered secret courts or off the record hearings. Even the occasional 'closed hearing,' is a matter of public disclosure. I can't even locate a sealed indictment."

Monroe didn't comment, his gaze simply boring into Crawford's eyes.

After an uncomfortable pause, Tim inhaled and went for broke. "I see. You'll understand, if I pursue a claim of missing persons... if my paper chases the mysterious disappearance of these citizens?"

The agent shrugged his shoulders, "Suit yourself," and turned away. He stopped two steps later and pivoted to face the reporter. "I can tell you one thing, Mr.

Crawford. In about five minutes, the United States government is going to offer a reward for your friend Weathers. It will be 25 million dollars, dead or alive."

Tim whistled, "That's unprecedented, isn't it? I mean, wasn't that the same amount offered for Osama Bin Laden?"

"Yes, it is." Monroe hesitated a moment, having intentionally avoided the reporter's barrage. Now it was time to turn the tables. The press could be used as a tool, and he knew how to do it. His vast experience at the higher levels of the nation's premier law enforcement agency had given Fred Monroe a lot of firsthand experience in manipulating the fourth estate.

Keeping in mind his recent discussion with Shultz regarding public perception, Monroe decided to make Durham Weathers Public Enemy Number 1.

"Look, Mr. Crawford, I can tell you've got some sort of conspiracy bug flying up your ass. If you really want to get a nice, warm-fuzzy feeling concerning Weathers, why don't you investigate his recent issues with the IRS? I understand they are investigating him for tax evasion. Why don't you drive out to West Texas and take pictures of his workshop and huge gun safe? Talk to the locals about his reputation for making super-accurate rifles – weapons that could only have one logical purpose – to kill. He's a disgruntled, divorced loner who blames his country for his own personal problems. He's a danger to every citizen, and I'm doing my best to bring him in before more people get hurt."

Crawford's voice was hollow, "I'll do just that. But what about Barns and Kennedy?"

"Again, sir, I'm not breaking the law. I'm well aware of what DOJ is doing, and it is perfectly legal. Rarely used, but perfectly legal. That's all I will say."

Monroe spun away, avoiding the temptation to look at the reporter's face. If he had, he would have seen a bewildered man, standing in the street with his gaze focused on nothing.

His statements about Weathers were calculated to sway public opinion. A large segment of the public didn't like guns – especially if there were a hint of radicalism involved. The same could be said of tax evasion. So, if you wanted the average Joe on the street to hate someone, paint a picture of a tax cheat toting a sniper rifle.

Monroe grunted as he walked up the steps. About the only thing that would make Weathers look worse was if they'd found a Nazi flag in his workshop. He'd have to think about stocking up on a couple of "throw downs," sporting the evil German emblem.

With her boss's ex making the front page on an almost daily basis, Paula had taken to buying a newspaper on the way in each morning.

Strolling in after her morning ritual of reassuring Eva, yet again, that everything was going to be okay, Maria saw the copy of the *Post* on the corner of her assistant's desk. With a casual glance, she said, "What's up with my outlaw ex-husband this morning?"

Maria's statement was crafted, just as her behavior had been the last few days. She now assumed the FBI was watching her every moment, listening to every word. She had taken to walking about the house naked, just to frustrate any pervert-Fed who might be watching. The activity had given her an outlet, until an embarrassed Eva had trouble sleeping and came downstairs unexpected.

Her façade included projecting an air around the office, a mixture of "I don't give a shit," accented with a touch of, "He's ruining my life by splashing my name all over the headlines."

She walked by, seemingly uninterested in the paper, which was mostly true. She had already read the article at home. Pausing, she smiled at Paula and said, "Do you remember that handsome, young lawyer we found the house for up in The Woodlands? You remember the one... he seemed fascinated with my bosom."

Paula grunted, "You're going to have to do a little better than that, Maria. They're all fascinated with your boobage."

"Oh, you remember the one. He drove that fancy sports car... the silver one... a Porsche I think it was."

"Ahhhh, yeah! I remember. His name was Steven... Steven Morrison I think. I also think he had a strong desire to attend an open house in your bedroom."

Waving off the comment, Maria asked, "Could you see if you can find his number and make me an appointment? Don't tell him why, but I think with Dusty raising hell all over the place, I might want to change back to my maiden name."

"Why don't you want me to tell him?"

"The young man was way, way too eager before. If he thinks I'm changing back to my maiden name, he'll double his efforts."

"I don't blame you for wanting the change, although it doesn't seem to be hurting business," Paula replied, holding up a stack of messages.

"It might be a while, but I don't want to take the chance."

She entered the inner sanctum, shuffling through the messages taken by Paula. There was nothing important or unusual that needed immediate attention. In reality, she wanted the lawyer for Eva, as she had no intention of changing her name.

That concept brought her around to the 25 million dollar reward. She knew exactly where Dusty was, could probably lure him out into the open where he could be arrested safely. She seriously pondered doing just that. Aside from the fact that Dusty was going to get himself killed, 25-large was a lot of money. She wondered if she could use part of the reward to pay for his legal bills, maybe get him off without jail time. That would be a good question for young Steven, if she could ever pry his attention from her chest.

There were other reasons to consider turning him in. Dusty was the type of man who could never forgive himself if someone got killed. As she followed the newscasts closer than anyone knew, she was amazed at the extra steps he appeared to be taking in order to avoid ending some corrupt cop's life. His luck couldn't hold out forever, and if she ended this entire nightmare, it would be better for all involved in the long run. Besides, a sum of 25 followed by six zeros was a shit-pile of money.

Then there was Anthony, their son. What chance would he have in life if his father became a mass murderer? She was sure Dusty hadn't considered that before taking off on this rampage. It was just like him — riding off on a noble cause, just like a knight in shining armor, without a thought to the worried-sick family he'd left behind. Besides, 25-mill was airplane, "never work again" money.

Grunting, she came up with yet another reason to turn Dusty in. If she was sourly tempted by that huge pile of cash, every bounty hunter, adventurer and wannabe badass in the country was probably booking tickets for

Houston at the moment. The city would be crawling with armed, dangerous men searching for poor Dusty. He'd probably be shot on sight. Besides, 25 with the "m" word was a ton of cash.

I wonder if Paula has found that lawyer's number yet, she pondered.

The jail's matron attached Grace's handcuffs to a metal loop securely bolted onto the conference room table. The woman assigned to deny the female prisoner's escape was close to 6 feet tall, no doubt tipping the scales at close to 200 pounds.

Grace, on the other hand, barely weighed 100 pounds, even with the shackles on her wrists. The routine of securing the smaller woman to the table was purely for intimidation and discomfort, not security.

Monroe sat watching across the table, nodding his head in acknowledgement at the jailer as she finished securing the feisty attorney.

"Orange isn't your color," the FBI man began, nodding at the ill-fitting jumpsuit issued to all detainees.

"I thought you might be gay," replied Grace calmly. "A man that notices fashion and requires a woman half his size to be tied down like a dog while in the same room leaves little doubt."

Ignoring the jab, Monroe pointed at the handcuffs, "That is purely procedure, Ms. Kennedy. I'm not scared of you."

"You should be, Agent Monroe, but not physically. You should be scared of losing your pension after I'm done with you and the bureau in court," she countered.

Monroe sighed, "If I only had a dollar for every time a criminal threatened me with that line, I wouldn't need my pension. But enough of this tit for tat, I want to talk about Mr. Durham Weathers."

The look on Grace's face actually expressed relief. The FBI wouldn't want to talk about Durham if they had already captured him. "Having a little trouble corralling that cowboy, eh? I could have told you to save your energy – he's a far better man than you, Mr. Monroe."

"So you do know Weathers quite well?"

"He is a dear friend and a client, sir. Given attorney-client privilege, that's all I can say."

Monroe sat back in the seat, a pencil at his lips. The look on Grace's face told him she was firm in her resolve to not provide any information about Mr. Weathers. In fact, he didn't believe she knew much if anything. Her attitude, however, pissed him off.

"Were you aware that he was developing a weapon of mass destruction?"

"My position as an officer of the court demands I not answer that question."

Sighing, Monroe bore in. "I disagree, Miss Kennedy. I too have a law degree, and as I recall, this privilege you keep spouting on about requires you to fully disclose any information regarding a pending crime. If you knew Weathers was building such a weapon, you're just as liable as he is, client privilege or not."

If she could have, Grace would have crossed her arms and smirked at his weak attempt to annoy her. As it was, she kept her bound hands flat on the table, her expression neutral.

"Ms. Kennedy, you're sitting there thinking that we have little respect for you. I'm sure you believe that we have taken these actions without regard for your capabilities. Let me assure you, nothing could be further from the truth. As a matter of fact, your involvement in this case had motivated my associate over in the

Department of Justice to up the ante as far as Weathers is concerned."

Again, Grace didn't react, her expression showing nothing.

The FBI agent grunted, "No matter. I do think you'll be interested to know that the United States government has put a $25 million reward on Durham Weather's head. My men at the airport have reported a virtual parade of bounty hunters, private investigators, and mercenaries arriving in town already. I wouldn't want to be in Mr. Weather's shoes."

He watched her eyes dilate at the announcement, unsure if it was fear or anger. Still, she offered no other reaction, verbal or otherwise.

Folding his notepad and standing, Monroe took one last shot. "I thought 25 million might be of interest to you, Ms. Kennedy. That's a lot of money. We've already picked up discussions by some of Weather's other friends talking about just that topic. If you know where he is, you should be the first to fill us in. You can save his life, collect the money, and keep additional charges from piling up against him. I would think about it, ma'am. I would think real hard."

And with that, Monroe walked out of the room.

A few minutes later, Grace was returned to her tiny cell, rubbing her wrists where the tight steel had chaffed her skin. She paced back and forth within the confines, trying to reconcile the reward being offered for Durham and what it meant.

Her dilemma was two-fold – a professional rejection of the government's actions and a personal cloud of emotion generated by her feelings for Dusty. While she knew he was more than capable of handling himself in a crisis, a manhunt on the scale Monroe was hinting at was more than most people had experienced. She feared for his life.

She recalled an encounter with Durham, an afternoon almost two years ago when he had volunteered to clear a patch of saplings and brush away from her new house. "You should take down those trees," he'd advised. "They're pinion pines and grow rapidly. You'll have moisture and limb problems with them being so close to your roof."

The next morning, she had been woken by his work outside, saw, shovel, rake and hoe busy doing the job. She'd tried to help as much as possible, but the heavy lifting was beyond her frame's design. Still wanting to contribute, she'd gone inside to make lunch.

Leaving him alone to continue the job while she prepared a meal, she decided a cool drink was in order, gathering a tray of tea and ice-filled glasses while the food finished in the oven. She'd walked around the corner and found a shirtless Durham swinging a heavy axe.

She'd admired his build before, tall and thin, a swimmer's physique. With shoulders twice as wide as his hips, he drew the eye of most women. He was, as she'd noted, a fellow worthy of watching as he walked down the street. What she had never witnessed until now was the power and grace of the man as he tested his frame to the extreme.

His skin undulated and bulged as he swung the axe, knotted cords and rippling waves of power moving across his back. His arms surged with honest muscle, cut and taunt, born of toil and hard work - not countless sessions on a machine in a gym.

She found herself watching, riveted, his display arousing a part of her that she had forgotten. For a brief period, she was a woman... a woman feeling a need, a physical need ignited by the kind man who was working so hard on her behalf. That craving had been dead in her for so long, unfelt and unrealized for so many years. Its reemergence was a shock, lust-hot and spreading through her core.

Again and again, he swung the axe, his body a choreographed combination of raw strength and unwavering focus. She couldn't help but picture him as a lover, his lean body against hers, unrelenting in demand, irresistible in its resolve. She wanted him – the first man she'd felt that way about since the death of her husband so long ago.

While she stood fantasizing like a schoolgirl, holding the tray of cold tea in a stupor, his mesmerizing swinging of the axe had paused. A loud cracking sounded from the trunk, and then the pine began to topple. She remembered looking up at the thick trunk... recalled how fast it seemed to be moving directly at her, the sight causing her legs to freeze. She was going to be crushed, struck down by impact. She was about to die.

It was all so cloudy after that. She remembered his shouted, desperate warning, startling her from the dream. Then he was moving... a blur... the tray of drinks flying through the air. She remembered the weightlessness and momentum and then the loud crash and thump of the tree as it slammed into the earth – right where she had been standing.

Dusty was holding her. Her legs suspended off the ground as he'd lifted her like a small child, swinging her to safety. She'd never felt so helpless, yet so safe. Reality rushed into her head, an awareness that she was whole because of the man who was now screaming her name.

"Grace! Grace! Are you okay?" his voice rang, cutting through the shock of her near-death terror.

Nodding her head rapidly, she managed a hushed, "Yes."

Satisfied with her state, Durham had pulled her close in an embrace of relief.

She wrapped herself around him, the driving emotion to cling to the hero – the savior of her existence. But that changed as she recouped, her renewed need as a woman quickly recovering – stronger now, enhanced by his rescue.

She clutched the back of his head and pulled his lips to hers as her legs tightened around his waist. He reacted as a man would, his rock hard chest seeking the softness of her breasts... bruising, desperate kisses.

Her hands moved down, traveling on their own and seeking his belt. Halfway down his back, she felt warm, sticky... wet. She raised her hand and inhaled sharply at the sight of her blood-covered fingers.

He was bleeding. "Dusty, you're hurt," she said, pulling back and meeting his gaze.

"It's nothing, Grace. One of the tree limbs scratched me a little."

She released her grip and pushed away, determined to see how badly he was injured. It wasn't pretty. The skin on his shoulder had been torn open for several inches, the blood pouring out of the wound. "I need to get you to the emergency clinic – right now!"

He didn't want to go. The spark between them had ignited a desire that wasn't going away over some minor injury. Despite the blood, he moved to hold her again, but she resisted, her voice growing stern. "You're not going to bleed to death in my yard. I'm going to get you a towel for that cut and then run you into town, and that's that."

She had stood and fretted as she watched the young doctor apply the staples to his shoulder. Again and again the painful device had snapped and clicked, Dusty never complaining once. His only protest came with the order to wear a sling for at least a week until the injury healed.

Self-doubt and insecurity weren't hallmarks of Grace Kennedy's existence. She had been on her own for too long – survived in the cutthroat world of business too many years for such weaknesses to have any room within her. Now, watching someone pay a heavy price for her stupidity, now those emotions began to take hold.

They had driven home in silence, Grace embarrassed and feeling terrible over the entire affair, Durham stoic, offering no commentary. She had helped him into his home, made sure he was comfortable as the pain medications began to make him drowsy.

Every day she went to visit him, often twice daily until the sling came off and the staples were removed. Every single morning she checked in, helped around the house and made sure he wanted for nothing. But they never talked about what happened – the events of that day left to fade away and grow cold.

Now, today, in her tiny cell, Grace was feeling those same emotions of self-doubt and insecurity. Had her actions resulted in a good man being threatened? Had her ego added to Dusty's troubles? She could have played nice with the DOJ and FBI. She could have negotiated in private with the cocky, young lawyer, let him save face in front of the judge. Had her calls to various elected officials pushed the Feds over the edge as Monroe had insinuated?

Now, a huge reward was going to endanger the man she cared about, and she couldn't help but feel part of it was her fault. The cell grew cold, the chill generated by her helplessness.

Dr. Witherspoon's cell sounded, the caller ID showing "restricted," a sure sign of someone important on the other end.

"This is Henry Witherspoon," he answered in a neutral tone.

"Please stand by for the President of the United States," a female voice responded.

Finally, the ex-professor thought. *I was beginning to think our conversation had been forgotten.*

Time seemed to drag on as he waited, anticipation building during the pause. After what seemed like an hour, he recognized the commander-in-chief's voice. The boss wasn't in a good mood.

"Henry, I assume you've heard about the incidents in Houston?"

"Yes, sir."

"I've got the governor, both senators, and a handful of representatives from Texas crawling up my ass. Everyone knows there is a madman down there randomly blowing things to hell. I want you to cease and desist all activities associated with the blue ribbon panel we discussed. This has become a law enforcement matter and is too politically charged for my administration to be involved."

The man's tone shocked the Secretary of Energy, the boss's statement seeming to blame him personally for the activities in Houston. "Sir, I tried to warn you of the device's potential. I must beg you to reconsider, Mr. President. We need to develop a strategy to limit the technology, or this will end badly."

"Oh, it's going to end, Henry. It's going to be over soon. I don't care about the device or the inventor. I only want that crazed individual off our streets and either in a grave or behind bars."

Rubbing his temple, the SecEng sighed, "I understand, sir."

Having received agreement, the president's voice softened. "Look... Henry... we can't be seen as weak here. My oath demands I enforce the law of the land and protect the citizens of this nation. If word got out that we were even considering negotiating with this Weathers fellow, all the folks with an axe to grind would be licking their chops. We would have every radical zealot in the world trying to extort us. Put your project on hold until things settle down. We'll restart after the drama has played out."

"Yes, Mr. President."

The call disconnected. Dr. Witherspoon stared at the silent phone, his eyes deep with concern. "You're making a big mistake," he mumbled to himself. "I hope we survive it."

Day 18

The six large delivery vans were painted with the logos and color schemes of a nationally recognized parcel delivery company. Piggybacked on trailers and pulled by over the road semis, the fleet was rushed to Houston after the Department of Justice was granted a FISA court warrant.

The truck's exteriors were identical in every detail to the thousands of such vehicles that delivered packages all over America. It was the perfect camouflage to hide in plain sight. The only noteworthy features on the outside of the units were an extra array of antennas mounted along the top, and the heavy-duty locking systems installed on both the rear and side doors. Even the drivers' uniforms were a perfect counterfeit of their civilian counterparts.

The interior of the cargo area was a different story. Rows of sophisticated equipment lined one side of the space, the electronics mounted in shiny aluminum racks complete with shock absorbing rubber feet and extra cooling fans. Flat panel computer monitors, fixed keyboards, tracker balls, and a host of switches, LED indicators, and meters adorned the consoles. The mobile mounting system had been copied from a Trident nuclear submarine.

Along the center aisle, two comfortable-looking executive chairs were affixed to the floor via stout-looking pedestals. The plush seating, designed for controllers to spend long shifts at the consoles, wouldn't have been out of place in any well-appointed corporate office.

The opposite wall contained a large battery bank used to supply power to the array of microprocessor-controlled systems, as well as climate control for the operators and equipment.

Next to the batteries was a purpose built storage rack that contained over 500 glass tubes. Similar in diameter to common laboratory test tubes, each container was almost two feet long and sealed with special rubber caps on the ends. Inside of these clear rods were the drones.

Slightly larger than a healthy Texas mosquito, each glass tube held a stack of the miniature surveillance drones, the insect-like devices stacked one atop the other like bullets in a belt of ammunition. Each container held 20 units, allowing the six trucks to launch a swarm of over 60,000 of the plastic winged camera platforms.

The torso of each tiny robot consisted primarily of a power cell, a battery slightly smaller than the lithium-ion units used in wristwatches. Small plastic wings, slightly larger than those that propelled nature's blood-sucking pests, extruded from each side of the body. These aerodynamic wonders served both to obtain flight and as to recharge the unit's battery with the miniscule solar panels embedded in them.

Instead of a skin-piercing, blood-extracting beak, a camera was mounted to the "head." A marvel of miniature optical electronics, each drone could snap low-resolution photographs in both normal and infrared spectrums of light.

The robo-insect's head was the control center. A small amount of computer memory, basic processor, GPS system, and transmitter were all contained within an area one quarter the size of a pencil eraser.

Each of the six legs was an antenna, two of the carbon fiber appendages used to communicate with the nest, or home van. The remaining four were utilized as a GPS receiver, proximity and inter-hive communicator, radio frequency identification (RFI), and parabolic microphone.

Each micro-drone could be controlled individually or programed to cooperate with a group. The standard operating procedure involved one of the vans slowly traveling the city streets, circling an area where observation was desired. At preprogrammed stops, normally intersections or traffic lights, a small sunroof slid open, and a tube of 20 "bugs" was released to fly away and begin their coordinated search patterns.

The range of the tiny flyers was restrictive, especially if the wind were anything but calm. Limited to 400 meters of travel distance without stopping and recharging their batteries, the delivery van had to be relatively close to the target. Deployment in rain or winds higher than 10 mph was forbidden.

The latest iteration of the micro-drone software allowed for multiple vans to work together in order to provide coverage for larger, more complex environments. The six units heading for the Medical Center area were an unprecedented test of this new scalability.

The electronic brain inside of each van was designed purely to control the swarm. Facial recognition, photographic reconnaissance, and sound interpretation were performed hundreds of miles away in Bluffdale, Utah, home of the National Security Agency's ultra-modern data center.

Any intelligence gathered by the swarm was transmitted back to the hive-van where it was bundled into long streams of binary data. Microburst satellite transmissions carried terabytes of compressed images, readings and sound, bouncing the signals off a low-earth orbit, military communications bird. Those signals were received by the NSA's supercomputers.

The NSA had once been the most secretive of any US intelligence-gathering entities. Unlike the CIA, or other field-active government organizations, the NSA was created purely to perform electronic eavesdropping on telephone, radio, and later, internet activity.

Plagued by scandals, whistleblowers, and congressional inquiries during 2013, many average Americans were shocked to learn that the all-powerful spying technologies possessed by the agency were being used to monitor domestic activity within their country's borders.

Email accounts, cell phone records, and internet sessions were being stored, sorted and analyzed on a scale that seemed like science fiction to most people. Politicians scrambled to publicly decry the agency's domestic spying as a violation of privacy, while at the same time, in private, supporting the expansion of the NSA's capabilities with secretive funding and lackluster congressional hearings.

One such investment was the construction of the world's largest data center in Utah. While specific capabilities were kept ultra-secret, some information did leak out for public scrutiny. Despite the warnings of independent experts, the size, scale, and scope of the new installation received very little press coverage in the mainstream media.

People who built large networks of computer systems were astounded by the size of the NSA's new facility. One Silicon Valley expert was quoted as saying that the agency could now store every detail, phone conversation, internet browsing session, and email for the entire population of the planet – times 10. In reality, his prediction was short by several multiples.

As the giant, skyward pointing dishes received the hive's streams of data, massive banks of supercomputers began processing the drone's output at the Utah location.

RFI signals embedded in credit cards, driver's licenses, toll road passes, and security system key cards could be crosschecked and verified against numerous databases. Newer model automobiles with satellite radios and location tracking systems could be scanned, identified, and tracked.

Every conversation and phone call could be monitored, the NSA's supercomputers correlating the signals provided by the cell phone carriers with the microphone built into the drone's tiny leg. Voice imprints could be stored, analyzed, and compared with existing records collected over dozens of years. As one intelligence analyst had said, "It is practically impossible to hide anything but thought from the drones, and we're working on that."

Monroe and Shultz watched the six hive-vans exit the staging area, each driver's route plotted in advance with logistical precision to provide as much area coverage as possible. The Medical Center was a downtown in its own right, complete with high-rise buildings, parking garages, and of course, apartment and condo buildings. It would require the enormous swarm to cover the entire area.

"If he's in the search area, we'll find him," commented Monroe.

Shultz shook his head, "That's what worries me the most."

The charlatan parcel van designated Hive One rolled to a stop at an intersection. After a check of the rear view mirrors, the driver pushed a hidden button on the steering column that signaled the controllers in the back that they were free from prying eyes and could deploy.

A small trapdoor in the roof of the cargo area was unhinged, a small peephole showing the yellow glow of the Houston night sky visible through the opening. One of the glass tubes was inserted into the small portal, immediately followed by a few keystrokes on one of the keyboards.

Without any sound or fanfare, the topmost mosquito drone disappeared into the atmosphere. One by one, the small machines exited the tube, each patiently waiting its turn. The container was empty in less than 20 seconds.

A small blue light flashed once on the dashboard, a signal that the driver could proceed to the next launch point. Similar launches were occurring all over the Medical Center area.

Less than one percent of the tiny robots failed – normally the fault of a manufacture's defect or improperly assembled component. Another insignificant number fell victim to natural predators, such as spider webs and birds.

Of those deployed from the van this evening, two were wiped out by a lawn sprinkler, another struck by a delivery truck speeding the opposite way. All in all, over 99% of the 10,000 drones survived the deployment and proceeded to dissect the grid that had been preprogrammed into their microprocessor brains.

Unit 2131 was launched three blocks from Dusty's condo. Staged at the 13th position in the tube, it powered up its wings and rose vertically 12 feet above the parcel van's roof, hovering there until it verified its position via GPS.

Using its camera and internal programming, it began its predetermined course toward the southwest, avoiding trees, lampposts, and other non-structural obstacles. Once every ten seconds, #2131 verified its position, altitude, and course, its electronic brain intent on finding the flat surface of a structure.

The first building it encountered was actually a small warehouse of pharmaceutical supplies. Sending a signal back to the van's controllers, the tiny drone was soon ordered to bypass the building as it was already being searched by 20 or so of its cousins.

The next image to be detected by #2131 was Dusty's condo building. Again, permission was sought from the van's computers, and this time the drone was ordered to begin scanning the third floor windows.

The northernmost balcony was the closest opportunity, so the drone corrected its flight path and made for the destination. Slowing as it approached the sliding glass door, the mechanical bug made for the upper right hand corner of what its primitive brain recognized as a window and gently landed on the glass surface. Its camera-nose began searching for the brightest point of light, movement of shape differential equations surging through its internal processor.

Just like its living cousins, the drone's legs were tipped with tiny suction cups that allowed it to defy gravity and remain flush against the glass. Light spectrum analysis quickly informed the #2131's brain that it was looking at a curtain, blind or other window covering. Infrared temperature analysis informed the logic circuits that the window was closed and that no air was flowing nearby.

The parabolic microphone couldn't detect any sound vibrations through the glass, so the mechanical bug started crawling from one corner to the next, its sensors seeking some differential in light, temperature, or sound.

Similar activities were occurring all over the search area. Some of the drones found open windows and entered offices, stores and residences without a second thought. Others detected doors being opened and invaded restaurants, bars, and even the abundant hospitals in the area.

A flood of data started arriving in the vans. Some of the information was voice recordings of everyday conversations, while other drones found valid video targets and started snapping pictures.

The vans compressed and transmitted the massive amount of sound and video to Utah, where the world's largest collection of supercomputers began analyzing the input, filtering through every conceivable human activity while looking for any sign of one Mr. Durham Weathers.

The NSA's processors didn't care that one couple was making love while the man and woman next door were having a fight. Two teenagers, sneaking out to the backyard to smoke pot never saw the drone that hovered above their blue cloud of smoke. Several men playing Texas Hold 'em poker were completely unaware of the mosquito-like robot on their windowsill.

Every voice was analyzed and compared to the phone call Dusty had made to the FBI headquarters. Every face was digitally measured to find a match with the images of the fugitive held in the bureau's memory banks. Every human frame was measured against the known dimensions of the West Texas gunsmith.

Unit #2131 eventually gave up on its first landing spot, unable to find anything for its sensors to record. Reinitiating its wings, the drone made for the next window and began repeating the process all over again.

~ ~

The NSA Analyst drained his coffee cup, setting the empty mug on the counter without his eyes leaving the computer screen. The manhunt in Houston was resulting in a lot of overtime and tired eyes.

His monitor was filled with images that the computer software had deemed "Worthy of human attention," meaning the digital brains ascertained that there might be something in an image, but couldn't be sure. No machine could match the combination of human eyes and brains. At least not yet.

Tens of thousands of man-hours were being invested on the project, teams of analysts such as himself scouring over photographs that ranged from innocent cooking utensils scattered on a countertop in the shape of a rifle, to a man cleaning his billiards queue while watching a television show.

Clicking on the next image on his list, the analyst peered at what looked to be a common apartment or condo, a dark object lying on the kitchen counter. With a bit of imagination, he could make out the shape of a long gun. Using the keyboard, he pulled up a description of what the computer had found interesting about the picture.

A red square was overlaid on the countertop, the machine-brain ignoring the potential weapon and focusing on the blob of dark color beside it. A few more taps on the keys and the image changed to a brightly colored thermal scan, again the computer focusing on the blob.

He enhanced the image, adding artificial light and converting the pixels to a dense gray-scale. The blob on the counter became a hat... a hat that matched one known to have been worn by the suspect on a previous occasion.

Inhaling sharply, the analyst moved the mouse and applied the same photographic magic to the rifle lying on the counter top. Once the image was cleaned up, he immediately reached for the phone.

The operator controlling the drone swarm answered immediately, the call being from an obvious source. "Yes."

"This is Magic Mountain, we have a high confidence hit from #2131 at the following location," announced the excited voice through the headphones.

After writing down a sequence of numbers and times, the FBI agent riding in the van replied, "Gotcha. I'll redirect additional units to that location."

After disconnecting the call, the drone-controller typed several commands into his console and sat back, waiting on his nosy insects to execute their new mission.

The sun was just rising in the east.

Dusty was sleeping in, the curtains open just enough to allow in a small line of light from the low angle sun. Still, it was enough to wake him.

Rolling his legs off the edge of the couch, he stretched the slumber from his frame and immediately made for the microwave to heat coffee water. A trip to the bathroom followed.

He'd been busy making a replica of his rail gun, using parts from the Goodwill's appliance section. An old blender, a non-working drill and parts from an alarm clock radio were scattered over the kitchen counter. He didn't know why a decoy seemed important, almost dismissing the project. Still, it kept his hands busy, a state that seemed more aligned with his temperament, especially after years of gunsmithing.

A 100 times he'd wished for the simplest tool, easily within reach on his workbench at home. Over and over again, he thought about driving the truck to a local store and purchasing a small kit of basics.

Dusty had developed another habit, one of pacing the length of the small combo and checking for odd behavior outside. Every few minutes he felt a need to check out the sliding glass door, peeking through the crack and watching the traffic patterns on the street below. He'd then walk to the back, checking the bedroom window for the same clues. In between, he'd stop and listen at the door, unsure if he'd hear the SWAT team lining up in the corridor or not.

You're a pacing animal in a cage, he concluded. *Eventually, you'll go insane or make a mistake - the end result being the same.*

Still, he checked the windows and listened at the door. Everything looked normal, another day on the dodge in south Houston. He sighed, returning to the toy gun and his tinkering.

"We've got him," said the excited agent on the phone. "We have 100% identification. He's in a third story condo. I'm transmitting the address."

That one simple call to Agent in Charge, Monroe, changed everything. A thousand activities began at once, men scrambling into action all across the south side of the city.

Orders were issued to hundreds of Houston policemen, instructions to quietly begin evacuating a wide perimeter around where the suspect was holed up. Dozens and dozens of patrol cars converged on the area, city computers coordinating bypasses, traffic control, and signal coordination.

The Predator drone was commanded to maintain a racetrack orbit above Dusty's condo, its powerful camera and instruments focused solely on the small flat. The FAA flashed bulletins, restricting the air space above the Medical Center area to law enforcement aircraft only. The Lifeline air ambulance pilots were grounded.

The HRT squads were alerted, scrambling to load the gear into the back of waiting SUVs that would rush them to the area.

Every FBI agent available headed toward the address flashing across the computers, command and control instructions being issued by the unit commanders and senior personnel.

Job one was to protect the surrounding civilian population. Roadblocks were constructed, police waving frustrated motorists into detours they didn't want to take. Storeowners were forced to lock their doors, shooing customers out and away from what became known as the exclusion zone.

The commander of the HRT arrived as the evacuation was in progress, eyeing the surrounding area with years of experience and an expert knowledge of his team's capabilities. After scanning the landscape for five minutes with a beefy set of binoculars, he calmly informed Monroe of his recommendation.

"Sir, I want to put my best sniper team on a high floor of that building. I think that will provide the best angle of support and observation."

Monroe followed the specialist's pointing arm, scoping out the 12-story Trustline National Bank building. Monroe acknowledged the expert's wishes, turning to a nearby police captain and barking, "We want our shooters in that building. Please move it up on the priority list to be cleared out."

The HRT commander followed Monroe to where a map was unfolded on the hood of a car. Pointing to a street one block over from Dusty's condo building, he announced, "I'll stage my entry teams here... and here. We'll be at his door in three minutes after the all-clear signal is given."

Nodding, Monroe looked at his watch and replied, "It will be at least another 30 minutes before HPD gets everyone out. I'll give the order personally."

The two men were interrupted by the arrival of the sniper team, each member of the three-man crew carrying heavy cases of equipment as they rushed past, heading for their assigned hide. Uniformed officers were already hustling confused, frightened workers out of the bank building with more reinforcements arriving on the scene every moment.

Sergei and his men were also moving quickly. The director had just entered the swimming pool when the captain approached and announced the deployment of the HRT squads. By the time the Russian had dressed, the SPETZ officer knew their destination.

The rental cars sped from the Houstonian's parking lot, the remainder of the captain's men changing into their counterfeit uniforms and unpacking American-made weapons. By the time they were approaching the Medical Center area, it looked as if three carloads of FBI reinforcements had arrived to bolster the dozens and dozens of federal agents already on the scene.

The captain had received directions for a rally point, the address texted from the team's first arriving members. With traffic snarled and gridlocked by the blockage of roads, it took some time to locate the abandoned warehouse just eight blocks from Dusty's condo, only two blocks away from the nearest police roadblock demarking the exclusion zone.

Scanning radios had been employed by the snooping Russians, eventually learning the address of the American farmer's location. After a brief conference with their captain, the team began to deploy.

~ ~

Dusty finished wrapping the pretend coil, holding the rifle at arm's length to examine his handiwork. Four paperclips, part of an empty superglue tube, and a half dozen salvaged parts had been pasted together on the toy rifle, the result remarkably resembling Dusty's original invention.

Were it not for the lack of an optic and aiming laser, he'd have trouble telling the fake from the real rifle. Looking at his watch, he realized he'd been absorbed at the task for almost two hours – a record in the close confines of his cage.

He picked up the empty coffee cup and decided to reward himself with another before starting lunch. Glancing at the toy again, he was kind of sad to see the project finished – wondering what he would find next to occupy his time. I guess this is better than being in a cell, he mused.

He filled the cup at the sink and then programmed the microwave. Habit moved him toward the sliding glass doors, his hand moving back the curtain just a bit so he could check the street below.

He stood motionless for almost a minute, waiting to see a car roll down the street, giving the traffic lights a chance to cycle. None came.

He then moved to the other side of the door, checking to the east where a more traveled street was just a block away. His heart began to race when nothing but empty, black pavement met his gaze. Something was wrong.

He moved back to his original spot, checking every sidewalk for as far as his limited angle would allow. Nothing – not a single person or car came into sight. Had they found him?

Several blocks away, Monroe's earpiece sounded with a calm voice, "This is Eagles Nest to all assets – I have movement at the suspect's window. Repeat, I have movement at the suspect's window."

Dusty pushed down the panic. There could be a million reasons why there weren't any cars or people, random circumstance being one of them. The microwave dinged, signaling his coffee water was ready, but he ignored it.

He needed a better vantage. Looking down at the real rail gun, he decided to use the weapon's powerful scope to check the area. Carrying it back to the window, he shouldered the device and began sweeping his surroundings using the optic's magnification. The microwaved again sounded its bell.

"Gun! Gun! Gun!" sounded the voice in Monroe's ear. "The suspect has a weapon, repeat, the suspect has a weapon. Appears to be a shoulder-fired rifle with a large optic."

Monroe keyed his mic, "Do you have a shot?"

A brief moment passed, every officer with a radio pausing to wait on the response.

On the sixth floor of the bank building, the sniper pressed a button protruding from the black box attached to his riflescope. The circular view inside the optic changed, red numbers flashing in sequence as a laser rangefinder scanned the doorframe next to Dusty's enlarged image. The readout in the sniper's eyepiece read 1260 meters, well within the range of the .338 Laupa Magnum chambered rifle.

"I have a shot."

Monroe didn't hesitate. "Take the shot."

"Sir," sounded the calm voice, "I need your authorization for the record."

"Monroe, Special Agent in Charge, BN171433 – take the shot."

"Acknowledged."

The ballistics computer mounted to the sniper's rifle was a marvel of modern technology. Fully integrated with the optic, rifle and even the actual round being fired, the shooter again pressed a single button, the action followed by small electric motors automatically adjusting the crosshairs for windage and bullet drop.

The spotter, watching Dusty's window with an even more powerful optic, looked at his teammate and instructed, "Send it."

The sniper pulled the trigger.

The .338 Lapua Magnum was named for the Swedish company that assisted in the cartridge's development. Designed as a possible replacement for the heavier .50 BMG round, the terminal ballistics of the bullet were considered by many experts to be the most efficient in the world.

By the 1990s, practically every military and police organization on the planet was evaluating weapons that fired the big cartridge.

A 250-grain bullet left the barrel, aimed 61 inches above the center mass of Dusty's chest, and traveling at 3,000 feet per second. After leaving the muzzle, there was nothing more the sniper could do but wait the nearly two seconds it would take for the round to impact on the target.

The microwave dinged again, the annoying sound reminding Dusty of the elevator's chime from down the hall. Frowning, he turned to shut the damn thing off so it would quit adding to his paranoia. He took one step toward the kitchen, and then the entire room exploded with flying glass and splinters of wood.

Dusty froze for just a moment, his racing mind unsure of what had just happened. Instinctively flinching into a crouch, he first thought someone had thrown a hand grenade into the room, but a quick glance at the door revealed it was still securely closed.

"Shit," mumbled the spotter, "I think he moved at the last moment. Switch to infrared."

The sniper nodded, pulling a small tubular device from his chest-rig and quickly snapping it onto the rifle in front of the optic. The view through the scope was now a world of bright hues, the new addition to his weapon displaying variations of color, each object reflecting different levels of heat. The human body, at an average of 98.6 degrees, normally showed solid red or yellow.

Dusty finally figured it out, a large bullet hole in the wall directly behind where he was standing just a moment before. "They're shooting at me from outside," he said aloud, and then he dove for the floor.

The curtains covering the sliding glass door blocked some of Dusty's body heat, but not all. While the thermal imager couldn't see through walls or solid objects, it could detect heat as it was transferred through fabric. The sniper caught Dusty's movement as he went prone, his mind thinking it was logical for the target to go low after the first missed shot. He pulled the trigger again, this time rushing the shot ever so slightly.

Ignoring the glass on the floor, Dusty was just starting to wiggle toward the window when the curtain puffed inward and a solid thud sounded behind him. The bullet's impact pulled the curtains partially off their rod, the uneven drapes creating a small opening that he could look through.

Glancing at the damage the bullet had caused in the wall, he judged the shooter was in a position higher than his condo, and that made sense. Any hunter preferred to be above his target if possible.

Despite shaking hands and short, nervous breathing, Dusty managed to move the rail gun to the opening and began searching the horizon, a desperate attempt to locate the man trying to kill him. It only took a moment to see the high-rise building in the distance, a bit more time and he realized that structure was the only possible option.

He was scanning floor by floor with his scope when a small flash and puff caught his eye. He rolled hard to his left as the bullet hit the doorframe not two inches away from his face.

Shards of aluminum stung his cheek, large pieces of the concrete sub-floor slashing his arm and shoulder. The pain changed Dusty. The fear seemed to melt away, replaced by a hot anger that boiled up inside him. They weren't even giving him a chance, not even making an attempt at an arrest. They were hunting him as if he were some animal, and it enraged him.

The green LED glowed bright, soon followed by the closing of a full breech. His hand brushed the power selector, turning it up. He really didn't know how much juice he was giving the rifle; he really didn't care at that point in time. Fully expecting another bullet to slam into his head, Dusty rolled back to the open window, centered the aiming laser's dot on the distant building and pulled the trigger.

The line appeared larger this time, its existence in earth's universe lasting longer. The darkest black streak ever witnessed by mankind flashed, drawing a super-black pencil mark between Dusty's wrecked balcony and the far-off bank building.

The stripe absorbed every color in the spectrum, sucking light, time, and all matter into another dimension. Then it was gone. Moving radially away from the core of the dimensional pipe, the blast wave shredded everything in its path.

A huge trench, over 20 feet wide and just as deep was plowed through the ground underneath the line of Dusty's shot. Trees were shredded; the roofs of buildings crushed inward, like the footprint of some giant monster had just walked through.

For blocks in every direction, a wall of supersonic air slammed into parked cars, street signs and pedestrians, knocking down anything in its path.

A cloud of dust, powdered concrete, pulverized pavement, and soil was thrown into the air. Rising almost 50 feet above the tortured ground, the airborne debris soon began mingling with the smoke of exploding automobiles, propane tanks and natural gas lines caught in the aftermath of Dusty's shot.

The inter-dimensional pipe met the bank building one floor below the sniper team. The FBI shooters experienced a slight shuddering, almost as if a small earthquake were rattling the structure. It was the last sensation they would ever feel. The entire building exploded, structural steel crumpling like tin foil, supporting concrete shredded into talcum powder.

Monroe was on the street below the bank building, watching and listening to the police communications through his earpiece. The small, tight-fitting, plastic speaker saved his hearing on that side, the other ear suffering a busted drum.

When the building above him started to collapse, there wasn't really any time to run. He managed two steps, diving for the back of a nearby car as chunks of cement, glass, and steel rained down on the area.

With his cheek against the cool pavement, Monroe cringed as the ground shook, the choking fog of debris burning his lungs and stringing his eyes. When it was all over, he pulled himself out from under the back of the car, kicking several large masses of wreckage out of the way.

When his vision finally cleared, the scene before him was unbelievable, the destruction stretching off into the distance. It was as if an enormous plow had swooped down from the sky, curling a furrow of devastation right through the middle of the urban area.

It took a few moments for the shock to wear off, a few more before the reason it had all happened to return to the forefront of his mind. Weathers!

After brushing off a thick layer of grime, he was stunned to see the radio transmitter on his belt still showing the red LED of power. He pushed to talk, "This is Monroe, any assault team on the command frequency, please respond."

He repeated the message a short time later, his voice becoming desperate. He thought they were all dead or badly injured. Finally, a weak voice sounded through the earpiece, "HRT unit one reporting, sir."

"Thank God," replied a relieved Monroe. "Go get that son of a bitch. Go right now."

"We're on our way."

Shultz appeared at his side, the junior agent covered from head to toe with a thick coating of dirt and white powder. A slight smile crossed Monroe's face, genuinely happy to see his co-worker had survived the attack.

Grabbing the still wobbly agent by the arm, Monroe said, "Come on, Tom, they're storming Weather's building. I want to be there to see the end."

Looking around, the two agents found every car in the vicinity heavily damaged. Not to be denied, Monroe hurried along on foot, determined to arrive in time to see his quarry either dead or in handcuffs.

Dusty chanced a glance around the doorframe a few seconds after his shot, uncomfortable with exposing himself and unsure if he'd eliminated the sniper threat.

What he saw caused his soul to go cold.

Starting below his balcony, it appeared as if a huge earth-moving machine had dug a trench from his condo all the way to the sniper's building. Anything that bordered the gash in the earth's surface was pushed away or toppled over, as if a massive downdraft had blown everything over.

Trees were snapped off at the base, entire sections of buildings crushed and crumbling, automobiles and trucks lying on their sides or roofs. The devastation was incredible.

The building... his target... was now a pile of rubble partially hidden by a column of smoke and dust. It was just gone.

Dusty looked at the rail gun as if to say, "You did that?" The power setting read 20%.

They'll be coming, he knew. *They'll really be pissed now.*

He jumped up and began throwing anything in sight into the pack. After it was stuffed full, he grabbed the messenger bag and began filling it. He started to leave his hat – the only thing he had left besides the gun from his previous life, but decided the cat was out of the bag and perched it on his head.

The rail gun was reloaded, the power lowered, and then he was out the door. Bounding down the steps two at a time, he expected to meet armed men at every turn, but the stairwell was empty. He ran out the back door and into the garage, the uneven load of his packs and weapon slowing the pace.

He unlocked the old truck, threw in his luggage and started the trusty V8.

He really didn't have a destination, no specific place in mind to run. His actions were born of desperation – a burning desire to just get away, as far away as he could. Again, distance equaled life.

Sergei and his men had been watching the law enforcement proceedings from the parking lot of the warehouse when the shooting had begun. When the FBI agent's voice had come through the scanner's speaker, ordering the snipers to shoot, the director had given the captain a glance showing respect for Monroe's tactic. He would have done the same.

They had been looking at the bank building when Dusty returned fire. At first, Sergei visualized a meteor slashing in from space and striking the area, but he quickly settled on the true reason. Despite their distance, the Russians' cars had been badly shaken by the blast wave. Again, a look of respect crossed Sergei's face – the weapon was truly a marvel, and he wanted to hold it in his hands.

It was clear that the American authorities had underestimated the backlash from the farmer. From his vantage, Sergei watched a line of HRT assaulters blown over by the shockwave, two nearby police cars now in flames, resting on their sides.

He couldn't blame the US commanders. After all, who knew this situation was a possibility? Who could have planned for such destruction delivered by a single man with a handheld weapon? He wanted to hold the device; he had plans for its proper utilization.

"We had better deploy," commented the always-stoic captain. "The Americans will recover and storm the farmer's building. We should be ready."

"Agreed. Make it so."

The director watched as his team deployed, their uniforms and equipment identical to the FBI HRT squads. It had been easy to equip them so, the patches and identification papers recreated from hours of news video on file at the agency, the weapons purchased from local gun stores in Houston. Helmets hid their face, fancy sunglasses covering their eyes. Even their own superiors would struggle to tell the difference.

Lighting a cigarette, Sergei leaned against the door of the rental, watching and listening as his men moved toward the farmer's building. He would have the gun soon, and then the world would change.

Dusty exited the parking garage and turned onto an empty street. He could hear sirens now... what seemed like thousands of sirens from every direction.

A block later, it dawned on him that the police had most likely closed the roads surrounding his condo. It made sense that they would evacuate people from the immediate area. With the vision of the destruction caused by his shot still fresh in his mind, the realization that the crushed buildings had most likely been devoid of people, helped him relax – a little.

The combination of random driving and the pattern of the streets pushed him south. He turned a corner and noted a roadblock up ahead, two police cars blocking the intersection, uniformed officers trying to control the flow of confused traffic.

Dusty started to turn away from the checkpoint at the first crossroad, but didn't. He had already spied another intersection controlled by the cops was just a short distance away. Again, it made sense that they would have cordoned off the entire area.

Glancing at the rail gun sitting in the seat beside him, a sick feeling began to creep into his stomach as he rolled slowly toward the cops. On the far side of their roadblock, a solid line of traffic was backed up as far as he could see. If he had to use the rail again, a lot of people were going to get hurt.

Two fire trucks and an ambulance were trying to make their way through snarl, desperate to reach the destruction behind him – their presence making the gridlock even more difficult for the cops to manage.

Evidently, not everyone had managed to get out before the battle. Dusty found himself in a short line of cars trying to exit the area but slowed by the manual control of the traffic by the officers ahead. One by one, the police were letting the cars in front of him pass – the officer leaning down and looking inside of each vehicle. A clash seemed inevitable.

With three cars in front of him, Dusty looked desperately for a way out. There was none – he was hemmed in. Beads of sweat formed on his forehead, his heart pounding in his ears.

Two cars now, a strong temptation to put the truck in park, jump out and run. It wouldn't work. They would converge on him from every direction and kill him. His arms were tingling, the back of his legs felt wet with fear.

One car left, his hand reaching for the gun. He didn't want to. He'd had enough for one day. A gross vision filling his head - what would the weapon do to a human being if fired point blank?

As Dusty rolled forward, he pulled the rail from the seat, bringing it across his lap. A figure appeared, out of nowhere, yelling something at the cop. Clad in black and carrying a battle rifle, the new arrival wore yellow patches declaring him FBI, smaller red swaths of cloth spelling the letters "HRT."

Before Dusty came to a complete stop, the FBI shooter was motioning for the cop, trying to get his attention, pointing at an approaching fire truck that was being blocked by a small sedan. The body language was clear, and Dusty could hear the voice shouting at the confused officer, "Fuck this – get those damn firemen into the zone – we've got shit burning out of control and people trapped."

Nodding his understanding, the cop turned away from Dusty's truck, moving with purpose toward the blocking sedan. Dusty hit the gas, accelerating past the police. He finally exhaled, as the checkpoint grew smaller in the review mirror.

Sergei flicked away the butt of his smoke, and then stopped – listening intently as an excited voice sounded in his ear. Something must have gone badly wrong because his captain was ordering an emergency recall back to the rental cars.

Looking up, the director could see his SPETZ team running at full speed back to the waiting vehicles. In front of the pack was their commander, shouting verbal orders for everyone to get in the cars – now!

Having confidence in the man, Sergei did as his captain wished. A moment later, the driver's side door flew open and then an assault rifle was flung inside. Reaching for the key and starting the engine, the SPETZ officer looked at the director and breathlessly managed, "The farmer is on the run," he gasped. "I helped him get out through a roadblock because the damn fool was getting ready to shoot it out with the American police. We have to hurry to catch him."

The captain spun the tires, without waiting on the rest of his team to arrive. Again Sergei approved of the decision, every second giving the farmer better odds of escaping.

As their lone car sped through the streets, Sergei listened to the captain's full report, finally nodding his agreement, impressed with the man's clear thinking. They could deal with the farmer on their own terms if they caught him away from the hundreds of policemen in the area. It would be better.

Six blocks later, they caught up with Dusty's truck, the American driving as if he were out for a casual day of shopping. A few minutes after spotting the old green truck, they were following close behind.

~ ~

Dusty was ill, his stomach churning and head pounding badly. He was driving slowly, convinced he was going to vomit at any moment. His body's protests at the recent turn of events demanded a quieter, more contemplative pace, that, or risk causing a fender bender.

He decided a drink of water might help. Reaching for the pack on the passenger floorboard, he ran a stop sign, a flash of blue paint appearing in his peripheral vision.

Slamming on the brakes and cutting the wheel, he watched in horror as a minivan barely missed his front bumper, the offended driver blaring on the horn.

Dusty straightened the truck and then glanced in his rearview mirror, hoping to see the van continuing on its way. The car immediately behind him had barely braked in time, almost adding a rear-end collision to his troubles. His glance revealed two men visible in the front seat, the bright yellow letters spelling out "FBI" clearly visible across the driver's chest.

Calm down, he ordered. *You don't know that they are after you. They might just be heading the same direction.*

Dusty started randomly turning, varying his speed and keeping a constant visual on the trailing car. After five minutes, he verified they were intentionally following him.

"He knows we're here," commented the captain, the obvious change in the farmer's driving making the statement unnecessary.

"Let's remain calm," replied Sergei, "this area is too populated for us to make any attempt. His vehicle is heavier than ours; he has superior firepower."

Dusty continued heading in a generally southern direction, his meandering path eating up time, but few miles. He was puzzled why they didn't try to pull him over. *They're scared of you*, he reasoned. *Maybe they're calling in reinforcements, perhaps even helicopters*. A quick scan of the sky showed no hovering gunships anywhere in sight.

At every turn, Dusty expected to see a roadblock ahead, but none appeared. Still, he knew the longer he allowed the FBI to stay back there, the less were his chances of escape. He started searching for some way to lose the tail.

A shopping mall loomed ahead, the facility not yet open at the early hour. Noting the parking lot was divided by several raised, concrete curbs, an idea popped into his head.

His truck had a higher clearance than the car behind. It should also have more tolerance for climbing over low barriers. He turned into the mall, accelerating ahead of his shadow.

Quickly discerning the pattern of the barriers, Dusty drew the tailing sedan into the maze. When he was close to the actual structure of the huge mall, he slowed and began driving over the curbs.

The truck lurched and ratted, its antique shocks and springs protesting the abuse - but it kept on going. Dusty prayed he wouldn't blow a tire as he was tossed side to side, forward and back. The car followed, but at a much slower pace. He was gaining distance, and that's all he expected.

Sergei's chest was pressed into the safety belt, and then he was thrown back against the seat. "Don't lose him," he gasped between jolting bumps. "He's just trying to make us stop."

"If we damage our car," replied the angry driver, "we'll never find him again."

Both Russians watched as the truck, now with a considerable lead, rounded the corner of the mall and disappeared from sight. "Go! Go! Go!" ordered Sergei, desperate not to lose their prey.

The pattern of curbs ended as the sedan accelerated around the corner of the building. No sooner than they had reached a good speed, the captain slammed on the brakes, sliding the tortured rental to a skidding stop. The Russians stared out of the still-rocking car, looking directly into the muzzle of the rail gun.

Dusty stood by the open door of the truck, pointing his weapon at the sedan, unsure of what to do next. He was tempted to just fire on the vehicle and take off, but some fiber of honor wouldn't allow him to pull the trigger.

The passenger-side door opened, an older man slowly exiting the car. He kept his hands in the classic, "Don't shoot," position.

"I mean you no harm," came the oddly accented voice. "My name is Sergei, I am Russian."

Tilting his head in confusion, Dusty replied, "What do you want?"

"I only want what you have in your hand. I have traveled with these men from Moscow in hopes of procuring that weapon. I want to bargain with you."

Grunting at the irony of it all, Dusty replied, "I'm sorry you traveled so far, but it's not for sale."

"Please, please hear me out. My country cannot let the technology you have discovered fall into the hands of the United States, or any other nation. We understand its potential, and to be honest, we're frightened of it. I want to destroy the weapon, not use it. I can offer you money, freedom, and a way to escape."

Dusty considered the man's words, a mixture of emotions flooding his mind. His initial reaction was anger

– pissed that a foreign government was offering to negotiate while his own beloved country hunted him down like a rabid dog. Distrust flowed next – everyone knew you couldn't trust the Russkies. He finally settled on the fact that it wouldn't hurt to let the man speak.

"Go on."

"I can obtain a large amount of cash in any currency you wish. I can provide passports and other documents under any country or name you choose. I can get you out of the United States safely. If you will exchange the weapon you hold for these things, I will promise to destroy it. After some time passes, we will contact your government and prove the device no longer exists. There will be no reason to pursue you further. Even if the US authorities do chase you, you will be a wealthy man. You could choose to live elsewhere, or come home and fight the charges against you. All of these things I can do."

Dusty pondered over the man's offer, images of Hank and Grace being released from their cells, visions of one day returning to his ranch filling his mind. "I have two questions," Dusty stated. "The first is why? Why would you do this? The second is how do I know you'll destroy the rail gun?"

"Da! These are excellent questions," the man smiled. "As I said, I do this because we cannot let the device loose in this world. My country, Mother Russia... we eat because we sell arms to other nations. Your gun would make obsolete everything we manufacture, and our people would go hungry. As to a guarantee of destruction, this I cannot provide. There must be some trust between us... no?"

The man seemed genuine, his argument somehow logical. The Russian's next action made even more sense. Looking around the expansive, empty parking lot, he said, "We cannot stay here. This place is too open, and soon your American police will spot us. I will give you a telephone number. Call me with your agreement and terms. You set the time and place, and I'll be there. Be reasonable with your demands, and I will do my best to meet them. Is this, as you Americans say, a deal?"

Dusty had to agree, the wide-open spaces of the lot making him feel exposed. He nodded, "Deal."

The Russian reached for his breast pocket, stopping instantly when Dusty tensed and re-centered the rail gun's aim. Moving slowly, Sergei produced a notepad and pen. He scribbled a phone number on the paper and then bent down, leaving the sheet on the pavement. Pausing for a moment, he slowly reached into another pocket and produced a cell phone. Showing the device to Dusty, he said, "This phone is untraceable by your authorities. Use it to call me at the number on the paper." Without another word, he pivoted and returned to the waiting car.

After a quick exchange inside, the engine revved, and then the sedan was rolling across the lot. Dusty watched it fade to a safe distance before walking over to retrieve the phone and number. He needed time to think, but wanted to get away from the mall as soon as possible.

Agent Monroe splashed cold water on his face, and then looked around for a towel in Dusty's ex-kitchen. He couldn't find one, which raised the level of his frustration even higher. Most of the forensics team wandering around the condo were avoiding him, his constant scowl and angry demeanor a clear warning to give the man some space.

At least his cell phone wasn't working, that in itself a positive situation. The suspect's attack with his super weapon had destroyed at least two electrical grids and one natural gas line. The Houston Fire Department was still fighting multiple secondary blazes. Cell service was down for much of the south side of town.

So far, the death toll had been remarkably low. The three-man sniper team in the bank building had perished in the line of duty, four other HPD officers killed by the concussion of the blast wave.

The number of injured was staggering, the close proximity to the vast number of hospitals in the area a blessing. The last count he'd heard put the number of wounded at over 150, many of them critical.

Traffic was now being affected all over the city. As word of the incident spread, many people feared another terrorist attack and decided to leave their places of employment. The ensuing exodus hit the streets at the wrong time. Between the cordoned off area around the condo and the powerless traffic lights, thousands of nervous, frightened commuters sat hopelessly gridlocked on the city streets. This caused a secondary issue – first responders struggling to make it to the people who desperately needed their help.

Shultz appeared at his boss's side, the look on his subordinate's face making it clear he was about to deliver more bad news. "No sign of him, boss. We've swept this building and everything else in the area. He obviously made it through our perimeter, which isn't surprising given the confusion after the attack."

Nodding without comment, Monroe wandered to the sliding glass doors, looking over the destruction below. For a brief moment, he considered resigning. He felt beaten... defeated by a lowly gunsmith from some hick town in West Texas.

Despite all of the resources under his command, he hadn't been able to capture one lone cowboy. The man hadn't even gone to college – had never held a professional job in his life.

The train of thought began to work on Monroe, reflectively surveying the decimation of what had once been an affluent, thriving area. Now it looked like a war zone – like pictures he'd seen of German cities during WWII. His anger began to burn, a drive to bring the person responsible for the scene below to justice.

He wouldn't resign – wouldn't quit in disgrace. He would not give Weathers the satisfaction. He would find the man and kill him – then resign. A fitting end for his career.

Turning to Shultz, he quietly said, "Tom, take me home. I need a shower and change of clothes. As soon as they finish here, have the team do the same. We'll meet later at the office."

~ ~

Dusty kept driving, the Russian's offer competing in his mind with the horrible images at the Medical Center. A dash of paranoia and the hangover of an adrenaline dump didn't help his attitude or his throbbing head.

He needed to find someplace to hide, but it wasn't so simple. Using Maria's listings was now definitely out. The cops would surely be onto that game by now. Hotels were also out of the question. That left campgrounds, underpasses and parking lots, none of which sounded attractive at the moment.

He turned down another road he'd never traveled, relieved at least to not be going in circles. He wondered how long it would be before the police figured out what he was driving – how he'd gotten away. He needed shelter... someplace to sit, relax, and work things through.

A sign ahead caught his eye, the neon announcing "Southwest Storage," and a possible solution occurred to him. He knew that many storage places were used as garages for project cars, campers, and boats. Would his truck fit inside such a place?

He signaled his turn and parked, sitting in the truck and garnering what information he could from the assortment of signs posted on the office windows. He had no idea if identification was required to rent space.

He turned off the truck and stepped inside, the elderly lady working behind the counter acknowledging him with a weak smile. Dusty noted her glasses were extremely thick, which might mean she wouldn't be able to identify him from the television pictures.

"I'm moving soon and need to store my project-truck," he lied. "Can I rent a storage shed for a few days?"

"Our shortest agreement is 30 days," she replied coldly.

"How much does 30 days cost?"

"That depends. Do you need it climate controlled? Do you need electricity inside the unit?"

Dusty had no idea such features existed for a storage area. "Climate-controlled might be good. Can I work on the truck while it's stored here?"

"You can do anything you want as long as it's not illegal, and you don't harm our building. You can sleep inside for all I care."

Little did she know, mused Dusty. "Okay, I'll take climate-controlled with electricity. How much?"

The woman nodded, and began punching numbers into a calculator. "That will be $180 dollars."

"Let's do it," he replied, peeling off two $100 bills.

The paperwork required the usual name and address, phone number, and other such details. He was ready for it this time, using the name of a high school teacher and a fictitious address in Houston. He was then assigned a number and given a gate code so he could enter at all hours. "You're responsible for your own padlock," she warned. "We've never had an issue here, but I advise all of our customers to lock their access door."

And just like that, the old Chevy was rolling through the electronic gate, heading for unit #905.

He parked in front of what appeared to be a common garage door. Turning and lifting the handle, he was greeted with a rush of cool air, a clean concrete floor and a single florescent light hanging from the ceiling. *Home sweet home*, he declared. *You're really moving up in the world, cowboy.*

A few minutes later, the truck was backed in and the door closed. Relief flowed through his body, the reprieve eventually allowing his stomach to settle enough to forage through his pack for something to eat. A package of jerky and a bottle of water would hold him for a while.

He had taken the battery out of the Russian's phone, a bit of paranoia making him wonder if the device didn't contain some sort of tracking mechanism or locater. It dawned on him that the unit might have more than one power cell, so he dumped it into the jerky's empty foil wrapper, content with his defeat of the sneaky foreign spies.

Next, he lowered the tailgate and began spreading out his few remaining earthy possessions, the hasty grab before exiting the condo now a blur. There really wasn't much to inventory.

He opened the door again, checking around the area more from habit than any perceived threat. It would be a while before the sun went down, the thought of darkness being more secure than broad daylight. Satisfied that the police weren't getting ready to storm his storage bin, he closed the door and trekked back to the tailgate.

Exhaustion began to take hold. He caught himself yawning, his eyes tired from the stress. He eyed the pickup's bed, remembering long days on the ranch and sleeping underneath a shade tree after lunch. He spread out the empty packs and made a cot.

Ten minutes later, #905 was filled with the gentle rustle of snoring.

Day 18 - Night

"We've filtered the Predator drone's image database, sir," the tech reported to Monroe. There were 116 cars and trucks that were videotaped leaving the exclusion zone between the time when the HRT entered Weathers apartment and his attack on the bank building. We only have license plates on about one quarter of these vehicles due to the angle; another 26 had toll road passes with broadcast chips – the rest we are analyzing at this time."

Monroe nodded his acceptance of the report, otherwise offering no comment.

The next agent to address the meeting passed around a one-page report, summarizing the information uncovered about the condo where the suspect had been holed up. "You'll notice who the real estate agent was on that unit," he pointed out. "We already have teams searching all of her other listings. I assume you want to interview Ms. Weathers personally, sir?"

"We have no evidence that his ex-wife knew of his habitation, or that she assisted him in any way. She's only going to claim that her ex knew her key code and could have found the listing on the internet. It's on my to-do list, but not a priority. My gut says she knew, but right now we've got more important leads to follow up," Monroe offered.

The low-key tone and outlook displayed by the boss worried several members of his team. Conjecture varied about the cause for his odd mood, none of the speculation positive. Some people believed he had been beaten by the case – a broken man limping through the motions.

Others decided he was getting ready to break down and go rogue – most likely shooting Weathers on sight, regardless of the circumstances.

A few felt sorry for the boss, sure he was being harassed by every elected official from the president on down to the city hall mail clerk.

Tom Shultz was the only one who had neither offered an opinion, nor believed the investigation was in trouble. While he never voiced his thoughts, the #2 man on the team believed that Monroe was upping his game, finally getting serious.

His boss's next statement was about to shake Shultz's commitment to the man.

"I'm going to ask the president to allocate military assets to this office. The device Weathers is using against us is more powerful than anyone imagined. We're still not sure of its capabilities. We may need more force than what the department is capable of fielding alone."

Mouths dropped open around the table, a few people audibly inhaling. To a US law enforcement agency, calling in military assets was akin to declaring martial law. The implication was a loss of control – the inability to enforce rule of law. Failure.

Interdepartmental squabbles over jurisdiction and authority were bad enough – bringing in the military was sure to invoke legal and procedural anarchy. It was already difficult enough to coordinate the ongoing manhunt across numerous departments; the military would make things worse.

To make matters worse, Monroe rose as if to leave the meeting, offering no further explanation or opportunity for questions. Seeing the look on everyone's face, he paused and scanned the room.

"I'm only seeking a few hi-tech helicopters, perhaps an armored vehicle or two. Don't worry, I'm not requesting troops."

The explanation helped a little, but the precedent had been set. Almost as an afterthought, Monroe turned and dropped the second bombshell.

"My apologies... I forgot to mention that I'm requesting the DOJ release Grace Kennedy. I'm not convinced that she had prior knowledge, nor is she involved directly with the weapon."

Before anyone could comment, Special Agent in Charge Monroe turned and left the room.

Shultz, stunned, rose up and followed his boss back to his office. Closing the door behind him, the junior agent said, "Sir, I'm sure you have your reasons, but I ..."

Monroe cut him off, "Let me ask you something – do you think Grace Kennedy and Weathers had a romantic interest going on?"

Shaking his head at the boss's change of direction, Shultz couldn't answer right away. "I... I don't know, sir. I guess it's possible."

"I think it's more than possible, Tom. I think it's probable. That's why I believe if Ms. Kennedy is released, Weathers will try and contact her. I'm letting her go to bait Weathers. We'll be ready to set the hook."

The nap made Dusty feel like a new man – sort of. While the few hours of rest were good for his mind and attitude, sleeping on the hard metal surface of the truck bed wasn't appreciated by his aching muscles and stiff vertebra.

Opening the garage door enough to bend and look outside, he found the sun had set. The cool air felt good, the lack of SWAT teams ready to shoot him down even better.

A short distance from the entrance to the storage facility, he'd seen a cluster of fast food restaurants. The slight breeze carried the smell of cooking hamburgers, so he decided to go for a walk. The exercise would help his back – eating some hot food would improve life in general.

On the way out of the storage complex, he passed a couple unloading a hatchback's small cargo area into their bin. The man was peeking inside a container, holding up an item, and yelling at his spouse, "Honey, I thought you didn't want to keep this box?"

The woman appeared at his side, peering at the contents. "Oh, damn it. I meant to throw those away. Carry them over to the dumpster, would ya?"

About then, the man noticed Dusty and smiled. Tipping his hat, mostly to cover his face, Dusty continued past without incident. *Nowhere is safe*, he said to himself.

The burger joint was a national chain, complete with a playground for the little ones and a wide assortment on the menu. Uncomfortable with the well-lit dining area, he placed his order to go. Safely away from the bright lights and endless cars at the drive-up window, Dusty enjoyed the walk back. There was little traffic on the route, his chosen path behind a strip mall and two empty lots kept him well away from the street.

The tailgate again acted as his dinner table, the paper food wrappers his plates. *With the lights out and door open, this is like dining at a sidewalk café*, he mused.

As he boiled it all down, there were only two problems he had to solve. First and foremost, he had to get Hank and Grace out of jail. Secondly, he had to find somewhere to live while Mitch worked his plan. Yes, the Russians were an issue, but he didn't know the extent of their commitment or involvement. If he disappeared, wouldn't they?

He still believed that the only way he was going to obtain his friends' release was by eliciting public outcry at the injustice of it all. The destruction today, no doubt blamed on him, would hinder that effort for some period of time. He had to have faith that the hungry reporter, Crawford, would do the heavy lifting on that front.

Dipping the delicious French fries into a small puddle of ketchup, he determined there wasn't anything he could do about the reporter for a few days. While the vision of Grace and Hank being locked up even one more day was discouraging, he couldn't figure out another method of securing their freedom.

His funds were limited. There was a considerable balance in his account back at Fort Davis, but he knew those monies were out of reach. Maria, at great risk, had helped, but he couldn't see her taking the chance of being arrested. Such a disaster would destroy her name - everything she'd worked for. Anthony would be crushed.

The lack of cash was everything - the fulcrum of the issue. Without resorting to a life of crime, he couldn't figure out how to overcome his cash crunch. If he were well funded, then travel, temporary residence in a foreign land, or even a secluded spot in the USA might be within reach. Poverty was not only hell, it was a set of virtual handcuffs restraining his freedom.

Chewing another bite of his sandwich, Dusty considered how he could raise money. With the rail gun, robbing a bank or business would be easy physically, difficult mentally. He could also pull a "Robin Hood," hitting a drug dealer or thief for his loot and redistributing it to the needy – namely himself. The problem there was he didn't know where such villains were located and didn't think it would be wise to drive around Houston's less affluent areas trying to obtain a target.

The Russians claimed to have money, but he had a sneaking suspicion they weren't easy men to take advantage of. *Stop being egotistical*, he chided, *all of these men know more about violence and the dark side of human nature than you do. You're an amateur playing dangerous games with professionals.*

He finished his meal, wadding up the paper wrappers and empty ketchup packets. He left the bin and headed for the dumpster with his garbage. As he approached, he noticed two boxes lying beside the large green trash receptacle. He was reminded of the couple he'd seen on the way to the burger joint. Curious more than anything else, he bent and opened the top of one. It was full of discarded clothing. The other, he soon discovered, contained old beach towels.

Dusty tossed his garbage over the top and then decided to do a little trash picking. Scooping up one box under each arm, he headed back to his cubby to investigate his newfound treasures. "You're really moving up in the world, Weathers. Dumpster diving is a sign of achievement in life," he whispered to no one.

The clothing wasn't even close to his size – no reward there. The beach towels, however, seemed clean and only slightly worn. They would make an excellent pad to sleep on, softening the old Chevy's sheet metal bunk. An old section of garden hose rounded out the treasure.

He sat the unwanted clothing aside, rags that might come in handy later. A stroll and fresh air seemed like a good idea, so he began walking the facility. There really wasn't much to see... three rows of low, single-story buildings – each looking like a wealthy car collector's dream garage. Other than that, the place was about as featureless as one could imagine.

One thing did catch his eye. At the end of each building was a ladder, welded onto the side of the building and leading to the roof. Curious, Dusty climbed to peer over the edge.

The first thing he noticed was the air movement. His building was sandwiched between two others, those structures blocking the slight breeze. He continued onto the pea-gravel covered roof, enjoying the cool wind on his face. He could hear the distant rumble of a freight train's passage, the sound a calming backdrop in the night. Car lights were visible on the horizon, so distant their pinpoint lights were as silent as the stars.

It felt better up here. He had a considerable vantage, all the way to the entrance of the facility and the road beyond. He'd have warning if anyone approached. There was something else though – some feeling of openness that resonated within him. He decided to sleep on the roof.

Before long, he was climbing back up the ladder, his bedroll of old beach towels, a bottle of water and the rail gun stuffed in his pack. He made a bed, used the empty pack as a pillow and pulled off his boots.

Dusty settled in and relaxed – a plan beginning to form in his head. He tried to work every angle, play out every move in advance. Fatigue finally overwhelmed his scheming, but not before he'd concluded it just might work. The comfort of a workable solution eased his stress and finally allowed him to drift off.

Grace heard someone walking down the hall toward her cell, an unusual activity at this hour. She'd been given a stack of books, reading the only thing that had allowed her sanity to remain intact during her incarnation.

The lights went out at 10 p.m. sharp, the advanced ritual and control of every aspect of her life a constant reminder that she wasn't a free woman. She couldn't imagine how anyone could spend years in confinement without insanity. Maybe that's why there were so many repeat criminals, she had decided.

Now someone was walking through the detention area after lights out. This hadn't happened the entire time she'd been locked up.

Her heart rate increased slightly when the lights in her cell came on, her pulse rising even more when a key entered the lock on her door. The face of a female jailer appeared in the small, chicken wire, reinforced window set in the door – a procedure to make sure the prisoner wasn't hiding in wait to attack the guard. Grace remained on her cot, a curious expression on her face.

The door opened, and a woman's voice said, "Grace Kennedy, you are to come with me."

"Where are we going?"

"You are being released. Now please come with me."

At first, she thought it was a joke – another cruel technique dreamed up by overzealous FBI agents – a weak attempt to get her to talk. Studying the guard's stoic face, Grace decided the woman deserved an academy award for acting if it really was a joke.

Fine, she resolved. *If they're resorting to sleep deprivation as a method of interrogation, they must be getting desperate.*

As she walked in front of the jailer, her faith in the guard's words increased with every step. By the time they entered a locker-room type facility, her heart was soaring.

On a counter lay the box containing her personal possessions that had been taken away the day of her arrest. The guard made her re-inventory its contents and sign the receipt, then she was left alone to "clean up and dress in street clothes."

It didn't take her long. Then she was escorted to another conference room where a young man waited, a stack of papers sitting on the table in front of him.

He introduced himself as a lawyer from the Department of Justice, here to expedite the necessary paperwork for her release.

The man droned on and on, warning Grace not to leave the country without notifying the authorities, warning her not to speak publicly about her case, as it had not been dismissed. She was given worthless instructions on how to hail a cab, in case she needed a ride home. He handed her a list of women's shelters in the Houston area, in case she didn't have a home to go back to.

Grace didn't care about any of it, listened to even less of what the man was saying. She had her car keys, purse, wallet and cell phone. She was going to be free.

Twenty minutes later, she was let out a door on the side of the federal building. She remembered where her car was parked and made for the garage. The streets were deserted, the area badly lit. She wasn't scared.

The Mercedes started without protest. Her cell was dead, but the car charger had the battery strong enough to call Maria before she hit the interstate.

"Maria, this is Grace. They've let me go. I hope I'm still welcome at your home."

"Oh, my gawd! Grace, that's such good news. Yes... yes of course you're welcome here. Eva and I were just having a cup of decaf."

"I'll be there soon. I'm dying for a long shower and change of clothes. A cup of good coffee sounds pretty good, too."

"I'll have it ready for you. This is such a wonderful turn of events!"

"Any word on Dusty? I'm wondering if they let me go because he was captured... or worse."

"You've got a lot to catch up on, but no, as far as I know, he's still on the loose. There's been another incident, a bad one. But he's still on the dodge the last I've heard."

After disconnecting the call, Grace's excitement began to fade. Why had they let her go? Why now? She was sure that Agent Monroe hadn't orchestrated her release without a reason; she doubted it was his kind nature. There had to be a motive.

Day 19

Dusty woke on the roof, the sun not yet clearing the horizon in the east. He took his time before standing, giving his stiff body a bit to circulate the blood and loosen tight muscles. He wanted coffee.

After checking the area and finding he was the only thing moving so early, he climbed down and entered the bin. After a quick brushing of his teeth using a few gulps of bottled water, he decided to walk back to the burger chain and buy a cup of coffee.

He arrived without drama. Glancing at the condiment counter, he spied a stack of small plastic cups, normally filled with ketchup from a hand pump mounted nearby. Making sure he was unobserved, he snatched one of the containers before entering the men's room.

After finishing his business, he filled the little ketchup cup with soap from the dispenser and sealed the lid tight. He'd use the suds later.

He was the first customer in, as far as he could tell. His order of hash browns, an egg sandwich, and the biggest cup of java offered was ready when he exited the restroom.

The walk back passed without incident, very little traffic yet on the road. He dined behind the wheel instead of sitting on the tailgate, his backside appreciating the softer seat. *The Maître' D gave you a better table this time*, he mused. *It pays to tip generously.*

Sipping his hot brew, Dusty picked up where he'd left off the night before – plotting like a rat desperate to escape his trap. It all seemed so much simpler now – the sleep had helped. Again and again he worked through it, step by meticulous step.

He glanced at his watch, the timepiece indicating it was 6:50 a.m. *There's still time to do this before it gets busy around here,* he decided.

Starting the truck, he drove the short distance to the strip mall and pulled around to the back. He removed the Russian's cell phone from its tinfoil cage and replaced the battery. Sergei answered on the second ring.

"Da," sounded the sleepy voice on the other end.

"This is Dusty. I've decided to take you up on your offer, but this is not going to be a dime store transaction. I will need resources to survive independent of my past life. Do you still want to do the deal?"

"Yes, yes of course. What is it that you ask?"

"I want a Canadian passport, driver's license, and supporting documents under the name of Anthony Maxwell Booker. Throw in 200 South African gold Krugerrands, one million in US dollars, and one million Euros, cash. Also, a .45 Glock pistol, two spare magazines, and 100 rounds of quality ammo."

For a moment, Dusty worried that he'd asked for too much, nothing but breathing coming through the earpiece. Finally, the accented voice said, "The gold will take a little bit of time, but it can be done. The rest is not such a problem. I will need two days."

"Two days is acceptable," Dusty replied, trying desperately to keep the nervousness out of his voice.

"Call me back in 48 hours. We'll make arrangements for the exchange at that time," and the line went dead.

Dusty repeated the process of removing the battery and sealing the phone in tinfoil, and then drove back to his garage-hideout. Step one had gone as planned, perhaps better. Now it was going to get tricky.

He had spotted a pawnshop on his way in. After parking in a secluded spot and waiting a while, the small business finally opened. Dusty walked out with a used laptop and a cheap riflescope a short time later.

He returned to the burger joint, the place advertising free Wi-Fi. It took him a bit, but he finally figured out how to connect his new computer to the service. Remaining in the truck, he began researching the next phase of his plan.

He needed someplace that would provide cover and yet allow for a reasonable chance of escape if things went wrong. He wanted the FBI to know the Russians were in the game, but the timing of their awareness was critical. As the old saying went, timing was everything.

The internet's capability to display satellite maps was a savior. The high-tech, bird's eye view of his surroundings an invaluable tool for his scheme. Patiently, he scrolled around images of Houston and the surrounding areas, a checklist of features in his mind. Notes were scribbled, locations bookmarked, the laptop's processor burning hot in his lap.

Inspired by the easy source of coffee, Dusty sat for hours in the parking lot. Twice he drained the laptop's battery – a situation that required a trip back to his storage-hideout to recharge his primary tool. He was okay with it, venturing away from the restaurant's lot keeping the manager from becoming suspicious. It also provided a chance for him to stretch his legs and walk around. *How do these people who work in an office all day long do this?* He wondered.

It was almost 6 p.m. when he finished, his back sore from sitting in the Chevy's non-conforming front seat for so many hours. He had one last task to accomplish before the stores started closing. Verifying his cup of coffee was still half-full, he started the truck and exited the parking lot. The game was about to officially begin, and once the clock stated, there was no turning back.

Day 20

The driver smiled at Paula, taking back his mobile terminal after she'd signed for the packages. She'd flirted with him practically every day for over a year now and he just wasn't taking the bait. Shrugging her shoulders, she looked at the three next-day envelopes he'd delivered and began tearing open the perforated ends.

The first contained a marked-up contract from a perspective buyer Maria had been courting for over a month. The man was from Seattle, completely anal over every minor detail of the home he was buying. She grimaced at the number of changes he'd requested on the document. The boss wasn't going to be happy.

The next package brought a frown to her face. A hand-lettered, common white envelope was inside, sealed and addressed as; "Personal and confidential – Maria Weathers only."

"Now, that's odd," she whispered. "Why would anyone do that?"

Shrugging her shoulders, she placed the item in Maria's inbox and continued on to the third delivery.

True to her word, Maria arrived at the office shortly after 10, her workout clothes evidence of the morning's activities. The broker stood at the corner of Paula's desk, shuffling through messages and then picking up the mail. The plain white envelope drew its second frown of the day.

Picking up her gym bag without another word, Maria entered her office and closed the door. She recognized the block print on the letter, and it made her stomach churn.

How clever, she reasoned. *No way the cops would intercept a next day package.*

She sat at her desk before opening it — looking at the letter as if it was a snake about to strike. Gently tearing open one end, she pulled out two sheets of paper and began reading:

My Dear Maria,

I wanted to drop you one last note before I depart. I have arranged for transportation on a foreign-flagged freighter leaving the United States. I'm saddened to be leaving my country forever. I will miss you, our son, and my land.

I know this news is probably welcome. I'm sure the authorities are pressuring you. I know you probably won't, but if there is any chance you can get away, my boat leaves from pier #19 tomorrow at 10:30 a.m., the Houston Ship Channel. I would like to see you one last time if you can push our history aside.

Tell Anthony his father loves him and is proud of him. One day, please tell him the truth about me — what I stood for, how I lived my life.

Yours Truly,

Dusty

What is he doing? He's up to something, she wondered as she turned to the second page. It, again, was another note, the block printing that was so Dusty scrolling across the page.

Maria — The first letter was for you to hand over to the authorities. I want them at the ship channel tomorrow. Turn me in for the reward. I want you to. I need you to. When the Dust (y) settles, you'll understand.

The letter was signed with a smiley face — a cute little secret code they had used during the marriage to let the other know everything was okay. He hadn't used it for years.

Exhaling, she separated the two pages and gathered herself. Pulling a pair of scissors from her drawer, she quietly cut the second page into small bits and then flushed them down the toilet. *Let the FBI men go swimming in the sewer if they want to see that*, she mused. The first page was folded and placed in her purse.

Paula knocked on the door and then stuck her head inside. "Are you okay?"

"No," the boss replied. "Something has come up, and I'm going home for a bit."

"You don't look good. Is there anything I can do?"

Maria considered her response for a bit, deciding to practice her act before a friendly audience first. Conscious that federal ears were probably listening, she reached into her handbag and withdrew the letter. "This is what was in that envelope," she said.

Paula scanned the note, her lips moving as she read. After finishing, she looked up at Maria and simply whispered, "Oh my God," followed shortly by, "What are you going to do?"

"I'm sick and tired of my ex-husband interfering with my life. I can't risk my business or reputation any longer. He's killed people and hurt the city of Houston badly. It will take years for the Medical Center to recover. That note is proof – he's gone completely over the edge. I think I'm going to call the FBI."

Nodding, the assistant handed the page back. "I don't blame you," she said, a supportive tone in her words. "I was worried you were going to actually go and meet him."

"No, I'm going home. I'm sure the police are going to want to see that letter, and I don't want a bunch of cops hanging around here and scaring off customers. Hold down the fort – I'll be back in after I've turned everything over to them."

Then as an afterthought, Maria added, "Get me the number of that cute lawyer up in The Woodlands. I'm going to have him meet me at the house – just in case."

Maria stood to leave, her friend and co-worker coming around the desk to hug the troubled woman. "Good luck – you're doing the right thing you know."

Grace's confidence grew every day, recovering quickly after being released. Her spirit and sense of injustice motivating her to invest all of her energies in order to obtain Hank's freedom. Since being let go, she'd drained the battery in her cell phone three times, calling every judge, attorney friend, and law school professor she knew. Agent Monroe had surprised her once, she was determined not to let that happen again.

Eva had helped as much as she could. Taking on the persona of a law clerk, the woman seemed competent with internet searching, happy to look up any subject and filter useless results. Grace was building a case, but it was a tedious, lengthy process.

Her progress was slowed by high emotions, both hers and Eva's. After reading reams of web-based news reports covering every angle of Durham's escapades downtown and at the Medical Center, she had struggled to correlate what was being said, with what she knew about the man. A man, she admitted, she cared deeply about.

Often she would find her mind wandering off Hank's case – wondering what had really happened...

how it had changed Durham. The vision of a frightened man, all alone and being chased by the whole world pulled at her heart. The fact that people had died, apparently due to his actions, confused the issue and frustrated her.

The two legal eagles had converted Maria's breakfast nook into what they had taken to calling "the war room." The large table completely covered with papers, two laptops, legal references checked out from the local library, a phone charger and coffee cups completed the effect. The sound of their host's car pulling into the driveway was unexpected, both women looking up with concern.

Maria entered her home, walking past the nook on her way to the master bedroom. Grace could tell something was wrong immediately. "Everything okay?"

"Yes… yes… everything's fine. I'm going to work at home today, ladies. I'll use my office so as not to interrupt your efforts. I may have some visitors stopping by later."

Odd, thought Grace. *The woman is out of character. Something is going on.* Shrugging it off as most likely something to do with Maria's real estate business, she returned to study the legal opinion displayed on the laptop's screen.

A few hours later, a young man rang the doorbell. Again, Grace noticed Maria carried herself differently, rushing to greet the gentleman. Rather than introduce him to her guests, the hostess guided the new arrival directly to her office and closed the door.

Don't make too much of it, she concluded. *We've been intruding here for days now, and I'm sure Maria has private dealings as much as anyone else.*

Grace continued with her work, the behind-closed door meeting passing without either party so much as exiting the private space to use the powder room. The doorbell rang again.

Now, her curiosity spiked, she rose from the table quickly, determined to answer the new call. Again, Maria beat her to the punch. Grace's heart froze when she saw Agent Monroe standing in the threshold. *Am I going to be arrested again?*

Just like the first visitor, Monroe and another of his henchmen was escorted into the home office. The door was closed behind them.

Grace's mind raced with the possibilities, but couldn't settle on an explanation for the weird goings on. She decided to do a little sneaking around herself. She stood and stretched as if the hours of study left her body extraordinarily stiff. Turning to Eva she announced, "I think I need to move around a little and get my blood circulating again. I'll be right back. I have to run upstairs anyway and retrieve a file I fell asleep reading last night," and headed for her second floor guestroom. Ascending the stairs as quietly as possible, she walked carefully across the floor, hoping to pass without any squeaking. She entered her temporary bedroom and closed the door gently.

Going to her hands and knees, Grace put her ear to the heating register installed in the floor. She'd heard Maria's voice once before, not surprising since her room was right above the office.

She could hear the conversation below clearly, but didn't believe the words that reached her ears. Maria was turning Dusty over to the FBI! For a reward!

She listened with a growing anger as her host's lawyer outlined the documents he'd created – legal papers that gave Maria immunity and outlined a trust account where the electronic payment of $25 million was to be deposited. The entire conversation made her sick.

She was about to storm downstairs and barge in. She wanted to grab Maria by the hair and slap some sense into the woman. What she heard next stopped her from going on the offensive.

"I also want you're guarantee that Hank Barns will be released immediately."

Agent Monroe's voice floated through the vent. "Yes, as soon as Mr. Weathers is no longer on the streets, I will release Mr. Barns."

Maria responded, "Then we are in agreement. I have a letter here that I received from Dusty this morning via next day delivery. As you can see, he has suggested that I meet him down at the Houston Ship Channel, before 10:30 a.m. tomorrow morning – pier #19. He claims he has found transportation out of the US."

Grace didn't hear the rest of the conversation, the blood rushing through her ears canceling all sensory input. She couldn't believe Maria was doing this, yet she didn't want to take any chance on jeopardizing Hank's release.

She sat with her back against the wall, trying to sort it all out.

Finally composing herself, she reached a determination. She'd get Hank out on her own – she had to warn Dusty of Maria's treachery.

Sergei stuffed the cigarette into the ashtray, bending the filter over the cherry to extinguish the smoke. The bathroom door opened, a younger, blonde haired woman crossing into the main part of the suite. She showed no sign of embarrassment that he was awake, casually walking past while drying strands of damp hair with a towel.

"They have an ingenious device called a blow dryer, I believe. It is used by females after taking a shower."

Grunting, she replied, "I'm well aware of such things, Sergei. I don't like using heat because it makes my hair brittle."

He continued to watch as she moved about the room, unashamed of her nakedness. Buxom, with strong shoulders and wider at the hip than most western men preferred, Arianna was typical of good, solid Russian peasant stock. Capable of working in the field all day, the kitchen all evening, and the bedroom all night, the young woman benefited from years of generic advantages.

She hadn't been recruited into the SRV because of her looks; raw sex appeal had nothing to do with her advancements. Arianna was brilliant with numbers and equations. The fact that she possessed a healthy libido and volunteered to exercise it with the director of her agency was a happy bonus for both.

She moved close to him, picking up his pack of cigarettes from the bedside table. After lighting her smoke, she sat beside him, a look of concern on her face. "I'm still not sure what it is you want me to do tomorrow," she stated. "I know you didn't go to the trouble of flying me in from Moscow just for good sex."

"Tomorrow there is going to be an exchange with the farmer who invented the rail gun I was telling you about. I want you there to examine the weapon during the trade."

Shaking her head, Doctor Sharapova replied, "There's not much I can do, really. Without equipment and a lab, about the only assurance I can render is entirely speculation. Besides, as I told you on the phone before, I don't believe the weapon is as powerful as claimed. It would defy the known laws of physics."

"I understand, Arianna. You are an insurance policy against the American playing any games. When we meet with him, I'm going to introduce you by your formal title. I want to watch his face... his eyes. If he is playing a game with us, then I'll know."

Nodding, she stood and moved toward the chest of drawers to retrieve her clothing. On top, next to her slacks and blouse, was a duffle bag full of money, gold, and a pistol. Glancing at the collection of wealth, she said, "Why don't you just kill him and take the weapon? It seems such a waste to use such wealth when a bullet costing less than a ruble would do the trick."

Smiling, then shaking his head, Sergei responded, "Have you been watching those western spy movies again, my dear? Word gets around when you break a deal – even a deal with a farmer. That amount of money is a fair price for what we will receive in return. I'll protect myself against skullduggery on the part of the American, but I won't instigate it myself. Such acts damage one's reputation."

"Okay," she shrugged, "I'll leave the methods and procedures up to you. I'll do the best I can with the science."

She walked back around the bed, using the ashtray to extinguish her smoke. Looking down, she touched herself and said, "Are you through with me, or can I get dressed?"

"If you keep walking around in the nude, I most surely will require more of your company. What about you – still feeling the need?"

Laughing, she smiled and said, "I'm cursed, Sergei. I always feel the need. It is such a distraction that I'm surprised I get any work done at all. It's a good thing I was raised in the sparsely populated countryside, or I would have never finished school."

They both had a good laugh over her comment. After the humor had faded, she moved her hand inside of his blanket. "Perhaps I can accelerate your recovery," she offered.

Monroe and Special Prosecutor Haskins left Maria's home, each man having a completely different opinion regarding the outcome. The lawyer was upbeat, his workload lightened with the promised release of Hank Barns, his political future in Washington looking far more positive if his name was associated with the capture of the world's most wanted man.

Monroe, on the other hand, was skeptical. After weeks of chasing Weathers, the end seemed all too easy. Many criminals had seen an end to their lives or freedom due to the betrayal of a woman they loved and trusted. John Dillinger was only one of dozens of examples the senior FBI man could name.

Still, something just didn't seem right about the entire situation. Finally shrugging off his pessimism, he decided he didn't have any choice but to do his best to ensure that Weathers didn't escape again. He was familiar with the Port of Houston, and he would put a wall of steel around pier #19. No ship would leave until he had Weathers – either in cuffs or a body bag.

The Final Day

Dusty woke up from a catnap, the loud rumble of yet another in the seemingly endless parade of trucks waking him from the light slumber.

He glanced around the main terminal parking lot, the same cars and trucks parked in the same spaces as before he'd dozed off.

He'd been inside the security perimeter of the terminal since late the previous afternoon, sitting in his truck, occasionally walking down along the water's edge just to circulate the blood. He figured Monroe would deploy his men early, so he'd made sure he was the first one in – the early bird, not the worm.

The night had passed slowly, Dusty's level of alert focusing suspicion on every car, truck and van that entered the busy port area. After a while, it had all become routine, and he'd managed some sleep. It wasn't quite daylight yet – probably another 20 minutes before the sun crested in the east. He was sure the law enforcement teams would be arriving soon.

It was time to call his Russian friend.

"Da," the now familiar voice responded on the first ring. "I hope after our exchange you will be a man who can sleep normal hours, Mr. Weathers."

Dusty laughed, actually beginning to like the foreigner's attitude. "So have you managed to gather everything I requested?"

"Of course, of course. I am eager to return home. Please tell me there won't be any delay."

"Meet me at the Port of Houston, Pier #19 at 10 a.m. Follow the signs for the free boat tour. I'll meet you at the east edge of the terminal parking lot – the side closest to the big bridge."

"This is acceptable. You will have the weapon with you, I assume?"

"Yes. It is sitting right here beside me. One other thing – this area is very secure. This is the only parking open to the general public. Just tell the guard you're here for that free public boat tour."

"Da. I will see you in a few hours then."

Again the line went dead, Dusty assuming that the Russians weren't big on salutations. Shrugging, he tossed the phone, no longer caring if anyone knew where he was. It was time to go.

He cleared out all of his personal items from the truck, the two packs bulky and awkward. Avoiding the pools of light created by the high overhead fluorescent bulbs, he strode calmly toward the 610 bridge.

A working port uses a lot of pallets, and pier #19 was no exception. A virtual forest of wooden frames stacked as tall as a man dominated one section of the loading area. Covering more waterside real estate than a football field, Dusty had played hide and seek with his son on this very ground years ago.

Disinterested in the school field trip's free boat tour, he and Anthony had slipped off to chase each other through the canyons of pallets while waiting. The size of the maze was just as he remembered, perhaps even larger.

It wasn't uncommon for a stack to be knocked over, the forklift drivers occasionally careless, or the random thunderstorm whipping up enough wind to push over a wobbly tower of wood and nails.

It was here, in a sea of old wood stacked in sloppy rows, that Dusty made his hide. Before the sun rose, he was concealed and comfortable under a makeshift pile of random pallets, the powerful optic of the rail gun scanning for the arrival of false-friend, the Russian, and foe, the FBI.

It all ends here, today, he determined. *I might be dead, in handcuffs or free, but I won't be a trapped, helpless rat in this city... this foreign place where I don't belong.*

After scanning the area for riflemen, observers or teams of law enforcement officers sneaking into position, he relaxed a bit. *They'll be here*, he reassured himself. *A watched pot never deploys its snipers.*

Looking down at his pack, he decided to don the Resistol, the crumpled hat having made the journey with him, looking as though it had suffered nearly as much as he had. Wearing a western man's hat just seemed proper, a fitting way to go down if it all ended badly.

Great, historical last stands filled his mind. The Alamo didn't end so well for the defenders, but most of the time things didn't work out. Places with names like Stalingrad, Bastogne and Thermopylae filled his thoughts. He wondered if any of the 300 Spartans had a favorite hat, pondered if any of the Airborne troops holding off the Germans at Bastogne were just sick of the whole thing and only wanted it to end – one way or the other.

Twice, he started to stand and leave – not sure if he had the stomach for the approaching confrontation, temporarily lacking the confidence he could pull this off. Movement caught his eye, grounding his retreat. A swirl of blue, out of place, rustled in the distance. *Here they come,* he sighed, his body locking into a motionless statue.

Dusty watched an FBI agent with an M16 rifle move along the edge of the access road. The man disappeared into a patch of waist high weeds, only the black barrel of his rifle visible from the hide. *I hope that guy is laying on a fire ant mount.*

A few minutes went by without seeing any other law enforcement. It was the glint of sun that exposed the next man – a Houston SWAT officer who hadn't seen fit to remove his shiny sunglasses. *He should get an ass chewing for that rookie mistake,* Dusty mused.

Slowly, carefully moving his scope back into place – weary of flashing the sun himself, Dusty began studying his surroundings carefully. There, where the slope of the ground met one of the bridge's support pillars, there was a sniper.

An empty semi-trailer was home to another. The black circle of the shooter's scope was visible over the edge.

He almost missed the guy in the stack of discarded cardboard boxes. A clever fellow, Dusty scanned right over the top of him twice and would have never spotted him were it not for part of a rifle sling hanging over the lip of a box.

He found several more while he waited on the Russians to arrive. He was also fully aware that for every cop he could see, there were probably three more he couldn't. *Let the Russians deal with them*, he thought.

The West Texan's experience with hunting had taught him that movement draws the human eye. Forcing every move to be extraordinarily slow, Dusty managed a glance at his watch. The Russians should be here any minute, and they weren't the only ones.

A steady stream of cars began entering the parking area, mostly visitors arriving for the free boat tour provided daily by the Port Authority of Houston. With the increase of incoming traffic, it would be difficult to detect the Russians until they exited their car. Dusty didn't care. He'd spot them before they found him.

Movement on the water drew his attention, a small Coast Guard gunboat slowly patrolling up the ship channel. He couldn't tell if that was part of the FBI's dragnet, or just a coincidence – and again, it didn't matter.

While he waited, he noticed the increasing traffic noise coming from the nearby bridge. Carrying six lanes of morning commuters, a background chorus of engine noise, singing tires and the occasional horn would continue to build as the day grew older. Dusty knew from his research that the crossing was called the Ship Channel Bridge by locals, its official title being *The Sidney Sherman Bridge*. Rising 130 feet above the water, the structure had been struck more than once by the cargo cranes of various ships. Two of these collisions caused the roadway above to be closed for weeks. *Keep your mind focused*, he chided. *Now's not the time to wander off on internet trivia.*

And then they were there. Dusty recognized the Russian from their previous encounter in the parking lot. The female walking beside him, as well as the muscular man a few steps behind, were both strangers. All three wore FBI logos on their clothing. The burly guy carried a large duffle bag – no doubt full of either newspaper, if treachery was afoot, or currency. *I didn't realize that amount of money would take up so much space*, he noted.

Dusty reached slowly for the Russian's phone lying next to him. He dialed a memorized number belonging to his last no-contract cell, and waited for the connection to go through. Both he and the Russians could hear the ringing, the cheap phone lying nearby on a bench. The older man shook his head and moved to answer the phone.

"Da."

"Sorry to be so dramatic, but I'm new to this game. Please bring the money and walk toward the pallets to the west. I'm waiting inside. Please come alone," Dusty said.

"This is unnecessary… but… I will play along. However, I do need to bring the woman with me."

"Why?"

"We are exchanging quite a bit of money, my friend. She is a doctor of physics…an expert. I want her to examine the goods I am buying."

Dusty analyzed the request for a moment, finally deciding it was a bluff. No one could be an expert on a technology that didn't exist. "No problem – bring the woman. Leave the big guy where he is."

"Da."

True to his word, the Russian turned and snapped an order to Mr. Muscles, taking the duffle and pulling it over his own shoulder. He then motioned with his head for Miss Big-boobs to follow.

Dusty slowly backed out of his hide, the toy rail gun in his grip.

One quarter of a mile away, on the roof of a warehouse, Monroe lowered his binoculars and turned to Shultz. "What the fuck is going on down there, Tom? Those people in the parking lot have on FBI uniforms. Are you sure we don't have a team that didn't understand their orders?"

"I don't get it, sir. Everyone received the same operational orders. Yet, they look like our people."

"Something's not right," judged Monroe. "Send in the teams. If our people have fucked this up, heads will roll."

Shultz interrupted his boss – a large optic still focused on the ground below. "Wait, sir. Something's happening. There're moving out of our sight."

As if on cue, both agents' earpieces sounded with a chorus of "I've lost contact with unknown team," and "They've moved off to the west; I can't see them now because of the pallets."

"Shit!" snapped Monroe. Keying his mic, he ordered, "All assault teams, this is Monroe. Move in. Move in now!"

Dusty let the two Russians walk right past him, the dense maze of stacked pallets impossible to maneuver in a straight line. He cleared his throat.

The older Russian jumped just a little and turned quickly. "Only in the movies do they do this sort of thing, Mr. Weathers."

Dusty shrugged his shoulders, "That's about the only example this old cowboy has to go by."

"This is the weapon, da?" he inquired, nodding towards Dusty's fake rail gun.

"That is the money and other items I requested?" Dusty replied, nodding toward the duffle.

Smiling, the Russian sat the sizable bag on the ground, tugging on the zipper and pulling apart the sides. He held open the edges so Dusty could look inside. It appeared to be a butt-full of money, complete with clear tubes of gold colored coins. "It is all here, including the passport. Our Canadian embassy assures me it is a real document, issued by a friend working in the government."

Dusty approached the stoic woman and handed her the rail gun.

The Russian physics expert hefted the weapon, appearing to examine the coils and other mechanisms. He then handed her two ball bearings, and answered her questioning look with, "The bullets."

While the woman examined the gun, Sergei watched Dusty. The man seemed relaxed. "Your hat – it is a real cowboy hat?" He asked.

Grunting, Dusty nodded. *What else would it be?*

"I wish to trade you something for it. You have plenty of money now to purchase another. I would like it for a souvenir of my travels. My friends back in Moscow will be impressed."

"What do you have to trade?"

The question seemed to give Sergei pause. He brightened after a bit, and pulled off his FBI jacket. "How about this coat? It is close to the real thing."

An idea formed immediately in Dusty's head. The jacket and its gold FBI letters might help if things got dicey during his escape. "Sure, he replied," and took off his hat.

Sergei donned the cover, smiling at his companion who was still mesmerized by the rail gun's configuration. "How does it function?" she asked.

Dusty opened his mouth to explain, but his words were interrupted by a gunshot ripping through the air from behind them.

Sergei and Dusty both uttered "What the fuck," at the same time, the former doing so in Russian. Snatching the rail gun from the woman's hands, the director began walking with purpose back toward the parking lot.

Dusty bent and grabbed the duffle, hustling away in a different direction.

More shots rang out, their report guiding Sergei back toward the parking lot. As he approached the end of the pallet-maze, he noted his captain prone on the pavement, his sidearm pointing toward an area of overgrown weeds nearby by. It quickly became obvious what his man was shooting at, as three uniformed

Americans jumped up and scrambled a few steps closer to his position.

Sergei didn't know what exactly was going on. His analytical mind quickly sorted through several possibilities, eventually settling with the logical assumption that the authorities had finally caught up with Mr. Weathers. He didn't care.

Walking boldly from the stack of pallets, he brandished the rail gun for all to see, and then pointed the device at the Ship Channel Bridge. Yelling at the top of his lungs, "Cease fire and back away, or I will drop the bridge with this weapon."

The law enforcement officers approaching the parking lot had been briefed on the rail gun's potential – a few of the team having been eyewitnesses to the destruction at the Medical Center. The man in charge of the closest assault group keyed his mic. "Sir, the suspect is threatening to shoot the Ship Channel Bridge with the super weapon if we don't back down. Instructions?"

Monroe was already on his way, the lead agent wanting desperately to be present when Weathers went down. The transmission reporting the huge bridge was now a hostage surprised him, the scenario not something they had anticipated. Now, as he sped across the parking area, it seemed so obvious. "Close down the bridge! Right now – both directions!" He ordered over the radio.

Dusty, still hiding back in the pallets, turned on the real rail gun, the glow of the green LED boosting his confidence. His angle and position provided a small window through the forest of pallet-stacks, enough where he could see the Russian who was now joined by his two colleagues. The trio of foreigners was retreating toward the cover of the pallets – probably not wanting to chance a sniper's bullet. They came closer, slowly backing away from the visible cops, the rail gun steady and pointing at the bridge.

"Sir, where are we going?" asked the nervous SPETZ captain, his sidearm scanning in brisk motions trying to cover their retreat.

"Move toward the ship docked over there," replied his boss, motioning with his head toward a tanker docked further down the shoreline. "We're going to hijack that vessel. It will be our ride out of here. They won't dare fire on it while it is so close to all of these people, the explosion would kill many innocents."

Dusty had planned to appear with the real rail gun, holding the Russians off until Monroe's men captured them. Using the bridge as insurance hadn't occurred to him, but now that he saw the effect it was having on the pursuing lawmen, he conceded it wasn't a bad idea.

He was just about to step out of his pallet-cover when a female voice rang out from the parking lot. "Dusty! Dusty!" yelled Grace, running to a man wearing the familiar cowboy hat. She didn't realize the misidentification until it was too late. The meaty Russian intercepted Grace as she ran to Sergei, pointing his pistol at her head. "Insurance," he announced to his boss.

Dusty stopped dead in his tracks, the whole situation quickly getting out of control. A low thumping sound bouncing across the channel added to the confusion.

The two Longbow Apache gunships pulled up and hovered just over the center of the channel, their undercarriages bristling with missiles and mini-guns. Looking like angry, giant wasps, each military helicopter carried more firepower than a World War II naval destroyer. The multi-barreled cannon under the nose followed the pilot's line of sight, which at the moment was clearly focused on Sergei's party.

"Surrender, and no one will get hurt," sounded a loud speaker from across the lot. "This is Special Agent Monroe of the FBI, lay down all your weapons, and you will not be harmed."

Dusty watched, the enormous firepower represented by the military attack aircraft freezing his soul. Even if he did step out to free Grace and show the FBI the real rail gun, the missiles under the wings of the two war birds left no doubt of the outcome of any gunfight. While he could knock down one of the gunships with the rail, the other would blast the entire area into oblivion.

It was a standoff. While Sergei had stopped his retreat, he still held the bridge and all the commuters on its surface hostage. The FBI was confused, not sure who the people were in their sights. Grace stood amongst the foreigners, a pistol held against her head while her body was used as a shield.

"Suspects have a hostage! Suspects have a hostage!" sounded the exited voice in Monroe's earpiece. "Negative on that," came another call, "That is an officer taking Grace Kennedy into custody."

"Kennedy? Who's the other woman if Kennedy is being held? I thought the lawyer was the first woman?" questioned one of the snipers.

Monroe looked at Shultz, frustrated at the obvious confusion surging through his teams. He clicked his mic to issue orders, but the words never left his throat.

From the water a horn sounded, the deep-pitched alert overriding the whining jet engines and rotor wash of the helicopters. A wall of steel appeared, a huge container ship barreling down the channel – the unaware Apaches directly in its path.

Again, the ship's captain blew the ear splitting air horn, but the pilots couldn't hear it. Dusty watched, stunned as the behemoth of moving steel raced directly at the hovering craft. The boat was attempting a turn, probably reversing its engines, but he knew it couldn't avoid the choppers. Big ocean going ships required miles to stop, almost as much distance to turn. Even with emergency maneuvers, there was no way to avoid the collision.

The ship struck the closest Longbow, the hull of the juggernaut slamming into the tail rotor just below the vessel's anchor chain. Everyone ashore watched in horror as the now-tiny looking war machine spun slightly before its fuselage was flattened against the ship's hull like a bug on a speeding car's windshield. A ball of boiling flame erupted, a deafening explosion tearing across the area.

Dusty was already moving, realizing the distraction caused by the collision might be his only chance to rescue Grace. Three steps to Mr. Muscles, the rail gun pointing right at the Russian's head. His message was clear. Bewildered and distracted by the freighter, exploding chopper, and the approaching lawmen, the big Russian didn't put up a struggle, actually shoving Grace toward Dusty like he was glad to be rid of her.

Dusty was pulling her back toward the pallets, screaming, "Run! Run! Run!" at the top of his lungs.

The remaining pilot saw the expanding ball of fire where his wingman had been just a moment before. Having been briefed on the power of the weapon he might be facing, the Army Warrant Officer was already on edge. Seeing the destruction of his friend pushed him over. He squeezed a button, launching a Hellfire missile just as the approaching freighter impacted his tail.

The Hellfire had been designed to kill thickly armored battle tanks. The 100-pound, rocket-propelled weapon jumped from its launch rail and wobbled for just a fraction of time before beginning its acceleration. The 20-pound, high-explosive warhead flew directly at Sergei's chest.

Everyone was in motion.

The Russians were scattering, Dusty and Grace running away at full speed through the pallet-canyons. Monroe was trying to issue orders over the radio. None of them had much time. It took the Hellfire less than two seconds to travel the 600 meters to its target.

The warhead impacted four feet behind the Russians, the Centex core expanding at 8,000 meters per second. A ball of white-hot fire enveloped the SVR personnel, the heat killing Sergei and his team instantly, their bodies shredded by shrapnel and shock a microsecond later.

The blast wave slammed into the wall of pallets with enough force to shred internal organs and collapse lungs. Grace, motivated by Dusty's push, hit the ground, and the whole world went black. She never felt Dusty's body land on top of her.

For a moment, everyone watching the scene froze – the destruction and chaos of such a scale, the human brain struggled to process it all.

The silence was broken by the sound of the tanker's horn thundering across the water, somehow resonating panic and desperation with its bellow. Again and again, the captain of the big ship let loose with his warning.

Dusty was pulling Grace up from the debris, pushing aside scraps of wood and kicking away pallets. He lifted the stunned woman to her feet, checking her up and down for injury. She appeared dazed, but unhurt.

Lifting the duffle with one hand, he began tugging her along with the other, "We've got to go. Come on, Grace. We've got to get out of here."

She didn't seem to comprehend at first, her gaze unfocused, her eyes darting back and forth between the tanker's blaring horn and Dusty's blaring voice. Her legs began to cooperate, finally moving through the pallets away from the impact of the missile.

Something about the repeated sounding of the tanker's horn drew Dusty's attention. Burning fuel and bits of the destroyed helicopters remained stuck to the hull, the flames and smoke making the huge ship appear like a giant dragon rolling smoothly across the water. Again and again the horn sounded.

"Why is he riding that horn?" Dusty questioned. "The helo's are already toast."

As Dusty and Grace cleared the pallets, they continued walking, quickly crossing an open area along the shoreline. He glanced up again at the tanker, still wondering why the captain kept blasting away with his obnoxious signal. Then he saw why.

The ship, as long as two football fields, had executed an emergency turn in a vain attempt to avoid the hovering war birds. Now, it was pointed directly at the main support of the bridge, closing the distance at such a rate that a collision was unavoidable.

Dusty looked up at the bridge's road deck, finding it still full of cars, trucks and... his blood went cold... a school bus. His mind raced, plotting the tanker's course, speed and momentum. Even if the big ship wasn't moving fast enough to collapse the support, there was a good chance the roadway would be damaged, perhaps opened to the water below.

Looking down at the rail, he made a decision. He and Grace were most likely free and clear. The FBI would find the toy rail gun, and it would take them weeks to figure out it wasn't the real deal – if ever. The small, charred bits of Russian flesh would make identification of the recovered bodies difficult.

Yet, he couldn't let the cargo ship kill everyone on the bridge. There were hundreds of lives at stake. He shouldered the weapon and scanned the roadway above. The school bus was filled with small faces, plastered against the windows, drawn to the action below. He adjusted his aim to the water, settling on a spot a few feet ahead of where the bow plied through the channel.

He pulled the trigger.

Like the biblical Moses parting the Red Sea, a narrow, empty corridor of black void split the channel. The effect was temporary as the dimensional opening pushed the dense liquid aside with incomprehensible force, and then collapsed into a vacuum. A wall of water rose from the 65-foot depths of the passage – a Tsunami moving faster than the speed of sound. Striking the bow of the container ship, the kinetic energy of the liquid battering ram crushed the hull, abruptly halting the mega-tons of steel and cargo. The entire ship shuddered from the impact, containers flying from the deck and splashing into the waterway.

Dusty was pulling on Grace again, convinced he had saved the bridge and wanting to expedite their escape. "GO! GO! GO!" he screamed, not sure if the dazed woman could comprehend his urgent commands. Regardless of her state, somehow his message got through and she began to run.

The tidal wave of water moved quickly across the channel, flooding the opposite shore in a few seconds, the surge expanding in multiple directions. With the closing of the dimensional portal, normal, known physics again came into play. The laws of fluid dynamics required the displaced water to return, and return with a vengeance it did, rushing back across the waterway after ricocheting off the banks and bends of the curvy waterway. The now-crippled cargo vessel was directly in its path.

Dusty and Grace were running, legs pounding and blood racing, trying to put distance between themselves and the carnage they'd left behind. A quick glance at the waterway froze Dusty's soul.

He watched wide-eyed as the returning tidal wave lifted the disabled ship, raising it like a cork in the surf. The oncoming wall of water continued rushing toward the shore, the huge freighter looking like a surfer riding the crest of a wave, barreling down on top of them.

He couldn't pull his gaze away, watching over his shoulder as the image of the tanker grew larger and larger. It was going to crush them, pulverize their bodies into smears of blood and flesh on its great hull.

At the last moment, Dusty reached for Grace's belt, holding on for dear life. The chasing water hit their bodies first, a swirling roar of black liquid lifting them like driftwood debris, suspending their bodies in a pool of raging darkness. Dusty held onto Grace, the torque feeling like his arm was being ripped from his body as they were tumbled head over heels by the force.

And then he was slammed into the ground, the momentum of the current suddenly reversed. As the wave drained away, he came up coughing, choking and spitting muddy liquid. Dusty made it to his feet first, spotting Grace as she tried to make it to her knees. Cursing and shaking her head, she managed to stand. Both of them turned to look at the massive ship, lying on its side not 20 feet away.

It took a bit to regroup. As they gathered themselves, Dusty rearranged the duffle bag still strapped to his back and stared back at a scene of utter chaos. The ship was listing badly, most of its hull now residing where the pallet forest had been just a few moments before.

The parking area was empty, all of the vehicles pushed to higher ground by the wall of water that had inundated the lot. Resting on top of one another in a disheveled wall of mangled steel and broken glass, Dusty couldn't spot the old Chevy, the small loss of little consequence compared to the devastation that filled his eyes.

For a moment, Dusty wondered how many of the policemen had made it to high ground. He questioned if Monroe had made it out alive. He was saddened when it dawned on him that other lives may have been lost.

Movement from the corner of his vision drew his attention, a man lifting himself from a pool of sloppy mud, looking around in shock. Gradually, other survivors began to show themselves – most moving as if in a daze.

He checked the rail gun, unsure of what the dousing had done to his invention. The green LED still glowed bright, his waterproofing efforts having paid off.

Dusty gently took Grace's arm and said quietly, "We have to go."

Dripping wet, disheveled and muddy, the pair began hustling away from the crippled vessel.

"You sure know how to show a girl a good time in the big city, cowboy," Grace teased between breaths.

"My pleasure, ma'am. But we're not done yet."

The End

Epilogue

Grace sat in the bow of the inflatable raft, wringing out her shirt, unashamed of Durham seeing her clad only in her underwear. Her pants were already drying in the sun, draped over the edge after she had rinsed out the mud over the side.

Trying to be a gentleman while at the same time steering the outboard motor, Dusty pretended to keep his eyes on the waterway ahead. Grace had already caught him casting an admiring glance once before.

"Where are we going?" she finally asked.

"I don't know. Where do you want to go? I've got lots of money, a new ID, and the world's most powerful weapon. This little boat ain't so bad either."

She smiled, and then replied, "You're also the world's most wanted man."

Adjusting their course, he peered along both shorelines looking for any sign of trouble. They had meandered down the now closed ship channel, darting behind docked container ships and sneaking around piers. The Coast Guard had rushed past over an hour ago, obviously responding to the events at pier #19. They hadn't seen another boat or ship since.

The last civilization had passed 30 minutes ago, the appearance of wetlands, marshes and rock lined shores replacing the refineries, piers and wharfs. The lack of industrialization allowed the couple to relax. They would be in the open waters of Galveston Bay soon, the Gulf of Mexico not far beyond.

"I think we've got a bit of a head start before they realize who was actually killed back there," Dusty said. "The exchange of the hat for the jacket was a stroke of luck. I hadn't planned for that. I hope the fake gun will allow Monroe to relax a bit. He'll think the primary threat is past."

"I think all the bodies and the fake gun are under the hull of that ship. That will take some time to move. But still, you shot the water after everyone was already dead. They'll know that — they'll figure out the sequence."

Nodding, Dusty's voice was optimistic. "I'm hoping they'll think it was the exploding helicopters or some cargo onboard the ship that caused the wave. You're right, they'll figure it out. I think we have a head start, not a clean get away."

Grace drifted off, pondering her future while gazing silently at her surroundings. As the tiny boat moved closer to the open waters of the bay, a flock of cranes glided low across the surface nearby. For the first time in her life, she understood the true meaning of freedom.

She turned to him and said, "I'm with you, Durham, if you want me along. I'll go wherever you want to go. It just seems right being at your side."

Her words brought a smile to his face. Nodding, he said, "I want you here. I realized how much I missed you during all this mayhem. I can't promise much of a future right now, but however it ends, I want you there with me."

Grace scooted back to sit beside him, and the two hugged. She maintained her embrace as Dusty returned to steering the boat, accelerating toward the open water.

"The coast up ahead is lined with marinas, yacht brokers, and boatyards. How about we find a nice little cabin cruiser that's for sale? One with a good shower and BBQ grill docked in a dark corner of a seldom used marina. We can hole up, clean up, rest up, and make up time. We'll decide where to go after things have settled down."

"Okay, Dusty," she replied, smiling as he realized she had finally called him by his preferred name.

Made in the USA
Lexington, KY
22 November 2013